WE STAND EQUAL ALONGSIDE THE FEW,
WHERE ONE DAY WE MIGHT BE FREE TO RISE
ROSALINE MACKAY : 2023

BLOODSTREAM OF MOONLIGHT

EQUAL RISE SERIES

BLOODSTREAM
OF MOONLIGHT

ROXAN BURLEY

Copyright © 2023 Midnight Moon Press / Roxan Burley

First paperback edition January 2023

Book design by Roxan Burley

ISBN 9781068787409

Instagram: @roxanburleyauthor
Website: www.roxanburleyauthor.co.uk

For my two daughters,
the determined one who believes, and the quiet one who listens.
For my husband who has allowed me to do this without
complaint.

Bloodstream of Moonlight is a dystopian fantasy where mythical creatures exist, and the boundaries of magic are possible. It is a brutal and cruel reality, be prepared to enter the rebellion of

Equal Rise...

GLOSSARY

Myth — Term given to creatures of magical and immortal origin.

Hybrid — The illegal genetic combination of two different species.

High Races

Elves — The first immortals to walk the earth. Great in power and influence.

Gargoyles — Forced to walk within the nocturnal hours of night, worshippers of Lunar.

Welkin — The instigators of chaos and order. Weather tamers of the skies.

Lesser Races

Trolls — The keepers of the tunnels and bridges.

Gnomes — The inventors and manipulators of magic and tech.

Dwarves — The traders and transportation.

Goblins — The keepers of coin.

Mischief makers — Imps, Sprites, Pikes, and Brownies.

Shifters — The ones which can take two forms.

CHAPTER I

||| EIRA

'Doctor, we urgently need your assistance!'

The voice was muffled, but still loud enough to reach her.

'Emma, wake up now!' The borrowed name roused her, piercing through the fog of sleep.

Her body was rocked by a shove, jolting her awake. Bleary-eyed, Eira stared into the unforgiving face of Nora, whose pig-nose and ruddy cheeks were aflame with anger. Sighing, she lifted her head from her outstretched arm, working the kinks out of her taut neck muscles.

'Falling asleep on the job again?' Nora sneered at her.

'So would you if you'd worked a double-shift without a break.' Eira sighed as she carefully opened her other hand which was clamped around her necklace. She had held onto it so tightly that an impression had been made on her palm of the small key attached to the chain. She gently traced the three vertical lines embossed on the opal stone with her fingertips.

'Ahem,' Nora coughed. 'Anytime now, Emma. We have an emergency on our hands. Life and death. Your talents are required.'

Nora's sarcastic tone made Eira look up from her contemplation, dropping her necklace against her chest as she shook the dream from her mind. Placing both palms on the scratched melamine table, she pushed herself up, shoving her chair back. She towered over Nora, who seemed to recoil inwardly, dropping her gaze towards Eira's dark-purple Doc Martens. Eira strode from the gloomy staffroom without a backwards glance to see if Nora was keeping pace with her long strides.

Eira could feel her heart rate increasing, but she made herself take a deep, steadying breath, and sent a pulse of magic to soothe her weary muscles. She instantly felt more alert, her head clear. The faces of the nurses they passed were tense and on guard; she knew that whatever she was heading towards was serious. Striding down the hall, Nora running to keep up with her, she asked over her shoulder, 'What's the emergency?'

'Three males have been attacked. Two are unconscious with no visible injuries. They've been booked in for an urgent CT scan. The last male has a broken arm and a severe laceration down his chest. He's bleeding out, and we can't get the wound to clot. His BP has dropped, and his breathing is ragged.'

Eira swiveled in the deserted corridor to glare at Nora as her words washed over her, before turning back and breaking into a sprint to the treatment rooms on the ground floor. Leaving Nora far behind, she flew through the double doors at the end of the corridor. Taking the steps two at a time, she thundered down the stairs, pulling her stethoscope from around her neck to stop it from falling to the floor.

The silk scarf neatly folded over her head to hide her ears slipped as sweat gathered on her brow. With her free hand, she grabbed the ends and pulled it taut across her forehead, adding to the pressure building in her head.

Why did I fall asleep?

But the truth was she was running on empty. A twenty-four-hour shift with no breaks, delivering a baby, healing two broken legs, and saving a man from a brain haemorrhage had drained her reserves.

Doing it all under the watchful eye of Nora had made it even harder. She often appeared out of nowhere during a consultation or treatment, getting in the way, and making Eira work harder to conceal the magic that she was wielding.

She would not lose this patient's life! Not like last time, she thought grimly.

Reaching the ground floor, she entered the chaos of the main foyer. The laboured breathing coming from the stairwell alerted her that Nora was right behind, determined to stay on her heels.

Weaving between patients and colleagues, Eira slammed through the battered double-doors to the treatment area. A brief glance around the opened ward showed dozing patients, and she could hear the constant beeping of many machines. The room was dilapidated with most of the windows blocked-up or smashed, the walls flaked with peeling paint. Two unconscious figures in military gear nearest the door were the new patients.

Observing the stillness and silence for a heartbeat, Eira entered the first treatment room noting the patient on the bed and the nurse standing over him, the smell of antiseptic and blood almost overwhelming. She processed all of this in the blink of an eye, before launching herself into action once again.

The patient was laying on his back, his black top shredded and saturated with blood. His skin was ashen, and his breathing came in ragged gasps. The heart monitor was beeping, showing his dangerously increased heart rate. His head was rolled to one side, black hair obscuring his closed eyes.

Eira shut the door with a deafening thud, rattling the frame in Nora's face as she tried to storm in. She firmly turned the lock and, advancing to close the blinds, acknowledged Nora's exasperated huff with a smug smile. Now for the task at hand.

Taking a deep breath, she finally raised her eyes to Elowen.

Eira sensed the mounting horror in her friend's dark eyes. These were the same injuries as before. The same knife wounds that killed their last patient. But they'd been inexperienced and hesitant before. They would not make the same mistake this time.

If his eyes were black like before… She swept the thought from her head. *Breathe. Think. I'm a professional now.*

The smell of his blood coated Eira's throat, making her gag. She stepped up to the side of the bed, watching Elowen's slender hands pressing gauze against the wound, trying to stem the bleeding. Her black-painted fingernails stood in stark contrast to the crimson blood coating her skin.

Elowen's black hair had escaped her ponytail, plastering itself to her sweaty brow. Her nurse's uniform was stained in blood. Eira could hear her heart, the erratic beating showing just how panicked her friend was.

'I think he has a pneumothorax in his left lung where the puncture wound was first made.'

3

Eira could clearly see that the laceration started above his pectoral and continued down his chest to his abdomen in a jagged sweep. A serrated knife had been used to carve him open, leaving his body a massacred mess. The wound looked to be seeping a black substance. His breathing was scratchy and laboured, which worried her.

She stretched towards the wall behind her for the hand sanitiser, cleaned her hands, and nodded for Elowen to move over slightly so she could gain better access. Laying a hand on her friend's shoulder, she said, 'This will not be like before.'

Pushing the man's leather jacket back, she tore open his shirt. Without the fabric in the way, the blood pooled and ran down his chest in dark rivulets.

With a feather-light touch she placed her hands palm down either side of the entry wound, closed her eyes in concentration, and directed her magic into his body. She would normally make a display of using her stethoscope whilst her magic flowed through the patient, so as not to arouse suspicion. Since the argument with Nora six months ago, she had learnt to hide her powers from prying eyes.

But not today. Time was not on her side. And even if it was, she didn't have the extra strength required to conceal her glow. Eira felt her hands heating and, behind closed lids, sensed the spark of light as her powers charged to her will. Opposite her, she heard Elowen's intake of breath.

The magic seeped from her cupped hands and spread into the patient's body. Like a seedling taking root, her magic coiled into his body, flowing through his arteries, and wrapping a protective shield around his heart, seeking his body's distress. With a physical jolt, her mind melded with his, and she was overwhelmed by his pain. Trying to ignore it, she carefully shaped her magic into long tendrils that coated his pain receptors and dulled his agony to a dull throb. The patient relaxed with a sigh, and she imagined the tension in his face easing slightly.

Elowen's judgement was correct. His left lung had partially collapsed when the weapon was first driven into his body. Blood trickled between his chest wall and lung cavity. *How was he still alive?* A kernel of her magic encased his heart, regulating the beat, and she extracted the rest of her power, stepping back into her own being. Her powers flared, catching a shimmer in his blood around the wound fighting against the dark substance oozing out.

'The knife pierced his lung, and he has a hemothorax. The blood is collecting in his chest cavity and putting pressure on his lung, meaning it can't inflate properly. I need you to perform a thoracostomy whilst I inflate his lung and heal the wound. Do you think you can do that?'

Elowen widened her eyes in shock, before steeling herself and nodding. She reached into the tray beside her for the equipment she needed to perform the procedure, pulling surgical gloves over her hands.

'Is there any pain relief in here?' Eira asked.

Finding her voice, Elowen answered, 'We ran out two hours ago.'

Eira nodded, accepting the consequences. Her magic was depleted, and she was unsure if she even had enough left to heal him, let alone block his pain as well. Already her legs were shaking, and her headache intensifying.

Elowen sterilised the man's chest where indicated. She stuttered, 'I've never done this without machine guidance before.'

'I'll direct you. I promise,' Eira stated, looking into her friend's nervous eyes.

Distracting them both, a light tap sounded on the treatment room door, followed by Moyra's calm tone; 'Emma, is everything okay in there?' Again, with that name.

'All's good, Moyra, we just need to concentrate.'

She heard Nora's rebuke outside the door and Moyra's raised voice as she ordered Nora to retreat down the corridor.

Rolling her eyes, Elowen stuck her tongue out in concentration and made an incision in the man's skin. A bead of red blood pooled between her gloved fingers. Eira closed her eyes and entered her trance state, her magic flowing once again into his body. She detected the incision and nodded to Elowen to insert the thin tube whilst directing her to the correct location to drain the excess fluid. Like a net, her power encased his lung in its grasp, inflating it slowly with its power. She started to knit the wound back together.

'He needs oxygen.'

She sensed Elowen moving behind her to the locked cupboard where the oxygen tank and masks were kept. Oxygen tanks were rare and hard to purchase on the Black Market, so they used them sparingly. Eira opened her heavy-lidded eyes as Elowen placed the mask over his head. She heard the man's heart rate regulate and settle into a steady rhythm. Leaving the tube in for the fluid to drain, exhaustion slammed into her like a tidal wave, dizziness overcoming her until she had to grab the side of the bed to steady herself for the last stage of the healing process.

Elowen wiped the sweat from her brow, sighing from her position at the man's head, checking his pulse. Nodding that all was constant, she looked relieved. Eira found herself smiling despite her exhaustion.

Taking another deep breath, she again placed her hands either side of the hideous gash on his abdomen, noting the firmness. Her magic stuttered to life, and she dispatched her will down the tendrils of power to bond the muscle and flesh back together. Hearing Elowen's intake of breath, she glimpsed admiration on her friend's face as she witnessed the miracle of her power.

'I've always known, deep down, that you could do this,' Elowen whispered with a smile on her face. 'Your secret's safe, I promise,' she vowed, placing a hand on her heart.

Abruptly, Eira's whole body snapped as a jolt ripped through her like a lightning strike. Her magic recoiled, and the wound between her fingertips, newly healed, started to open again. A thick black substance started leaking from the wound.

No, no, no, no, no. Not like before.

6

The monitor showed the acceleration of the man's heartbeat as Eira's protective casing was dispelled from his body. Stepping forward slightly, she removed her pen torch from her pocket and, sweeping his dark hair away from his face, she tentatively opened an eyelid, shining the torch in. His eye was a dark void with no pupil.

Unwilling to accept the outcome, she reached further forward to examine his other eye. As she bent over him, the pendant on her necklace swung out and rested on his upturned cheek. She opened his eye as a pulse of light and a sonic boom propelled Elowen against the wall.

Grabbing hold of the bed, Eira managed to keep herself upright. Panting, she seized her necklace to remove it from the man's face, halting as her fingers skimmed the stone. The white opal was pulsing, and black tendrils snaked their way across the man's pale skin towards it. Gradually, the opal heated up as the dark substance flowed into it, darkening from a dazzling white to a murky, insidious black.

His heart rate had increased to an alarming rate, and his body thrashed on the bed. Shaking off the shock, Eira surged her power into the man's body to encase his heart, sending calming impulses through his taut muscles. The tremors in his body diminished. At the same time, she grasped her necklace and gently tried to prise it from the man's face.

'Elowen, I need your help!' she gasped as the drain on her magic became unbearable. Her head was swimming, and she was barely clinging to consciousness. 'We need to lift the opal from his face.'

Hair in her eyes, uniform crumpled and blood-stained, Elowen tentatively approached from the wall she had been propelled against. Together they managed to wedge their fingers under the opal and, like a plaster, peeled it off. The instant the pendant left the man's face, the connection was severed. A great pulse shuddered through his body before he relaxed instantly on the bed. The man's eyes fluttered open and, unseeing, he stared into Eira's emerald eyes. His left eye was still black, but his right eye was a stunning sapphire-blue, the pupil dilated. For a heartbeat, she gazed into that blue eye, before oblivion claimed him again.

Eira felt her own vision blurring as her knees finally gave way and she slumped to the ground. Her last memory was the sight of the tube in his chest, a leaking tap. Instead of pure red haemoglobin blood, the drip was an oily black.

CHAPTER 2

||| EIRA

Eira endured the heaviness pressing on her, as if she was weighted down by invisible pressure. Gravity must be crushing her bones, her very soul. She could see only an endless void of darkness. An echoing boom in her head was the only sound tying her to reality.

Gradually she became aware of her body. First her fingertips, then the backs of her legs and knees. She felt the ground beneath her body, an anchor to the real world. Eira reluctantly opened her eyes, her hands going straight to her temples where a severe headache was throbbing. Banging and raised voices reached her from the other side of the locked door. Hissing, she shrank away, covering her sensitive ears and bringing her knees to her chin.

'Emma are you okay?' a voice whispered. Two cold hands took her arms and gently pulled until Eira was sitting upright.

'Here, drink this. It'll make you feel better,' Elowen said, pushing a glass of clear water into Eira's hands.

Eira gulped down the cool liquid as her mind replayed the events that had brought her to this moment. Inhaling, she stood suddenly and staggered to the bed, thinking the worst.

The steady beep of the machine was still there. The slow rise and fall of **the man's** chest still there. Stunned, she looked at her friend.

'He's stable. His left lung appears to be fully healed, and he's breathing fine. BP good,' Elowen stated as she went back to her task. 'I didn't know how long you would be out, or if you would have the energy when you woke up. So...' She gestured to her surgical needle and thread with a shrug.

Looking at the man's chest, Eira could see Elowen's neat stitches pulling his flesh together.

Giving her friend's arm a squeeze, Eira went to the man's head. Crouching, she found her pen torch abandoned under the bed. Steadying herself, she opened the man's eyes one at a time. One black and one blue. Both reacted to the light, even if the pupil in his fully black eye was camouflaged.

9

Sighing, she straightened and then noticed the three vertical lines engraved onto the side of his cheek.

Shocked, Eira cradled her opal necklace in her cupped hands, tracing the lines on its surface, pale and cold to the touch once more, with no sign of the implosion it had caused. She tucked the necklace safely under her jumper, relieved that the key hanging from it appeared to be undamaged. She could feel Elowen looking at her from under her lashes.

'That isn't the only scar he'll have,' said Elowen, gesturing at his wound. Eira was beyond shocked. She opened her mouth to reply and then thought better of it, turning to the window, and peering through the slats.

The thudding on the door had subsided but the raised voices were still audible.

'How long have they been trying to get in?' Eira whispered as she hugged both arms around herself.

Through the timber slat she made out the back of Nora's platinum-blonde hair pulled tight into a military bun, not a strand out of place. She stood with her arms folded, legs apart in her bright-pink Croc slip-ons, glaring at Moyra. Shaking her messy, grey bob with her red glasses perched on the end of her nose, Moyra rewarded the matron with her sternest headmistress scowl. Eira was confident that Moyra would not demand the door be opened until they were ready, but she could only push the woman's respect so far.

'They knocked when the boom happened and then became more urgent when we didn't answer.' Elowen shrugged. 'I think they're just worried about us and want to check everything is okay. Moyra at least, anyway. Nora is just sticking her nose in.'

Eira smiled. She had liked Elowen from the first moment she met her. As slim as a willow, with jet-black hair and a straight fringe, she worshipped bands such as Linkin Park and Evanescence. Most people avoided her based on appearance alone, with her black nails, kohled eyes, and cobweb tutus, they judged her to be sullen and mournful. Eira had found Elowen to be thoughtful, funny, and a great person to have in her corner when in a fight. She owed so much to the first friendship she had ever known outside of her isolated life. It was a shame she couldn't be as open with her in return.

Eira watched as Elowen carefully placed a dressing over the man's neatly sewn wound.

'You do know you're glowing?' Elowen muttered, looking up from concentrating on her work.

Holding her hands out in front of her, Eira saw the radiant light surrounding them, and cursed. She pulled harder on her glamour, wrapping it tighter around herself, and feeling her power settle into a gentle tug in her gut. Her glamour had never failed before. She found her hand covering her necklace under her jumper, wondering if whatever happened earlier had interfered. In the centre of the power surge, she hadn't even felt her magic slipping, and that worried her.

'The glow is a sign of magic. The intensity of the glow shows how much power you possess,' Eira told Elowen truthfully.

'So, you have a faint glow. That means...?' Elowen left the question hanging.

'Believe me, I could light up this block like a firework,' Eira said with a spark of humour that she didn't feel. 'To be able to hide your magic is also a sign of great power. I've worked hard to glamour my magic and, under Nora's watchful gaze, I've learnt to hide my spark too. It's something that would endanger my life.'

Worry filled her again as she turned back to their patient. 'What are we going to do?' she asked in exasperation. The man was still unconscious, though his breathing was regular, and his skin looked healthier. She still needed to investigate if everything had healed internally, and was worried about what she might find. What did this all mean? And what did she carry around her neck?

'First, we make this patient comfortable and finish doing our jobs,' Elowen stated, grabbing Eira by the shoulders to stop her pacing and gazing directly into her eyes. She looked exhausted. Her face was drawn and there were purple smudges under her hazel eyes, though they were bright with determination.

'Doctor, what are your orders?'

Eira chewed on her bottom lip, thinking.

'I need to go back in to make sure that he is truly stable. My magic is spent, but I should be able to repair his broken arm. Can you monitor his ops as I work?'

Elowen nodded her approval, taking her position at his head again, whilst Eira placed a hand on his chest. White light flared on her fingertips, and the throbbing in her head intensified as she reached deep into her magic reserves one final time.

Abandoning herself fully to her power, she detached herself from the room around her and focused on the man's body beneath her fingers. As before, her power explored the structure of his bones, the pulse of his heart, the rush of his blood, and the reaction of his pain receptors.

Eira's healing magic reinforced his wound, adding strength and binding to Elowen's stitching. He would always have a scar, but the risk of infection was minimal with her power increasing the healing process. The invading darkness and the shimmering glow that fought it had both disappeared.

His lung was inflating and deflating well, and his heartbeat was strong and steady in his chest once more. Moving her hand to his left wrist she tensed and, through touch alone, located the fracture. Targeting her magic to the broken point she fused bone, mended muscle, interweaving his veins and testing the receptor movements.

Eira swayed on her feet, feeling a trickling sensation from her nose. When she reached up, her hand came away coated in blood. She knew if she were to hold her hand up to the light, she would see a glimmering radiance. Elowen rushed to her side, catching her before she crashed to the floor. Supporting her friend, she helped her to the nearest chair.

'You'll be the one on the bed in a minute,' Elowen joked, handing Eira another glass of water. Wiping her face with a tissue, Eira quickly pocketed the evidence.

'He's stable and will survive. You did that, Emma,' Elowen said with admiration, staring down at Eira who was shifting uncomfortably.

'No, we did it, Elowen,' Eira stated firmly, holding her friend's hand.

'How is this time different than before? The boy had the same injuries. The same black eyes.'

An image of the limp body flashed through Eira's mind. She could almost sense the ghost of his weight in her arms, the tang of his blood on the back of her throat. It was one of the deaths that she had witnessed which had left a scar on her. Left a scar on them both. But it had also cemented their friendship.

'The boy was brought to us too late. His wound was too deep, and he was very weak. When I used my powers to investigate, I could sense death on his breath,' Eira explained sincerely, releasing her friend's hand. 'Believe me, I tried to heal him, but what happened today happened then as well. Now we know that my powers alone cannot heal this black virus sweeping the city.'

'What do you think it is?' whispered Elowen, hugging her arms tightly around herself.

'I'm not sure. But I know who invented it and released it into the city,' Eira boldly stated. 'Now, let's go and face the others.'

Feeling some resolve and fight coming back to her, Eira inhaled as she opened the locked door of the treatment room. Her headache had dulled to a low throb at her temples, and her magic was depleted, but at least she could stand without shaking. She needed a good night's sleep to order her muddled thoughts. Elowen stood behind her, a sentry at the man's treatment room. Eira admired her friend for not prying into her powers. For the first time in her life, she finally knew loyalty.

'What in All Souls has been going on?' Nora demanded, her eyebrows raised, and a scowl twisting her features.

Standing there, arms folded across her ample chest in her immaculate, dark-blue nurse's uniform, with her left foot tapping in its pink Croc, her fury was palpable.

Nora had been on Eira's case since her first day at the clinic. Highly suspicious and constantly seeking praise, she was always trying to stay close to the action. Her complaints to Moyra six months ago, about Eira's methods, and how she always treated patients on her own, had been the climax to their silent feud.

As the clinic's director, Moyra had sided with Eira's approach stating that if it saved patients' lives then it didn't matter if she did it on her own. Like a poker player, Nora had switched tactics, complimenting the star Doctor and asking to shadow her. A compromise had been struck that Nora would shadow Eira twice a week.

Today was one of Nora's designated days.

Lifting her chin and not even looking in Nora's direction, Eira addressed Moyra directly. 'I was under pressure to make a quick diagnosis to save his life. Sister Elowen was already in the room in a critical position with the patient. If she had moved, he would have bled out. We would have had the Batman boy all over again.'

Bringing the boy's death into this was low. Moyra nodded once, understanding the significance.

'So, Matron, I apologise for locking the door, but I needed to concentrate,' Eira said through gritted teeth, finally meeting Nora's eyes.

'That still does not explain, Doctor, why you didn't unlock the door after the thud and flash we heard,' Nora snarled at Eira.

'Ladies, we are professionals here.' Moyra's ever calming voice sliced through the tension. 'Nora, back off and let Emma and Elowen explain.' Though her tone was even, Eira could see that she was beginning to get frustrated with Nora, exasperation written clearly on her lined face.

Eira exhaled the breath she had been holding, glancing around the hushed ward at the sleeping patients and constant beeping machinery humming like a giant beehive. Sunlight crept through gaps in the plywood covering the shattered windows, indicating that hours had passed since she first entered the treatment room.

'Our patient was in a critical position. He had a laceration to his chest, and his lung had been punctured by the weapon. We have drained the fluid from his lung and chest cavity, given him oxygen, and stitched up his wound. He is stable now, but the next twenty-four hours are going to be critical,' Eira finished her assessment.

'That still does not explain the loud boom and...' Nora stopped abruptly at the sharp stare from Moyra.

'That was my fault, Matron.' Eira shrugged, gesturing to the room behind Elowen, attempting to use Nora's respectable title to ease the situation. 'Sister Elowen was in a critical position putting pressure on his wound, so she couldn't move. We didn't have the correct machinery with us to perform a clear thoracostomy, so I guessed by listening to his chest.' She gestured to the stethoscope around her neck.

'That was extremely risky,' Moyra stated, 'but ultimately it saved his life.'

Nora inhaled and pointed at Eira, ready to argue again, but Elowen stepped forward before she could continue.

'If Doctor Backwater hadn't acted the way she did, we would have lost a life today.' Elowen looked each of them in the eye, daring them to challenge her. They glanced away from her fierce stare, knowing that loss all too well.

'I couldn't move, so when Doctor Backwater collapsed on the floor, taking the light and monitor with her, there was nothing I could do. So, Matron, *that* was your bang and the reason why I didn't unlock the door.'

Eira put a hand on her friend's arm. 'I've worked two days straight, without much food or rest, so I passed out from exhaustion,' Eira concluded. 'We dedicate ourselves to the care of others and can neglect ourselves sometimes.'

Moyra nodded in agreement, some of the tension easing from her shoulders.

'I had no option but to continue and stitch him up,' Elowen said, 'hoping Emma would come around. She was out for a while. I managed to get her to the chair and give her water once I had finished with the patient.'

'Have you any injuries?' Moyra's evaluating gaze slid over her.

'Only my head.' Eira indicated the dressing on her right temple.

'I'd still like to examine you, just for my peace of mind.'

Moyra guided Eira to the nearest chair, shining her pen torch in her eyes and rotating her neck to check for injury. Eira prayed that Moyra wouldn't lift the dressing; on reflex, her magic healed any injury she might sustain, leaving no evidence behind.

Straightening her back, Moyra announced that Eira was fit and well. Adjusting her folded headscarf and smoothing her blazer, Eira stood.

'Who is he then?' Nora blurted, her thirst for gossip overtaking her anger.

Eira gestured for them to enter the room, watching their reactions as they took in the smashed light on its side and the dented monitor which was, surprisingly, still beeping.

Elowen gave her a secret wink as she stood in the far corner, making room for the others around the bed. Smashing the light silently had been a challenge. The bed sheet and the side of the monitor had been their choice of tools.

Eira took the position of authority at the man's head, with Nora and Moyra flanking either side of the bed. They had removed the man's blood-stained top and neatly folded his leather jacket on the bedside table. His breathing was steady with the oxygen mask over his nose and mouth. Colour was slowly returning to his cheeks, and he looked peaceful in his sleep. Eira's fingers tingled with the desire to investigate his awareness and pain.

'Very neat stitching and plaster cast, Sister Elowen.' Moyra's approving tone sliced through the tense silence as she placed her glasses on the end of her nose, smiling at Elowen, who blushed.

'His name is Captain Cole Hawkins of the Metropolitan Police.' Eira handed them his official ID.

'I thought Captain was a military term?' Nora voiced her opinion.

'It is indeed,' Moyra answered, handing the ID back to Eira. 'He looks young to be a captain in charge of a unit of men.'

'I wonder what happened,' Elowen said, fingering the hem of her light-blue nurse's uniform. One black biker boot rested against the peeling plastered wall.

'We do have another problem though,' Eira said, lifting the man's unruly black hair from his face and opening his left eye. Shining her pen torch, Moyra leant forward, glasses on her nose, then gasped. Nora placed a hand over her mouth.

'The virus hasn't taken full control,' Eira showed them his bright-blue right eye. 'As far as we can tell, he isn't fully infected. As it's something you can't catch, he should be safe. This makes him the first survivor we've had.'

'H-he might still become infected though,' Nora stammered, stepping back as if she could catch the parasite from just being in the same room. They had no face masks or protection. When the NHS was disbanded, product supply was the first casualty.

'He needs a full scan when he's out of the danger zone to establish if the virus is only partially infecting him,' Moyra said, taking control. Her eyes met Eira's, knowing the results they'd found from scanning the dead Batman boy.

'He can only tell his story when he's awake. This situation stays between the four of us,' Moyra ordered. 'All non-infected patients need to be relocated. This door and the main ward door will stay locked. I would like to assess the people he came in with.'

Moyra leant over the patient again. 'How about these marks here?' She indicated his cheek.

'He already had those,' Elowen said quickly.

Moyra raised an eyebrow but didn't make any more comment. She strode from the room with Nora on her heels, a lapdog at its master's beck and call. Raising her eyebrows and pushing off the wall, Elowen followed. Eira traced the vertical lines on the man's cheek one last time, before exiting the room and locking it behind her.

Approaching the two silent figures outside the treatment room, Eira found herself crossing her fingers behind her back hoping that they were mistaken.

The first patient was stocky with a mop of ginger hair and a matching goatee; he had a hooked nose and laughter creases in the corners of his eyes. Eira imagined that he was the joker of the group.

Moyra bent over him and shone her torch in both eyes. Shaking her head, she looked rueful. Elowen did the same with the second patient. He was built like a bouncer, his face flushed with fever. The despair on Elowen's face was nearly too much.

Both patients had black eyes.

'Nora get both of these gentlemen to the CT scan now,' Moyra commanded. 'Emma and Elowen with me.'

Nora sprang into action, stampeding through the main doors where they could hear her commanding the troops. Moyra exited the same way with Eira and Elowen close behind.

Moyra caught a passing nurse and, to their surprise, instructed her to remove three patients from the ward. Where they would be relocated to, Eira couldn't imagine. They were already at full capacity and were being forced into the unsafe upper levels of the disused office block that housed the clinic. Most of their patients were from the lower classes who were struggling under the new regime.

Moyra found a nook in the abandoned corridor, skirting around cracked ceiling tiles and rubble from a ceiling cave-in.

'We all experienced the death of the Batman boy,' Moyra said, folding her arms. 'We were able to keep it hidden from the Dark.'

Eira looked down at the floor, unable to keep the sadness from her face, and the tears from welling in the corners of her eyes. The abandoned boy had staggered into their clinic a week after Eira started. He was thirteen; barely old enough to be on the streets on his own. He had died in her arms, her power unable to save him. She had questioned why her magic hadn't worked, blaming her inexperience. Today's events told her that this wasn't the case.

Moyra had carried out the post-mortem herself. They had kept his frail body in the morgue for months, placing adverts in the papers and on posters around the local area. But no one claimed him. So, Moyra had paid for a simple funeral out of her own money. They had nicknamed him the Batman boy from the picture book they found in his pocket.

'This time, I don't think we'll be able to keep it quiet. Especially if they are police,' Moyra stated, looking down her nose at them.

'What are you suggesting we do?' Elowen asked.

'First, we keep an eye on the two infected patients to see if they rise again, like the rest.'

Stunned, Eira's head snapped up, her green eyes sparkling, and cheeks wet with tears. Her mouth hung open in shock, and she saw the same expression on her friend's face.

'That could put us and everyone else in the clinic in danger!' Elowen countered, throwing her arms in the air.

'Aren't you fed up with not fighting back?' Moyra said calmly. 'Day after day we treat patients who, because of the Dark, can't even get simple health care. I fund this clinic from my own pocket and those of our charitable benefactors. Emma, you don't even receive a salary.' Moyra gestured towards Eira. 'I'm tired of our situation and having no future to look forward to. What I'm suggesting will not put anyone in danger. I simply propose that we observe and see what happens. Then, we take the scientific information we have gained and use it to research a cure to the darkness spreading in the city.'

Elowen glanced at Eira before dropping her eyes to the floor. She knew that Eira carried the cure around her neck, but Elowen's silence was enough confirmation that she wouldn't betray Eira's trust.

I know how to heal them. I know how to stop this.

The words were on the tip of her tongue. Here were the two people she trusted most in her life. New friends who had helped her more than they knew. Her body seized up, the words locked in her mind. She had promised her aunt that she would protect herself, hide her powers, and not draw any unwanted attention.

Well, after today, that was out of the window.

'You're unusually quiet, Emma,' Elowen said, eyebrows raised.

Swallowing, Eira set her face into a tired smile and brushed the tears from her eyes.

She was fed up with hiding who she was, weary of witnessing the poverty and struggle of the people around her in their everyday lives. But she knew firsthand the danger of going up against the Dark. She had to draw a line in the sand and protect this fragile life she had created.

'I agree with Moyra,' Eira began slowly, almost in a whisper. 'But...' — she held up a slender finger — '... we take the two infected males somewhere else, away from the clinic. We monitor them from afar, see where they go, or if *they* come for them. They can't be protected, not now they're fully under the parasite's control.'

Both women nodded in agreement.

'What about Captain Hawkins?' Elowen asked.

'When he wakes, we listen to his story and then we move him somewhere safe as soon as he has recovered enough,' Moyra suggested.

'I ask only one thing,' Eira said. 'That Elowen remains at home for the next week or so until the situation has resolved itself.'

Elowen scowled and took a sharp intake of breath, a look of hurt crossing her face. 'I will not be sent home! Not when the rest of you are risking so much.' She stamped her heavy black boot, which made the ceiling shudder, causing a dust cloud to rain over them. 'Perhaps you should take some time off too, Emma. You're exhausted,' Elowen begged.

Moyra raised a wrinkled hand before either of them could protest.

'Both of you are correct. Emma, I do not want to see you here tomorrow, you need to recover. But I want you to interview the captain when he wakes up,' Moyra stated with authority. 'Elowen, you are my youngest and most enthusiastic member of staff. You are my responsibility. If I had my way, I would send you both home for protection. I have no authority over Doctor Backwater as she is my volunteer, but I am afraid that I do have authority, as your employer, over you. I beg you to remain at home until I send word that it's safe to return.'

Moyra's pleading face shattered Eira's heart. Elowen ran her hands over her face in frustration, smearing her makeup even more. She blinked behind her thick fringe, nodded once, and turned on her heels, leaving without a backward glance.

Eira felt the new thread of friendship between her and Elowen fray, and she hoped she would be able to make up for it soon.

CHAPTER 3

||| EIRA

Through the cracked double-doors, the day outside appeared inviting. Although it was the beginning of October, the sky was bright and crisp, with only a few wisps of white clouds sailing by. The blissful blue was in stark contrast to the destroyed urban landscape upon which it shone.

Eira paused on the threshold with her pass in her hand.

The thought of returning to the deserted streets, the empty shops, the time curfews, and constant monitoring of her life daunted her today. This was why she stayed in the clinic.

The hard, plastic pass in her hand displayed a picture of her, but even that was a lie. Most of her honey-coloured hair was covered by an azure-blue band around her forehead and ears. The headscarf had become her trademark uniform at the clinic. It kept her messy hair from escaping and the sweat from her eyes. But it was also concealment and protection against her real identity.

It disguised her slender, pointy ears which would distinguish her as an outsider from her human colleagues. She was descended from elves, though she wasn't full-blooded. She was worse; a half-breed, a mongrel, something to fear, something to spit at in the street.

The government term was "hybrid". An illegal combination of two gene pools which had been outlawed since the end of World War II, due to the immense power and unpredictability they supposedly possessed.

Even the name printed on the pass had been stolen. EMMA BACKWATER.

Her whole identity was a fabrication to protect her against the corrupt government, which would make her disappear without a trace if she was exposed.

Eira was tired of pretending, of hiding in plain sight. Today she had just blown two years' worth of careful manipulation, guarded secrets, and possibly the life she had become accustomed to also.

With a confidence she didn't feel, she swiped her card in the slot, pushed the buzzing door, and stepped out into reality. Throwing her bomber jacket's fur-lined hood over her head, she eased her satchel over her shoulder, and stomped down Epworth Street.

The disused office block with its smashed glass façade and graffiti on its doors was a lifeline to most of the inhabitants of central London seeking aid with any health-related problems. Since the collapse of the NHS ten years ago, four clinics had replaced the major hospitals in the capital, each clinic self-funded by charities and benefactors. It was even rumoured that some of the rebel groups funded them. The Dark, the current government which had come into force a decade ago, mostly left the clinics alone.

They were all desperately understaffed and lacking in medical equipment and resources. Eira's clinic, the Wallflower, was the largest in capacity and reputation, and patients came from far across the city seeking their aid. The success rate of their clinic, which was down to Eira's magic, made the place even more popular, and the rising number of patients had placed a strain on the staff. But it had also increased the funding from the secret benefactors. Eira wondered if they would continue if they found they had a magic user in their mix.

Eira kept an unhurried pace. To any onlookers she appeared to be a normal commuter walking home. She had spent years learning how to blend into society, suppressing her lightning-fast reactions and sharp senses. It would take her two hours to walk home at her current speed; she knew she could run it in half the time.

She felt on edge after the events at the clinic. Eira found herself listening for any sounds of drone pursuit and staring at anyone who gave her more than a passing glance. She had left Moyra to arrange a safehouse for the two patients infected with the Dark virus. Unfortunately, she had missed Elowen in the staffroom and so couldn't explain her motives.

She clenched her hands into fists and increased her stride. She needed to get home to the safety of her small bedsit. But first, she had to make a detour.

At least the fresh air had cleared her headache.

Eira passed through the black, wrought-iron gates and imposing columned entrance to Bunhill Fields. The weak sun penetrated the canopy of leaves overhead, turning the ground at Eira's feet into a kaleidoscope of reds and yellows.

She could hear the chirping of blackbirds perched on the crumbling gravestones long forgotten by the residents of Islington. Their solemn stones cast long shadows across the gravel path in the fading light of the afternoon. In milder weather, Bunhill Fields was Eira and Elowen's favourite spot to gossip about Nora's latest tantrum over steaming flasks of coffee on their bench under the twisted oak, which still held its green leaves.

She continued onto the main road, keeping her eyes ahead. If she stopped for too long to look at the boarded-up shops with the smashed windows and rebel graffiti on the walls, she would break down in the nearest doorway. Some buildings were vast craters with ashen skeletal frames reaching skywards.

She mourned the London of her childhood.

She reminisced about the bustling streets and the open markets her mum used to take her to. The sheer volume of noise and number of bodies pressed into a confined space was overwhelming at the time, but she would give anything to be back there now. But even then, she could still remember the shadows beginning to develop in the backstreets, the whisperings of a growing power in the depths of humanity. Her mother had been a light in the narrowing dark of her childhood, standing up for her rights of equality in a corrupt society.

Eira's hand drifted to the necklace under her sweater.

The Dark was the reason why the vibrant city she had once known was now a grey smudge on the horizon. Being back in London had brought it all back. The anger, regret, and loneliness. The unanswered questions surrounding her mother's death. If she let that anger take root again, she wouldn't be able to do what now needed to be done. To protect her little slice of happiness in a sea of darkness.

Rounding the corner, Eira heard the monotonous low tone of a drone gliding overhead. The constant humming had been one of the changes she had found hardest to adapt to, her heightened hearing amplifying the sound until it vibrated inside her skull. The drones were harmless. It was the heavily-armoured, blacked-out trucks following them that you had to watch out for.

Eira's hearing was her saviour as she could pick out the low hum from a mile away. Ducking into the nearest doorway she pressed herself into the shadowed recess. The drone zoomed by, rotating a camera monitoring the street inside its helical body. She had passed at least two other people on her journey, and she knew that they would be stopped.

Counting to twenty, she heard the crunch of tyres and sprinting feet. Holding her breath, she prayed the runner wouldn't choose her doorway to hide in.

On returning to London, she had spent weeks monitoring how the Dark operated. The constant stop-and-searches were one of the main ways they inflicted terror and captured hybrids.

To their great arrogance they didn't know what was right under their feet. Her anger simmered to the surface again.

Clutching her satchel to her chest, she heard the roar of the engine as the truck accelerated after the sprinter. She knew the scene all too well. They would be thrown to the ground by agents in black uniforms with black, lifeless eyes, handcuffed and bundled into the back of the truck, never to be seen again. Hearing the final thud of the truck's doors, Eira counted to fifty before tentatively stepping back into the street, heart hammering.

No evidence of the soul smuggled into the back of the truck.

Knowing she had a small window of time to reach her destination before the next search, Eira broke into a jog, passing the entrance to Angel Underground.

To take the underground was tempting. To enter you had to have nothing to hide, you simply had to prove you were completely pure of blood. Fully human.

When the Dark seized control of the capital, one of their first legislations was a blood tax on public transport and spaces. Within the first few months, the Dark had captured hundreds of hybrids and Myths. Anyone who visited the library, took the train, or went to the local supermarket and didn't submit to a blood tax was interrogated.

"Myths" was a slang word humans used to describe mythological creatures or immortals. Some were magic-users, others weren't. The one thing they had in common was that they were persecuted by the Dark. Even humans were not immune to the horrific treatment.

Eira slowed to a quick walk as she approached the bridge over Regent's canal. Halting on Danbury Street, she looked ahead to Islington Tunnel. She glanced along the street and saw a delivery van speeding past, and a man with his hood up, walking on the opposite side of the road. This was as quiet as she could hope for.

Slipping off her hood, she reached behind her neck and undid the clasp of her necklace. She let the opal drop into her palm, feeling its weight. Eira slid the tiny key off the long chain and placed it inside her back pocket. The key was the reason she had returned to London. The reason why she had remained for too long: her fear of the answers to the questions she needed to ask.

Taking a breath, she stepped up to the brick parapet. Ahead, the Islington Tunnel loomed like a giant void, sucking in light. A few abandoned barges lapped against their moorings in the churning water below.

She had to be brave. She had to do this to protect her life here, her identity. If she didn't, they would come after her, endangering the clinic and everything she cared about.

The chain, as delicate as silk, glided between her fingers as the opal's weight descended towards the murky water below. Catching the light, the opal refracted sparkling colours onto the water's surface.

Reflexively, Eira's slender hand closed around the chain, halting its fall. A single tear slid down her nose and dropped into the brown stagnant depths without a ripple.

What was I thinking?

With shaking hands, Eira clutched the opal to her chest. Her mother's legacy, her only inheritance, and she had nearly tossed it into the canal like a murder weapon, to selfishly protect her life in London. A place where she had already overstayed her welcome.

For a split second, her hands were smaller, covered in dark red blood. Hands helplessly trying to cover a wound she didn't have the ability to heal yet. A chest struggling for air and an opal smeared red in her palm.

Eira caught her breath, coming back to the present moment as she heard the distant roar of traffic and felt the caress of the breeze off the water. She immediately scanned the area around her; she had dawdled for too long.

Sliding her necklace into the pocket of her bomber jacket, she walked briskly down the worn flagstone path towards Regent's canal, trying to shake the lingering dread of what she had nearly done. The canal, at the height of the industrial revolution, served as a trade link to Paddington and the Grand Junction Canal. Now forgotten by most, it was overgrown, with deep, dark waters and decaying barges.

An unremembered part of London, not used by the current government, had become the lifeblood of another.

The weed-infested water rippled beside Eira. Glancing to the side, she smirked to herself as she saw fins and a spiny tail. She knew she was being monitored.

The rotting barges raised the hairs on the back of Eira's arms. The gaping portholes in the hulls gave the impression of spies in the deep darkness. Peeling shutters banged and screeched in the wind, with the water lapping against the keels. Any average human would turn back now, but Eira could see into the darkness and was able to discern that the fear she was feeling wasn't natural.

Looming ahead was the Islington Tunnel. The arched portal, defined by its geometric keystones, sucked the surrounding light into the centre void. Even Eira's sharp vision couldn't penetrate the darkness of London's longest tunnel.

A smacking sound like a wet fish followed by a belch reached Eira's ears, and she grinned at the horrid sound.

'Ma gul,' hiccupped the tramp, reclining beside the tunnel's entrance.

'Hey, Issy.' Eira waved. Snuggled under layer upon layer of blankets it was hard to make out Issy's form. All Eira could see was her weathered wrinkled face, gummy mouth and thinning grey hair under a tartan hat. Her alert amber eyes shone with mischief.

'Wha' ou doin' ere?'

Issy was a bridge troll and the protector of the Islington Tunnel's entrance. The secret tunnels were used by the Myths as a network for trade, passage, and protection to move unseen around the city. The entrances could be anywhere, you just had to look for the waymarks. The Islington Tunnel was the central hub of the underground maze, a place where precious objects could be kept safe.

26

'I've come to deposit an item for safekeeping.'

Smacking her bloated lips, Issy replied, 'Ou don' ormly posit, ightingale.' Eira smiled at the affectionate term that Issy used. The other Myths called her Nightingale after Florence Nightingale. They all knew about her healing skills and had benefited from them more than once.

Kneeling, Eira asked, 'How is that toe of yours, Issy? Have you been keeping your weight off it?'

She knew that the troll had been — she barely moved off her vast behind. She couldn't wander far from her bridge, being magically tethered to it. She might appear fully human to any passerby, but beneath the human glamour was a wart-infested exterior with the consistency of slimy toads. Despite her appearance, Eira knew that the troll could match her for speed if she needed to. She was sitting on the magical trigger, in case of an attack. If she moved off the trigger, the bridge's defences would activate, securing the entrance from invaders. Something that Eira hoped would never happen.

Issy huffed, wrinkling her amber eyes in amusement. 'Do ou ave ayment?'

Eira reached into her satchel, wrinkling her nose at the rotting smell wafting from the closed container she was carrying. Issy's podgy arm was already outstretched, fingers working like the beak of a baby bird desperate for its next meal. Her fingers grabbed the fish out of the container greedily. Eira averted her eyes as Issy swallowed the fish whole, but that didn't stop the wet smacking sounds and the crunch of bones reaching her ears.

'At wos ood. Ank ou ma gul,' Issy said with a massive, toothless grin. 'Ou no wear tu go.'

Straightening, Eira thanked the ancient troll and stepped out into midair across the water. If she had never done this before, fear would have taken over, and she would have been a nervous wreck on the bank. Even with her experience, her stomach still plummeted like she was on a rollercoaster.

Her foot met a solid surface even though she knew she appeared to be floating in the air. Glancing back and waving to the bridge troll behind her, Eira made her other foot join the one on the magical pathway under the bridge. She knew that Issy could quite easily send her plummeting into the watery depths to be eaten by her other pet. As if sensing her thoughts, scaly fins breached the surface of the water, sending ominous ripples out in front of Eira.

Peering into the deepening dark, Eira placed her palm on the tunnel's damp stone wall. Her touch activated the glowing embers in the apex of the tunnel, creating a sinister twilight. Her hand traced the engravings on the stone surface, foretelling the story of the bridge troll's enslavement to that bridge. Issy's was a sad one of betrayal and heartache.

Eira finally reached her destination. Halfway along the tunnel, a passageway revealed itself, sensing that she had something to deposit. The space was only wide enough for one person to enter, and even then, it was a squeeze. Carved into the white stones were roman numerals depicting the available safety boxes. As Eira entered the endless passageway, the magical embers gradually flared to life above her head.

The numeral XX caught her eye. The date of her mother's death seemed like an apt place to store her necklace. Drawing a scalpel across her finger, she traced the crosses, paying the required blood tax. The brick slid sideways, and a drawer popped out, waiting for her necklace. Blowing out her cheeks with relief, Eira gently placed it inside, pushing the drawer closed with a click. The XX immediately vanished before her eyes.

Eira gasped with the suddenness of the drawer closing with no visible mechanism to reopen it. *What have I done?* For a moment she was back on the bridge, her hand poised above the water, about to make a life-altering mistake. Eira knew that to gain access to her box again, she would need to make another blood payment.

A sense of desperate urgency overwhelmed her, and she dragged the scalpel roughly across her finger again, already placing her finger on the wall before the blood had even started to drip. She watched with relief as the numerals flashed up again, and her drawer sprung open. The desperation left her as she confirmed that she would be able to get to her necklace when needed, and her shoulders slumped as though a weight was lifted off them. She knew that, with the tunnel's defences and magical shields, her necklace wouldn't be detected by the Dark. Now, hopefully her link to the captain's recovery would go unnoticed.

|||

Weary to her core, Eira emerged from a brick wall near Half Penny Steps along Harrow Street in North Kensington. The doorway automatically sealed behind her, vanishing from view, the rebel graffiti melding together again. It was now early evening, and the pink sun was dipping behind the skyscrapers of central London. Curfew was an hour away.

She had left Islington after bestowing another treat on a smug Issy who swore she wouldn't tell a soul that she had been there. She had found the nearest waymarker, which took her home through the underground network, heading for the Grand Canal. She crossed the rusty blue footbridge over the canal which was congested with weeds.

The Dark changed shift just before curfew, when they would come out in greater force. But it also gave any stragglers a better opportunity to sneak home without meeting any patrols.

Reaching into the last of her magic reserves, Eira sent a pulse of magic through her veins to give herself enough energy to jog home. The burnt cars of Kensal Road blurred past, and she eventually rounded the corner and saw the brutalist tower block that she called home.

Trellick Tower was a savage structure of exposed concrete, broken only by the glint of windows from hundreds of flats confined within its main rectangular block. Accessed via the floating bridges to its service tower, the ninety-eight-meter tall building penetrated the darkening sky and cast a long shadow across the ground.

29

Eira normally dreaded the return to her bedsit, the loneliness and quietness stark after the buzz and stress of the clinic. Today she couldn't wait for the shabby comfort she called home on the twenty-sixth floor.

Entering through the main atrium, she marveled at the architect's abstract design. Whilst the exterior was dark and foreboding, the main lobby was punctured by primary-coloured stained-glass blocks refracting the fading light into rainbows on the floor. All other surfaces were hard and functional, including the dark-blue metal lifts which she called down.

Eira stepped into the lift, quickly becoming aware of a presence behind her. Taking a quick sniff, she was able to identify the figure, and she glanced over her shoulder and down. But she quickly raised her eyes with a gasp to meet the gaze of the dwarf stepping into the lift.

'Something tickling you, Nightingale?' rumbled the dwarf.

'Sorry, Franklin, no offence meant,' Eira admitted. 'It was just a surprise to see you taller than usual.'

Franklin huffed his great chest, rolling his shoulders and cracking his knuckles. 'Well, it is your potions that allow this to happen,' he said, gesturing to his large bulk.

As Nightingale, Eira's other persona, she acted as the Myths' doctor and potions master, treating their ailments and enabling them to disguise themselves in human form. Her height-enhancing spell, taught to her by Etta, was one of her bestsellers.

Franklin was one of her best customers. He worked on barges transporting goods for the Myths, and often raided the Dark's warehouses for much needed supplies. His work provided welcome medical equipment to the Wallflower. Occasionally he would step from the safety of the tunnels to do some scouting in the human realm.

It made her heart hurt that such courageous Myths had to resort to altering themselves simply to survive.

'Have you been above today?' she asked.

A grunt was her only reply. She knew better than to pry. Secrecy was important in the work that they did.

Eira leaned against the walls of the lift, crossing her purple Doc Martens at the ankles. She found her eyes roaming from Franklin's large black boots to his ample belly tucked in with a rusted belt, his clan insignia of two crossed hammers as the buckle. His mighty bronzed hammer appeared small against his increased height. Knowing that he was also observing her, she met his coal-dark eyes wrinkled with amusement within his weathered face.

'You know, chick, because of you I need two different wardrobes.'

Despite the exhaustion and utter despair that she felt, a giggle bubbled in her throat until she was doubled over with laughter.

'You wouldn't know how confusing it is to have size three and size nine boots in the same cupboard. Don't get me wrong, I enjoy the height. Means I can reach the top shelf in the kitchen. But it does sometimes get confusing here.' He pointed a thick finger to his temple, shaking his head.

Eira lifted her head and felt tears welling in the corners of her eyes again. Franklin stroked his plaited beard, giving her a sympathetic look.

'Rough day, hey, chick?'

'Something like that.'

The lift jolted to a halt at floor twenty-three, shifting with Franklin's weight as he moved to exit. Slamming a dinner-sized plate of a hand on the closing doors, he grumbled, 'If you ever need me, Nightingale, you know where I am. You give enough to us. It is about time we gave something back.'

In the humbled look staining Franklin's aged face as the lift doors closed, she saw the dwarf's sincerity, and it nearly shattered the last of her self-control. As the lift shook to life again, she pinched the bridge of her nose, closing her eyes to keep the tears at bay.

In no time at all, she was walking along the link bridge to her flat. Smelling of piss, with sprayed scribbles over the walls, she glimpsed London's spectacular silhouetted skyline in the twilight as she emerged into the dank endless corridor of her floor. The leading wall was tiled in olive-green mosaics punctured by sickly-green front doors. She paused at number three, inserting her key in the lock. She was finally home.

The shiny blue floor of the communal corridor continued into Eira's flat, blending with the turquoise walls. Not her choice. But since this was only temporary, she didn't mind. There was a tiny kitchen to her left as she entered her flat with the same olive-green doors, peeling and shabby. The only time she used it was to microwave her meals. A drab bathroom took up the space to her right, with cracked, white metro tiles and a dated avocado suite. The main room had a sagging antique-leather sofa by the window overlooking the balcony. The unmade bed pushed against the far wall and a rail of clothes were the only signs that the place was lived in.

She made sure the door was securely locked, fastening the top, middle, and bottom bolts.

Her only treasured possession was her chemistry kit which was carefully set out on the dining room table against the far wall opposite the bed. She took great pride in this and used it to concoct her potions. On the other side of the table was a monitor rigged up to the block's CCTV which she used for her safety. Stashed underneath, was her sturdy medical bag and potions kit, which was always packed in case she had to escape quickly.

Bending, she fished the bag out from under the table and slid her key into the front pocket, withdrawing the creased photo which she kept there. Sighing heavily, Eira retreated to the bed, laying on her back to look at the image. She had looked at it so often that she could conjure it in her mind without the picture, but she liked the comfort of holding it in her hands.

The photo, ripped in half, depicted a woman with a curly mess of chestnut hair smiling with joy at the camera, cradling in her lap a toddler who was sticking her tongue out at the camera. The toddler had strawberry-blonde hair, slightly pointed ears, and stunning green eyes. The rip cut off the toddler's right arm, but it didn't detract from the love radiating from the photograph. A younger, happier photo of herself with her mother, one sunny day before her world imploded.

Eira closed her eyes, for a moment lost in her past anguish and current hopelessness. She slowly drifted into a deep regenerative sleep, fully clothed, her only photograph of her mother clutched in her outstretched hand.

CHAPTER 4

Δ COLE

As Cole's consciousness crept back, pain hit him like a tidal wave. He couldn't move his limbs, and he felt as if he was stuck in quicksand. He could recall snatches of memory as they flitted through his mind, but in his confusion, he wasn't able to grasp hold of any to examine further.

He still felt the unnerving sensation of control of his body and mind being wrenched from him, an invading force stealing through him.

The pain was so intense that it pushed all coherent thought from his head.

Finally, he was able to move a little. and he tried wiggling his toes and stretching his legs. Cole flexed his right arm, clenching the soft sheets under his palm. His left arm was encased in something hard, and he couldn't curl his fingers properly. But the pain wasn't radiating from his arm.

The searing pain was concentrated in his chest and travelled down to his stomach. An image flashed in his mind: a pale hand holding a serrated onyx dagger.

Cole's eyes fluttered open; his head lolled to one side as a moan escaped his cracked lips. A new panic gripped him like a vice. The vision from his left eye was blurred, fogged like a black mist.

As he turned his head, Cole saw her sitting on a chair, knees pulled up to her chin, the glowing screen in her hands lighting her features from underneath. Before he could open his mouth to speak, she moved, flitting from her chair to stand next to him.

Her palms met his flesh and a calming sensation washed through his body, abruptly stopping the pain. Gasping for air like a drowned swimmer, his mind cleared, and he became aware of his surroundings. He took in the room as the woman eased him into a sitting position and tipped a cool glass of water to his lips. He spluttered, gulping the pleasant liquid, and spilling it down his chin.

'Easy. Drink more slowly.' Her voice was soft and gentle, putting him at ease straight away.

His eyes closed as he focused on his breathing, calming his mind as if he were in training, loading his gun before he took aim at the target. Cole cracked open his good eye, struggling to form the words to ask where he was. His throat was so dry.

The woman in front of him held his stare. Her eyes were stunning, deep-green, reminding him of the lake from basecamp, calming and serene. She wore a jade fabric band around her head, the length of it woven into her long braid, which slid over her slender shoulder as she cocked her head to one side. Her hair was the colour of honey. As he opened his damaged eye, the room was cast into shadow, and he saw the copper, gold, and white tones running through her hair. An image of her hair spread around her face, glowing, crossed his mind for an instant.

'Where am I?' he croaked after a second sip of water.

'You're at the Wallflower clinic. You were brought in two days ago,' she replied calmly.

He had been unconscious for two days. Fear gripped him. *My team!*

He recalled an explosion. Men with black lifeless eyes. Sam's body had been thrown back.

He couldn't locate Flint and Tagger in the jumble of his memories.

Lofty. Lofty was the traitor. He caused this.

'Were any others brought in?' he rasped with his unused voice. He closed his eyes again as nausea took over. He couldn't focus his bad eye, and it was making him feel sick.

'How are you feeling?' the doctor enquired, tactically avoiding answering his question. It must be bad.

'Like I've been beaten with a red-hot fire poker in hell.' Cole grimaced.

'I didn't mean your injuries. I meant your new symptoms.'

Cole leant his head back on the comfy pillows and opened his good eye to peer at the doctor. She had a smirk on her lips.

'What's your name?' he asked.

'For someone who has just woken up from a major injury, you do ask a lot of questions.'

34

'I can't help it, I'm the curious type,' Cole joked. 'Seriously, what happened? I'm worried about my team. Are you sure no one came in with me?' He paused. 'And I'm about to throw up!'

The doctor held a cardboard pan under his chin, just as he hurled up from the shock of it all. His dark hair was plastered to his forehead as the bile rose, his whole stomach contracting in agony.

Catching his breath, he sank into his pillow nest again. 'Well, that was embarrassing.'

'I've seen worse, believe me.'

Cole raised an eyebrow as he swept his mop of hair from his eyes.

'My name is Doctor Emma Backwater.' Cole thought that the name didn't suit her. 'You were brought in with two others: one with ginger hair and a large bald man. Neither had injuries and are currently on a recovery ward.'

Relief flooded through Cole. Tagger and Flint were fine. *How about Sam?*

'Do you know their names, Captain Hawkins?'

So, she knows my identity then.

'Please call me Cole, Doctor Backwater.' If she was being formal, then he could be as well. 'They're part of my unit. Lieutenant James Tagger is my second-in-command, and Private Ben Flint is our muscle. Are you sure no one else was with us?'

Doctor Emma shook her head and shrugged her slender shoulders, flipping her plait across her back. She was a beauty. Pale as a snowdrop, tall and slender with a lovely curve to her hips and breasts. He didn't let himself finish that thought. He needed to focus on how badly their mission had gone wrong and find out what had happened to Sam. Major Stone was likely to shoot him at dawn.

'You're part of the Met, aren't you?'

Cole nodded, wincing at the shooting pain racing up his chest. He hadn't dared to ask about or look at his own injuries yet, knowing that they would put him out of action for a while and result in another verbal bashing from Major Stone.

'How come your titles are Military then?' the doctor enquired.

'Now who's asking all the questions, Doc?' he joked, grinning despite himself. How much could he tell this civilian? He was in enemy territory and needed help if he was to make it out of this situation. He was in no fit state to just walk out. His first priority was his men and then informing his Major.

'We're a special task force made up of police and army, so it was easier to use the military terms.'

Doctor Emma gave a curt nod, not meeting his eyes. There was something she wasn't saying, he could tell. He had spent enough time interrogating suspects to know when he was being lied to. He also knew when not to push.

'So, Doc, what's the verdict? Am I going to live?' He gestured to himself, finally glancing down. His plastered wrist and eye were the obvious signs of injury, but that didn't explain where his pain had initially come from, or how it had subsided so quickly. Slowly pulling down the sheets, he examined his body through his good eye. His chest, down to his belly button, was wrapped in neat bandages. His skin prickled with goose flesh as heat rose in his cheeks. The doctor was staring at his banged body, a look of faint horror on her face. Do I look that bad?

She gulped and then sat on the chair near the bed, dragging the legs across the floor to better talk to him. She finally looked him in his good eye. Cole found he couldn't stand her sympathetic expression and looked around the room, needing to focus on anything but her face. He found her closeness suddenly stifling. He didn't want to know the outcome.

He was in a simple room, with paint peeling from the walls, and cracked ceiling tiles with a bright light which was insufferable. A sink on the wall, a locked storage unit, and a bedside drawer, were the only furniture other than his bed. Spying an object on his nightstand, relief surged through him. His battered leather jacket, folded with care, looked completely intact.

'You were bleeding out when you were first brought in. You had a punctured lung from the laceration made in your chest. We drained the fluid from your lung, which saved your life,' Doctor Backwater stated calmly, leaning forward, and placing both elbows on her knees. She looked guilty, like Cole should be asking her for an apology. She chewed her bottom lip.

36

'You also had a fractured arm, which we've set and plastered. I'm afraid we have no pain relief readily available so the tightness in your chest is due to that. We should have some paracetamol available by this afternoon.' He was aware of the lack of resources the clinics faced. Was that why she looked so culpable?

'And my eye?' Cole gestured to his left eye with his broken wrist. Hurt reflected in her own eyes for a split second. 'It's making me feel sick. When I open it, I can't focus. All I can see is black mist and shadows.'

In answer, she held a hand mirror to him and gestured for him to look.

Preparing himself, he studied his face with his good eye. As always, his hair was unkempt and falling in his eyes. He swept it back to see a face he barely recognised. His cheeks were hollow, black smudges had appeared under his eyes, and stubble was growing on his jaw. His good eye was still the intense blue it always had been. The left side of his face had no injury, apart from a small scar on his cheek, and he traced his fingers along the three vertical lines. He looked at Doctor Backwater with a question on his face, and she clutched her neck, fingers searching for an item which wasn't there. She gestured for him to open his other eye.

What greeted him sent a pulse of pure horror down his spine. His eye was fully black. Leaving it open for longer this time, he managed to focus enough not to feel sick. It was like having split vision. His black eye brought everything out in relief, in shade and depth, no colour.

'Have you heard of the dark virus?' the doctor said quietly, pulling Cole's attention away from the mirror. Taking his stunned silence as a no, she quickly continued. 'The dark virus appeared ten years ago. No one knows how it spreads or where it came from. But like a parasite, it takes over the host, controlling...' She stopped when Cole raised his hand.

In a flat voice, he muttered, 'I know,' through gritted teeth.

Doctor Emma Backwater kept silent as the reality of what had happened settled in Cole's gut. If he was infected, it would only be a matter of time before he was lost. His heart was hammering in his chest, the increased beeping from the heart monitor was evidence enough. He felt a cold hand resting on his upper forearm, and a soothing sensation spread through his body as his heart rate normalised.

'We think that you're only partially infected. You haven't shown any signs of the expected control.' Her calming voice helped to settle his rising fear. 'We need to do a CT scan to see where it has spread.'

'Why do you think it only partially worked?' Cole asked.

'We don't know, Cole,' Doctor Emma replied. 'That's why I need to understand what happened. How and why was your team attacked?'

He liked the way she said his name.

Before Cole could formulate a reply there was a light tapping on the door, diverting Emma's attention. As the doctor approached the door, Cole noticed for the first time how quiet and dark the wider room was. Closing his blue eye, he focused his infected eye and made out deeper, intense shadows which slowly cleared, showing him the dark room in greater detail than his normal eye would have detected.

Cole focused on the doctor's back and, to his astonishment, detected a faint glow surrounding her. He also found that he could make out the shadow of the person she was speaking to through the wall, dumpy with a hazy grey outline.

Before he could comprehend what this all meant, Emma stepped back into the room looking distressed. 'I must go. There's an emergency. I'll be back as soon as I can, I promise.' Glancing back once, she hurried from the room, locking the door behind her.

As the serenity of Emma's presence disappeared, Cole's fear intensified. His pain amplified, and he clutched his chest in agony. His confusion about his partial infection increased, muting his rational thinking. He thought he could feel the parasite worming its way deeper into his brain.

He reached for the glass of water on the nightstand, knocking it off and shattering it on the floor. That was when he noticed the glowing screen left abandoned on the chair. Groaning in pain, he managed to hook the screen with his good hand and pull it onto his lap.

Adjusting to his new eye, he focused on the lit-up pad. The main screen showed a full body scan of a patient, male by the body's proportions. He was no medical expert, but even he could tell that something was wrong. The veins, where they met the heart and brain, were black. He swiped the screen and found another much larger body scan with the same black infection.

Realisation dawned on Cole as he studied the images. He swiped again to a fuzzy video feed, dated a day earlier, showing two patients asleep in beds in a dark empty room. He could just about make out a huge body with a bald head and another, slighter body, with longer hair. Cole would bet his captain's pay cheque that the other patient's hair was sunset-red.

He flicked through the images again, to what appeared to be a live feed of unfolding events. Both patients were walking around, the stockier of the two hammering on the door and demanding release. As the patient turned to face the camera, Cole cursed, raising his hand to his mouth. A face he knew so well. The only difference was the black, hollowed-out eyes boring into the screen.

Suddenly, the door was unlocked and both figures surged forward. Cole watched as his two comrades — his friends — disappeared. He had to act, had to do something to protect his unit. Sam was most likely lost to him already, but Tagger and Flint were still alive. If his infection had somehow been stopped, surely there was hope. He had to get to the doctor. He paused as he pushed himself up, realising that the doctor had known about this all along. *Why had she lied?*

Shifting his full weight onto his good arm, he pivoted his legs to the floor as nausea threatened his vision. He pushed through, and on shaking legs, eased his feet onto the floor and tried to stand. Pain shot through his stomach, and his vision swam.

Sheer determination and adrenalin kept him upright as he staggered to the door, but his unsteady feet twisted beneath him, and he fell crashing to the floor. Gut-wrenching pain lanced through him and took his breath away. Glancing down, he saw red spreading across his white bandages.

Cole surrendered to oblivion once again, but before he passed out entirely, he registered a pair of purple boots rushing towards him, and strong slender arms grabbing his shoulders, sending a soothing pulse into his body. Delirious, he could have sworn he saw a flash of white light as her palms connected with his flesh.

CHAPTER 5

‖‖ EIRA

Eira puffed warm air into her cupped hands. It was early afternoon. The day was clear but there was a bracing breeze. She raised the fur hood of her jacket and stuck both hands under her armpits. Leaning against a stone chimera on the rooftop on which she was balanced, she glanced at her phone for the umpteenth time.

The tracker app showed that they were close to the Dark's headquarters in central London. They had nearly made it to the Shard, and it would only be a matter of time before they knew if their gamble had worked.

Sighing, she adjusted her shoulder against the creature anchored to the parapet of the Victorian terrace she had chosen for her vigil. The building was a perfect blind spot from the spying eyes of CCTV cameras at ground level and, if a drone flew over, she could crouch behind the raised parapet. Eira hoped that the drones wouldn't be the new heat-sensing ones the Dark had started using.

The gargoyle adorning the once elegant townhouse had avoided the vandalism and destruction of the main house. Completely intact, its squat face had a forlorn expression with a turned-up nose and jowls like a boxer dog. Its membrane wings were tucked in as it perched on the parapet leaving claw marks in the stone. *At least I have a friend for the afternoon.*

She was focused on another abandoned, red-brick mansion in the middle of Battersea. The once grand property would have been worth millions of pounds before the rich fled to the country to escape the reign of the Dark.

Hatred churned in her gut for the ones who had left. The upper-class snobs who had run instead of staying to recapture the capital from the corruption stewing in its pit. The lower classes had been left behind to face the consequences alone.

41

Eira's mobile buzzed, which meant they had reached the target. She still couldn't believe Moyra's contacts. She had managed to obtain a safehouse as far from the clinic as they could find, it was unregistered and had no link to Moyra or the clinic. Eira never asked Moyra how she did it, just accepted the plan to keep the situation under control and away from the clinic's doors.

It had been the best course of action for the safety of the clinic. For them all. It didn't have to sit right with her that these were people's lives that they were gambling.

When Captain Hawkins had given names to the two unconscious men, they had stopped being an experiment against the Dark. They had become real people.

Lieutenant James Tagger.

Private Ben Flint.

Tag and Flint. People.

Eira couldn't shake off the unresponsive stare on the video feed from Moyra's office, as they staggered from the very building she was staking out. The tracking device inserted into the soles of their shoes, the latest tech on the market, untraceable, was just a precaution. They were all aware of where they would be controlled to walk to.

Eira had witnessed the virus's control only once before. On the fallen Batman boy, who had died in the grip of the virus before he could tell them how he became infected. That's why the captain's testimonial was so vital. If he was ever in a fit state to deliver it to her.

She cursed herself again for her carelessness on leaving the screen abandoned on the chair. She had been preoccupied with his symptoms — as soon as he came round, it was obvious that he was in a great deal of pain and distress.

I've never been over-involved with a patient before.

Eira knew that what her necklace had done was a miracle. It might be their only hope against the dark virus eroding the capital city of Great Britain. It also terrified her. She would have to step into her mother's shoes and break rank, which would put her, and everyone she treasured in danger. She needed allies, and Cole could be that to her. It was clear he had strong connections with an organisation, but at present he was isolated in the clinic without any help.

Perhaps that was the only connection she felt towards him, and her guilt was confusing things.

Her phone showed two blinking dots, stationary at the Shard. Cole's parting words echoed through her head.

Eira had returned from Moyra's office to find the captain slumped on the floor, his legs twisted beneath him, and half his stitches ripped out. His clean bandage had been bleached red.

With her elven strength, she had managed to haul him back onto the bed. Cole had stared blankly at her, his grief prominent on his face. Eira had seen the overturned screen showing an empty room and realised that he had witnessed the whole event. He refused to meet her gaze. She would have preferred him to shout at her for not telling him because now, the easy rapport that had been building between them had reverted back to a formal doctor-patient relationship.

When Eira had unwrapped his bandages, he had physically tensed, and she wasn't sure if it was from pain, or from her touch. Despite his injuries, he never made a sound. At that point she had been past caring if he witnessed her powers or not. She had been racing against the clock to heal him before he fully lost consciousness, and before rushing to the safehouse to observe who returned.

Her powers were at full strength, so making her glow disappear had been effortless. Eira couldn't hide his flesh knitting together between her fingertips, but he was so distracted by what he had seen on the screen that he didn't notice.

Cole had stirred when Eira cursed, his flesh parting as her magic receded. The virus was dormant within him and still fought her power, which meant that she'd had to do it manually.

As she worked, she had tried to break the tension by apologising for not telling him, admitting that she was about to confide in him when the emergency had occurred.

43

His next words had stung, more so now as she replayed them, waiting patiently on the cold rooftop. Her phone showed the two dots were still stationary at the Dark head office; they were obviously being interrogated. Eira wondered if the hosts could feel anything that happened to them now. Blinking away threatening tears, Eira curled her hands into fists, as fury took over, the desire to break something overwhelming. She turned, avoiding the gargoyle, and slammed her fist into the dilapidated roof, shattering the slates.

How dare you make decisions on behalf of my team? Their mishaps are mine to solve. You clearly don't care what happens to them. You've just handed them over to the enemy.

Captain Cole's words swirled around her head.

If she didn't care, she would have run away; she had promised her aunt that, at the first sign of trouble, she would return home. If she didn't care, she wouldn't have protected Elowen and the clinic. She wouldn't be feeling this angry about hurting the feelings of a man she barely knew.

Eira knew that Cole's anger hadn't been directed at her but was more a reflection of his own feelings towards his inability to help. It still hurt though. Her pretend life here was on the line, as was the safety of the clinic. If the Dark traced the infected patients to the clinic... She pushed the thought away; she couldn't be thinking like that.

Glancing down at her phone again, she gasped. The two dots were moving quickly in her direction. Based on how far away they were and how quickly they were moving, they would reach her in twenty minutes.

You don't care. You don't care.

Eira closed her eyes and remembered Cole's pleas. She had re-stitched his wound, forcing herself not to use her powers to numb the area. He had endured without complaint.

We had our reasons. The clinic had to be protected. Believe me, there was no other way. I will do everything in my power to make this right.

Only then had he looked at her, his remarkable blue eye shining like an endless sea, his midnight hair obscuring his black eye.

Make sure they're safe.

She had promised him that she would.

The sound of mechanical buzzing carried across the city, Eira's first warning of the approaching patrol. She could easily tell which direction they were coming from, and checking her phone again, she saw that they were only a few streets away.

Though her healing powers were unmatched, her ability to use her powers to fight were woefully lacking, and she couldn't attack from a distance. Because of this, she had to rely on technology in these situations. She reached into her pocket and pulled out a metallic sphere. Pressing her index finger against its surface, the sphere hummed, emitting a pulse of light as the orb scanned its surroundings.

Gently placing the orb on the hard parapet, it pulsed once before lying dormant. The sphere was an Incognito, a device which used magic and high tech to create an illusion over the wielder. She was invisible to prying eyes, but not to thermal radar. Payment for her services to a Myth client.

Eira plunged behind the parapet despite the cover that the Incognito gave her. She detected four drones approaching. One rotated, spinning on its gyroscope right above her hiding place. Her panic subsided slightly as she noticed the blinking red light. Red meant a standard camera, whilst green meant a thermal radar.

Still crouching, she leaned over the parapet, scoping out the scene below.

Two armoured trucks screeched to a halt in front of the safehouse. The doors exploded as agents in military clothing and carrying automatic guns flooded out of the vehicles. Eira's attention was drawn to the front cabs where two figures in mismatched shirts were hauled out. Both looked dazed, but automatically obeyed the commands they were given. They both appeared unharmed.

At least I can offer Cole some closure.

The buzzing of the drones intensified as all four swarmed towards the house, and Eira instinctively ducked. As she looked down again, her attention was caught by a suited figure, taking his time to exit the cab. Her blood turned to ice in her veins and her sweating palms were unable to gain purchase on the stone in front of her.

His dark shades reflected the light of the fading sun. His buzzed hair showed his ear, mutilated, deformed by a scar that ran from the side of his skull and down his neck. Eira could make out the twisted, reddened tissue. Gulping for air, she slumped behind the wall, trying to calm her racing heart.

A rain-soaked stage. A flash of white teeth. A maniacal man with a hideous scar on his face.

Not here, not now.

Regaining her composure, Eira pushed up onto her knees in time to see the agents enter the house below. She watched as flashes of light from their torches spilled through the broken windows. In a matter of moments, the agents reappeared, shoving Flint and Tagger into the back of the first truck, which sped off. The suited agent removed his glasses, revealing his black, void-like eyes scanning the surrounding street. Mercifully, he climbed into the cab of the second truck before it left, with the drones following behind.

Eira found her fingers searching at her neck for her mother's necklace and was reminded of the tunnel when her fingers couldn't find anything. The Incognito vibrated, indicating the illusion was about to fade. Remembering her purpose, she picked up her phone again with trembling fingers and watched as the red dots travelled towards central London.

Her fingers ran quickly across the keypad as she typed the encrypted message to Moyra.

All was safe. The agents have returned to the hive.

✕ COLE

Restless, Cole flexed his legs, the only part of him that he could move without pain lancing his body. At least he had pain relief now, but it only dulled the sharp agony instead of eradicating it completely. His chest felt tight, and he flexed his good hand as he resisted the urge to scratch his wound.

A snooty nurse with bright, dyed-blonde hair tied back in a bun had shuffled in with a tray of food midway through the afternoon. He was hungry, but the anxiety knotting his stomach made the thought of eating almost unbearable. The dry toast had tasted bitter on his tongue, but he had forced himself to eat it anyway, knowing he would need his strength to help him heal. She had fussed over him like an overbearing mother, prying into his business. He had automatically closed down and pretended to fall asleep.

There was no clock in the room, so Cole was uncertain if it had been minutes or hours since the beautiful doctor had left with the promise of checking if his comrades were safe.

He had been a class A jerk towards Doctor Backwater. Blaming her for his team members' contamination and for sending them away from the clinic. Even though he would have done the same if he were in her position.

Rule one in the League was that any infected members of the team were to be terminated immediately.

How he would have killed his brothers-in-arms didn't bear thinking about. They had all made the pact together, but the thought of carrying it out sent Cole spiralling into a cloud of misery. At least Doctor Backwater had saved him from that.

The League was in danger with Tagger and Flint alive. If they were interrogated or had their minds searched, they would find him and then the League.

Fear gripped him like a vice. He knew that he was incapable of eliminating the threat in his current state. His best chance was to get out of London and warn Major Stone. Cole heaved a sigh, trying to figure it all out in his head.

I wish the doctor would come back.

To pass the time and dispel some of his unease, Cole experimented with his vision. His black eye was better focused and had stopped making him feel sick. Despite himself, he was intrigued that it appeared he could see through objects and detect people's "inner shadows" as he had started calling it. The distance he could see was limited — so far, out towards the adjoining ward — but he had only tried it from the confines of his room.

Cole's face was screwed up in concentration as he focused on the window to the wider ward when he heard the rattle of keys in the lock. Doctor Emma Backwater strolled into the room, her shoulders slumped, and some of the brightness from her green eyes dimmed. Cole noticed the knees of her skinny jeans were smudged with dirt.

Viewed through his black eye, she had the same muted grey hue as everyone else, but he was sure that he could detect a faint white glow around her when he wasn't looking directly at her.

She flopped onto the chair beside the bed, a defeated sigh leaving her lips.

'Look, Doc, I'm...' He hesitated when the doctor spoke as well.

'They're...' She bit her bottom lip, glancing down at her hands tucked in her lap.

'Doc, I was out of order before. You aren't to blame,' Cole mumbled to his cast, avoiding her eyes. 'I just feel so trapped in here, knowing that I can't help them.'

Cole glanced up when Emma didn't reply. Her body had lost a little of its tension at his apology.

'They are safe and unharmed,' she replied gently, in her soft, calming voice. 'The tracker showed that they went straight to the Shard and then returned to the safehouse where they were being kept. I waited another hour to see if any agents returned. All was quiet. To my knowledge, they're still at the Shard.'

They aren't coming here; he sensed the unspoken words.

Cole sighed and nodded.

'Did they act, you know...?'

Understanding his meaning, Emma said, 'They're fully under the Dark's influence and obeying commands without question.' She quickly added, 'The tracker embedded in their shoes will last a month if they don't change footwear.'

Cole glanced up at this information. The question hanging on her lips. *Are you going to rescue them?* She had registered his motives straight away.

Emma leaned forward, her fingers splayed on the bed next to his plastered hand. Cole caught his breath.

'Now, Captain, I need to know how your team was attacked.'

He could see the pleading look on her face, and her body taut with apprehension.

Something happened when she was observing the agents.

'I've been trying to remember what happened, Doc, but it all seems a bit disjointed.' He blew his cheeks out in frustration. 'There was an explosion. At the door of our safehouse, I think. I remember… Sam… Sam got thrown back. I think.' *Where was Sam?*

Cole huffed in exasperation, absentmindedly scratching the wound on his cheek. Emma watched him with understanding and pity.

'It's like that part of my memory has been blocked. All I can see is blackness.'

'What was your mission?'

Cole hesitated. Their mission had been highly classified, only he and Major Stone had known the details. The months of prep and training they'd done … it was all for nothing. Now, the largest threat was the information that the Dark would glean from Tagger and Flint. He needed to inform his Major. But he needed help to do that. He could barely walk, so it wasn't like he could do it himself. They were probably looking for him now anyway.

He didn't know what to do. Should he tell the doctor about his mission, and probably get in trouble with Major Stone, or keep his secrets and let her down? The doctor waited patiently whilst the debate raged in his head.

He asked instead, 'What's going to happen to me?'

'Tomorrow, we'll take you to another safehouse where you can recover. We can't risk the clinic.'

Right, he was putting them all in danger. Sighing again, Cole made a decision.

'My mission was highly classified. I can only tell you part of it. If I told you everything, it would put a lot of people in danger if you were ever caught and interrogated.'

Cole stared at her intensely. He had to make her understand the risk he was about to take, and the danger he was putting her in. To her credit she never flinched, but stared back just as intensely, her lips parted slightly in anticipation.

'We were tasked to monitor the Dark at their HQ. We'd been given some intel about a new device they'd invented. Our mission was to monitor and, if possible, intercept. One of our team...' Cole paused and swallowed, '... was compromised. We were evacuating when the agents raided us. I need to get word to my team leader and to collect the information stored at the safehouse.' Doctor Emma was silent, considering his words.

Then, without hesitation, she asked, 'What do you need me to do?'

CHAPTER 6

||| EIRA

Eira crouched behind a wall overlooking the charred remains of the warehouse that Captain Cole and his team had used as a safehouse. The door had been blown in, and half the tin roof had collapsed. The hidden warehouse was located on the bank of the Thames, discreet, and easily mistaken for a ramshackle, disused unit. It was well placed for covert access to the river churning below. The salty smell of fish drifted to her in the breeze.

The night was overcast with a thick layer of cloud and mist swirling off the Thames, casting everything in shadow. A perfect night for going unseen.

Cole had point-blank refused to tell her the location of the warehouse and had appeared shocked that she would even entertain the idea of going there. He had insisted that he should go, not wanting to endanger her. He had even thrown the covers off, stepped down from the bed and staggered toward the door.

The stubborn man had made it two steps before collapsing back onto the bed. For his sheer determination, Eira had sent a pulse of healing magic through him as she guided him back. She knew he was desperate when he finally relented and gave her the location, putting his trust in a complete stranger.

Eira knew that he saw her as a civilian, a human who was incapable of undertaking the task. Why was she even putting **herself at risk for a stranger? But Moyra's words had ignited** something in her. She was tired of being dictated to, not having a say over her own life.

Her eyesight pierced the veil of the night, and she was able to make out the shape of the building ahead. Only the front of the vast building appeared damaged, which meant that the information stored inside might still be intact.

She stepped from her hiding place behind the wall and, dressed all in black, melted into the shadows. Eira had returned to her flat to change her clothes and collect her daggers, now sheathed on either thigh, a parting gift from Pyke, her mentor. They were elven steel, indestructible, light, and fast in her grip. She had never killed, but Pyke had made sure she had the skillset to do so. The thought of it made her nauseous.

She carefully pulled up her hood, obscuring her braided hair and the black band over her ears. She checked the pockets of her new leather jacket, the smokey smell from the tannery still clung to it, and wafted around her, tickling her nose. She wished it smelled like the captain's jacket: warm cinnamon and sulphur.

The disused streetlamps were smashed, keeping the road swathed in inky darkness. Her elven senses were on overdrive, alert to the lack of agents around. *Where were they?* Eira had expected at least a blacked-out four-by-four parked down the street. She had waited behind the wall for a long time to see if anyone turned up.

Silently, she crossed the tarmac and mounted the side wall of the warehouse's courtyard in one fluid movement. Entering via the destroyed entrance would be suicide if there was a trigger switch to alert the Dark. Keeping her arms stretched in front of her, she skirted the courtyard wall.

Eira reached the back of the building and crouched to listen for any sounds inside. A metal shutter at the back led onto a slipway into the murky depths of the water. Lifting the shutter would make too much noise.

She scanned the corrugated roof until she spied what she was searching for: a smashed skylight. Eira continued to where the wall joined the building and hauled herself onto the roof. On silent feet she ran across the roof, crouching low, monitoring the sky for drones.

As she approached the skylight, Eira sent a pulse of power through herself to heighten her awareness even further. Kicking out with her boot, she made the gap in the skylight larger, causing the shattered glass to fall, glinting, to the concrete floor below.

She waited. Still no sound from below, so she let out a breath, squashing the unease in her stomach. In the dim light, her keen vision picked out a mezzanine walkway suspended across the width of the building on rusted steel. Eira searched for her destination. Under the mezzanine, she saw the outline of a dark van.

Eira judged the drop and the angle and, taking a few steps backwards, took a run-up and launched herself through the glass. Landing on her feet, she rolled into a half-crouch, surveying the area immediately. The years she had spent as a young teenager scaling and jumping on the rocks on her island had made her agile and a fantastic judge of distances.

Still nothing happened. She wasn't sure what she was expecting. Maybe luck was on her side.

Eira slid a dagger from its sheath, palming it, and using her other hand, she slid out the keycard the captain had given her and placed it between her teeth.

She had one chance to do this.

The smell of destruction choked her, making her eyes water. Ash hung in the air like dust mites, soot coating every inch of the mangled steel frame, and below it all, she could detect the coppery tang of blood. The blasted impact from the front had imploded into the workshop area, incinerating crates and boxes.

Sam had been thrown back.

Cole's words echoed in her head. He must have been killed on impact. How the captain and his fellow comrades had survived she would never know.

From the mezzanine, she grabbed the corroded rail, dropping like a stone in midair, and landing with a slight thud on the roof of the van.

A thin dividing wall under the mezzanine separated the van, and what appeared to be the group's living accommodation, from the front workshop. The explosion hadn't penetrated this deeply into the building, but it was clear that fighting had taken place.

The table and chairs were turned upside down and one of the metal bunks had been shoved away from the wall. The absence of bullet marks was curious since the agents normally went in heavily armed. It was almost like they had wanted them to survive.

Why infect them and then leave? There were too many unanswered questions.

Eira hung down and peered into the opened doors of the van. Immaculate, no gear or supplies. Cole had stated they were leaving when the attack happened. Looking closely, she saw that there was no paperwork or data in the building. It was like a forensic sweep had been made, collecting only the critical elements.

She slid her dagger back into the holder, swinging her legs around, ready to drop down to the concrete floor, panting through her nose with the keycard in her mouth. She had identified the wall the captain had described to her.

As Eira's boots touched the hard floor, a green laser pulsed through the large warehouse, the light reflecting above the mezzanine. Her whole body tensed as her elven senses expanded to find the source of the disturbance.

She had minutes.

A low buzzing reached her ears.

Eira sprinted to the brick wall, counting as she slammed into the rough stone. Her fingers sought the hidden panel that Cole had told her about.

She removed the keycard from her teeth, blindly trying to find the slot as the humming intensified and the door buckled. Multiple low-flying drones zoomed in.

Eira risked a glance. Five drones, green lights flashing, sped towards her. She registered that they were the heat detection kind, so hiding was out of the question. But they didn't have the live camera feed, so they wouldn't catch her on film. They were acting without human control, which meant that they had been programmed to achieve an objective.

With a quick movement, she flipped a dagger into her hand, whilst the other finally located the slot. The panel slid open on hidden hinges. Blindly, she extended a gloved hand into the dark void, her fingers wrapping around the object inside.

The drones had spread into a v-formation, speeding straight towards her. She paused for another heartbeat, bending her legs, and focusing her breathing. Suddenly the drones opened fire.

Holding herself still, she waited as the bullets peppered the wall behind her. Then she threw herself to the side, ducking and rolling away. Two drones flew straight into the wall, immediately bursting into flames.

Face down in the dirt, she shielded the rescued tablet underneath her. Glancing down, she watched her skin knot together again as magic pulsed through her body.

But before she could even catch her breath, the remaining drones swung back around and zeroed in on her position.

She had to move now.

Dagger in hand, Eira thrust upwards as one of the drones hummed overhead. Sparks flew as she pierced the mechanics within it. Heat spread across her hand, making it difficult to keep hold of the dagger, but she pressed on.

She didn't wait to see the outcome.

Rolling out of range again, she jumped to her feet, swatting at the remaining drones as though they were bothersome flies instead of life-threatening machinery.

She had to find a way out before the agents showed up. She raced towards the shutter at the back of the building, sheathing her dagger as she went.

Using her enhanced strength, she heaved the shutter open, before throwing herself to the ground and squeezing through the opening. Pivoting around, she slammed the shutters closed, just as the drone impacted with it.

Stopping only long enough to catch her breath, she slid the tablet into its protective waterproof casing inside her leather jacket.

Eira could feel her heart hammering inside her chest, and she sent a pulse of magic through her veins to help calm her.

She staggered down the slimy slipway, wading up to her hips in the glacial water, which immediately stole the breath from her lungs and chilled her to the bone. Eira gasped in a deep breath before she plunged into the blackness.

Even with her keen eyesight, the murky depths were impenetrable. Trying not to panic, she pushed forward, diving deeper.

Eira's hand brushed a large scaly body, and she almost exhaled in relief.

Hand over hand, she dragged herself up the creature's humped

body until she reached the bag it had strapped around its chest.

Embracing the creature with her thighs, she opened the waterproof bag and pulled out a diving mask and oxygen tank. Lifting the mask over her head and securing it around her mouth, she sucked in a breath with relief. The mask stopped the water from stinging her eyes and she was finally able to get a better look at her ride home.

Like a torpedo, the creature powered through the water, the current flowing over its aerodynamic fins and body. The marine creature was a giant, the last of its kind, a Mosasaurus. A prehistoric reptile thought long extinct. The intelligent creature had a head like a crocodile, and dagger-sharp teeth that could snap a bus in half. It had a long body with protrusions and scales, and battle scars from centuries of fighting for its territory.

Eira worked her way to the Mosasaurus's head and leant down to gaze into its giant amber eye. The eye blinked back in acknowledgement, and Eira could see the centuries of wisdom within the creature.

Mosasaurus was a guardian of the Thames, and had been so for thousands of years, long before humans arrived with their overfishing and pollution. She served her own agenda protecting the waterways and the creatures within, but she did have an understanding with the bridge trolls, which meant that she would sometimes do them favors in exchange for extra food.

She powered them undetected through the heart of central London.

CHAPTER 7

||| EIRA

The morning mist had yielded to drizzle, but grey clouds still hung in the sky, muting the landscape. Eira's headscarf, patterned with peacock feathers today, was plastered to her forehead, and her wet hair curled around her face.

Eira was running late. She had arrived at the Islington Tunnel soaking wet and freezing cold in the early hours of the morning. She had fed Mosasaurus a sack of fish, which she had eaten in one gulp, swishing her tail as she dived back down to the deep. Eira had stowed the captain's tablet in her keep-safe drawer with her necklace. Waving Issy a fond goodbye, she dragged herself back to her flat via the hidden tunnels, took a scalding shower, and then fell into a deep sleep.

Eira had slept through her alarm, woken in a panic, and dashed to the clinic. Her magic was at full capacity, but she knew that her tiredness and lack of breakfast could lead to mistakes. She was feeling tense and on edge after the attack with the drones, and barely making it out.

She knew the captain would be anxious too. Her priority was moving him to a safe location today.

Sliding her key in the lock, she pushed open the door, which buzzed to announce her entry. The smell of disinfectant greeted her as she walked the staff-only corridors. Head down, she stepped into the sterile room, the dented lockers lining the wall.

Eira hesitated as she opened her locker, the scent of another woman wafting into the room. It was a smell that she was familiar with: an exotic, woody, smoky incense.

She spun on her heels. 'Elowen,' Eira blurted before she even faced her. Stepping forward, she held out her hands to her friend, ready to give her an embrace, and dropped them immediately as she took in Elowen's guarded expression, edged with anger. Or horror. 'What's happened? Why are you back?'

Her friend straightened, wrapping her arms around her slim frame, peering at her from beneath her thick fringe. Eira found it hard to make out her eyes under the thickly applied makeup. She tried to close the distance between them, but Elowen retreated to the open doorway.

Eira felt her own shields sliding into place at the rejection, her posture mimicking the other woman's. The only human outside her inner circle who knew about her magic was shocked with what she had uncovered. Or maybe she was disgusted. Before Eira could retort with a remark she knew she would regret, Elowen muttered in a hushed voice, 'They're here.'

Eira didn't understand. Her expression must have conveyed her confusion as Elowen whispered, 'Moyra said it was safe to return. She said they wouldn't come.'

Eira felt as if she had been plunged into an ice bath as the revelation settled inside her mind. *Have I led them here?* The clinic was in danger!

The bottom dropped out of her world. Cole was in danger. She couldn't comprehend why that unsettled her so much, but she didn't have time to question it.

She rushed to her friend, surprising her as she grabbed her shoulders. Elowen was physically shaking.

'When?'

'Thirty minutes ago. Moyra saw you on the cameras and sent me to get you. They're in her office.'

Eira exhaled, calming herself. She could do this. She had prepared for this meeting. Releasing her hold on Elowen's shoulders, she rushed to her locker and, slipping her satchel over her head, fished her stethoscope and flask out and then stashed it. Her mind was racing, preparing for the encounter.

She reinforced her glamour and her mind's magical shield; to wield any power in their presence meant certain capture. Eira paused as a dread she hadn't experienced since childhood crept over her. What if *he* was upstairs? The man who haunted her dreams. Who, until the night before, she hadn't seen in twelve years?

With her mind whirling, she stood inhumanly still. Eira didn't sense Elowen's approach until she felt cool hands wrap around her wrists.

'Don't go upstairs, Emma,' she begged. 'They will capture you as a … you know. You need to go now!'

Her stare was panicked and pleading. What Eira had read as disgust in her friend was actually unease. Not at her powers, but for her safety. The same concern Eira had shown towards her.

Her friend's apprehension halted the rising terror in Eira.

Looking Elowen in the eye, she said calmly, 'I have to go. The captain. Moyra. I need to protect them.'

'You suggested that I leave. Practically forced Moyra into that decision!' Elowen said through gritted teeth, releasing Eira's wrists. 'I was so angry at you that first day, but then I understood that you did it for my safety. The same as I am suggesting this to you now!'

So that was why Elowen had ignored Eira's texts.

Eira just stared at her friend, marvelling at her determination and her care. In answer, she unwound the scarf from around her ears, draping it around her neck with her stethoscope.

Elowen's sharp intake of breath and the wonder in her eyes was her only answer. Eira's ear tips felt cold after the warmth of the scarf, and she fought the urge to trace the delicate points of them.

'I'm so sick of hiding from them.'

Before Elowen could answer, she sent her power surging up to her ears. An itching sensation travelled along them as she reduced her ears in size, making them appear human. For effect, she even let out her messy bun, her honey-coloured hair cascading down her back. Holding her ears in this shape with her magic would take a lot of effort and concentration, but she had practiced for this moment.

Elowen clamped her hands to her mouth.

'I've prepared long and hard for this meeting. They will not detect any of my powers, I promise.' Eira held her friend's shaking shoulders. 'I'm more skilled than you know. They will not capture me.'

Now, the harder part.

'Moyra needs my support to get these agents out of here without jeopardising the clinic. For your own safety, I ask that you return home again or even leave the city. Do you have any family in the countryside?'

Her friend opened her mouth then closed it again, standing in stunned silence. Eira knew that her own face was pleading now, desperate to show her friend how much she cared. She would beg on her knees if she needed to.

'I don't have any family outside of London.'

Eira chewed her bottom lip, contemplating. *Would it be safe for her? For them? Would they even take her?*

'I know a haven within this city, but you need to be prepared. My kind live and work there. You won't see many other humans, if any. I'll send word that you're under my protection and they will keep you safe.'

Elowen looked nervous but nodded.

They clasped hands, and Eira used a pen from her pocket to write the address on Elowen's hand. Eira felt some weight lift from her shoulders, knowing that her friend would be kept safe. She knew that Elowen was smart, and she would have weighed the risks if she was to remain.

If this all went south, the whole clinic would be at the mercy of the virus; she knew the Dark wouldn't hesitate to infect every human in this building. As a hybrid, she hoped she was immune, but all the humans would be at risk.

'I promise that when we're safe, I'll tell you my story,' she whispered, sharing a smile with her friend.

Without wasting another moment, she rushed from the room, turning to smile at Elowen one last time. She was glad that they had mended what was broken between them before she had to face the agents.

A stillness Eira had never felt before greeted her as she entered the main reception foyer. The constant flow of patients at the clinic's main entrance had been stopped by two agents stationed at the front doors. Military gear on, radios crackling, guns held at their chests, they were enough to deter even the most desperate.

Two more agents with void-dark eyes monitored the corridor ahead. Eira felt the tension building in her veins as her concentration wavered on her ears. Instead, she sauntered between them with cat-like grace, swaying her hips as she went. A backward glance showed her that one of them was staring at her bottom. *So, they can think for themselves to some degree?* She stored that information away for consideration another day.

Moyra's office was located just off the main corridor, in a room barely big enough for a desk and two tub chairs. She paused at the door as her ears, altered but still able to detect the slightest of noises, heard an intense debate on the other side.

Eira threw open the door and then stopped, taking in a harassed looking Moyra, perched on the edge of her seat with her red glasses pushed up onto her head. Worry etched her eyes, and her stern mouth showed that she was not best pleased to be entertaining her current guest. The packed bookcase behind her, bearing all her medical journals, looked as if it would topple any moment, increasing the tension in the room. Moyra's beloved plants were scattered across every spare worksurface, taking up even more room in the already cramped space.

Moyra's eyes darted to Eira with a look of warning as their unwelcome visitor turned to her. *Oops, I should have knocked.* He was high ranking within the Dark, as demonstrated by his immaculate suit. Only the grunts wore military gear. It was rumoured that most of the police officers and Armed Forces had been converted, making Cole's team a mystery.

She risked a glance at the side of his head. No mutilated ear.

He wore sunglasses, of course, which he removed with a swish of a cufflinked wrist, to examine Eira from head to foot. It took all her self-control not to avert her eyes from him. She was playing a game right now.

Hooking her hair behind her normal ear, she ignored him as she padded behind Moyra's desk, scooting around a spiky yucca, and said, 'Here are the papers you requested, Doctor.'

Moyra's hand automatically reached out and took the papers, but she looked puzzled. With her back to the agent, Eira winked at her.

'So, Moyra, who's our guest? Does he need treatment? I've just finished with a patient upstairs so I'm available to examine him.'

Moyra, still stunned, looked at Eira as if she was insane. Her gaze lingered on her exposed ears as confusion flashed in her eyes.

'This is agent…' Moyra began.

'Agent Jones.' His smooth voice made the hair on Eira's arms stand on end. He offered her his hand, and she took it, shaking it firmly, but not too firmly. He was unremarkable, forgettable, with no distinguishing features. But Eira made sure to take in everything about him, from his brown hair to his shiny black shoes. His cufflinks, shaped as two overlapping circles, were the only personal touch. Not that he had a mind of his own.

'You are?' he enquired drily. His black eyes bore into her as if he were trying to see into her soul.

'Doctor Emma Backwater,' she said, finally removing her hand from his grip. 'The Wallflowers' doors are open to all. What are your ailments? You do not appear sick?'

'I am not ill, Doctor. Far from it, I've never felt better. Or more alive.' Eira almost shuddered. 'As I was just informing Doctor Watts, I'm here looking for someone. A couple of rebels have slipped through our net. We're visiting all the clinics in London to see if you've admitted any patients matching their descriptions.'

'Oh,' was Eira's only reply.

'As I was just saying, Agent Jones,' Moyra said, 'people come and go all the time. We don't always get a chance to account for all our patients. Do you have a description?'

'Oh, I can do better than that,' he said smoothly. 'But first, you know the procedure, *ladies.*' He pulled a silver disc from his pocket.

'Really, Agent Jones! I can vouch for the identity of all my staff! We have a very strict vetting procedure.'

Before Moyra could object further, Eira gently placed her finger on the disc and smiled at her boss. 'Really, Moyra, I don't mind.'

Eira felt a sharp prick on her finger as the device extracted some of her blood. Pure red blood seeped from the wound, and she sucked it to hide her fast healing.

The disc beeped, and a blue light flashed, confirming her status as a full human. Moyra obliged with her own finger as she stared at Eira, a look of disappointment on her face. The device beeped and flashed blue again.

Before Eira had returned to London, Etta - another of her mentors - had gone into worst-case-scenario preparation mode. Etta had taught Eira how to create a potion which suppressed her elven blood and increased her haemoglobin, allowing her blood to show up as human for a certain amount of time, depending on the strength of the dose. She always kept a potion made up in her bag and locker, for the worst-case scenario. If Etta knew what was happening right now, she would have a fit. Eira suppressed a smile as she imagined what exactly the brown-haired elf would say. And what about her aunt? She hadn't been in contact with them for a long time, so she made a mental note to give them a call.

Agent Jones smiled, flashing his white teeth. 'Well, ladies, you both passed.'

Moyra huffed, deflating as she sat back on the chair. Eira crossed her arms and leant against the desk, not risking saying too much.

'Where is the dark-haired nurse? The one with the fringe?'

He was observant, and Eira found herself gritting her teeth with anger and concentration as she maintained her ear shape.

'She nipped out on an errand for me,' she said defensively.

'How very convenient,' the agent muttered. 'Two days ago, we raided a rebel safehouse. We apprehended two members.' Eira knew that apprehended actually meant infected. 'But there are two members still at large.'

He withdrew his slim phone and angled it to them both so they could see the photos. The first image showed four men sitting around a picnic table, iced beers in hand, clear blue sky behind them. The nearest to the camera was Tagger, with a massive grin on his face as he lifted his beer in a mock cheer, his ginger hair and goatee glinting in the sunlight. Leaning on his shoulders was Cole. He had his cap on backwards, his black hair curling at the ends, and his crystal-blue eyes sparkling. He looked so carefree compared to the anxious man upstairs.

The other two men sat across the table. One was a large, bald man, much older than Cole and Tagger, caught in the act of swigging his beer. *Flint,* Eira thought. Under Ben Flint's raised arm was the sullen figure of a lanky young man, his brown hair ruffled, and his face pitted with acne, focused on a laptop.

Eira knew that one of Cole's comrades was missing. *Could this man at the back be him?*

'We're looking for this man with the baseball cap,' the agent stated, pointing at Cole.

'How about his friends?' Eira couldn't stop the question from forming.

'His comrades were all apprehended in the raid.'

Interesting. That must be the one who betrayed the team, the one with the laptop.

'We have a better photo.'

Agent Jones flicked to a more recent one of the team, minus the computer nerd who must have taken the photo. Captain Cole was clearly visible in his battered leather jacket, black hair hanging over one eye, proud in the centre of his team, arms crossed. Tagger stood to his right, his arm slung over his best friend's shoulder, with Flint like a brick wall to his left. Which meant the remaining man must be the dead comrade. *Sam.* As tall as Flint, against whom he was half-leaning, grinning, proud to be part of the team. Sandy-haired with blue eyes, he was Cole's opposite in appearance.

Sam had been thrown back. Cole's words. *Killed on impact given the devastation she had witnessed.*

'The blonde one on the far left is our other suspect. And we think the one in the middle is the ringleader. Now, ladies, do these photos jog any memories? May I remind you that you have a legal responsibility to help us as well as the wellbeing of this clinic to think about. These men are dangerous.' He left the threat hanging in the air.

'What are these men accused of?' Moyra asked calmly.

'They have plotted against the Dark, to infiltrate our headquarters and steal information from us. We have uncovered plans of their mission on the raid. But we are missing key data, which is why we would like to … talk to the ringleader.'

Eira's whole being fought to lash out, to scream in his face, scratch out those lifeless eyes. She concentrated on her faded purple boots and her breathing, maintaining her camouflage.

'We can easily look around the clinic without you. But I would prefer it' — he placed a hand over his cold heart — 'if I had your permission. It would be easier on all parties.'

Again, the malice and threat in his voice was obvious.

If Moyra refused them access, they would probably arrest them all, close the clinic, and even infect them. There was no way for her to save Cole now.

The stare from Agent Jones was intense, ominous. Eira shrugged at Moyra, as if it didn't matter to her. She hoped Cole would understand.

CHAPTER 8

⋈ COLE

Even with Cole's limited human senses, he knew something was amiss. The main ward and corridor beyond were far too quiet.

Cole could now stand without the nausea clouding his vision and making his head spin. He was able to focus his black eye, which showed everything in greyscale, whilst his normal eye still picked up full colour. If he had to live with it, then so be it. He was secretly hoping the tech at the League basecamp might be able to reverse his symptoms, but he wasn't betting on it.

His whole upper body was stiff and achy, and he couldn't bend without the threat of ripping his stitches. He had stopped using the painkillers because they made him feel drowsy, but he was suffering because of it.

Cole had woken early after an agitated night. He had been restless and worried about the doctor getting caught. As his fear spiralled, he couldn't stop the nightmare creeping into his head. His mother falling. He hadn't had that dream in years, but he was instantly transported back to the shadowy stairwell, a scream echoing around the space, highlighted by the sick thud of his mother's body hitting each stair. The large looming figure at the top.

Cole bent his head, breathing hard, both hands braced on the window frame as he tried to shake the memory from his mind. With nothing else to occupy his time, he had been pacing since dawn. If shuffling could be classed as pacing.

Dragging himself to the bathroom, he stared down at himself, looking in disgust at the blood-stained clothes he was wearing. He would have to ask the doctor to bring him more clothes if she survived. *No, not if.* When *she survives.*

Cole had washed as best he could in the chipped sink, grimacing at his reflection. He had dark circles under his eyes, and his chin was covered in scruffy stubble. He added a razor to the list of things he needed. He knew he had far more important things to be worrying about than his appearance, but it would make him feel better.

He had never been one to spend too much time focused on his appearance. It was enough for him to look clean and smart, like he had been taught in his training. It didn't mean he didn't know he was good-looking, only that he didn't play on it too much. The one feature he really liked was his eyes: striking blue just like his mother's. But now they had been ruined. The mystery scar on his cheek was raised and white, healed already. Cole had noticed that the doctor's gaze seemed to linger on that scar a lot.

Shuffling backwards, Cole leant his head against the cool windowpane, feeling a scream building in his throat. He raised his plastered hand and thudded it against the dark glass.

Where was the Doc?

Something was very wrong. He could feel it. Anxiety gripped his gut. He felt like a prisoner, cornered with nowhere to go. He had experienced similar feelings after his mother's death, which led him to make some stupid decisions that he lived to regret. He needed to keep his head clear.

Grief for his lost comrades tortured his every thought. He had let them down, both as their captain, and as their friend. He needed a plan, a clear way forward before he spiralled into that pit of misery like he had before. He had been a teenager then, barely old enough to fend for himself. Then he had been manipulated.

With an exasperated grunt, he pushed off the glass in frustration and balled his hands into fists. Looking at his reflection in the dark window, he saw the neat bandages crisscrossing his torso. He grabbed hold of a corner at the top and carefully peeled it away, pulling the dressing down to his stomach.

Raw skin greeted him, cracked with dried blood, and held together with neat black stitches. Looking down, he traced the jagged line. He knew he would always have a prominent scar. No more than he deserved, a reminder of his failings.

Cole lifted his eyes to stare at his reflection again. But instead of meeting his own gaze, his eyes caught on the green ones staring back at him.

Pure relief flooded through him, making his legs weak.

As soon as Doctor Backwater entered his room, Cole knew she was different somehow. Her hair, which she usually kept meticulously swept up, was down, the messy curls flowing gracefully over her shoulders. He could see the copper and gold tones reflected in the artificial lights. She appeared self-conscious and brushed a strand behind a perfectly shaped ear.

His hands tingled to do the same.

But that wasn't the reason that he felt unnerved and hesitant.

She had a swagger to her hips, which she hadn't had before. She fluttered her eyelashes and giggled, behaviour that was the opposite of her regular quiet intensity.

'You're up then, I see,' she said loudly, her tone curt. 'You shouldn't have pulled your dressing off. Now I'm going to have to do it all again.' She even tutted.

The doctor had left the door open, and he spotted movement in the corridor. She moved into his line of sight, blocking his view as she placed her hands on her hips, and drew his full attention with her raised eyebrows and scowl.

This was not the doctor he had come to know. He opened his mouth to speak, but she cut him off before the words left his mouth.

'And look at you, you *rebel scum*. You've soiled yourself. Do you need help with everything? Into the bathroom now!' She sneered at him.

Rebel scum!

Cole was speechless. He stared at the doctor who had selflessly helped him, even when he had refused. He barely even recognised her now. Focusing on her eyes to make sure they weren't black, he read an apology in them even though the rest of her face was set in that hideous sneer.

Realisation dawned on him like a crashing wave. He used his black eye to penetrate the shadows of the dark hall and made out the smudged silhouettes of five male figures and a female.

Every nerve in his body cried out to run as adrenalin surged through him. He quickly looked around, clocking the exits at the same time as his mind ran through the best way to fight these people off. But then he paused, as his training had taught him. Cole could barely walk or move his torso. How was he expected to fight?

Cole focused instead on his breathing, calming his pounding heart.

Clear head, focus, think!

Doctor Backwater seemed to know what was happening in his head, as her expression had completely changed to one of alertness and understanding.

'Are you deaf, *rebel?* I said into the bathroom. Now that we know your identity, you're no longer welcome here.' She raised her voice, making sure the people in the corridor could hear. Those words conveyed everything else she couldn't say.

It was a game that he had no option but to play along with for now. 'I've only soiled myself because your *pathetic* nurses have left me in here without any food or help for two days!' Cole mocked back, stretching his arms in the air. He discreetly nodded once, conveying to Emma that he understood this verbal lashing between them.

It hurt him to even say that. The nurses had been nothing but gentle and caring towards him, and he knew that he owed them his life. But he owed his life to Emma the most, for keeping him out of the clutches of the Dark, so he swallowed his pride and played along with her ruse.

Doctor Backwater huffed, crossing her arms, and tapping her foot. Amusement danced across her face; she was enjoying this.

'How did you discover my identity?' he asked.

'The *very* trusting gentleman from the government has informed us of your crimes.'

'What'll happen to me?'

'You'll be charged and interviewed. Do I look like a question-and-answer search? I don't give a damn about what happens to you. Now, as I've already asked twice, get in that bathroom, we're short of time.'

He knew her words were not real, but they still stung.

With no other remark to make, he turned on his heel and entered the small bathroom.

Emma followed with a pile of clothes in her hands and a tray of medical supplies. She clicked the door closed behind her gently. At least their exchange had quelled his panic.

Not knowing what to do, he sank down onto the toilet seat and leant his head back against the cold tiles. The doctor knelt by the sink, her supplies on the floor. Cole felt her close presence, her scent of jasmine invading his senses. Still, he couldn't bring himself to look at her.

She whispered urgently, 'You understand why we ... why I said what I did.'

Cole nodded once, his eyes still closed. He did understand, he truly did. She had to act as if he was the enemy, distancing herself from him. If anyone in the clinic was caught sympathising with their cause, the practice would be shut down, the staff arrested, and the patients shoved out onto the street. It was his life in exchange for that of hundreds.

Cole felt her fingers gently touching his cast, but before he had even opened his eyes, she had cut it open with one swift flick of her wrist.

His flesh prickled as the cast fell away. Instinctively, he flexed his fingers and was shocked that there was no pain. He looked at Emma in question, but her head was bent, concentrating on her work. The copper highlights in her hair shone under the harsh electric lights of the bathroom.

'Don't I need that?' he asked. She didn't even pause, just held up a slender finger for him to wait. So, he did.

Cole watched as she carefully spread his cast on the floor in two sections. Staple gun in hand, she attached elastic along the parted split, stapling it to the other side. Bracing it in her hands, she tested the stretch. Cole was confused as she slid it back over his hand.

'Now flex it open with just that hand,' she commanded.

Pushing his fingers up and his thumb down, he marvelled as the cast expanded.

'Why doesn't it hurt?' Cole murmured.

'I'll show you when I next see you.'

Cole's head shot up from his healed hand. Her eyes were sparkling with determination.

She then slotted a scalpel between his palm and the bottom of the cast.

'It isn't perfect, but I'm hoping that they're in too much of a hurry to interview you to check.' She gulped with anticipation.

'It's perfect,' he breathed. She had given him a slither of hope. He had a weapon and a chance to break out of any restraints they might use on him. The rest he would have to figure out.

'Now...' She puffed out her cheeks. 'You can't be tearing this off. It won't heal if you do.' She rose in one fluid motion that Cole couldn't help but follow with his eyes. She towered over him, smiling for the first time since she entered the room, and the tension seemed to drain from her body. Cole's cheeks grew hot as he glanced at her slim waist, trying not to look at what was level with his eyes.

She nimbly applied another dressing, her body heat making the flush on his cheeks spread even more.

Mute with desire, he closed his eyes. His hands were twitching to hold her waist, but he kept them in his lap through sheer force of will.

Emma sniggered.

'What?' Cole countered.

She just shook her head, not answering.

'We only have a few minutes, Captain. I was hoping that we could get you a whole new outfit, but the dressing has taken too much time. Arms to me, please.'

Cole obeyed as she stretched a navy-blue, cotton long-sleeve over his head. It felt soft and comforting after being exposed for so long, even though the pressure on his chest throbbed.

Promptly, she had his feet in new socks and boots, which were, surprisingly, a good fit. She had a good eye for detail.

Then she handed a familiar item to him. The roughness of the cracked leather beneath his hands comforted him as the smell of cinnamon and tobacco washed over him. He was overwhelmed with memories of his grandfather. The one bright spark in his otherwise dark childhood.

'Now, Captain, you're ready for war.'

He felt grounded, ready for whatever was coming next.

A thought suddenly hit him. With the shock of the day's events, Cole had completely forgotten his request.

'My tablet?'

'Safe.'

There was a brisk but violent knock on the door. Time's up.

71

The doctor turned to answer; Cole reached out with his un-plastered hand and gently held her wrist. She paused, shouting,

'Nearly ready! The rebel has just puked up everywhere.'

A snigger on the other side of the door was the only reply.

'Why are you helping me?'

'I'm fed up with them dictating and controlling our lives. The divisions between us need to stop.' Her jaw was set with a fierce determination.

He truly hoped that they would meet again. He asked, 'How?' His voice was no louder than a breath.

'You have the answer on you,' was Emma's only reply.

'But, Emma,' he started, his voice laced with confusion.

'Cole, my name…' She gulped, looking unsure, then shrugged and lowered her voice further. 'My name is Eira.'

With that she threw the door open wide, stalking out without even glancing back. 'He's got some cheek! Begging me to help him. Get him out of my sight.'

Feeling cold without the press of her skin on his, Cole stood on surprisingly steady legs and stared at the agents before him.

One suited man and four camo-wearing thugs. They all smirked and didn't even bother to level their weapons at him.

Eira.

Her name is Eira.

It suited her.

He barely registered as the handcuffs were fixed over his wrists and he was patted down for weapons.

A black hood slid over Cole's head, and he was prodded in the back to start moving, causing spasms of pain to rip through his chest.

He must have been mad as a smile tugged on his lips under the hood.

Eira. Hope.

CHAPTER 9

⋈ COLE

The scalpel beneath Cole's palm was warm from his own body heat. The gentle pressure against his wrist was the one thing that was stopping him from spiralling into a meltdown. His firm grip on it steadied him as he was shoved, still hooded, into a chair, feet and arms bound by leather straps.

On the journey, Cole had been surrounded in the truck, but with his head still covered by the hood, he hadn't dared risk trying to break free. He only had one opportunity. Instead, he had practiced small movements with the expanding cast to check the confines of his restraints.

As he was bundled out of the van, Cole knew where he was. He had studied the plans in detail for months and knew that there was only one way in and out. One stairway down and one service lift, in which they had brought him down. His team had worked out the route and the process for obtaining their objective.

He was below the Shard in the Dark's hidden laboratory.

Cole had then been left for what felt like hours, fastened to a chair, still hooded, unable to see or extract his wrists from the handcuffs. That was when the panic crested to a level which had made it hard to concentrate, his ragged breaths sucking in the itchy fabric of the hood.

Finally, he had been hauled from the holding cell and strapped to a reclining chair, which by a sick twist of fate, was the instrument that his team had prepared to break in to find.

Cole tried and failed to slow his racing heart, sucking in deep breaths which tugged at his stitches. Concentrating, he focused his black eye trying to penetrate the dark hood, but the light on the other side was so intense he couldn't make out any shapes.

Suddenly, the hood was whipped from his head and the searing light blinded him. He resolved not to plead.

He sat perfectly still, a list of names cycling through his head. *Tagger, Flint, Sam, Eira.*

He had to focus on the people for whom he was enduring this. Lost friends, and the new hope that he had felt fluttering in his belly mere hours ago.

Cole slowly cracked open his good eye to reveal a brightly lit, sterile lab. The chair he was strapped to was in the centre of the room, and all around him he could see glossy floors and pristine work surfaces covered in dangerous looking tools. There was a massive monitor on the wall behind him.

He didn't speak, but sat staring at the central agent who seemed to be in charge. His dark suit and sunglasses contrasted with the stark white of the room, and the light glinted off his double-circle cufflinks. He was flanked by two military-gear-wearing grunts.

Sleaze suits.

Cole and his unit had nicknamed them weeks ago. It wasn't quite so amusing now that he was facing one. Formerly high-level governors, military personnel, and police, they were now simply puppets in this game of the Dark's complete mind control. Where the virus came from and how it infected people was still a mystery, but it seemed to target people of influence and status. It was spreading rapidly, and soon lower-level officers like himself would be the next victims.

'Captain Cole Lucas Hawkins, we finally meet!' The agent's voice was as smooth as silk, and he had a way of holding onto his syllables when he spoke.

Tagger, Flint, Sam, Eira.

Cole held the scalpel, stroking his finger along the handle, biding his time. He expanded the cast, analysing the restraint holding his wrist. It was tight, but if he could ease his hand around it, he could start to cut through the bindings.

He needed to hold the agent's attention and keep him distracted.

'The one and only, at your service.' His voice was surprisingly steady, and a smirk curled at the corner of his mouth, his hair falling in front of his closed eye.

The grunt on the left, handed the agent a file.

'You're Captain of the Unit Delta Special Operations Team of the Hampshire Constabulary.'

'If you say so.'

'You're originally from Peckham, south London. Mother deceased. Father in prison.'

Cole tried not to flinch at the mention of his parents, concentrating instead on the list of names which had become his silent prayer as he slowly angled the scalpel to the leather.

'Criminal conviction at the age of fourteen for minor graffiti. Oh my, Captain Hawkins, you have a colourful past,' the agent chuckled. 'Petty theft, accomplice to arson where—'

'What's your point? Am I here for you to read my life history?' Cole snapped. He couldn't stop himself from rising to the bait. He wasn't ashamed of his past; he had done most of it for survival or out of blind loyalty to the gang that he had been involved with.

'I am merely wondering how a petty criminal like yourself ended up as a police captain at the age of twenty-two. Please indulge my curiosity, Captain Hawkins.'

Cole remained silent, his mouth a thin line as he focused on slicing the leather binding. Time was ticking.

'Your past is enlightening. How did a member of a gang hell-bent on the destruction of the hybrid rights movement become headhunted by the League?'

Cole took a sharp intake of breath before he could stop himself. *How did they find out?*

Of course, they knew. Tagger and Flint.

The information they could glean from him could threaten the League's entire existence. He was well respected and had been given too much clearance. He knew too much, and if the Dark got their hands on that information, it could be fatal to hundreds of people.

Cole weighed up his options if escape wasn't possible.

'Not talking, huh? Believe me, Captain Hawkins, we have ways to make you cooperate.'

The agent clicked his fingers. One of the grunts opened the heavy steel door, and a large man entered the room. He wore black camo gear, his large feet planted apart as he saluted the agent. That gesture alone pulled at Cole's heart. Ben Flint, dark sunglasses over his eyes, stared straight ahead, showing no sign that he recognised his captain strapped down in front of him.

Cole was relieved to see that at least his friend had no visible injuries.

'Agent Flint, can you inform me of your relationship with Captain Hawkins?'

'Yes, Agent Jones, he is the former captain of my previous Unit,' Flint answered in a monotone voice. Flint had always been the serious member of the group, slow to anger, and the one who held them all together. But this puppet before him wasn't the man he knew and respected.

Cole tried not to show any emotion as his heart splintered at the sight in front of him. Instead, he stoked the anger inside until it was raging like an inferno.

He gritted his teeth as he sliced through the leather. His whole body was shaking with the desire to drive the scalpel into the agent's neck.

'Agent Flint, can you tell me the organisation that you worked for?'

'Yes, Agent Jones, I worked for the League.'

They were so damn polite to each other, it was its own form of torture to Cole. He was used to the swearing and banter which came with his group of friends.

'What was your mission, Agent Flint?' Agent Jones tucked his hands behind his back and paced slowly towards Flint. Cole became more alert with every step.

'Our mission was to obtain information on Project Extract Image, Agent Jones.'

'And were you successful, Agent Flint?'

'No, Agent Jones, my previous team was compromised by Technician Jack Lofty, who decided to defer to our agency.'

'And what agency was that, Agent Flint? Just to make sure Captain Hawkins understands completely,' he asked with a smug smile.

'The Dark, Agent Jones. The saviour of humanity, the one true government for all kinds.'

Cole nearly sniggered at the ridiculous declaration.

'Agent Flint, can you tell me the location of the League's basecamp?'

Cole's gaze snapped to his friend, his good eye widening in a silent plea to keep the secret, even though he knew it was futile.

'No, I cannot, Agent Jones.'

Cole felt his tense muscles relax.

'Now you see our complication, Captain Hawkins.' Agent Jones pivoted on his shiny shoes to glare at him. Cole halted his cutting.

'No matter how I phrase the question, they can't answer. They have even sat right where you are and have gone through the same process you are about to go through, and they still won't answer the damn question.' He threw his arms in the air in frustration, before composing himself and linking his hands behind his back again.

'What about you, Captain Hawkins? For the sake of your comrade, I'd suggest you answer my damn question.'

Agent Jones picked up a pair of scissors from the counter, twirling it in his fingers before driving it into Flint's shoulder. Not a life-threatening wound, but enough of a warning that Cole flinched. Flint didn't even react.

Agent Jones removed a white hankie from his pocket to wipe the blood from his hands, leaving the scissors embedded in Flint. With a casual flick of his wrist, he gestured to the two low-level grunts to remove Flint from the room.

'We no longer need the old methods of persuasion,' he said, gesturing to the chair. 'But I thought I would demonstrate the might of the agency if you do not cooperate. It would be a shame though; trained military personnel are so hard to come by.'

Cole froze, his anger rendering him mute. Fear also washed through him. He knew what was about to happen. He tried to focus on the training that he'd had, channelling his fear into courage.

The agent advanced towards his head from behind, his white teeth flashing in the light and his sunglasses reflecting against the light in the room. Cole refused to lean back and strain to see what the agent was doing.

His head was suddenly pulled backwards and secured into position with another strap, so he was forced to look up at the dazzling lights. The agent secured a headset to his forehead, and Cole tensed, still refusing to open his black eye.

'This machine, as you're aware, extracts answers straight from your mind. The Extractor Image as your team has named it. It has a far more sophisticated name than that, but I won't bore you with details.' He waved his hand in dismissal.

'Every new agent gets tested before they embark on their new role within the agency. You see, new recruits normally come straight to the hive, unlike Agents Flint and Tagger who revealed their unexpected whereabouts at the house in Battersea. But you'll give us all those answers in good time.'

Agent Jones purred as he ran a taunting finger up the left side of Cole's face, tracing his scar and forcing open his black eye. 'Starting with how you managed to avoid our virus's hold.'

Cole sneered and spat in the agent's face. He would go down fighting.

The Agent smirked back and used his hankie to wipe the spit from his sunglasses. 'I feel sorry for you, Captain Hawkins. This is going to feel as though your brain is on fire. We've never tried it on a human who isn't under the influence of our virus.'

With that statement, he pressed a button on the side of Cole's headset.

Cole couldn't help the scream which ripped from his throat as his whole body jolted on the chair. Sheer willpower allowed him to hold onto the scalpel between his fingertips. He felt as if pure electricity was being pumped through his veins. The gash down his front pulled with the impact, creating its own pain which threatened to send him into unconsciousness.

Cole rode the wave and gritted his teeth, bearing the pain as he fought to stabilise his body and control his mind.

'Let's start with a basic test. Show me your most recent memory.'

The agent's voice commanded Cole's whirling memories. Like a firefly in a forest, one memory flitted to the forefront, and Cole gasped as he viewed it both within his mind and on the monitor above his head as it took shape.

'Good, good,' the agent cooed as if to a crying baby. 'Now let the memory take form.'

The image on the screen showed Cole staring at his reflection in a windowpane, his chest bare.

The agent pressed a few buttons and, like a film, the image fast-forwarded to show the doctor kneeling on the bathroom floor before Cole. Her head obscured what she was doing.

With a huge effort, Cole pulled his mind away from that memory and focused on a memory that was buried so deep within his mind he wasn't even sure if he could reach it.

He remembered the rain dripping off his school jumper, pooling at his feet on the threadbare rug. They could never afford a coat. The front door was still open. He could hear the traffic sloshing through the puddles on the road.

He was cold, chilled to the bone, *the reason he'd gone* home.

Raised voices were the norm in his household. By that stage, he didn't even care what the argument was about. He just wanted to have some warm soup and hide in his room.

His mother appeared at the top of the landing, black hair clinging to her face, blue eyes distant. She was still in her nightgown which was hitched up her thigh, one of the straps sliding down her slender shoulder.

She reached a hand towards him. Her body tipped forward in slow motion, her scream echoing in his ears as she fell. Cole watched in horror as his mother tumbled down the stairs, the impact ringing sickeningly in the air.

The puddle of rainwater on the carpet now merged with her red blood as it seeped from her broken body. Her arms and legs were at the wrong angle, and her neck was twisted to the side. Her startling blue eyes were lifeless as they looked up at him.

He sank to his knees, his too-short trousers landing in her blood as he reached out to hold her body.

A swaying shadow loomed at the top of the stairs, too drunk to care, or even realise what he had done.

Cole panted heavily through his nose, his teeth gritted as he let the painful memory fade. The screen behind him went blank.

'Interesting. Very interesting.' Agent Jones's stunned voice broke through the buzzing in Cole's ears. 'It would appear that without the virus coursing through you, you have a small amount of control. Very interesting.' The last sentence muttered, almost to himself.

'Let's try again. Show me your first memory when you awoke at the clinic.'

Cole gritted his teeth as the command surged through him and he gripped the armrest with his good hand. He tried with all his might to fight the impulse to bring the persistent memory to the surface.

He was transported back to the room at the clinic, hazily regaining consciousness. Cole's eyes focused on a pair of purple Doc Marten boots, but before the memory could unfold further, he pulled his mind away to another painful memory.

A terraced house on fire. The flames were heating his skin, and soot and ash were coating his throat as he choked, placing a sleeved hand across his nose and mouth. He backed away as the second floor ignited, the red and golden flames licking the twilight sky. That was when the screaming started.

Someone was still inside. It was meant to be empty, an easy target!

Without thinking, Cole sprinted to the side window just as it shattered, sending shards of smouldering glass towards him. He raised his arms to shield himself as the dagger-like splinters slashed his face.

'Stop! That's an order!' The commanding voice of Agent Jones stopped the memory in its tracks. He was in deep trouble.

Cole felt the scars lacing the inside of his forearm throbbing as the memory faded. His hand flexed, desperate to run his fingers up the inside of his flesh, as a reminder of the path he nearly stumbled down. For a moment, he wondered how his life would have gone if he had stayed in the gang. Probably following in his father's footsteps.

'Tut-tut, Captain Hawkins. You've forced my hand. I did warn you what would happen if you didn't cooperate.'

From the inside of his suit pocket, Agent Jones produced a black, serrated stone dagger.

For the first time since being forced into the chair he pleaded, a weak, *'Please,'* escaping his lips as Agent Jones raised the dagger.

The monitor flared suddenly to life, murky to start with, and then becoming clearer as Cole surrendered to the hidden images racing through his mind. Eyes screwed tight, body arched, Cole had no way of controlling the memory which filled his mind.

Cole leant down and picked up one of the duffle bags, chucking it across the empty space to Flint, who snatched it one-handed and threw it into the van. They had to evacuate.

Tagger was disassembling their guns at the plastic table. Even he couldn't make light of the situation, how badly it had gone *wrong.*

A boom sounded at the front of the warehouse, shaking the partition wall between the areas. A smaller thud followed, and then a flash of orange flame ignited towards the ceiling as the front door imploded. Sam was Cole's first thought. He had been on watch out the front.

Flint yanked open the separating door, only to be met by roaring flames licking the corrugated roof, and shadows forming through the gaping entrance. Flint spun on his heels, closing the door behind him. Tagger flipped the table and they both dived behind it. They had no weapons to hand as Tagger had already disarmed their larger rifles. Flint had a pistol in his steady hand as he knelt behind the table, taking aim.

'Hawk, you need to go now!' Tagger blared.

Tagger's words spurred Cole into action. He ducked and spun, racing towards the side brick wall and the hidden compartment. Jamming the keycard in the lock, he slid his tablet into the safe, sealing the door shut again.

He whirled around as the door burst open and canisters were thrown in from the opening. Black vapour poured from the missiles as black-clad figures stormed in. Choking, Cole raised a sleeved hand to his mouth. He read the urgency on Tagger's face as he gestured for him to run.

Their protocol, the golden rule that they had agreed to follow if they were attacked.

He had to get away no matter what, even if it meant them sacrificing their lives for him. For the League, for the greater good.

Cole looked into Tagger's eyes one last time as the room filled with nauseous gas. He heaved the metal shutter at the back open and sped away into the dawn.

He was immediately thrown to the floor by a force which pinned him to the slipway. A knee in his gut, a hand raised with a serrated black stone dagger. Cole could barely breathe with the pressure on his stomach, and he tried to heave the knee away from him before the dagger plunged towards his chest.

He couldn't make out the face, only the black soulless eyes staring back at him.

Cole had never felt pain like it as the dagger penetrated his chest. Driving the air from his lungs, searing hot pain spread down his front as the dagger was wrenched through his flesh.

He felt a wetness spread across his chest as his whole body went numb and his eyes became unfocused.

The searing pain paralysed him as he gulped for air, and the memory faded from sight. The wound to his chest pulsed as if it had just been inflicted on him. He couldn't breathe, overwhelmed with terror and shame.

'Now, that's more like it!'

But Cole barely heard the agent's words. His body spasmed, and his eyes rolled back in his head as he submitted to another memory which jolted through his mind.

The memory was unclear and foggy as his eyes snapped open, catching a flare of bright light. Rendered in colour through his good eye and monotone through his black eye.

'Freeze!' Agent Jones snapped, approaching the monitor.

Everything suddenly went to hell. A siren blasted somewhere in the building, a constant ringing which made Cole's head pound. Agent Jones went to the intercom, speaking hurriedly to another agent. Cole, physically weak and still restrained, forced his mind and body back under his own control.

Agent Jones approached the chair, leering at Cole. He removed his sunglasses with a swipe of his hand, black eyes boring into Cole, stripping him of his identity.

'This day just gets better and better. We're about to capture the golden egg, and you've just proven our suspicions were correct. Too bad you won't be in control to see it,' Agent Jones sneered.

He lifted the black dagger in his hand again.

'I wonder what will happen when you—'

Cole swiped out with his hand. The agent choked, blood spurting from his throat as his hands clawed the wound blossoming across his neck. With a garbled sigh, he collapsed against the chair, sliding to the floor, and leaving a red smear in his wake.

Hand shaking, Cole ripped the headset from his brow, adrenalin pumping through him. He sat up and sliced his other hand and legs free. Slowly lowering himself from the chair, he tested his weight on his legs.

Glancing at the slackened face of Agent Jones, the blood still spurting from his throat, Cole felt no regret. He did what he had to do to survive. He ran his hand across his face, trying to wipe away the blood he knew was spattered there.

Knowing what he would see on the paused monitor, he forced himself to look.

He saw Eira's face in frozen shock, emerald eyes wide, gazing into his. *Stunning,* he thought. But her beauty wasn't what made him trace the three vertical lines on his check. In her pale hand she held an opal amulet, white ombre to grey as it pulsed with an inner glow, three vertical lines in relief on its surface. Eira herself seemed to be pulsing with an external aura, filling the room around her. His black eye captured the bright white glow around her silhouette.

CHAPTER 10

||| EIRA

Eira entered the quiet foyer of her block, the primary-coloured glazed rectangles reflecting the streetlamps.

Her peacock scarf was once again secured around her forehead, her hair in a messy bun on the crown of her head. Her powers were spent from maintaining her human ears for over an hour. Agent Jones had left with two of his minions, leaving two behind to watch the clinic. Eira found solace in the staff locker room where, to her great relief, she had permitted her ears to transform back and given herself a moment to reflect on how close she had come to being discovered.

Eira had crouched against the lockers and laughed hysterically to herself for what felt like hours, until tears dripped from her eyes and her throat was sore.

She trembled with shock and surprise. Etta's careful plans and training had worked, but only just. Every sense in her body told her to escape. To run away. Now. But she had responsibilities to Moyra, and to the clinic that they had just saved from the Dark's clutches.

So, she had worked a full shift to keep an air of normalcy.

They treated any patients brave enough to enter the clinic and had secretly moved the most vulnerable away using Moyra's network. There was no discussion about her decision to sacrifice the captain. Eira couldn't bring herself to blame Moyra — she knew that she had no other option.

Eira kept herself busy treating patients, but she couldn't shake Cole's face from her mind. His stunned expression when she had acted contemptuously towards him, his playful banter as he had caught onto her game. The expression which haunted her the most though was when they took him away. His pure and honest acceptance of his fate.

Eira entered the lift, sighing. She had to pack her meagre belongings, make an overdue pitstop, and check in on her other responsibility.

84

She had texted Elowen to make sure she was safe, but she hadn't received a reply. Moyra had promised that she would lay low for a while; Eira knew there was no point trying to convince Moyra to leave. Like the captain of a sinking ship, she would remain until the end. Nora's absence throughout the whole thing was suspicious though, and she filed it away in her mind to come back to when she had more time.

One small mercy: she hoped that the scalpel she'd given to Cole would be enough to save him. Eira was being honest when she said she would see him again. He was part of her larger plan.

She had been an idiot to give Cole her real name. She had acted on a whim, feeling guilty about selling him out.

Eira, without taking in her surroundings, walked briskly along the bridge joining her tower, relying on her elven instincts to alert her to anything out of place.

One thought kept nagging at her. How had the Dark known to come to the Wallflower to check for the missing rebels? Moyra had checked with the other clinics, and none had been visited by the Dark. Had they been the first on the Dark's list? Eira had observed them long enough to know that they would have struck all the clinics at once, not giving them any time to pass messages between each other.

Something didn't feel right.

Unlocking her door, she entered the temporary tranquillity of her flat, securing the door behind her, using her heightened hearing to detect any intruders. She advanced to the main room on silent feet, the dim interior exactly as she had left it this morning. She sensed no other presence. Relaxing slightly, she slid her satchel to the floor.

Eira knew the Dark would follow her home. So, instead of cutting straight home using the hidden tunnels, she had led them on an unhurried trip west across London, painting a picture of a well-behaved human who obeyed the rules.

Whilst doing her shopping in the one remaining department store on Oxford Street, she had given the agents the slip after locating a secret entrance within the store.

Now, in the safety of her dark flat, Eira opened her bag and carefully removed her treasured necklace. She put it over her head, tucking it under her grey jumper. She felt whole again, as if part of her had been missing.

The detour to the Islington Tunnel, where she had retrieved her processions, had cost her time and energy. She should have made tracks before curfew — roaming the city at night was dangerous.

Eira let out a breath through her nose. Everything had gone to hell. Biting her bottom lip, she pulled out the captain's tablet. She knew it was useless even trying to hack in — it was high tech and probably programmed to his biometrics. Accessing the information that she had risked her life for would have to wait. Eira slipped it into the hard-case backpack she always kept packed as a precaution in case she had to make a quick escape.

She did a mental checklist of the contents of her bag: notebook, medical kit, blood samples, travel chemistry kit, and finished potions. Her most personal objects were secured in the front pocket: the key and the photo of her mother.

Eira put her hands on her hips and scanned the rest of her flat. Her home for the last two years, her first haven away from her isolated family island. She would have to get a message to her aunt; she would be worried if Eira simply disappeared. The flat had been rented under another fake name, so she was confident that she was safe, but it didn't dampen the urgency she felt to leave the capital.

Her eyes roamed over the herb planter on the windowsill. If she had informed Moyra she was leaving, the plants would have found a caring new home; now, the poor plants would have to survive on their own. With a second thought, Eira picked up the wooden box, opened the sliding door, and carefully placed it on the concrete plinth of her balcony. Stepping back inside, she allowed the fresh air to wash over her flat which had suddenly become stifling.

Eira knew she was delaying. Advancing around the unmade bed, she pulled clothes off her hangers at random. Stuffing them, and a selection of underwear and headbands into her bag, she straightened and took stock of what was left. Pulling open her top drawer, she fished out her cash wallet, extra identifications, and her last Incognito. Bag fully packed she moved it to the hallway.

Taking a few beakers to the kitchen, she emptied the contents down the drain. The chemistry set had been her first indulgence and would be the one item she reluctantly left behind. Knowing her powers needed replenishing, she searched the fridge and cupboards for food. She found a lone apple in the fruit bowl, and a yoghurt pushed to the back of the fridge. She ate the yoghurt, debating her next move.

Eira was devouring her last mouthful when there was a gentle rap on the door. She slid her dagger behind her back, confident that the Dark wouldn't politely knock.

Glancing through the spyhole, she saw the top of a head, coarse, soot-black hair swirling from the crown.

Grinning, despite her need to hurry, she unfastened all the locks and peered down at the stout dwarf.

'Well, that makes a change not having to look up at you, Franklin,' Eira said with a laugh whilst crunching into the apple. She needed the healing of a regenerative sleep which was impossible with the Dark looming down her neck, so fuelling her body with food was the next best way. Eira already felt her power surging within her, making her more alert and tense, although anxiety still burned through her, making her antsy.

The dwarf huffed, pulling his brass belt higher and stamping his feet.

'Well, that's no way to greet a neighbour, Nightingale,' Franklin grumbled.

Holding her hands up in submission, dagger in one and apple core in the other, she laughed. 'Please don't stand on me in your huge size nines, Master Dwarf!'

Franklin's deep laugh rumbled through the apartment. Eira enjoyed the distraction for a moment, savouring the dwarf's glee as reality hit. This would be the last time she saw him and others she had grown fond of.

'What can I do you for, Master Dwarf? More growth potion?' Eira guessed.

'Spot on, Nightingale,' Franklin's tone grew serious. 'The Myths need more help carting goods down the canal. Some nasty business seems to be going down lately, rumours of the League in the city and increase in suit-patrol. Dangerous times.'

Franklin shrugged his great shoulders. The joy drained from Eira's face. Swallowing, she asked, 'What League rumours?'

The human rebel organisation consisted of military and police personnel who had escaped the Dark's parasitic virus. They were the only force against the Dark, widely known to be protecting humanity's interests. They weren't pro-Myth or -hybrid though and had never stepped up to help their plight.

Hybrids were completely cast out by most organisations, even ones run by other Myths. Eira's mother was the only one who had cared about their rights.

Why Eira had been accepted by the few full-blooded immortals she sold her potions to, she didn't understand. There were so few left in the capital, she supposed her rare talents enabled them to live above without fear of discovery. She never pretended she was anything but herself, someone with a foot in both camps.

'Their computer hacker was seen in Covent Garden shooting his mouth off on how he had retrieved some top-secret intel on one of the Dark's experiments. You can imagine how quickly it was picked up by the CCTV cameras and drones. They swooped in within minutes. The League have lost their touch if you ask me. There's fewer converting to their cause these days.'

Eira felt herself still at Franklin's words, bile rising in her throat. Cole's words echoed through her head: *We were compromised.*

'You alright, Nightingale?'

Eira swallowed. Franklin must be referring to Cole's unit. This complicated her plan.

'*Eira, are you okay,* bird?' Franklin asked, stepping into her apartment, and reaching for her arm. Franklin's use of her real name shocked her out of her thoughts.

'How do you know my real name?'

The dwarf appeared chagrined, as if he had just been found out. 'You told me once, chick. Do you remember when you blacked out that time in the tunnels? Our first meeting?'

Eira was sure she had never mentioned her real name to him. That day was still a distant blur in the depths of her memories. It had been her first week in London, and she had become disorientated, lost for hours in the underground network. Franklin and the triplets had found her, escorting her back to their alchemy quarters, where Eira had been delirious with dehydration.

'I'll get your potions,' Eira said stiffly, turning away.

Eira returned and piled four bottles of tonic into the dwarf's arms. 'No need to pay,' she said, trying to close the door in Franklin's face, as a small-booted foot halted her.

'You're leaving, aren't you?' He gestured with an elbow to her packed bag. Eira just stared at the dwarf. She needed him gone, not sticking his nose into her business.

He knows my name. That's two people now.

'That is none of your business, Master Dwarf,' Eira gritted out.

She was shocked and upset that they were quarrelling. She got on well with him usually, but the fact that he knew her name and seemed to be lying about it made her suspicious and defensive.

'I really must go, Franklin.'

Using her elven strength, she forced the door closed. She calmed her breathing and entered the main room of her flat, monitoring the live camera feeds. One camera showed the dwarf waddling back towards the lifts.

A glint in the top corner of the screen, from a camera directed at the main road, snagged her attention. Eira leant forward and cursed before launching herself across the room and slinging the bag across her shoulders.

She yanked open the front door and sprinted towards the service tower, her Doc Martens squeaking on the glossy, blue floor. The disadvantage of this building was that the two main exits were in the same location. Her heart hammered as she sped towards the bridge to the tower.

How?

The glint on the screen in her room had been the propellers from a mass of drones, hovering in front of the main door. Looking closer, she had spied three black trucks idling on the pavement.

How did the Dark locate me?

Curse Franklin for distracting her.

Eira slammed open the doors to the stairs and stared down into the void. The lifts would be suicide, but the sound of thundering feet echoing within the stairwell suggested that the stairs were little better. For the first time in a long time, Eira felt fear; her luck had run out.

Doubling back, she heaved a fire extinguisher off the wall and wedged the black metal trigger between the double-door handles, buying herself some time.

A low continuous hum filled the air. Glancing to the dark horizon, Eira saw a mass of beeping green and red lights swarming towards her like bees to a hive. Without pausing to see the swarm take shape, she launched herself back down the corridor towards her flat.

Securing the door shut behind her, Eira rushed to the already open patio door leading onto the balcony, gulping the cold night air into her lungs to calm herself. Taking hold of the handrail, she vaulted onto the parapet, pausing to judge the drop down to the balcony below.

'Eira! Eira! Nightingale,' a voice boomed into the cold night.

Three floors down to her left, Eira saw the flash of a bronze hammer catching the moonlight, as it was waved back and forth like a beacon.

'Down here, Nightingale. To me, chick,' Franklin thundered in his bass tone.

Eira crouched, ready to spring to the balcony to her left, when a great force slammed into her, propelling her backwards into the glass window. As the clear pane shattered, slicing her flesh, Eira was blinded by a bright light suspended in midair, as she watched her carefully placed herb planter fracture into pieces on the concrete below.

CHAPTER II

||| EIRA

Eira's head collided with the partition wall, her vision blurred as she sank to her knees amongst the shattered remains of her precious chemistry set. The dining room table was upended, providing her a little cover. Palms flat on the floor, she steadied her ragged breathing and tried not to feel the irritating sensation of the flesh on her face and arms knitting together.

The blinding light was still in front of her, the whirring resounding in her ears. The hover copter moved forward, and Eira braced as it opened fire on her.

An incandescent white light erupted in front of her, enveloping the flat. As the missiles reached it, they stopped mid-flight and shattered into tiny pieces of glittering starlight. If she hadn't been so scared, she would have been amazed at the beauty.

Suddenly, the light shrunk into a ball in front of her, shooting through the night sky towards the hover copter. The copter's left propeller exploded in a spark of orange flames as the pilot lost control and it nosedived towards the ground, spinning aimlessly.

Eira was aware of the attention of something focused solely on her, and fear gripped her tighter. She froze, straining with her elven senses to make out the threat. She saw nothing in front of her, even the mesmerising light had winked out. Eira smelled embers and the underlying tang of sea salt on the night-swept wind.

But she wasn't a defenceless animal; she could be a wolf if she needed to be. Eira palmed both daggers from her thighs and straightened to her full height, planting her feet in a fighting stance as she raised her weapons, aiming for where the light had disappeared. She waited five heartbeats, anticipating an attack. Eira was about to demand who was there when there was a thud, and her front door buckled under the impact of a battering ram.

Eira dived behind the table, the unknown presence forgotten as agents streamed into her front room, weapons drawn and sweeping the room. They would see her, any moment.

She could probably take on a couple of agents in hand-to-hand combat, but not all of them at once, especially with guns trained on her. Eira searched the floor, looking for something she could use to her advantage.

Her hands grasped the metal tube of her Bunsen burner as her eyes tracked its gas pipe to the source. Still connected. Now to find a way to light it.

The scent of embers and sea salt invaded her senses again, as a force on her shoulder pushed her to the floor. Eira flinched, trying to shove away from the pressure, but even her elven strength **couldn't budge it.**

Her keen hearing amplified the click of many guns as the agents cocked their weapons. Eira screwed her eyes up tight, her hand searching blindly for something to ignite the Bunsen.

This was it. Even with her increased ability to heal, multiple bullet wounds would weaken her significantly.

A noise like a firecracker exploded in the confined space as the agents opened fire. Splinters of wood from the table flew up as masonry dust showered down, the bullets ricocheting off the walls. Eira pushed her power through her veins, increasing her healing. She knew that if a bullet hit her, she would have to act quickly before she became too weak to heal herself. Both daggers, as well as the Bunsen, bit into her hands as she held on until the agents had emptied their clips.

Silence engulfed the destroyed room. Her hammering heart pounded in her ears. A panting breath from behind tickled her ear. Eira forced herself to look. The wall directly to her side was completely undamaged, but above her head, the wall looked as if it had been peppered with small stones. Dust floated in the air, and the turquoise wall, now a grey void of bullet holes, looked like some sick impressionist art.

Stunned, Eira turned towards **the loud panting, but couldn't** make anything out. She thought she saw the light catch on an outstretched membrane wing, but the bang to her head might have been more serious than she thought.

Stardust twinkled in the debris.

Were they the dissolved bullets? Whatever had done that was a powerful being, one she had never experienced before. And it was protecting her, not attacking her.

92

Eira took the opportunity to break the creature's hold, sheathing both daggers and thrusting her body up sharply. She peered above the shattered remains of the table and saw eight agents in military gear with shocked expressions on their faces, their cold black eyes penetrating her very soul. Some of them were reloading their guns for a second round.

'I need a spark,' Eira said to the room, her mouth struggling to form the words of the old language.

The agents stared at her, blank-eyed and confused, but it wasn't them she was asking for help. Given the power of the being in the room, she gathered that it must be old and would understand the native Elven tongue used by the more ancient Myths.

Eira raised the Bunsen burner behind her back, angling the opening away from her body. In answer, a small silver ball of moonlight drifted to the tube and, as she twisted to ignite it, the tiny flame sparked blue.

The agents, distracted by the floating silver orb, had taken their eyes off her for a second. Eira sliced her dagger along the gas pipe, the smell of gas immediately hitting her. Hoping that the Myth would smell it before it was too late, she stepped towards the smashed window, her boots crunching on broken glass.

Eira saw the agents' faces change as they finally registered the smell of gas. She threw the flaming Bunsen into the space in front of them, before turning and sprinting towards the balcony.

A ball of blue flame erupted in the apartment as the gas ignited. The agents were thrown back against the wall, their bodies hitting the ground as they were engulfed in the fiery blaze.

Eira, bag on her back, launched herself off the balcony and into the frigid night sky, twisting in midair to find something to grab hold of.

For a heartbeat, as the world spun around her, panic consumed Eira. Maybe the creature that had been in the flat with her couldn't fly, and she had sent it to its fiery death. Either that or it didn't want to help her anymore, content to see her splattered on the concrete below.

The world suddenly stopped flashing by, and Eira's stomach dropped as her descent was halted abruptly. Sharp claws wrapped around her wrists, and she felt herself lifted into the air as the creature beat its powerful wings. She risked a glance back at the tower block. Through her shattered window, she saw the living room being destroyed, the flames already licking towards the other apartments.

Horror and guilt washed over her, and she pleaded to the night that everyone would escape. She knew that most of the flats housed humans. Franklin and the few other Myths within the building would surely help. Wouldn't they?

How had it come to this? She had traded the lives of many to save her own.

Cole's life for many.

Eira glanced up at her saviour, the claws around her wrists firm but surprisingly gentle. She still couldn't make out the creature's form — it seemed to be engulfed by the night itself. The waning, gibbous moon emitted enough light to cast the streets below in ghostly shadow. Flexing her stiff fingers, Eira gasped. Where her fingers should be, she could see only the starry sky.

Glancing down at the rest of her body, she flinched. Her body wasn't there, and she had a straight view to the ground, dizzyingly far below. The creature must have found a way to divert her glamour and make her invisible as well. *Why can't I see it?*

Casting her powers like tendrils within her body, Eira explored her glamour's weakness where the creature might have penetrated her defences. The one limitation of her power was that she couldn't cast it out from her physical body; there had to be a physical connection as a conduit for her power to flow through.

Eira's shield was a matrix of interconnecting tendrils of glowing white light, her healing power in its raw form. There she located it: a hairline fracture where the creature's moonbeam light poured in, coating her exoskeleton in an invisible barrier which fully reflected the surrounding environment. A more organic version of the Incognito's high tech.

Her power naturally started attacking the foreign body shielding her. Eira understood the risk. If she was suddenly exposed, suspended in midair, she would be an easy target. So, with all her might, she pulled her magic back into herself, allowing the other river of magic to flow around her. Instead, she sent her power creeping along the connection to investigate.

Eira focused her power, shutting her eyes, and explored the link between them. She forgot about the wind whipping her hair, the cityscape racing by below her feet, and the utter terror and thrill of flying.

Eira physically trembled at the vastness of the creature's power.

His power — because he was distinctly male — was hard to describe. She had never delved into another Myth's body before. She had healed Myths like Issy, whose power was ancient and linked to the bridge she was tied to, limited to her physical form and the distance between it and her bridge. Her power wasn't natural; it had been forced upon her. The humans she healed had no traces of magic within their veins, and as this was what she was most used to, this expanse of power was astonishing.

The Myth's power was like stardust and moonbeams coating a core of rock, ignited with embers of light and gravity. So vast and natural that she was lost to it.

Eira automatically kept pushing her power through the link, unaware of the threat surrounding them, unable to think about anything else.

A jolt as the creature started to plummet snapped Eira from her investigation. A low humming split the night as a swarm of blinking, green lights surrounded them. The creature growled. It seemed that even his powers couldn't hide from the high tech.

Eira raked the old language in her mind to explain. 'Heat-seeker,' she threw to the wind. 'Detection.'

The creature then banked, causing Eira to swing wildly in the air. She glanced down and saw that they were flying over Hyde Park, the dark treetops within skimming distance. Connected to the creature as she was, she felt him tense as a surge of power rumbled through him.

Sparks like fireworks sprang from him, shooting towards the drones. As the sparks collided with them, small explosions erupted, sending them spinning off into the distance. He dodged them, artfully swinging his body left and right.

It wasn't enough, a few irritating drones still tailed them. With a mighty heave, the creature accelerated through the clouds.

A whooping sound joined the low, monotone buzz of the drones, and Eira's heart fell. A sleek metal hover copter appeared in front of them, the drones having signalled their location. Levitating on its twin propellers, it was more agile than the average helicopter. The creature again surged a sparkling sphere of moonlight at one of the propellers, but the pilot was either better skilled than the last one, or had learnt from their failings, as the craft dropped down, tilting to avoid the missile before opening fire on them.

A shrill scream broke from Eira's lips as they went from hanging in the night sky to dropping like a stone towards the ground. The creature must have tucked in its wings as gravity propelled them downwards. After a few seconds, they levelled out again, and Eira's stomach churned as her pilot started to weave in the air. Cracking open her eyes, she pulled her legs up to her chest, just in time to avoid breaking them on an oncoming chimney stack. Her movement caused the creature to unbalance, and they wobbled in the air before he was able to regain his momentum.

The diving and weaving continued for what felt like miles as the creature flew low, using the urban landscape as obstacles to throw the hover copter off their trail. Eira gritted her teeth and tried her best to be as streamlined as possible, not wanting to slow her saviour down. The wind tore at her, and she was surprised to note that her headscarf was still in place.

They had just spiralled between Westminster Abbey's gothic twin pillars, barely avoiding crashing into them, when the hover copter reappeared, bullets raining down on the abbey's roof as it approached them. The creature stopped abruptly, jerking Eira in its grasp. She felt a swelling of its powers as it drew on his inner light.

Pure light expanded across the horizon, shielding them, encasing them in a shimmering glow of starlight. At the same moment, a beam of moonlight surged through the roof of the abbey, incinerating the metal and cracking beams. He simply opened his claws and dropped Eira through the hole.

The air ripped from her lungs as she free-fell through the damaged roof, glimpsing a winged figure take form in the air, glowing white in the shimmering light, and punching an arm through the hull of the hover copter.

Arms windmilling, Eira forced her body under control and turned to land on her feet as tile and brick rained down around her.

CHAPTER 12

⦀ EIRA

A second crash vibrated the stillness of the inner sanctum, causing another dust cloud to spread throughout the dark interior. A mighty grinding sound rang out as the hover copter plummeted through the roof, splitting beams, and scraping along the south aisle, grating on stone, scattering pews, and decapitating statues in its wake. Its trajectory was halted by the huge arched columns which supported the ornate ceiling before it could pierce the external wall.

Eira held her breath, curled on her side as she waited for the **inevitable. In her current state, she knew she wouldn't be able to** fight anyone off. An eerie quiet settled within the abbey as the hover copter terminated its scraping arc towards the south wall. The dust smog lifted enough for Eira to see the gaping void in the abbey roof, where the night shone, unperturbed by what had just happened.

Eira had landed heavily on a wooden pew in the north aisle of the nave. By pure luck, or the skill of the creature, the hover copter had fallen on the opposite side of the abbey.

Exhaling through her nose, she panted as searing pain shot through her leg. She looked down, feeling the damage with her magic. Her leg was trapped under a substantial wooden pew. She sent a wave of magic to it to lessen the pain and start the healing process. She knew that she had to remove the pew before she **could fully heal, but she couldn't stretch far enough to get** purchase on it.

Sighing, she sagged against the flagstone floor. Where was her guardian angel now? He must be close, probably buried under a beam. She had last witnessed the Myth striking the craft with his bare fist.

I wonder what his agenda is. He could still be an enemy.

The Dark would find her if she remained here. They had been flying too fast for any ground team to keep up, but it was only a matter of time before they tracked them here. The giant explosion would probably be a big giveaway. Eira pushed up on her elbows and tried to use her other leg to move the pew. Grunting, she poured all her strength into the kick, but it didn't budge.

Eira was about to shout for help when she sensed a shifting in the rubble near where the craft had landed. Poking her head above the broken pew she beheld a hulking figure approaching her.

The moonlight behind the figure cast his features in shadow. His height was imposing, but even more impressive, were the huge wings that sprouted from his back.

Despite herself, Eira recoiled in fear. She knew that he could probably smell it pouring off her in waves. What if he did mean her harm? She was entirely vulnerable, trapped, and useless.

The pressure suddenly eased from Eira's leg as the Myth heaved the pew up and threw it behind him.

Then he stepped into the moonlight and Eira couldn't hold in her awed gasp.

He was bipedal with the hind legs of an animal, his feet, clawed like a dragon, clicked, and scraped on the smooth tiles. The claws which had held her wrists so gently appeared strong enough to disembowel a human with ease. Above the knees, he wore tight-fitting leather trousers, pearlescent daggers topped with crescent-moon handles strapped to his athletic thighs. He was tall, at least seven feet, with strong, broad shoulders and chest. Her eyes drifted towards his iridescent scaled armour, each shoulder capped with a crescent-moon-shaped carbon disc. Light and agile for quick movement, interlocking like snake scales, it seemed to absorb the night and reflect the moonlight.

He was a creature of the dark and shadows, of starlight and moondust. His skin, as pale as alabaster, glowed in the dim light filtering down from above. As he stepped closer, Eira got a better look at his white, membrane wings, both tipped with a talon like a hawk's claw. He snapped them in, tucking them neatly behind his back where a staff peeked out from behind his right shoulder.

Face still in shadow, Eira could only make out his eyes, which seemed to reflect the moonlight. In a swift movement, graceful for someone his size, he crouched and offered a human-shaped hand towards her, bringing his face fully into the light.

Eira gasped in surprise, her hand hesitating in front of her. She had been expecting a grotesque face, something from Hel.

Instead, his face was humanoid. He had high cheekbones with a long nose, and crescent moons raised on the flesh either side of his curious white eyes, where no iris was visible. Small bone-like protrusions at his hairline were the only demon features he bore. He wore his platinum hair in a mohawk style, shaved on the sides, and long and braided on top, with trinkets interwoven throughout.

His ears, though, were what caught Eira's attention and made her take a sharp breath. His left ear was pierced in several places, but that didn't disguise the fact that they were pointed. Elven blood ran in his veins.

He wasn't a Myth, he was—

'You're like me!' Eira blurted in the old tongue.

No wonder he understood Elven.

He dipped his head to the side like a feline, parting his pale lips to show small fangs, his hand still held out towards her. Grabbing his hand, Eira felt herself pulled to her feet. She braced all her weight on her good leg, wincing at the shooting pain. He steadied her with his strong grip and glanced down at her useless leg, analysing how best to treat it.

A cheeky grin ghosted across her lips as she pushed her power through her leg, letting her white healing light glow on her skin. She had healed her leg internally whilst trapped, so she let her power take control, binding her torn flesh. She saw wonder in his eyes as he watched her leg repair itself.

'You have mixed-species genetics like me,' she whispered into the silence. 'I'm half-human, half-elf.' Searching for the word, she had to switch to her native tongue to explain. 'A hybrid.'

His eyes widened at that, and he stepped back, though he kept hold of her hand.

'What are you?'

A monotonous buzzing filled the quiet between them. His wings flared and, baring his teeth, he crouched, watching the gap above as four drones span through the hole.

(ORAN

The irritating buzzing noise which reminded Oran of swarming bees was so intense that he shook his head. He wanted to focus on the words of the female in front of him.

What are you?

He wasn't sure he could answer that, adrift between the species as he was with his biological father's revelation.

At least she hadn't baulked at his appearance, though it was obvious she had never seen anyone like him before.

You're like me.

As the buzzing noise drew nearer, he reacted, dropping the female's hand and springing into the air. Focusing on the light within himself, he created a spark and, igniting it, let it fly. It broke into small light balls, propelling towards the machines. As soon as they made contact, the mechanisms were short-circuited, and they fell to the ground like bees drunk on nectar.

Until arriving in London a week ago, he had never fought machines. Finding their weak spots had been trial and error, but a well-placed zap or spark would kindle a more intense explosion.

His light was unique among his kind. Other creatures of the night manifested their elemental powers as shadow or rock manipulation. The welkin, who were sun gods and weather tamers, had power that manifested as bright beams of scorching sunlight.

His light was softer, purer, a reflection of the moon and stardust. There was no heat to it. He had learnt through decades of practice to manipulate it to his will, strengthening, expanding, or contracting it, based on whatever he needed it for.

He did just that as he exhaled, swelling the light as it poured from his body. He sent it upwards, coating the holes in the roof to create a shield and stop any more unwanted visitors. Oran knew that maintaining the shields would drain his power quickly, but he had no choice.

He had been reckless with the aircraft. His rage that the technology was able to see through his invisibility took over for a second, and the resulting destruction to this sacred monument was inexcusable.

Oran glanced down, shy, when he heard a gasp and saw the look of wonder on the female's face as she stared at the shimmering discs embedded within the roof.

She wasn't the only one impressed though. She had certainly stunned him with the demonstration of her powers. From his vague knowledge of elven history, he would bet her powers were as unique as his.

No wonder interspecies breeding was illegal.

What was he going to do? He had become involved in a situation that was none of his business. He had been sent on a mission to find the source of a power surge that his real father had felt, and if Oran was right, he was looking right at it.

Oran landed gently on the ground, avoiding the worst of the rubble. He looked around the space they were in, easily checking the shadows for any movement. A perk of being a creature of the night.

'That will stop those flying, mechanical bees,' Oran rumbled in the old language, his mouth hesitantly forming the words of the ancient dialect. He knew the female in front of him wouldn't know his language — the language of gargoyles.

She blushed, looking at her feet, her scarf sliding over her shoulder. He couldn't smell fear on her, and her eyes were shining brightly with determination.

She stepped closer, a small smile lighting up her beautiful face. Oran picked up the overwhelming smell of antibacterial sanitiser, but underneath, he could detect sea salt and jasmine.

'They're called drones,' she replied.

He nodded once, waiting for her to accuse him of kidnapping her, to start shouting at him and maybe even try to hurt him. But she seemed calm. Grounded. He should introduce himself, put her at ease, but he was struggling to form the words.

Just as Oran was about to speak, they heard the buzz of dozens of drones overhead. Like flies around a heater, they flew at the shields, sparking and short-circuiting on connection. Oran was astonished as some backtracked and hovered above the shield. They were able to observe and learn.

'The agents will be here soon. We need to block the other entrances or get out of here,' she said with some urgency.

Oran growled, cursing himself for not thinking of that. With all his training, it should have been the first thing he'd done.

'Can you use your power to shield the other entrances? I'm confident that I can find another way out, I just need time!'

Oran raised his eyebrows at that, tilting his head to the side in question. She regarded him straight on in challenge, hands on hips, without backing down. She had trusted him, even when he was completely invisible and unknown to her, so out of respect he didn't question it.

'My light is getting low and depleting rapidly from maintaining the shields.' Oran gestured above. 'But I have another idea.'

Now it was her turn to look surprised.

Oran reached behind his back and, in one fluid movement, pulled out his staff. As always, he marvelled at its balance and weight, the way it felt like an extension of his arm. One hand on top of the other, he twisted a hidden mechanism, causing the staff to extend. Setting the staff vertically to the floor, he planted his feet, snapping his wings tight to his back, and inhaled.

Drawing on his moonlight, Oran used the staff as a conduit to amplify his power. Below his fingertips, the insignias on the staff lit up, the story of his clan engraved in ancient wood. Immersed within the pull of his power, Oran vaguely registered the female's intake of breath.

A sonic boom echoed within the abbey as his power snaked from the staff, tendrils of starlight spiralling out from the source before exploding and flooding the area with light. Oran's arms started to shake as he closed his eyes and concentrated on shaping his power to his will. Maintaining his hold for another heartbeat, he dropped his power, and the light immediately shut off. Awareness flooded back to his senses, and he fell to his knees.

Oran opened his eyes to a feather-light touch on his forearm as soothing calmness spread through his exhausted body, replenishing his energy levels.

How had she bypassed my shields?

He met her eyes.

'What's your name?' He switched to the human tongue of English.

'Eira Mackay,' she said softly, removing her hand.

She paused, waiting for his response.

'I am Oran, Light Bringer of the Crescent Clan.'

There was something about her that made him want to be honest, and he blew out his cheeks; this stranger deserved the truth. More than what he had revealed to his chief and clan. Apart from his soulmate, she was the only one who knew the very depths of his soul.

'And yes, I'm a hybrid. But my clan doesn't call it that. My crossbreeding is frowned upon amongst my kind, so only a few know my origins.' Oran traced a pointy ear self-consciously. 'I'm half-elf, half-gargoyle.'

Oran felt a weight lifted from his shoulders. He didn't have to pretend. With this stranger, he was free to be himself, to let his power flow freely and unashamedly.

Eira was staring at him with a look of fascination on her face. Maybe she too had to hide who she truly was. She sucked on her bottom lip, hands clasped in front of her, rocking back on her purple boots. She looked like a fledgling on the precipice of their first flight, bursting with excitement and anticipation.

Oran cocked his head, smirking.

Eira parted her lips, but then shook her head and started again. 'What exactly did you do?' She pointed to his staff, which was still faintly pulsing with light.

Picking up his staff, Oran raised a long finger, indicating for Eira to wait.

A sound akin to grinding stone resounded through the silence, and the drones dipped closer to the roof.

Eira tensed, pulling out two daggers which glinted in the moonlight. *So, she has some fighting skills then?*

The stone statues within the abbey slowly climbed down from their plinths and lumbered towards them. Glancing over, he could see the shock written across Eira's face and couldn't help smiling. There was an array of statues: hooded bishops, monks, and renowned warriors. Most were in pristine condition; some had stone features distorted from erosion. Their eyes glowed, filled with his moonlight.

With a simple thought, he commanded them to guard every entrance. They would remain at their posts until they were either dust on the floor, or he released his magic.

Eira's mouth hung open. 'Th-that's Queen Elizabeth I,' she stuttered, pointing at a stern-looking statue in a corseted dress and Tudor ruff carrying a sceptre and orb. Oran shrugged. Human history held very little interest for him, apart from the events surrounding World War II and the forced exposure of immortals.

'I feel our time is running short if you would like to investigate that idea of yours,' Oran said, glancing skyward. Lights up!

Eira sped into action, her backpack swinging as she turned on her heels, tracing the floor along the north aisle.

He kept quiet so as not to disturb her, despite his burning questions, focusing his mind on his stone warriors instead. The sensation was unnerving, no matter how many times he did it. He could see through their eyes, giving him a 360-degree view of the room. It would have been overwhelming if he hadn't been trained in mind separation. He hadn't stretched his power this far with so many stone manipulations since the clan wars decades ago. Then it had been animals, hewn from his imagination, charged with their own light source to enable self-control away from the host.

This was different. Oran had to maintain their life source, continuously pumping his magic into them to keep them animated.

Closing his eyes and resting on his staff, he slowed his breathing and relaxed his mind. Like a game of air-tag from when he was a fledgling, he darted from fake mind to fake mind, capturing and analysing the reported findings then moving on.

Oran was so absorbed in his mind's power that he didn't hear the crack of the gun being fired. The bullet impaled his right wing-socket. The impact sent him reeling forward, the staff barely keeping him upright.

His mind reeled, and adrenalin coursed through his veins, rage muting the pain. He spun on his clawed feet and bared his teeth in a low growl which vibrated the ornate, stained-glass windows.

Another crack. Another bullet embedded itself in his thigh.

How were the bullets penetrating his flesh? Gargoyles' rock-hard skin could deflect standard-issue bullets. Unless... Oran charged, raising his staff and throwing it with perfect aim, letting it fly towards the aircraft. The staff pierced the hull and imbedded itself in the head of the pilot.

His chest heaving, Oran staggered, wing-tips dragging on the floor as Eira rushed around the pulpit and ran towards him.

CHAPTER 13

⋈ COLE

The constant siren made it hard for Cole to concentrate on the task at hand. His hands still shook, both from what he had just done, and the secret memory revealed on the screen. Though he had been trained to kill, the guilt he felt after every death never lessened, though he tried to justify his actions by thinking about what had been done to Flint and Tagger. Not only that, but he had been close enough to watch the light drain from his enemy's eyes and feel his blood on his hands.

Cole forced himself to bend down, straining his wound to remove the agent's phone, access key, and gun from its holster. Activating the phone, he held it in front of the agent's face, using his face ID to unlock it. Using the hacking skills that he had learned from Lofty, he disabled the tracker, embedding the encrypted script within the phone's software to make it secure for him to use. Pocketing the phone, he flipped the body and removed the black suit jacket.

Slipping the gun into the back waistband of his jeans, Cole straightened with some effort and glanced at Eira's face on the paused screen.

It appeared that she was holding back some vital information. That the scar on his face was the same design as her necklace couldn't be a coincidence. On reflection though, Cole admitted that she hadn't had the time to tell him, what with his arrest and everything.

The other thing he couldn't understand was the silver-white aura flaring around her body.

Captured the golden egg.

The agent's words vibrated in Cole's mind. Did he mean Eira?

I wonder if the siren was for her.

A sense of urgency filled him, and he jumped back into action.

Turning to the main console, he searched for a way to obtain the recordings. Cole groaned as he saw the biometric access panel. He didn't have the stomach to cut off…

Nausea swept through him at the thought, but he knew he had to do it.

Bracing his feet, Cole gritted his teeth and dragged the dead agent towards the console, smearing a blood trail across the spotless floor. Slamming the agent's useless hand on the panel to be scanned, the console flared to life, lighting up his face.

Cole removed his leather jacket and draped it over the console. Angling the scalpel still covered in blood, he bent and wiped it on the agent's clean shirtsleeve, the red stain stark against the white. Piercing the lining of his grandfather's beloved jacket under the buckle, Cole pushed his fingers inside until he found the hidden micro stick. Withdrawing his hand, he saw that the stick was wrapped in a small piece of paper.

What the...?

Cole unrolled the paper, revealing a neat script of dots and dashes. Morse code. He quickly decoded the message.

You will have the answer on you.

Cole was lost for words. How had she known his micro stick was hidden in the seam? Then he remembered Eira had known his identity. *She must have found my hidden ID card.*

Folding the paper safely into his back pocket, he smiled to himself as the console lit with the recording of his memories. Slotting the micro stick into the port, he hoped that the software wouldn't reject it. Fingers flying across the screen, he copied his recordings over and permanently deleted them from the hard drive and cloud network.

Their mission had been to gather this intel; Cole had never thought it would turn into a solo mission. Raising his hands to his pounding temples, he pushed on, knowing that he could be interrupted at any moment.

He searched for the words: *Agent James Tagger.*

Sighing in relief as Tagger's recordings appeared, he copied and then deleted the files, before doing the same for Flint.

On a whim, he copied the files from the last two weeks of recordings, hoping that there might be some useful information in them. Shoving the micro stick into a pocket within his leather jacket, he allowed the familiar scent to wash over him as he pulled it on.

Reluctantly, he pulled the oversized suit jacket over the top and scanned the room. He grabbed the headset and smashed it against the console, shattering it into a thousand pieces before dropping it at his feet in disgust. He wished he could do something to destroy the chair, but he knew he didn't have time.

Not wanting to waste any more time, he cut the hand off the dead agent and held it to the scanner on the door before grudgingly storing it in the pocket of the borrowed suit. He snatched up the discarded sunglasses from the shiny floor, squared his shoulders, and blew out a steady breath as he swung open the door. The lack of agents in the corridor unnerved him. The siren was still ringing deafeningly, a flashing red light casting everything into scarlet relief. His black eye sparked into clarity, bringing the shadows into focus.

Now to blend in. Cole sauntered into the corridor like he had a purpose, one hand casually behind his back in easy reach of the gun. Picturing the map of the building in his head, he reached an intersection and took a left.

Passing more sealed doors, he carried on at a leisurely pace until his black eye snagged on a pitch-black darkness spilling through the viewing panel of a door at the end of the corridor. Walking closer, he glanced into the room, stumbling back in shock. The deep room was lined from floor to ceiling with metal racking stacked with gun canisters and black, serrated knives. Each weapon hummed with savage intensity and a darkness which seemed to suck the light in. Cole had stumbled upon the Dark's arsenal of weapons. This was how they infected humans.

Cole racked his brain; he was certain this room was not on the plans. Distant thudding resounded along the corridor as Cole pulled back from the door and proceeded right towards the sound. Shoulders held high, a blank expression on his face, Cole strolled past three grunts without any acknowledgement, even though his heart was hammering in his chest.

They rounded the corner without a backward glance. Another corner, and he arrived at the service lift and stairs, both of which needed an access card to enter. Here was where it became more difficult. Cole debated which form of escape would be easiest, and decided that, in his current state, it would be best to take the elevator. Both were likely to end with his arrest once he swiped the card, and the **command identified he wasn't Agent Jones, but** at least he would have a bit more strength to fight.

Stepping into the lift, Cole pulled out his gun, cocking it towards the door. Counting the floors going up, he focused his breathing, stilling his shaking hands, and telling his quaking knees that it was only a training exercise. Cole felt completely alone without his comrades who had been by his side on every mission he'd commanded over the last two years. They were his backup, his safety net.

As the doors slid open, Cole aimed the gun and tentatively stepped out into the dim light, anticipating an ambush. The siren **couldn't be heard on this level. All was** quiet, no gunshots or shouting. Aiming his gun, Cole surveyed his surroundings. He appeared to be in an underground train station — thick concrete pillars supported the curved ceiling, and navy-blue tiles lined the walls, with a recognisable sign, London Bridge Underground, ringed in red.

No wonder we couldn't find the entrance.

Months of staking out the main Shard had been futile.

It made complete sense now. A secret entrance with direct rail access, hidden below ground away from curious eyes.

An underground train was kerbside, automatic doors already open, and two grunts standing guard, flanking the doors. Cole stepped further into the station and purposefully walked towards the escalators at the end, keeping them within sight. They didn't respond. The lack of agents was distressing.

Cole reached the top of the escalator, gun still level as he analysed the street, flinging the sunglasses onto the pavement. A glance at the street sign enabled him to gain his bearings, *London Bridge Street.* The dramatic, angled-glass facade of the Shard was behind him, and in front stood high-rise buildings. A clear crisp night encased London with enough moonlight to see by, which would make hiding difficult.

He needed a plan, a place to lie low. A way of contacting the Major.

An explosion ripped through the night, illuminating the sky west of the Thames. A dazzling, pure white light flared and then dimmed.

Maybe that was why the Dark were preoccupied.

Every fibre in his body told him to leave central London far behind, head in the opposite direction, get away, but his heart urged him west. Years of training and discipline had him ignoring his heart, turning south, and running into the shadowed streets.

An hour after leaving London Bridge, Cole, London-borne, found his feet returning him to a familiar estate. The streets had been eerily quiet, and the drone patrols were easily avoided. The Dark seemed to be preoccupied with activity in central London.

He hoped it wasn't Eira, but his gut told him otherwise.

He snuck through the abandoned streets, ditching the suit jacket in a dustbin with the severed hand, keeping out of sight of the cameras at an even jog which was starting to send spasms of pain through his stitched-up wound. Cole paused to catch his breath, hands on his knees as he took great gasps of air.

A smashed phone booth stared at him from across the street. Relief nearly made his knees give way. Exactly what he had been looking for as he ran through the streets.

Corroded paint, more rust than red, greeted him as he heaved open the glassless door. The phone in the interior looked in working order. Slinging his leather jacket over his shoulder, he lifted the phone and dialled the emergency protocol direct to Major Stone.

The dialing tone sounded. Cole rested the phone in the crook of his neck, easing his panting, rolling both his sleeves up to expose his forearms.

The gruff voice of Major Rick Stone filled Cole's ear. 'The stone strikes the flint.'

'The hawk plays tag over the mountain,' Cole replied, the coded message instinctively rolling off his tongue.

'Hawk, is that you?'

'Yes, Major Stone.'

'Has your team been compromised?'

'Affirmative.'

Silence on the other end of the line. Then a barked, 'Report!'

Where to start. Cole ran a hand through his messy hair, scraping it back from his forehead.

'At 0300 hours four days ago, Delta was extracting on your orders, following Technician Lofty's disappearance. We were ambushed by agents who captured and converted Tagger and Flint. Sam, I believe, is dead.'

'Why has it taken you three days to contact the base? Are you compromised?'

Cole grimaced, catching his reflection in the dark window, his black iris not even reflecting in the bright light of the booth.

'I was severely injured and detained at the Wallflower clinic. Full protocol was followed, and all data protected. I can confirm I am not compromised.'

'Can you prove your position, Hawk?'

Cole sighed, glancing at the rusty, gum-covered ceiling of the booth.

'I can't, Major, until you physically see me, and I can prove otherwise. All I can state is that if I were under the Dark's influence, the base would have been attacked by now, as I'm the only one in Delta Unit who knows its location. Or I might be trying to lure you in? Your call, Major. I don't have a secure video link to prove my appearance to you.'

There was a long pause, and he imagined Major Stone weighing up the options, stroking his grey moustache like he always did when contemplating.

'Is our data secure?'

'Yes.' I think!

'Anything more to report?'

'The mission's full objective is in my possession.'

Another long pause, and then finally, 'How?' in Major Stone's hushed whisper. Cole was in deep trouble. How to spin this one?

'There is a major incident afoot in the capital. I will be honest, I wanted revenge for Tagger and Flint, so whilst their headquarters were vacant, I infiltrated their laboratories and undertook the mission solo.' The lie came easily.

Major Stone's shocked breath on the other end of the phone was the only sign he was still listening.

He ploughed on, playing his trump card. 'I know how to gain access to their laboratories via a hidden entrance. I also know how they infect their hosts.' And maybe an idea on how this virus can be defeated.

It was the biggest breakthrough in the last decade in their fight against the Dark.

Cole waited patiently, keeping an eye on the street around him. It must be at least four in the morning by now.

'What you did was reckless and out of character,' Major Stone said, the ice in his tone freezing Cole's ear. 'I'm concerned that you are indeed compromised and are not acting without instruction. Despite that, it's a risk we must take for the vital information you have gained. I need to refer to command and get their opinion on this development. Extraction is impossible at present until we've done a full risk assessment. Do you have a safe place to stay?'

'Yes, Major, I have somewhere that I can lie low.'

'Captain Hawkins you will be disciplined for this.'

With that, Major Stone hung up. Cole replaced the phone on the receiver and stepped out of the booth and into the cold night.

That went well then.

He suddenly felt weary, heavy to his bones.

Throwing his jacket on, Cole slid the pistol from his waistband and crossed the road heading down Ledbury Street. It had been a risk returning to his old estate. Agent Jones had told him that they knew his history, but he had nowhere else to go that was safe. Cole was gambling on the crisis in the capital keeping them occupied long enough for him to rest.

Cole couldn't help glancing up at the huge, sand-coloured tower block dominating the skyline, that he had called home for fourteen years. The memories that had been dragged up recently threatened to resurface again. His mother had died in that block. An abusive marriage, which resulted in her addiction and eventually her murder at his own father's hand. Cole had led his life in the shadow of that memory for the best part of a decade. His main goal was to not become like his father. He had succeeded, hadn't he?

Bracing his hands on the garden entrance, he tried to calm his racing heart. The squat brick terrace in the shadow of Bromyard House appeared unlit, the front garden a jungle of weeds.

A memory slid to the surface in Cole's mind.

The immaculate garden, row upon row of vegetable plants in raised planters, a potting shed in the far corner. An old gentleman bent double tending to his prized cabbages, shirtsleeves rolled up, flat cap on, and pipe puffing from his mouth.

His grandfather. This place had been his salvation away from the abusive flat he had grown up in behind his grandfather's house. The red door was now chipped with age, and the boarded-up windows held an air of neglect. Cole was saddened at the state of the once pristine house; he should have taken more care of it. He bent down and lifted the plant pot, removing the spare key.

The door squeaked open, and stale air wafted through the open doorway as Cole stepped inside, sighing. He had abandoned his grandfather's house eight years ago after spending two weeks hiding out following his mother's death, in fear that the social workers or police would come and find him. No one had bothered with the skinny kid who had run away, the only witness to his mother's death. Then the world had gone to hell with the virus, and he was forgotten about entirely.

This maisonette had been left to him in trust under his mother's middle and maiden name, a secret identity invented by his grandfather to give his only grandson some security.

Grandfather, what would you think of me now?

Knowing the electricity was off and not wanting to draw attention to the vacant property, Cole firmly shut the front door, securing the safety chain. Using muscle memory, he found himself marching up the tight stairs on shaking legs and turning into his grandfather's bedroom. Cole collapsed face first onto the musty divan, slipping the gun under the pillow.

CHAPTER 14

||| EIRA

Eira watched the scene play out in slow motion. She had heard the crack of a gun fired twice and sprinted around the corner in time to see Oran launch his staff at the hovercraft and then collapse on one knee, clutching his thigh.

Eira was immediately at his side, her magic flaring, stunned that a bullet had penetrated his defences. Hours ago, she had witnessed his ability to dissolve bullets into stardust. Black blood came away on her hand as she touched his right wing. A quick assessment showed no exit wounds.

Oran sagged in her grip. Eira was still stunned by his revelation. *A gargoyle! Not just that, but a hybrid.* As a teen, she had sought any mythological history book she could beg Etta to bring with her from the mainland. She had never heard of gargoyles before, but then she wouldn't put it past Etta to keep such a race from her. How was she going to treat him? His genetics would be completely different to anyone she had treated before.

She sent her power towards the pinprick gap in his shield. She gasped, feeling a kernel of her magic still inside him. Her magic analysed the wounds with ease. Eira reinforced Oran's strength and eased his pain. She needed to remove the bullets. The wound in his wing was critical — it had shattered the humerus. One wrong move on her part, and he might never fly again.

Shaping her magic into a fist, she nudged the bullet in his thigh. Oran hissed in pain, and Eira jolted as her magic was repelled.

'The bullet isn't normal, is it?' Oran panted.

Eira recoiled. Her power had only ever been repulsed once before. Recently. *Cole.*

Eira helped Oran sit on the floor, his knees bent at odd angles. Seated, Oran was her height. She watched as he wrapped his wings around his shoulders like a bat cocooning himself.

'I think it's infected with the Dark's virus. My magic is repelled by it. I need to get them out of you the old-fashioned way, but I can't do it here.'

Eira straightened as confusion filled Oran's angelic face. Of course, he was an outsider so he wouldn't be aware of the virus. He glanced at the shimmering web of magic above their heads, watching the reflected stars shine and wink in the darkness.

'I've eased your pain and increased your strength. Given your magical ability, I'd guess that you have more resilience than the average human,' Eira said more to herself than to Oran, and then added, 'I've never treated a gargoyle before.'

Eira turned to start the desperate search for the waymarkers again as a vice-like grip tightened around her wrist.

'You need to get out now, Eira. My time is limited.'

Eira looked down at Oran's sincere face.

He continued, 'There is an elven colony in Yorkshire. Go to Rievaulx Abbey, say my name. They will protect you and know what to do with that pulse of power I felt from you.'

Eira didn't understand, a pulse of power? Was that why he had come to protect her? He must be delusional with his wounds.

'You need to go now! Before the humans in suits come here.'

As if on cue, the large timber doors at the front shuddered from impact. The stone statues with the glowing eyes, braced against them, securing them as another thud trembled through the building. The drones above intensified their attack on the shield, many short-circuiting on impact. It was only a matter of time before the Dark infiltrated their sanctuary.

Eira came to a decision as she eased her hand from Oran's grip, determination set on her face. She purposely strode to the hover copter. Reaching for the staff, she gripped it with two hands and set a foot on the craft to pull against. For a moment, she glanced inside and saw the full extent of the pilot's death. The staff had embedded in his skull, a gruesome wound like something from a horror movie. Oran's shot had indeed been true. She wouldn't like to get on the wrong side of the gargoyle.

Grunting with all her elven strength, Eira eased the staff free, its release sending her stumbling backwards. Blood ruptured from the pilot's wound, spraying the cracked window. Without a second thought, Eira bent in to grab the gun from his lifeless hand and tucked it into her blazer. Breathing hard with the exertion, she looked down at the blood covering her hands.

The ebony staff was surprisingly light, well balanced, but far too long for her to ever wield. She marvelled at the engravings along the shaft. It hummed in her hands as she used it as a walking stick, the top spike glinting in the moonlight. Oran emitted a low growl of warning, then shook his head as if surprised at his reaction.

Apparently, he was possessive of his weapon.

Eira carefully handed the staff to Oran, who clung to it as if his life depended on it. It began to glow and vibrate at the contact. Another thud echoed through the arched space.

She quickly untied her peacock scarf and, with nimble fingers, used it as a tourniquet above Oran's wound. He winced as she double-knotted it as tightly as possible. Eira became aware of his gaze on her pointed ears, his eyes widening with acknowledgment, and she dropped her hands from his firm thigh.

Oran grimaced, pulling himself up using the staff to brace most of his weight and hopping on his good clawed-foot. The black blood pouring from the wound on his thigh had slowed to a trickle, but the wound on his wing was still steadily leaking.

'You need to go, Eira. Now! I have limited time.' He raised his head to the sky again, his silver braids catching the moonlight.

'A doctor never leaves a patient behind,' Eira stated firmly as she laid her hand on his forearm, releasing a tidal wave of healing power into Oran's core.

He straightened, relaxing the tension in his shoulders with a sigh as the blood cascading from his back eased. She had given him an hour's reprieve by draining some of her magic into him.

Without a backward glance, Eira stalked forward, staggering slightly as dizziness blurred her vision. She had drained her power too quickly. She shook her head, risking a glance at Oran, who was indeed following without more protest. She could hear the uneven scrape of his claws and the thud of the staff, an uneven beat.

The banging on the front door became distant as Eira led them deeper into the abbey. She flanked the north aisle leaving the destruction of the hover copter behind, and approached the gilded, triple archway of Scientists' corner leading into the Quire.

Eira ached to read the inscription, to spend an hour wandering these magnificent halls. She knew that Sir Isaac Newton and Charles Darwin were buried here. History had been her saviour as a teenager, a reprieve from her grief. Her fascination with the world she was protected from for a decade came alive within her imagination and only grew as she learned more. The real world was nothing like the texts she had read.

Eira set a steady but even pace for Oran who staggered at her side. His head tilted up in wonder as he surveyed the mural above their heads, an azure sky depicting stars woven with golden fretwork. The low ceiling gave a moment of reflection before it climbed to a heavenly height.

Oran snorted in amusement.

'Not impressed?'

Oran scanned the Quire, looking from the black and white chequered floor to the tiered pews rising against the ornate gold framework, dividing the Quire from the wider space. The Dark had, surprisingly, left the abbey intact. They allowed entry via blood tax, and understood the importance of the monument, even if they had banned worship.

'Our sacred temples dedicated to the goddess Lunar are not as...' Oran hesitated, trying to find the words. '... Ornate, fussy. We do not need all this stuff.'

Eira sniggered at that.

'Our temple is natural, hewn from the rock itself. Coloured glass penetrates the ceiling filtering the starlight directly onto the moon dish in the centre. The space hums with the crescendo of waves, the reflection of the full moon.' Oran spoke with such wonder that Eira wanted to visit.

A demon in an abbey. That would be how the humans saw him.

'What are we searching for?' he asked, pulling Eira back to the immediate danger of their situation.

Eira indicated a small marking on the column near the last pew, roughly engraved and worn with age. Westminster Abbey was crowded with so many inscriptions, symbols, and religious emblems that the waymarker would go unnoticed to untrained eyes.

'The V-shape indicates the direction, and the circle increases in circumference the closer you get to the portal,' Eira replied, pointing at the marker. The circle was a third of a circle with a quarter missing.

Oran, who had leaned down to view the marking, grunted as he drew himself up to his full height, his presence in the vast space intimidating. His head suddenly turned to the left, monitoring. He hit his staff once on the polished floor, igniting the symbols down the shaft. As one, the statues closest to the north door surged forward. Oran growled, the raw sound vibrating through the tranquil space.

At the same moment, he grabbed Eira's hand and plunged them both into his concealment as shadows appeared on the other side of the glazed doors. The central, stained-glass window at the front of the nave exploded in a rain of crystals, as drones zoomed straight towards them.

Grating stone echoed within the arched hall as statues launched themselves skywards to infiltrate the drones. Eira, shocked, watched a templar knight strike a stone sword through the main body of a drone before it plummeted to the floor in an explosion of shattered stone, to never rise again. The knight's glowing eyes dimmed as Oran's magic left him.

Oran's hand contracted in hers, a pulse to gain her attention, to urge her to move. She sent a surge of healing power back through their connection, tugging him towards the entrance to the cloisters. Thudding footsteps sounded on the flagstones as Elizabeth I's statue flew towards them, sceptre and orb swinging overhead in a warrior's cry as she entered the fray.

Eira thundered down the hallway, the first rays of dawn spilling through the gothic windows, lighting their way. Oran staggered beside her, his hand clammy in hers as he drew on his remaining power, anticipating an attack from the open windows.

Oran panted hard as they skidded around the corner, entering the twined, arched entrance of the octagonal Chapter House. This had to be it. Eira's guess that the Myth portal would be located in the oldest part of the abbey had to be right. If she wasn't, they were both doomed. She knew that the Chapter House dated back to 1255, commissioned by Henry III.

In the gathering light she admired the imposing central pillar, fanning out to a vaulted ceiling, murals depicting scenes from the Apocalypse below. But she didn't guide Oran up the stairs into the inspirational gathering place of monks past. She slowed her pace and approached a small oak door nestled within a stone arch to the right of the Chapter House entrance. It was no wider than four feet and barely tall enough to fit the average human male.

How am I going to squeeze Oran's bulk through the door?

She was aware of Oran's hot hand shaking in hers, and his breathing was laboured. His body had gone into shock. Eira squeezed his hand and felt a tsunami building within their connection. Oran's whole body constricted as he released the hold on his power. Eira suddenly saw his trembling hand in hers as his invisibility dissolved, chest heaving with his weight fully on his staff, head bowed. Blood dripped down his back in a slow splash which leaked onto the flagstones.

The sound of falling rubble echoed down the hallway as hundreds of stone statues lost their lives. They only had moments left.

Eira drew her blade, angling it across her palm to draw blood whilst still maintaining her grip on Oran with her other hand. She slammed her hand against the ancient five-panelled door right above the discreet waymark symbol before her hand could heal, admiring the softness of the timber she knew was covered in cowhide. From a side note she had read in a history book, the door dated back to Anglo Saxon times when myth and religion were blurred.

Her suspicion regarding the door worked. The door absorbed her blood and swung inwards on ancient iron hinges without a squeak. The pitch-black void within smelt musty and foreboding, but it was a risk Eira had to take.

She carefully steered Oran, eyes hazy with pain, to the portal door. He obediently bent, wings still wrapped around his shoulders, and retracted his staff so it could fit through the door. His movements were stiff, almost robotic, as if every movement cost him energy.

Oran curled his burly frame to cram it through the threshold, and as Eira turned to check that they weren't being followed, she noticed the trail of blood leading straight to them.

Tugging Oran's hand so he paused, she cast her tendrils of power into the abbey, invisible to everyone but her, to scout the trail of black blood, searching for every drop. Eyes closed tight, she focused, syphoning more of her power to flow like a river until it arrived at the source. She sensed hazy movement, low pitches of noises, observed as if through a distorted mirror. Eira plunged her palm flat onto the floor and, like a riverbed sucked dry by the sun, she absorbed the blood into the stone. Oran glanced at the window, a grimace on his face as he muttered, 'Sol's up.'

When she was sure every precious drop was gone, she retracted her hand from the rough floor and opened her eyes, astonished. In her decade of wielding magic, she had never experienced a rush quite like that. She still retained her grip on Oran, who was panting hard, confusion on his face. In the approaching dawn, she could see every sparkle on his alabaster skin, like crystal embedded into rock, and gasped at the wonder of it. In the blink of an eye, his confusion turned to horror, and he shoved himself through the door and disappeared into the darkness.

Without a moment to spare, Eira yanked the medieval door shut behind them, firmly securing the iron latch. She repeated the process of paying her blood tax to the portal door and, using her dagger, slashed the waymarker symbol.

'That will secure the door shut, sealing it from all. No one can get in as I've shattered the portal spell,' Eira whispered to Oran.

As her eyes adjusted to the acute darkness, she started to panic. She couldn't hear Oran, not even a whisper of breath. Had he turned invisible again? Eira knew his power was exhausted. Panic turned to anxiety as she used her heightened elven senses to locate him, fearing the worst. *Has he collapsed?*

Eira surveyed her surroundings in the gloom. The room was arched, more tunnel than open space, with rough bricks covering the ceiling and cobblestones covering the floor. The scent of stale mould and incense drifted to Eira as she stepped away from the comfort of the door. Any sounds on the other side were muffled. Eira was confident the Dark wouldn't find the door; not even their heat-seeking cameras could penetrate the thick stone wall.

The tunnel expanded into darkness which even her night vision found hard to infiltrate. Eira set her palm on the irregular bricks and proceeded along the wall, hoping she would locate Oran. *Where are you?*

Her hand collided with a smooth irregularity on the wall. Holding her breath, she felt a spike, the spine of a wing. A cold chest not rising.

Hands shaking, her breathing heavy, Eira extracted her phone from the hard-cased backpack which she lowered to the ground. Making sure the phone was still in safe mode and untraceable, she turned on the torch, but made sure to angle her body to hide the light from the door behind her.

Eira placed a hand over her mouth in shock, as the light traced the contours of Oran's frozen face. Leaning against the arched wall, hands gripping his staff, head bowed in silent prayer, he looked like a sculptor's impression of a mighty god. With a trembling hand, Eira reached for Oran's forearm. Cold polished stone met her fingertips where once there was soft skin. She sent her power probing their connection and found a wall of granite restricting access.

'Oh, Oran.'

Tears welled in Eira's eyes. What was she going to do?

Sol's up. My time is limited.

Oran's words. His protests and urgency for her to leave were now clear. Gargoyles, creatures of night and shadow. So, what had happened?

Light. The day. Sunrise.

They must live at night and turn to stone during the day. Why hadn't he said anything more direct?

She would have to wait until dark. But to stay in this tight space, with her enemy only a few feet away, would be a risk even with the door sealed shut. Could she leave and then come back? But Eira wasn't sure of the Myth tunnels this side of central London. She might get lost, captured even, and then Oran would bleed to death when he woke up. He had saved her, protected a stranger. As a doctor she had a duty of care and morals to follow.

Eira made her decision. Sinking down the wall, she sat on the damp cobblestones next to Oran and slid her phone back into her bag, plunging the tunnel into darkness. She could just about make out Oran's still figure. She tentatively wrapped a hand around his ankle to alert her when he awoke.

ORAN

Oran always found the sensation of waking uplifting. The forced state of being turned to stone was one he had never gotten used to, even in his hundred years of life. To have all your limbs become heavy, the organs you relied on growing laboured as they went into hibernation, was unsettling. The gargoyle existence hadn't always been like this, forced to endure the night and never appreciate the sun.

Before Oran's birth, they once had a sacred stone, which permitted a never-ending night across the kingdom. Then they were strong, many in number, healthy in magic, and confident in their leadership. But since the stones disappeared at the end of World War II, they were forced back to their primitive state of guard duty during the hours of slumber.

Oran felt every surface of his body begin to crack as he woke from his regenerative sleep. The first rule they were taught as fledglings was to open their eyes, be alert for danger. It was dangerous for a gargoyle to sleep in locations other than their protected clan.

Oran raised his head and opened his opal eyes to darkness. *This can't be correct.* As his night vision adjusted, he saw the curved brick ceiling of a cramped tunnel leading away to a door at the far end.

His lungs finally filled with air as they turned back to flesh, and sharp pain shot the length of his wing. He winced, a low growl of discomfort rumbling in his chest. He didn't feel rejuvenated as he would normally when emerging. Then he remembered.

The abbey, an encounter with a hybrid. Eira who was half-elf, half-human. He was still shocked to have met another who appeared to have unique gifts like him.

Oran became aware of a warm comforting pressure on his ankle and soft breathing to his left.

'Nelka.' His unused voice boomed in the dark.

But it wasn't his Starlight, his soulmate. A head of golden coppery hair, encrusted with grit and dust sprang to wakefulness as Eira opened her bright green eyes, the colour of the ocean outside the keep.

'Oran,' her voice was rough, husky. She rotated her neck, easing the stiffness from it.

Oran was astonished she had remained the whole night, honoured in fact. Her familiar power immediately flowed through his defences, easing his pain, and seeking an update on his condition. Eira's magic was addictive – it took all his hurt away and relaxed his body immeasurably. Was she aware that she had automatically sought his wounds? How had she even infiltrated his shield so effortlessly? That disturbed him. She was strong, maybe as powerful as him or…

As strong as his biological father.

He shuddered to think of the threat she might pose to him.

'I'm concerned about your wounds, Oran,' Eira whispered into the silence as she chewed her lip. 'The bullets are trying to spread the virus through your veins. Your magic is halting its progress, but I need to try at least removing the one in your leg.'

Oran blinked, gulping. Eira took his expression as ignorance as she explained. 'The Dark have invented a virus, which is spreading among humanity. The virus doesn't kill, but controls the host, creating a living slave to do the Dark's bidding. I've never seen it infect an immortal before.' She shrugged. 'So, I don't know how you'll react.'

The silence stretched between them.

'I know about the virus.'

Surprise lit Eira's face in the darkness.

'How?'

'It's not important right now,' Oran muttered, heaving himself up from his crouched position, his muscles burning with the strain of being trapped that way all night.

'Not important?' Eira hissed, grabbing Oran as he turned. He growled in warning to her, but she stood firm. 'You mean the high races, the elves, know and have done nothing to aid their plight?'

'When we last got involved, it ended in our casualties, a civil war within our clans. Humans are a destructive race who have brought this on themselves.'

Oran bared his teeth, his elongated canines flashing in the dark. He suddenly felt all his indignation fade. Did he believe that? His biological father's view? Callan, his chief and real father, believed it to some extent, so that must mean it was true, right?

His chest was heaving with fury; Nelka would have been ashamed of his outburst.

'I was brought up by humans,' Eira whispered sharply, pointing to her chest as she stared him down. 'By good people who sacrificed their lives so I could have mine, a half-breed mongrel who didn't fit in. Until you have lived among them, you have no right to judge.'

With that, she slung her bag across her back and strutted off into the darkness, towards the other door. Stunned, Oran reflected on her words.

A half-breed mongrel.

Is that what she had been called?

His half-illumini existence was unknown in his clan, only Nelka knew the truth. He was unique in appearance with his pale skin, where most gargoyles were of darker stone. His gifts alone set him apart from the rest, which caused the suspicion and guarded looks he received. Callan had made him Keystone to give him authority, which meant he had their respect and loyalty, but he was never viewed as one of them even though he had mated with the chief's daughter.

What must it have been like for Eira? At least he had a home, a clan to associate with. The sense he didn't truly belong had always been at the root of his feelings of loneliness, made harder when he was finally told the truth by his elven father. A decade of avoiding the truth of his elven heritage hadn't improved their relationship.

His real father was the reason he was in this situation.

Oran squared his shoulders, exhaling the last of his frustration. He should apologise. He followed her slowly, placing one unsteady foot in front of the other, bracing most of his weight on his staff. At least he felt no pain with the healing magic surging through his veins.

Oran reached the door at the end and heaved it wider for his large frame. This door was constructed from iron, with exposed metal hinges. An even smaller tunnel greeted him, and he could smell sea salt and jasmine mingled with stale mould and damp air.

Easing through the opening, taking great care not to knock his wings, Oran took a deep breath, trying to stamp down the rising panic that threatened to overwhelm him. The walls were closing in around him, he needed to fly, break free, inhale the fresh, cold air of the night. The musty air choked him as he wrapped his arms around himself. The iron door thudded shut behind him sealing his escape route.

'Oran, breathe in and out, slowly. That's it. Inhale and then exhale.'

Calming his racing heart, Oran followed Eira's instructions. The claustrophobia receded slightly.

'Do you have enough energy for a sphere? Light might make you feel safer.' Eira's pacifying tone washed over him.

Extracting a trembling hand, Oran willed an orb to float on his palm. The pure white light spread warmth along his skin, ebbing the tension. It threw the background into shadow and lit his face as he moved the sphere between them.

'It probably helps to focus on something as well,' Eira whispered soothingly. His tranquil light reflected her pale skin making her hair shimmer like molten copper.

Finally, regaining his composure, Oran stuttered, 'I-I didn't mean what I said. The high race situation is political and complicated. You deserve answers, and I will try to tell you as much as I know.' He lifted his orb and rested it on the tip of his staff where it remained, shining like a distant star.

Eira nodded curtly, glancing towards the ground as if she didn't quite believe him. She stepped back, gesturing for him to sit. He leant his precious staff against the curved wall, its starlight casting a glow of light around them in a protective bubble. With some difficulty, Oran took his full weight on his arms and rested his back against the smooth wall, bracing his right wing off the apex. His legs were inches away from the other wall, and he felt fear threatening again, but he swallowed it down and focused on Eira.

Eira unzipped her case, producing a ready-made workstation, and started to lay out instruments he had never seen before. The healers in his clan used primitive, natural forms of medicine, not these shiny utensils before him. Finally, she unclasped a pendant from her neck, and he saw a shining opal before she placed it tenderly alongside her other tools.

'I won't lie, this is going to hurt like hell. I can't dull your pain and heal you at the same time. My power is as depleted as yours.'

Oran nodded, bracing himself.

Eira carefully sliced the leather binding the entry wound. He shuddered. His alabaster skin was pitch black at the point of entry, veins of black transversing away from it.

Eira swiped an ointment across the wound which made him tense and growl. She chuckled to herself, green eyes sparkling in mischief.

'Glad you found that funny,' Oran grunted.

A knowing smile tugged on her lips. 'Tell me what first caused your claustrophobia.'

Unexpected question: a distraction. Oran could indulge her curiosity.

He leant back against the damp wall bracing both hands on his thigh near the makeshift tourniquet which was saturated in his blood.

'My light power manifested itself early as a fledgling. The invisibility didn't develop until early into transithood.'

Eira sniggered.

Oran glanced at her. Her eyebrows were raised as she laid the opal on his thigh. The cool surface became heated from his skin as Eira's white healing glow spread throughout the confined space.

She must be using it to channel her power like I do with my staff.

'Do you want to hear the story or not?' Oran replied with a grin.

Colour washed over her cheeks as she nodded at him to proceed.

'As humans would say, I was a *teenager.*' He snorted to himself at the use of that word. 'The invisibility took me by surprise. I found at the beginning I could only disappear for short periods of time. So, I practiced in secret until I could sustain it for longer.' The distant memory sent spasms of pain through his wing.

Closing his eyes, head tipped toward the arched ceiling, he let the pain subside until he could focus again.

'I slipped into Callan, my chief's, war room and hid in a giant chest as I couldn't hold the invisibility for more than an hour back then. I prayed to Lunar they wouldn't look in the chest as I was keen to hear the elders' debate. Well, you can guess what happened. Someone closed the lid. I didn't dare call out as I would have had to explain how I got into the room undetected, and I wasn't ready to share that part of my power with anyone yet. They already found my light power strange enough.'

Oran gasped as the opal heated to an almost unbearable degree. Eira still had her hand over it, head tilted to the side half-listening to his monologue, lips moving as if she was counting.

'After the elders left, I tried with all my might to lift the lid, but it was sealed shut. I must have been contained in that dark box for hours, desperately calling out, terrified that the walls would collapse, and I would die trapped inside. Echo... Nelka ... found me.'

Eira was so still, Oran thought she hadn't heard until she whispered, 'What happened next?'

'Nelka kept my secret like she always has,' he said with so much sincerity that Eira's eyes snapped back to his as she removed the opal. All traces of the black infection were gone. Oran was astonished.

Eira smiled once more to herself as she quickly replaced the pendant over her head, concealing it from view. Her slender hands now braced either side of the wound and Oran constricted at the uncomfortable sensation of an object moving within his body. He watched as the black bullet slowly appeared from the hole and popped out into Eira's waiting palm. It was barbed to create maximum damage and pain.

Oran's skin twitched as it was knitted back together before his eyes, leaving no evidence behind. Observing Eira's healing magic when she mended her own leg was one thing, but feeling it, himself was ... incredible.

Eira's pale, drawn face bobbed in the moonlight as she slumped against the wall herself. 'I'm so glad that worked.' The relief in her voice was evident.

'Thank you for healing my leg,' Oran muttered into the silence. 'Also, thank you for staying with me. Look, I was a bastard before with what I said. You're right, I don't know much about humans.'

Eira's eyes sparkled with understanding and acceptance. Oran felt a tingle in his stomach he had never felt before. Here was someone else who understood the suffering of not being fully whole, not fully belonging anywhere.

Arching over in sudden excruciating pain, Oran hissed through his teeth and clutched his shoulder. Eira was instantly at his side, her cool hand pressed to the wound. He could feel her power pouring into his body, but the pain refused to recede as before. Blinding light sparked from behind and a warming sensation flooded through Oran.

Eira cursed, pulling her hand back as if burnt. As Oran turned, Eira's hand shot out and caught the necklace by the chain. The opal swinging from her hand was no longer bright and shining, but dark and cold.

'It didn't work,' Eira said to herself. 'We need to go, Light Bringer. I need to get you to a safe place where I can heal you.'

She quickly packed up her bag and slipped her pendant under her top. Eira offered Oran his staff, which still twinkled with starlight, and braced her arm on the wall to help him to his feet. The confined space and intense pain threatened to send Oran into another panic attack. A now familiar power flowed along their connection, taking the edge off his pain. His legs were steady and took his full stooped weight as he proceeded to advance down the tunnel. Eira braced his right side, minding his wound. They could barely fit two abreast, but it would have to do.

'Tell me, who called you a half-breed mongrel?' Oran needed the distraction as every step sent a wave of pain searing up his spine. Why was Eira's power not blocking the pain anymore? Perhaps he was becoming immune to it.

The tap and scrape of his clawed feet and staff were the only sound as the globule of light wobbled in front of them. When the silence stretched on, he resigned himself to not getting an answer.

Finally, Eira spoke. 'When I was a child, my mother and I moved around a lot. We never stayed in a place long enough for me to go to school, so I was home-schooled by her around her other commitments.'

The grief in her voice made his heart constrict. Eira exhaled, then proceeded in a hurried tone.

'One day, when my mother's other commitments left me in the house on my own, I went searching for the school located in our neighbourhood. It was playtime, and I watched as the children chased each other, laughing and having fun.'

Oran gulped, knowing too well the sense of others having fun.

'A few children noticed me and beckoned me to the fence. Like the naive child I was, I went. They saw the pointy ears, my height, and my slightly different appearance, and started taunting me. "Half-breed mongrel" was one of many names they called me before one threw a rock at my head.'

Oran went rigid with anger; his free hand fisted at Eira's shoulder. Sensing his fury, she stated calmly, 'They were only children. They were following their parents or teachers' example. They knew no different. It's a vicious circle that only a handful of special people have ever dared break.'

Eira spoke with such acceptance and forgiveness that Oran felt ashamed of his initial reaction, wanting to attack anyone who would make such comments.

'From that abuse and mistrust, you still freely choose to help them?'

As they walked, he felt the tunnel changing around him. He could see it widening ahead, the air becoming fresher and more welcoming.

'I help those who have no voice, who've been mistreated by the current government. I do it in secret, behind a false identity because yes, if they discovered I was a hybrid, they probably wouldn't want my help. I do it because, one day, their views might change, and by some miracle we might be accepted.'

Hope infused every word, and Oran couldn't think of a response. He knew the viewpoint of both the gargoyles and the elves. It hadn't changed since the war, which had made the divisions between the races even more obvious. Only one ancient immortal had ever held them united, and he had disappeared, his name and leadership scattered to the winds.

Lunar, he was one to talk; he couldn't even tell his chief, his adopted father, that he was half-illumini, for fear of rejection.

Oran was so wrapped up in his pain-infused contemplation that he didn't register the change in their surroundings, until Eira gasped in wonder.

They stood in the centre of a double-vaulted space, ornate columns spanning the perimeter of the octagonal chamber. The walls were bare lime plaster, cracked and peeling with age, but the ceiling was a masterpiece.

'It's the same shape and similar proportions to the Chapter House at the abbey,' Eira remarked. Oran wasn't too sure of the space she referred to as the last moments before he turned to stone were still hazy.

The curved, sectioned roof depicted winged figures in various poses, some with balls of intense light in their splayed hands. Some were taming great tornados or creating clouds of fog. The faded, crimson background graduated to an intense black on the only painted wall with an arched door set between two columns, a full moon above.

Here, a starry sky was shown with two figures with horns and membrane wings holding up stones of a crushing weight, sentries at the door.

'They look like demons and angels,' Eira stated. She would see it that way, growing up in the human world.

Oran shook his head. 'They are gargoyles. You can see them worshipping Lunar, they even have our insignias.' He gestured to the complex star and moon constellations down their flesh. Eira's eyes swept over his own raised marks either side of his eyes.

'Those figures above are welkin; they have intense weather powers.'

'Who?' Eira asked.

'Those behind..."' Oran pointed back to where they had just entered the chamber.

'Elves,' she gasped.

Either side of the tunnel they had just exited, figures had been drawn with pointy ears, long tunics, and great swords hanging from their waists, strolling beneath ornate trees on an azure background with books and orbs in their hand.

'The three high races. The immortals as illustrated by early man and forgotten to time,' Oran declared.

Oran winced as another bout of pain shuddered through him. Eira, who he knew was reluctant to leave the chamber, led him straight to the other door. He scented blood and looked down to see red blood smeared on Eira's palm as she pressed it to the door. The flecks of silver in her blood glinted brightly in the light from his orb.

The great door swung noiselessly out, letting in an intense light which blurred Oran's vision and set his flesh on fire.

CHAPTER 15

ORAN

Eira sealed the door against the blazing light as Oran stumbled backwards deeper into the chamber, rubbing his eyes with the palms of his hands. In the commotion, he had abandoned his staff on the ground. The starlight spread its luminous glow across the flagstones.

His skin felt as if it was sizzling on his bones, heated and then cracking in the intense light. Removing his hands, he risked squinting in the comforting dimness of the chamber. A figure hovered in front of his dazed vision. Oran let Eira guide him to an alcove where she carefully lowered him to the floor. A familiar reassuring presence was pressed into his hand.

He focused on the ebony staff in his grasp, pushing away the building panic and trying to slow his heart rate. He put his head between his knees and took deep steadying breaths.

'What was that bright light? Do we have to go through there?' His questions were met by silence. 'Eira? Eira!'

Oran lifted his head so quickly that his vision swam, and shooting pains jolted down his back.

'I'm here,' she said calmly, placing a comforting hand on his knee as her now recognisable power swept into his body. Oran sought the complete numbness it brought, but the pain intensified to an uncomfortable crescendo which made his body shake and sweat pour from his forehead. He felt sleepy, his eyelids so heavy.

'Oran. Oran!' Eira lifted his chin, pulling him back from the edge of unconsciousness. 'You need to stay awake. My power can't numb the pain, there's too much of it. You've lost too much blood.'

Fighting the drowsiness clouding his mind, Oran opened his eyes. Eira's face was clear, her hands cool on his chin, solid, whole. Her eyes were intense, a bright forest-green. His staff still glowed its pulsing light, casting the octagonal chamber into shadow. A tiny slit of light spilled through the crack in the door, and Oran's whole being shrank away from it.

'I need to leave you, only for a moment, to get supplies,' she said. His head dipped again, eyes drifting closed. 'Oran you need to stay awake,' Eira pleaded.

'What's on the other side of that door?' he murmured.

'It's outside.'

'What do you mean? Why is it so bright?'

Eira didn't reply. Oran lifted his head, staring at Eira as he registered her surprised expression, mixed with regret.

'It's daytime, Oran. It's not bright out there, it's overcast.'

Oran opened his mouth to reply as he finally processed her words. *Daytime? That's impossible!*

'I can't be awake during the day. It's physically impossible.'

The look in Eira's eyes was so sincere that he knew she was telling the truth.

'How?'

'I don't know.' Eira shook her head. Her hand tilted his head toward her again, tenderly stroking his jaw. 'We'll work this out. You need to stay here, safe and awake. Do you hear me, Oran? Awake!'

She released his chin, the sudden disconnection leaving Oran feeling empty. He heard her quiet footsteps as she crossed to the door, and the smell of fresh air wafted over him for a moment before the searing light engulfed the room again. He hissed, tilting his head to the side.

He was awake during the day, and the pain was just adding to his disorientation. Resting both hands on the one solid object within the space, he intensified the soft starlight spinning on the sharp point of his staff.

Stay awake.

Oran traced his eyes over the murals, highlighting features he had missed before to keep the dark void at bay.

Three figures within the elven mural stood apart from the others as if worshipped from afar. Each held a different object: one a book, one an orb, and the female an hourglass. Elves were the keepers of time and knowledge.

Oran glanced to the heavens and beheld the leader of the welkin in battle armour, a shield with a sun symbol emblazoned on the front strapped over his back as his great, golden-feathered wings glinted in the inferno he was casting, twin swords raised in a battle cry. Welkin were the masters of chaos and destruction.

134

Oran looked to the left and could see the gargoyles, cursed to walk the night as protectors and seekers of the truth, warriors who hid in the shadows. On closer inspection, he could distinguish Lunar's phasing in the background. The mural told the story of their transformation from stone every night.

He gritted his teeth as another pulse of needles shot up his spine. He was sure that the virus was moving, slowly spreading up his back.

Perhaps it was the virus that had affected his ability to change to stone. His body's way of defending itself. He knew he was unwell, close to the dark side of Lunar.

He thought of Nelka and wondered what she would say when she discovered he had lost the one and only trait they shared. He should never have left her in her current state. He had abandoned his mate for a reckless mission given to him by his biological father based on a spike of power that he'd felt. As always, his father was doing all he could to gain power over the elves and other high races. Now that Oran had found the power source, he was reluctant to hand her over to be used by his father.

'Oh, Echo, I'm sorry my Starlight,' he said in Gork to the empty void knowing that she wouldn't be able to detect him from this distance. Unlike when he had needed her help stuck in the chest, then, she had heard.

Thinking of Nelka, a primal instinct flickered within him, numbing his pain. His yearning and need for her overwhelmed the desire to sleep. He had to survive for her, for his family. Their soul link, so faint from the miles between them, snapped and tugged like a life support. Oran wondered if Nelka had felt it. Encased in stone as she was at present, he didn't think so. She would have sensed his fatal wounds though, and that scared him. She could be wild and reckless at the best of times, and the thought of her coming here, to this vile city, filled him with dread. He would get a message to her tonight before she acted.

He needed support and eyes out there in the daylight if he was to survive. Oran had never used his power during the day and didn't even know if he could. Focusing the dregs of his remaining power into his staff, he opened his mind to the ever-present kernel of magic which gave him a connection to his companion in London.

Where did I leave the chimera? As he connected with his companion, he could see that he was still outside the clinic where he had been set up to keep an eye on Eira.

Being in the creature's mind gave him a brief reprieve from the pain consuming his body. He activated the small creature and ordered it to fly to his location. He would normally retract his mind from the creature at this stage, but instead, he sat and watched as a passenger, pleased that it was working. Oran marvelled at the multi-coloured landscape passing beneath the creature's feet. Everything was so intense and sharp. At night, Oran could perceive colour and tone with his night vision, but it was always muted compared to this true rendition of colour.

Then the noise registered. The sound of car engines rumbling, drones humming, and the buzzing of telephone wires overwhelmed the creature's senses. Even hearing it second-hand was painful for Oran, and he shuddered to think what it would be like if he were out there himself. The absence of humans on the streets was disconcerting. The few that they did see were on edge, sallow, and sullen. Compared to the vibrancy of the keep, this urban landscape was depressing. Appetising smells drifted to him on the wind mixed with the pollution and decay from the abandoned buildings.

The chimera followed the meandering strip of water as it banked and angled through the grey clouds descending towards its master's location. Oran, still hitchhiking, enjoyed the thrill of the dive as it dropped, air whipping past as it plummeted towards the ground. Wings suddenly flaring, the chimera slowed its descent and alighted on a dustbin with a clatter.

Oran was keen to take in his immediate surroundings without being blinded by daylight. Through the chimera's eyes, he observed the alleyway, noting the overflowing dustbins, rusted fire escape, and brick facade. He didn't know the city well enough to establish where the tunnel exited. He could be anywhere.

Oran positioned his pet next to the hidden entrance to the chamber, instructing it to keep its eyes on the alleyway entrance. Oran pulled his mind back, coming back to awareness in the chamber. His body screamed at the agony tearing through him. At least he felt more awake.

Oran waited for what felt like an eternity for Eira to return. He tried to keep himself awake by watching the alley through the eyes of his chimera, trying to keep tabs on anyone and anything that passed by the entrance. He was just giving in to the darkness when he picked up movement at the end of the alleyway. A female with jet-black hair strutted into view, heading straight for the door. The chimera growled a warning, and the female yelped, jumping back in surprise. She was distinctly human in appearance, but something familiar in her manner and clothes tugged at Oran's memory.

Recovering, the female stood with her hands on her hips, a bundle braced in one, and said in a voice he knew, 'Oran it's me, Eira.'

The chimera rumbled a low growl, its hackles raised as it stood on the lid of the bin, getting ready to pounce. Eira raised her hands, taking another half-step back.

'Oran, we've just been through a night of hell in Westminster Abbey. You made the statues come to life to protect us. You have a grave injury and...' — she searched for the correct response to make him believe that it was her — 'you told me about the time you got locked in a chest in your chief's war room. Nelka found you.'

Eira. It was definitely Eira. But how?

Oran instructed the chimera to stand down and allow Eira to enter through the door. She kept a watchful eye on the tiny beast as she slipped past.

Eira hurried to his side, stepping fully into the glow of his starlight. He made out deep-brown eyes, straight black hair pulled up into a messy bun, and human ears. If he looked closely enough, she still had the same shaped face: long nose, high cheekbones, a dusting of freckles on her nose.

How? He tried to utter the enquiry, but his throat was so parched that the only sound that came out was a cough. He could smell something delicious that, even through his pain, made his stomach rumble.

'Who's your friend?' Eira gestured behind her with a bottle full of water which she handed to Oran. 'I've seen that creature before on a rooftop in Battersea.'

Oran swigged the water, draining the whole bottle though most splashed down his chin and onto his chest. 'His name is Oswald, and he's one of my first creations.'

'Like the stone statues you brought to life?'

'Kind of, he lives off a Heart Stone fuelled by my power. It never runs out and doesn't drain my resources. He's as close to a living thing as you can get. I shaped him myself from rock. We're linked so I can see through his eyes,' Oran answered.

'He's very cute.' She held out a wrapped package, and the mouth-watering smell wafted over him, but before he could grab it, she took it back again. 'Was he on a certain rooftop in Battersea a few days past?' Eira asked, raising an eyebrow.

Oran sighed. 'Yes.'

'How long have you been spying on me? And why?' She waved the paper bag in front of him, making him growl in frustration. If he was at full strength, he would have had that paper bag out of her hands in a flash. Oran rolled his eyes.

'My elf father felt a rippling in power, a surge from the capital. He sent me to investigate. I tracked the source to the clinic and staked out the building. Oswald recorded the day movements, and I took the nightshift. One of my tracking skills is to sense when others have magic. Creatures who can use magic have a glow around them.'

Eira thrust the bag into his grateful hand, and he ripped it open to reveal a sweet-smelling pastry. Like a rabid animal, he devoured the chocolate-filled pastry, crumbs coating his fingers and chin. He glowed with contentment as he felt his energy flowing back. Oran shifted, pushing himself to his feet with his staff, but instantly cried out in pain and crumpled to the floor again.

Breathing hard, he looked to Eira for support, but her eyes seemed distant and surprised.

'I glamour my power so it can't be sensed. How did you know I was the reason for the power surge?'

'Do we have to do this now?' Oran replied, irritated.

'Yes, we do. I need to know that I can trust you. That you are not about to abduct me and...' She shrugged, waving her hand in the air. 'Steal my power and bend me to your will.'

I would never do that. But I know others who would.

Oran rolled his eyes. 'My light power, like your healing power, is unique. It can detect power within a creature even if it's faint or glamoured. Because of my half-illumini blend, the invisibility and the light work in harmony. I can detect the tiniest drop of magic in humans. Oswald is programmed to track such power ripples, so that's why he followed you. You were the only one at the clinic who had a strong enough power ripple to be the candidate for the power surge. Your glamour is sophisticated and hard to detect.' Oran paused, letting her know he was impressed. 'We observed the Dark's arrival at the clinic and knew something was about to happen, so we followed their movements in the hope that they would lead us to you, which they did. Just in time, too. Earlier that day, Oswald lost your scent and could no longer sense your power. I presume you used one of your sneaky tunnels?'

Oran's turn for questions. Eira nodded.

Eira seemed satisfied with his answers and stepped closer as Oran bent double, wrapping an arm across his middle. Grunting, he panted through his teeth as another wave of pain shuddered up his spine.

'It feels like it's moving within me,' he grunted and turned pleading eyes to the healer.

||| EIRA

There was real fear in Oran's eyes as he bent double in pain, drawing in huge lungsful of air. Eira glanced towards the back of his neck, carefully peeling away the top of his scaled armour. Her eyes widened in shock; black veins crept up his pale skin. Bracing Oran's arm, she pulled him onto his trembling feet and carefully scanned his right wing. Black veins expanded from the wound like ivy spreading along a tree. It had started to weave itself along his white membrane wing.

Oran appeared unaware of this development.

She shouldn't have tormented him with the pastry. She barely knew him, although there was an instant connection, and she needed some answers before she could trust him fully. He seemed to be telling the truth though. She owed Oran a life debt for protecting and rescuing her at the apartment, so it was the least she could do.

Oran being able to detect her power was unnerving though. What if the Dark could fully control him? No one would stand a chance with him on their side. She just hoped that her plan would work.

Treating his thigh had been easy and had only taken about a minute for her opal to extract the virus from the wound. The surprise was that on Oran's back, it had burned and refused to connect as though it needed time between removals to regain its power. The opal still hummed against her skin, its warmth seeping into her chest.

Keeping a firm grip on his muscular arm, Eira flared out the bundle of fabric she was clutching. She draped the black material around Oran's shoulders, clasping it gently under his throat. Eira was relieved the cloak fit his large bulk.

'This will keep the sun off your skin until we can find an alternative solution. Now for your eyes.' She presented a worn pair of aviator goggles to him with glass which refracted the light. It had been pure luck spotting them in an antique shop on her way back to the alley.

Oran gave Eira his staff as he took the goggles and, without question, slipped them over his eyes, adjusting them where necessary. He proceeded to tug up the cloak's hood, grunting with the strain to his back.

'Thank you,' Oran muttered as he held his hand out for his staff. Taking a deep breath, Oran moved toward the door, and Eira could tell that even the tiniest movement sent pain flaring up his back. She regretted relieving his pain as much as she had. If she carried on topping him up, she was afraid that it might numb him for good. His pain threshold as a hybrid was beyond even the toughest of humans.

A low grumble of warning was heard as a clunk and the sound of a car reversing filtered through the crack in the door. Oran instantly tensed, his sphere of light fading out as he plunged them into the darkness of the chamber.

'It's okay,' Eira reassured him, steering him toward the door. 'That's our ride. She's a friend.'

Eira heaved open the heavy door, keeping a guiding hand on Oran as she felt his whole body go rigid. He had never seen daylight before. Eira couldn't believe that something she took for granted was so confounding to him.

Oswald bared his teeth, his pudgy face drawn back in a snarl as he hissed like a cat, his spiny back standing on end, and his small leathery wings flapping with distress. Oran, completely covered from the sun, exhaled as he stood in the grey overcast daylight. Eira let out a sigh of relief that it had worked.

The chimera's complaints cut off abruptly, and he flew over and perched on the top of Oran's staff. His eyes were trained in the direction of the black van, whose red reversing lights were casting an eerie light into the alleyway.

The driver's door opened with a thud, and they were greeted by a female in black platform boots, a cobwebbed tutu skirt, and a Linkin Park T-shirt under a leather jacket. Eira had to give Elowen credit, she didn't scream at the sight in front of her. She staggered backwards slightly as she took in the hunched, cloaked figure of Oran, noting his clawed feet, and the stone beast perched on his staff. As Eira stuck her head around Oran's shoulder, Elowen let out a gasp.

Eira wasn't surprised. The human guise that she had taken was strikingly similar to her own, and anyone would have struggled to tell them apart. It had been the first time in a long time that she had completely changed her full appearance so dramatically. Oran's cloaked head snapped back and forth between them; confusion written in his features.

When she called her friend, Eira had told her that she needed urgent help with transportation and had simply given her a road name. Elowen didn't question her or ask why, she just said that she would be there.

Eira, knowing time was against them, blurted, 'This is Oran. He's a hybrid like me and has a fatal wound on his back.' Eira thought if she said wing it might very well freak her out. 'He rescued and protected me from the suits. It's been a night from hell, and I'll tell you all about it once we've saved him. Can you take us to the clinic?' She paused, adding with an apologetic smile, 'And yes, I might have borrowed some of your hair for this appearance.'

The corners of her friend's mouth twitched, her eyes sparkling with amusement under her thick fringe.

Without further comment, Elowen slid open the side door and helped Eira guide Oran inside. They both winced as he growled in pain, his wound pulling taut as he was bent almost double inside the small space. Oswald glided onto his master's knee, letting out a low rumble as Oran stroked him for reassurance. Eira pulled the door shut, casting them into comforting darkness. She didn't dare switch on the piercing overhead light, for Oran's sake.

The van was equipped as a small ambulance with a fold-out bed, some minor supplies, and oxygen tanks. Eira debated laying Oran down and then dismissed the idea; she didn't want to risk him falling asleep and not waking up again. Instead, she carefully pulled his hood back to reveal his silver mohawk and ossicones, flushed with sweat. He was clammy. His head rolled forward. Eira hesitated before pulling the aviator goggles from his eyes.

'Elowen, we need to leave now!' Eira banged on the privacy screen separating them. 'Are the Incognitos charged?'

'They're at 60 percent which will be enough to get us back,' Elowen replied as she gunned the engine and sped out onto the road. Eira braced herself on the bench opposite Oran.

The small ambulance with its emblem on the side wouldn't be stopped by the Dark. They refrained from interfering in the clinic's business, but under current circumstances, Eira didn't want to take the chance. The van had Incognitos on its bodywork, which made them invisible to the city cameras, and the deserted roads increased the illusion.

Oran's eyes were closed, his eyeballs moving erratically under the lids. Eira rested a hand on Oswald's rounded head and rubbed behind an ear. The beast swished his scaly tail in contentment.

'Oran, I need you to focus and stay awake.'

He jerked slightly at the sound of her voice.

'Can you tell me about Nelka?'

His nostrils flared, his lips pulling back to reveal elongated canines as his eyes snapped open. Something animalistic filled his eyes, a predator ready to do whatever was needed to protect those he cared about. Eira waited, hardly daring to breathe. His white hand clutched hers and squeezed once.

'We call her Echo,' Oran whispered.

'Why does she have that nickname?'

He let out a deep sigh, closing his eyes momentarily. 'Because of her unique gift. Like her mother, she can distort sound as a weapon, hear and receive pitch differently, and carry messages on the air. She can always hear me.'

Which made sense if she was the one who found him inside the chest. He whispered something in an abrasive language which sounded like pebbles grating on a beach.

Elowen swerved the van, sending Oswald flying off his master's lap, hissing as he dug his claws into the side of the van to steady himself. Oran grunted and held Eira's hand tighter, almost crushing her slender fingers.

'Nelka's powers sound as unique as ours. Is she a hybrid as well?' Eira enquired.

'No, she is a full-blooded gargoyle. The exceptional talent is a manifestation only found in the Crescent Clan's female gene pool. It's passed down from daughter to daughter. Its origin is lost to history. Echo's sister doesn't have the trait, but it could be passed to our daughter.' Oran spoke with such tenderness and longing that it cracked Eira's heart. She needed to keep him alive so he could see Nelka again.

Maybe one day she would experience that same love and connection with someone. So far, her only experience of romance came from the books she had read.

'We're nearly there,' came Elowen's muffled voice as they turned down a ramp.

'Nelka would like you,' Oran whispered, eyes trained on Eira as he traced the back of her hand with a rough finger. Holding a male's hand should feel strange, especially one as attractive as Oran, but somehow, with him it felt different, natural. Not in a romantic way, but as if they had already developed a deep connection that she couldn't quite place.

'I'd like to meet her one day,' Eira muttered into the silence, and joy overtook the pain on his face for a moment. Her own face lit up with a grin in return.

The van halted and, a second later, Elowen slid open the door, a dim light filling the interior. Oran tensed, but the light was subdued enough that it didn't blind him. Oswald shot out through the open door with a whoosh, startling Elowen, who now gaped openmouthed at Oran.

Eira didn't give her friend a chance to drool over the stunning male, before she took command. 'Can you tell Madam Scudamore that I require the first floor of the gatehouse and my private suite? All curtains shut.'

'Good to have the old you back again,' Elowen replied before turning on her heels and racing to the stairwell.

Eira glanced at her reflection in the van's blacked-out window. Her honey hair had reappeared, and her ears had elongated to a point once again. She had been too distracted by Oran's words to notice the normal itching sensation that came with an appearance reversal. She looked haggard, with deep bags under her eyes, and grit and dirt smeared across her face.

'Where are we?' Oran asked, taking in the subterranean garage with its roller-shutter door and shiny new lift. Now she had her appearance back, she could use her powers again, so she sought the link between them and was immediately overwhelmed by his pain.

'We're at the Nightingale, my clinic for Myths and hybrids in the city.' She gestured towards the lift door at a small symbol of a bird silhouetted in flight.

Supporting Oran by the forearm, hand clenched tightly within his, Eira helped him to the lift which she called to take them down. His breathing was ragged, and he was bent almost double over his staff. The lift door slid open, and they stepped inside. It was wide enough for a bed to enable the transfer of patients to all the floors, and was one of the first items Eira had installed when she moved in. Oswald's eyes glowed from afar as he rumbled.

'He will remain there until I call for him,' Oran said as the lift doors closed. He leant against the lift wall, his breath misting on the metal panelling, his great chest heaving. 'How does this place exist?' Oran gestured to the metallic lift.

'When my mother … died,' Eira said, Oran's horrified expression focused on her, 'she somehow left me a vast inheritance. I have been cared for by others for the last decade without any expense. So, it had just been sitting there. I put it towards caring for others.'

The look of sadness which swept Oran's features was tinged with sympathy — he must know what it was like to lose people too. He hesitated to ask the next question which she knew would spark old wounds.

'That was a very selfless thing to do, Eira,' he said instead. He had read her guarded expression well; she wasn't ready to open up about the circumstances surrounding her mother's death.

The lift doors glided open, and she stepped into a nondescript hallway. Placing her hand on the biometric scanner, a secret door swung open on her left. With a knowing expression on her face, Eira guided Oran through. She secretly smiled when she saw the wonder on his face.

'St Bartholomew's Gatehouse dates to Tudor times. It's had many uses over the centuries. I purchased this, and the adjoining building, a year ago. I've made a few modifications by joining the buildings together, but the gatehouse has pretty much been left intact.'

The room they entered was panelled in mahogany, its mismatching windows obscured by crimson velvet curtains, timber beams exposed in the low ceiling. Madam Scudamore had turned on the wrought-iron wall lights, which cast a soft glow within the interior. Herringbone flooring led to a practical workroom screened off from a cosy sitting area. Eira led Oran up the tight staircase to the attic bedrooms above, praying that he would fit. He staggered, puffing hard behind her.

She should have taken him to the Nightingale next door, but she would have had to answer some awkward questions about what and who Oran was. Even though she had only known him for a short amount of time, she knew that he would prefer privacy, especially given what she was about to attempt. Madam Scudamore was like Nora, she interfered at the most inconvenient times. It was a shame that she came with the house, but Eira just had to accept it. Elowen must have been very firm in telling her to stay away.

The attic was divided into two snug bedrooms. She opened the room at the rear, which was furnished in dark panels, muted by the soft glow of the wall lights and the regal velvet curtains drawn against the daylight. The room wasn't large, with only enough space for two single beds and a chest of drawers in the middle. Eira found the gatehouse more welcoming and comfortable than her sterile flat. The flat was a front, an illusion in case the worst happened. Eira released her breath. She couldn't imagine the outcome if the Dark had traced her to the Nightingale, but at least the security was higher here.

Oran slumped on the bed without invitation and unclasped his new cloak, which he lowered to the planked floor, leaning his staff against the bedpost. He left the aviator goggles on his forehead. Nimbly, he unbuckled the sleeve for his staff, adding it to the heap on the floor. Eira waited on the threshold, suddenly nervous. What would happen if her opal didn't extract the virus again? Her powers were useless in decreasing its spread.

A roar which shook the very foundations of the historic gatehouse escaped from Oran. Any anticipation that Eira felt dissolved as her professional facade snapped into place. She rushed to his side, lowering her backpack to the floor, and watched as Oran extracted his right wing from around his shoulder, trying to stretch it out. The light from the wall lamps highlighted the black veins creeping along the main joint. The wing sagged as Oran collapsed forward, bracing his forearms on his knees.

Eira crouched at his side. 'I daren't give you more pain relief because I'm worried that you'll never feel pain again. All I can do is make you sleep whilst I heal you.'

'Not feeling pain sounds like a mighty fine outcome to me,' Oran muttered. Looking at his face, Eira knew that he was being serious.

'Believe me, you need to feel pain to live. Even when you think you can't bear it. Now, can you move your left wing out of the way? Fold it back if you can.'

Oran obeyed, retracting his wing, and folding it against his back without difficulty.

'How do you remove your armour?'

Easing himself up, Oran unclasped the secret fixings along his left side. 'I don't think I can unclasp the other side,' he said with a hiss as he tried to raise his right arm.

With instruction, Eira managed to find the clasps. She gently removed the front part, pulling it down and off his muscled arms. Eira marvelled at the lightness and flexibility of the armour even though it looked as though the scales were cast from chips of stone and diamond.

She had been prepared for Oran's physique. It was obvious he was a warrior and had honed his body as a weapon. What she hadn't anticipated was the embossed marks decorating his upper body. Not tattoos inked onto flesh like humans would, but actual raised patterns in relief. A work of scientific art, it appeared most of the star constellation was displayed on his chest. The black veins bruising his right side destroyed the constellation of the great hunter Orion. Oran appeared self-conscious, wrapping his arms around his torso.

She hastily draped his armour over the bedpost and indicated for him to lie down on his front, trying to hide the flush rising on her cheeks. He barely fitted on the narrow bed. Now for the tricky part. The back panel of the armour was welded to his flesh with dried blood, and she had to navigate it over his wings.

'There are more fixings near my wings, it breaks into three panels,' Oran supplied, head leaning to the side, long hair swept back.

Eira unfastened the clips, peeling the left panel away with ease as Oran flared out his translucent wing, the spread so large she had to step back to avoid being hit. Puffing out her cheeks, she placed her hands on her hips, debating the next move.

Chewing her bottom lip, she said, 'I'm going to put you to sleep at this stage. It will dull the pain and increase your ability to heal your body and your power.'

Face in profile, Oran's eyes shuttered as he nodded once in acceptance before tucking an arm under his head as a pillow.

Eira flared her power, her pure white light glowing through her fingertips. Looking at it, she saw that it was similar to Oran's but without the heat. Her power flowed along their established connection, which was still intact. His vast power spread along their bond: starlight, moonbeam, and an obscure silvery thread, which must be his invisibility cloaking. *Is this how Oran traces power,* she mused. It was awe-inspiring.

Oran sighed a mighty breath which eased all the tension in his body, and Eira smiled, knowing he was no longer feeling the excruciating pain.

Eira nimbly set to work extracting the right panel of his armour by gently manipulating his wounded wing, admiring the softness and stretch of the membrane, translucent like tracing paper but as strong as spider silk. The colours from the artificial lights turned pearlescent as they passed through his wing, making the black webbing of the virus even more dramatic. Oran grunted in his sleep with the motion.

Now for the back panel down his spine. The entry wound had penetrated through the main wing spine where it connected to his shoulder blade, splintering flesh and bone. A lucky shot to an exposed area. If the wound had happened to a human, they would have died instantly. Eira gritted her teeth as she carefully eased the panel away from the wound, cringing as flesh pulled away with it, causing another river of blood to trickle down his back. Oran jerked with the movement but did not wake.

She would have to get Madam Scudamore to clean his scaled armour. She was glad that she wouldn't be responsible for working out how to clean the stone and crystal without damaging it.

Oran's back exposed, she could see the full extent of the virus spread. The veins had twined around his wing and shoulder blade and were snaking up his neck; it had also wound around the right side of his chest, merging with the start of his markings.

Anticipating more embossing, Eira couldn't help herself as she ran her fingers along the Lunar phase carved down his spine, starting with the new moon and ending in the full moon above his waistband. The relief was so smooth and precise she wondered how it was done and how they stopped his body from healing before the art was complete.

Shaking her head, Eira tried to refocus. It was so strange to finally find another hybrid, let alone treat one who matched her in power and uniqueness. From her bag, she extracted a scalpel and test tube. The scientist in her couldn't miss an opportunity to analyse the virus and its impact and spread within a host. She hoped Oran would understand as she obtained some of the flesh and blood from the entry wound.

Removing her necklace from under her top, she blew out a breath as she stared at the opal. It had become dull, and ivory in colour again. Shrugging to herself, she knew she had to attempt it again or risk Oran being turned into a pawn for the Dark.

Gently setting the opal on his wound, she waited. A surge of power pulsed around them. Not as large as the one with Cole, but enough to lift Eira's hair from her shoulders and cause Oran's to flutter across his face. The opal heated under her palm. Eira counted, not wanting to leave even a trace of the virus in him the way she had with Cole.

Cole. Eira had forgotten the captain in the chaos of the night's events. Her heart squeezed with tension. What if he hadn't made it out? Maybe he was the reason the Dark had come for her? She couldn't rule that out.

The opal hummed. She risked a glance; the virus was seeping into the stone as it swirled deep-black beneath her fingers.

Two minutes.

Three.

Eira gritted her teeth in effort as the heat increased under her hand.

Come on. Five minutes.

The opal pulsed once more and then went cold.

Eira flipped the stone over. The normal glossy surface was matte black. Placing the stone carefully on the chest of drawers, she examined Oran's exposed back and wing. Smooth alabaster flesh met her fingers, as hard as granite but completely uninfected now.

Tilting her head to the heavens, she thanked a God she didn't believe in, then corrected her silent thanks to Lunar, the moon goddess that Oran had mentioned.

Now for the hard part. Flexing her numb fingers, Eira sent her power to seek the bullet from his flesh, checking that the virus wasn't lurking within his internal organs. As before, the black bullet squeezed from his flesh with a horrid suction noise. Adding the second bullet to the plastic bag along with the first, Eira flared her diluted power. She suddenly felt very lightheaded.

How to fix a wing? She had only attempted such a procedure once before on a tern which had crashed into her aunt's greenhouse. But a bird was a completely different species, Oran's wing was more bat-like.

Like most of her healing experiences, she let her intuition guide her. Eira could hear Etta in her ear; stop agonising and let your powers lead you.

149

So Eira did. Instead of controlling her magic, she let it flow and drift towards the injury, and watched as it connected and mended the wing. Eyes closed, white light flaring, her power sought Oran's starlight and, like before, it pushed towards his mind, confusing his granite shield.

Her breath hitched as her power showed her snapshots of his memories.

Enjoyment and anticipation of his first flight, airborne within the clouds, the breeze caressing his wings.

A hand wrapped around his ebony staff as it vibrated and glowed with moonlight which lit up the stunned faces of his teachers.

Horrified looks mixed with envy from the other fledglings as he used his power to defend himself.

The approval and fear of an older, gnarled gargoyle to his emerging powers.

Like fast play on a film, the memories became distorted. Eira tried to extract her power from the invasion of Oran's mind, but their powers were too interwoven. She could sense her powers start to capture his memories, draw them in as if they were her own. They intensified inside her head until she felt like screaming.

Overriding fear which controlled all his senses and rational mind as he was trapped in the dark. The stunning face of a gargoyle girl with midnight-blue hair peering down at him.

Watching, cloaked within his invisibility, a full moon party on the beach. A tall figure dancing, blue wings splayed and loose hair cascading down her back. She turned and blew, instantly finding him within his concealment.

Pulling back, Eira finally extracted herself from Oran's memories, but not before being overwhelmed by the feelings of sorrow and loneliness. She fell to the floor, heaving in huge gasps of air. She hadn't known that she could do that.

Eira felt disgusted with herself for violating Oran's private thoughts. Like her own mind shield, his had seemed an impenetrable fortress, but she had simply stepped over the walls with ease.

The gargoyle appeared none the wiser in his slumber. His face was no longer contorted in pain, and he finally looked calm and peaceful. She didn't have the power to check that he was fully healed, but judging from the way he slept soundly, she thought that she had done a pretty good job.

Exhausted, she rested her back against the chest of drawers, her emotions a tangled mess within her.

CHAPTER 16

||| EIRA

Eira padded into the twin room in the gatehouse, drying her hair with a towel. It was just before sunrise on the fifth day after Cole's attack, and with any luck, she would be meeting him tonight, if he had found her hidden note. If he had escaped from the Dark. *All unknowns, all ifs.*

She had slept like the dead for the rest of the day and all night after treating Oran. Her body had been pushed to its limit, and her power was completely drained. But when she woke up, she felt anything but refreshed. She was still in turmoil over the fact that she had pried into Oran's private memories. Eira had left the gargoyle fast asleep and headed for the shower. His armour had mysteriously disappeared, and if she had to guess, she would have said that Madam Scudamore had snagged it to give it a good clean even though she wasn't technically allowed in the bedrooms.

Eira was busy scrolling through her phone, catching up on messages from Moyra. The doctor's texts had become more frantic as the day had progressed. She said that Nora had been found dead, her body floating in the Thames, and that Elowen was missing. Eira replied with an encrypted message, reassuring her boss that she was with Elowen, and they were both fine, but they would have to remain in hiding for a while, and asking for more information on Nora's death.

Eira didn't immediately register the empty bed until she smelt the fresh morning air and felt the gentle breeze entering the room. She felt oddly disappointed that he would just leave without seeing her, especially after all that they had been through together. Then she noticed Oran's staff still leant against the chipped headboard. *He wouldn't leave without that, would he?*

Approaching the staff, she saw a familiar fabric knotted around the ebony shaft. Reaching her hand towards her peacock scarf, she noticed it was damp and clean of the black blood that had coated it.

'Oran,' she called through the open window.

In answer, a pale white hand reached towards her, a clear invitation. Stepping onto the chest of drawers, she wrapped her hand around his forearm, and he pulled her up one-handed. She gasped and looked up to see his smug grin. He settled her next to him on the moss-covered roof tiles.

'You thought I'd left, didn't you?'

He tipped his head to the side, watching her curiously. He was topless, his embossed markings on full show in the approaching dawn, shining pearlescent in the morning light. His membrane wings were wrapped around his shoulders, the tips of his talons locked under his neck. He drew his leg up, resting a clawed foot on the roof.

Eira chose not to comment on the fact that she had come to rely on him so much in such a short space of time. She never normally trusted so easily.

'How are you feeling?'

Oran was concentrating on his thigh, his hand pulling a fine thread in the air, and then pushing it back down towards his leather trousers. He was patching up the rip.

'You'd make a mighty fine doctor with sewing skills like that.'

Oran sniggered in response. 'I have learnt many mundane skills. Would you believe I am a fantastic cook?'

Now Eira sniggered. Why did she feel so comfortable with him?

She peered down at the ancient rooftiles beneath her legs. She loved the back elevation of the gatehouse the most. The front was regal, sandwiched between two buildings, with an arched stone entrance framing the historic church behind, St Bartholomew the Great. Above the archway, the lattice of exposed black timber was on show, inlaid with white plasterwork, and crisscrossing lead windows flanking its very own coat-of-arms. The rear elevation was imperfect, wonky with mismatched proportions. A curved turret rose from one side, and on the other side, the lower floors jutted out from the ones above.

Oran looked alert and clear-eyed. She sensed none of the loneliness and sorrow she had felt from him the night before. Her magic instinctively sought his, and she had to make a conscious effort to pull it back within herself.

Oran was staring at her intently. 'Something's happened, what's wrong?' He was perceptive. Eira moved away from him slightly, his magical essence tugging at hers. But she couldn't allow herself to let it reconnect. She would never break his privacy again.

She shrugged and looked away, avoiding his question.

Instead of pushing her, Oran turned back to stare at the horizon and, sensing the impending sunrise, wrapped the cloak around himself and pulled the goggles over his eyes, leaving only the smallest slit within.

'I didn't want to miss this. I have never seen a sunrise or sunset before.'

Eira settled back too, pulling her damp hair into a braid running down her back. It wasn't the most breathtaking sunrise she had ever seen, but Oran's delight was infectious as he stared in awe at the pink and red hues smudging the sky.

'The colours are so intense and vibrant. It is so different from a moonrise.'

They both watched in silence as the sun fully emerged, marking the start of another day.

'You should see the sunsets at home; the light playing across the sparkling water can be stunning.' Eira felt the familiar pang of guilt that she got whenever she thought of home.

'You miss your home?'

Oran's head turned to her, and even though she couldn't see his face, she knew his eyes were locked onto hers. It seemed that he was able to sense her sadness. She wasn't used to being around people with such skills; being around humans had made her complacent.

Eira simply nodded. Again, Oran didn't push. It was a quality of his that she was beginning to respect.

'I'd hoped that, with the virus removed from my body, I would be able to turn to stone again,' Oran stated, watching the sun light up the clouds.

Without thinking about it, Eira found her hand moving towards his. She forced her hand into her lap instead, and clamped down on her power, locking it behind her walls.

'We will figure it out,' she muttered, and then added, 'I have friends who might be able to shed some light on why you've lost your ability. I'm going to see them tonight.'

Oran shifted, nodding his acceptance.

'To answer your first question, I feel fine now. I think everything is working, though I haven't tried my wings out yet.'

Eira knew he would be smirking under his hood. She sighed, rolling her eyes, and sweeping her long braid behind a pointed ear. 'I did honestly think you'd flown right out the window never to return, or that last night was all some kind of hellish nightmare.'

'I'm afraid it was all very real.' Oran grew serious. 'How close to death was I? Or being a host to that parasite?'

Eira blew out her cheeks.

'You weren't that close to death. If you were human, you would have died instantly, but being a hybrid gave you a huge advantage. Your main problem was blood loss. On reflection, I think it was probably a good idea that you didn't turn to stone as being asleep would have made it spread more quickly. That's why I made sure to keep you awake. In truth, I don't even know if it would have taken full control. I've only seen it inhabit a human host. Without analysing and testing it, I can't be sure.' She was grateful for the sample that she had taken yesterday.

Oran nodded, reflecting on her words.

'What are your plans now?' Eira asked, not sure she wanted to know the answer. 'You've found the power source you set out for.' Eira gulped, worried that he was going to follow through with his orders.

Oran's hooded face turned to her, and she saw the shine of the goggles beneath. Could he sense her anxiety?

'For the first time in a long time, I'm without answers, Eira,' he said solemnly. 'I follow orders, I don't normally make decisions. I'm duty bound to return to my clan. But I can't do that until I've worked out why I've lost my ability to turn to stone. I wouldn't even know how to explain it to them.' He shrugged and turned to face her more fully. 'As for your worries about why I was sent here in the first place, I have no desire to send you to him.'

Eira let out a relieved breath. 'But you ordered me to leave you and locate an elven colony at Rievaulx Abbey last night.'

'Did I? Some of last night is very hazy.'

'Is that where your orders came from? Someone there?'

Oran nodded. 'It's complicated.'

Eira paused, giving him the space he needed to organise his thoughts, remembering the feelings of envy and repulsion towards him in his childhood memories.

'To not belong is like having a part of your soul missing,' she said, shocking herself. But since she had started, she decided to carry on. 'After my mother died, I drifted for a couple of years. I was surrounded by family, but it wasn't the same, they weren't her. They were all human, they didn't understand' — she gestured at herself — 'this. The fast reflexes, the heightened hearing and sight. Then, when my powers finally manifested, it was obvious that they were terrified, though they tried to hide it. I first found out I could heal when my aunt cut her hand whilst gardening. I simply held her hand and willed the cut to close.'

Eira clasped both hands within her lap, allowing the memory to wash over her, aware of Oran's intense gaze.

'From that point onwards, I finally felt whole and content with who I was. I knew I would never fully fit within the human or the elven world, but I could belong in my own world and form my own path.'

A warmth seeped through her hand. She glanced down to find Oran's hand clutching hers within the folds of his cloak. He had moved closer to her without Eira even noticing. Her power surged, searching for the connection between them. Biting her tongue, she fought against her power, trying to keep it under control.

'As a babe, I was abandoned in a gargoyle war camp on the eve of the end of World War II. No one knows where I came from or which clan I belonged to.' Oran's voice was rough, raw with emotion. Eira could tell that it was something he rarely talked about. 'Callan found me. He raised me, trained me, and never questioned my heritage. As far as I was aware, I was a full-blooded gargoyle, just with unique gifts. It wasn't unheard of within our kind.'

Oran gulped, squeezing Eira's hand.

'A decade ago, I was promoted to Keystone. I am his second-in-command and have jurisdiction over our army, Dax, their training, who gets promoted, responsibilities like that. It also gives me greater say in our meetings and should have given me more respect. Callan requested that I create an alliance with the elves, since the relationship had been strained between us since the end of World War II. There, I met my biological father, and he filled in a few blanks. Some of his and Callan's views are backward-looking, left over from the end of the war when we tried to help humanity.

'I'm tied to Callan's commands by magical bindings, loyalty, and protocol. If he had been the one to send me on this mission, I would have no choice but to return you to my clan. But Callan's motives would be understandable, defined. My real father has hidden agendas, he's power hungry and will protect the elves' reputation above all else. I won't subject you to their corruption and schemes,' he finished, sighing deeply.

'Oran, how are you aware of the virus?'

'You do ask a lot of questions!' Oran nudged her with a wing-wrapped shoulder.

'You avoided that particular question last night too,' Eira mused.

'Nelka and I were returning to the keep from my father's colony when we were forced to spend the day in York. It's safer for us to sleep amongst urban landscapes, especially ruins. We awoke to five figures spread out just down from the main city wall. They looked like they were asleep. It was very odd,' Oran chuckled. 'Echo wanted to investigate even though I told her it wasn't a good idea. Like I said, she's a force to be reckoned with, which is why I think you'd get on so well with her.'

Eira grinned at his comparison.

'When we approached, they weren't aware of our presence as I had cloaked us. When Nelka checked their pulse, they were still breathing. Upon closer inspection, we saw that their eyes were completely black. As we watched, they simply stood up and walked off. We followed them at a distance until they all climbed into two blacked-out vans. Since then, I, Nelka, and her sister Gaia, have been investigating similar reports from other major cities.'

The hairs on the back of Eira's arms stood on end. It was so much worse than she had thought. If it had spread that rapidly in the last ten years....

'The high races won't do anything about it?'

Oran shook his head. Eira understood Oran's words, but she couldn't quite believe them. The high races, the immortals, had risked everything during World War II when they had shown themselves to humanity to help the allied forces against Nazi Germany. Then, they had united in a common cause, to stop the destruction of humanity. Surely this was just as important.

Eira felt the weight on her shoulders again. The loneliness of the mighty task at hand. Her mother's necklace weighed heavily around her neck. Could she risk sharing its powers with Oran? Was this new partnership something to trust? He had just been open and honest with her.

To stop the deflated feeling that she knew they were both experiencing, she threw a plastic tube in his direction, knowing he would catch it.

'What is this? Some healer's potion?'

'It's suncream from the local shop,' Eira answered, trying to hold back a laugh.

Oran stilled, tilting his head to the side in confusion. Eira couldn't hold it in any longer, and she sputtered a laugh at his reaction.

'Here, give it back, I'll show you what you do.'

Oran gave the tube to her. She wasn't sure it would work, but she still wanted to try it. She lifted Oran's arm and, squirting some cream into her hand, started rubbing it into his alabaster skin. Moving back, she let the sun hit his arm, but instead of hissing in pain, Oran just stared in wonder.

'How does that feel?' she asked, knowing she wouldn't get an answer. 'The power of factor fifty,' she teased. 'I suspect your skin will get used to being in the light, but you'll need to protect it for a while.'

Oran yanked the tube from her hand and, within the shade of his hood, applied it to his face. Tentatively, he removed it and sighed, his expression one of satisfaction as he turned his face to the daylight, grinning from pointy ear to pointy ear.

'I thought I would have to wear this hood forever.'

Gaining confidence with the cream in his hand, Oran stood, cloak dropping open as he spread it across every surface of his upper body. Eira's attention again snagged on his markings, and she caught herself staring.

'What do all your relief markings mean? How are they done?'

'Some of them are clan tradition and identification.' He traced the crescent moons either side of his aviator goggles. 'Others are bindings and promises to someone.' He showed her his ring finger, where instead of a wedding ring, a band of stars with a crescent moon were engraved.

'They're made by magic to stop them healing. I'm the Light Bringer, so to honour my unique gifts, Lunar's phasing and the constellations seemed appropriate. Now, I need to test these newly healed wings if you wouldn't mind.' Oran indicated his muscled back, unclasping his cloak.

For the second time in a few days, she found herself staring at a familiar part of him, his muscled back with his wings unfurled, catching the light of the rising sun, elated with the freedom he might have. Cheeks aflame for who knows what reason, Eira worked the remaining cream into his broad back.

'Your wings are too thin and sensitive for suncream. Do they feel uncomfortable in the daylight?' Eira enquired, stepping back.

With a mighty gust of wind, Oran launched skywards, sending Eira flying back to land on her bottom, as he disappeared amongst the clouds. Eira sat back, watching the sky to see if she could catch a glimpse of him. She didn't even notice straight away as he landed in the courtyard of the gothic church opposite. Bending, he plucked something off the ground before flying up and landing next to her once more, snapping his wings behind his back.

Hair windswept, a huge grin on his face, he looked like a kid who had just been on a rollercoaster.

'I'll never get over that feeling,' he said, shaking his head in awe. 'Everything is in working order, healer. It's a miracle. If I couldn't fly, I couldn't live.'

'What have you got there?' Eira asked, ignoring her blush at his words.

Oran peeled his fingers back to reveal three large stones. His palm glowed as he willed his magic into form. Before Eira's eyes, Oran transformed the stones, dissolving the surface with his light, shaping, carving, and manipulating until three nightingales sat on his palm. Each with glowing eyes. They were the colour of stone, but so lifelike that Eira was lost for words.

He brought two of them to his mouth and whispered in a language Eira didn't understand. Once he finished, he opened his hand, and they took flight, weaving through the sky.

'This one's for you, Eira. To send a message home. Just speak your message and its destination, and it will follow the instructions.'

Eira stared in shock at him, her throat choked with emotion and her eyes full of tears. She carefully held out her hand as the tiny bird hopped onto it. Cocking its head, it puffed out its stone feathers and chest, chirping brightly.

With one last glance at Oran, she bent over the bird and quietly whispered her message home. Placing a kiss on its head, she held out her hand and watched it jump into the air and then soar off, starting its long journey north.

'Are you two going to stand on that roof all day or do you want some breakfast?' Elowen said, sticking her head out of the window below.

ORAN

Oran hesitated on the window threshold, crouched to enter. The exhilaration he had felt from his flight was gone, and now apprehension filled him. He gritted his teeth, resisting the impulse to turn invisible.

He watched as Eira, who had jumped to the jutting roof below and lithely swung herself through the window of the first floor, embraced the human with black hair. Elowen, that was her name. Their driver.

Eira stepped back, talking intently to Elowen. Why was he not entering the room? With the curtains open, the small room looked inviting with a fire blazing in the far corner and deep-buttoned, rolled armchairs. The panelling absorbed the light with the low ceiling, but it felt cosy and homely. The smell of bacon wafted through the window, and his mouth watered. He hadn't realised how hungry he was.

He faltered, not ready to face a human and see the judgement on her face. He knew how she would see him — as a demon. All humans judged gargoyles in that way thanks to their religious renderings. His presence always drew stares and suspicion, even within his clan, so he couldn't expect to be accepted by a human. And he was used to feeling like that, but somehow, with Eira, it felt different.

You're like me.

Her opening words.

She hadn't judged him.

Looking at her now, Oran could see that she was rested and refreshed, and looked completely at ease with the human, smiling cheerfully with her. The worry stirred in the pit of his stomach, and he knew he had sensed it within her too — the cost of being different. The fear of not being accepted.

But here she was, her pointed ears on display, not showing an ounce of self-doubt. He traced his own ears to the pointed tips, an old habit hard to break.

'Have you turned to stone, gargoyle, or are you going to stop letting the heat out?'

Only his decades of training stopped Oran from toppling backwards in shock. The only reaction he allowed himself was a slight ruffle of his wings as he stared at the female who had materialised through the floorboards.

He grinned to himself, then folded his body through the small window, raising to his towering height, making a show of closing the window.

'My apologies, poltergeist,' he said with a dramatic bow.

He knew that Elowen and Eira were staring at him, their conversation forgotten for now.

'I would think so, gargoyle,' huffed the housekeeper. She was wearing a grey corseted dress, high-necked with flowing sleeves. Her brown hair was pinned in a tight French plait, and her stern amber eyes shone brightly.

'Madam Scudamore, I presume?'

The poltergeist's manicured eyebrow rose. 'You're an observant one.'

'I believe my thanks for your hospitality in this wonderful house are in order. It is the most impressive establishment.'

Oran had dealt with spirits in the past and he knew that flattery was normally the best approach. She would be bound to the house, and she could have been that way since its foundations were laid.

A thin smile played on her ghostly lips. She floated towards Eira, whose shoulders were shaking with silent laughter.

His encounter with the housekeeper had helped to rid him of a lot of his apprehension, and the thought of breakfast cured the rest.

Oran stepped further into the room, noticing Elowen's constant glances. He could feel her fear rippling off her like moonlight on a millpond.

He knew this was a mistake. He couldn't help his appearance or how it affected others.

Oran then detected another underlying emotion, dread laced with guilt. Not from Elowen, but Eira.

He was instantly at her side. *Why am I reacting like this around her?* Oran had only ever been this protective around Nelka. He knew that Nelka was his one true love, and that what he felt towards Eira wasn't romantic love, but he was still confused about his reaction to her. His overwhelming need to protect her.

Eira glanced at Oran, her green eyes sparkling, aware that he must have picked up on the tension. She raised one eyebrow in question, before she slid her coppery braid over her back and sat at the farmhouse-style table. Elowen nervously sat down near her friend, still glancing at him.

The counter ran along two walls creating an L-shape behind the massive table. It looked like it was part kitchen, part laboratory. The shelves were littered with all manner of objects ranging from standard kitchen utensils to sharp metallic objects which looked like they could dice up internal organs.

Madam Scudamore bustled about at an ancient-looking oven, plating up scrambled eggs and bacon which she set in front of the females. They had all gone quiet, watching him. Oran stopped in the doorway, confused at how normal it all felt for him.

'Have you now lost the ability to move, gargoyle? Do you want to upset my hospitality?' Madam Scudamore asked bitterly. This time, both Elowen and Eira sniggered, causing the ghost to raise her wooden spoon in mock outrage.

Oran quickly grabbed a stool opposite the females before he could draw any more attention to himself, relieved that he could fit his wings in.

A plate arrived in front of him and, remembering his manners, he nodded his thanks to the housekeeper before picking up his cutlery and diving into his food. The poltergeist was a good cook; the eggs were fluffy, and the bacon cooked to perfection, so much so that he nearly picked up the plate to lick off the grease.

He glanced up to find Elowen staring at him open-mouthed.

'Excuse my friend, Oran. Apparently, she's never seen a half-naked male before.' Eira nudged Elowen, whose cheeks flamed red. Oran, caught equally off-guard, smirked, bowed his head, and made a show of raising his orange juice to his lips. He slid his goggles onto his head, hoping that he would be able to cope with the light inside.

'Unfortunately, my armour seems to have gone missing,' he said, glancing at the housekeeper with a smirk, 'and I have nothing else to wear.'

Madam Scudamore clicked her tongue and laid another plate full of food in front of him. 'You mean that piece of rock and sparkling crystal is yours? I thought it was a new form of cheese grater.'

Oran couldn't help himself; he threw his head back and laughed, the deep sound rumbling through the room. Eira snorted too, clutching her stomach as she laughed. Elowen just glanced between them both, stunned.

'Yes, that cheese grater is mine and is a fundamental piece of my attire,' Oran snickered.

Madam Scudamore waved her wooden spoon at him, brandishing it like an iron smelter. 'Well, that foul garment is impossible to clean, it smells like sweat, and it's made a dent in my floor. You will get it returned when it is laundered to my standards. It has blood where no blood should be.'

Oran bit his bottom lip, nearly drawing blood in his attempt to stop himself from snorting. 'You would be doing me an incredible service, it has been many years since it was last washed.'

The housekeeper's mouth twitched, and she evaporated through the floor before she could utter another retort.

Eira was looking at him with amusement and intrigue. The ghost's reaction must have been a positive one then. Shrugging, Oran returned to his plate, contentment filling his stomach alongside the food. They were quiet as they took their fill.

'So, Nora's dead then,' Elowen voiced. Oran snapped his head up at those words. Elowen's shoulders slumped, and she looked at Eira wide-eyed. He could feel the fear radiating from the human, and a sense of regret from Eira.

The fear Oran had felt from Elowen wasn't directed at him, but the news that she had just heard. Oran relaxed his shoulders, letting out a breath.

'I know we didn't care for her much, but it was still a...' Elowen quietly added.

A Life.

Oran had never spent time with a human before, so he sat and watched. They really did wear their emotions on their sleeves. Most gargoyles were stone-faced with a solid core of rot. The other clans anyway, especially the Quarter Clan. Elowen seemed upset by the death of someone she hadn't liked, which, to Oran, was odd. She had been fully open about both her emotions, which were conflicting.

Oran observed Eira, who had her teeth gritted. He could tell that there was something she didn't want to say. She chewed on her bottom lip, contemplating, a habit of hers that he had already noticed.

'Moyra's text said she had black eyes,' Elowen said. 'Why would they kill her? I thought they kept their hosts alive.'

'We don't know all the facts yet, Elowen. Don't worry, you're safe here,' Eira reassured her friend, squeezing her shoulder.

'You are safe, protected, whilst I am here,' Oran added.

'I ended up saving you last night,' Eira snorted, a grin plastered across her face.

Oran huffed, fighting the impulse to stick out his tongue.

'What actually happened? Where's the captain?' Elowen probed.

'Who's the captain?' Oran jumped in.

'There's a lot to fill you both in on,' Eira sighed.

Eira pushed back her chair, leaning forward, and interlacing her fingers under her chin. Oran leant back, ruffling his wings, and folding his arms across his chest, conscious that he was still topless.

'The suits took Captain Cole Hawkins. Moyra had no choice but to save the clinic by handing him over to them.' Elowen placed a pale hand over her mouth at that.

Eira raised her startling green eyes to Oran's. 'The captain and his unit were attacked and infected with the virus. They were treated at the clinic. Two were fully infected. Cole survived and is only partially infected, like you were, Oran. When Oswald was spying on me in Battersea, I was making sure that the Dark didn't link the two infected comrades back to the clinic. We were just about to move Cole to a safehouse when the Dark came knocking.'

'So, the captain is important because…?' Oran asked, trying to understand.

'He's the only witness we have who has survived a Dark attack. He could have vital information on how they infect a host and how they could be stopped.'

'But if he was arrested?' Elowen questioned.

'I gave him the means to escape.'

Oran caught the glint in Eira's eyes at those words.

'We're to meet him tonight … if he was able to escape.'

'That's a big if. What happens if he has been reinfected and is under the Dark's control?' Oran challenged.

'I'm confident that he cannot be reinfected,' Eira replied with a sharpness to her voice that told him not to push further.

A tense silence followed, and they both stared at each other, waiting for the other to challenge them.

Elowen broke the ice. 'So how did you two meet?'

She was a brave human for attempting to step into this stare-off.

Eira was a determined one. Luckily, Oran had a hundred years' experience of dealing with strong-willed females. He normally lost, but at least he could be there as her protector, something his instincts kept pushing him to do.

'This gargoyle and his pet had been spying on me for days,' Eira chuckled, folding her arms to mirror his stance. Oran listened to Eira's brief account of how the Dark managed to locate her, how Oran saved her from their clutches, their flight through London, and then the barricade in Westminster Abbey. She made it sound epic and not nearly as frightening as it had been, and she left out many of the parts where magic was involved or certain hidden tunnels. She didn't once mention anything about Oran's unique gifts or his heritage, for which he was grateful. 'So, that was our exciting night. What we do know now is that the Dark has weaponised the virus and it can infect immortals. To what extent I do not fully know.'

Elowen blew out her cheeks. She hadn't asked any questions throughout Eira's monologue and seemed to understand the situation. The fear radiating from her had ebbed slightly.

'So, what do we do now?'

A question I would like answered myself, Oran thought.

'I'm going to do my rounds at the Nightingale and prepare for meeting the captain tonight. I would also like to analyse the samples I took of Oran's infected blood.' Eira pushed the chair back and stood, dismissing them all.

'My what?' Oran blurted, springing up in one fluid motion.

'Oh, didn't I mention it? Whilst you were out, I took a sample of infected blood,' she tossed over her shoulder as she walked out. Elowen quickly rose and followed her friend.

Oran rolled his shoulders, snapping his wings around them, cocooning himself in their translucent safety. He felt violated and undermined that she hadn't asked. But he had been in no fit state to give permission. Blowing out an exasperated breath, he followed the two females, tracing Eira's sea salt and jasmine scent to the hidden door.

He slammed a hand within the opening and proceeded through.

Grabbing Eira's forearm he forced her to stop. Why am I so angry? It was only a small amount of blood. And it could help. The rational part of his brain battled with the animal side of him.

Blood held power; blood held knowledge.

'Please ask my permission next time you go harvesting my blood,' Oran growled. 'Blood can be powerful, and if it falls into the wrong hands... Well, let's just say we don't want that to happen.' He bared his teeth and snarled down at her, but Eira didn't even flinch.

A small gulp brought his attention to Elowen who was huddled against the wall of the corridor, shaking. Breathing hard, he let go of Eira's arm, embarrassment washing over him. *What have I done?* He wasn't training new recruits or enforcing his authority. He was...

What am I doing here?

'Don't you dare question why I have done something. If I didn't grab the opportunity to take a sample of infected blood, I couldn't test it and create an antidote. Do you want hybrids to fall into their clutches? If they control us, they can control the high races!' She was on her tiptoes, glaring at him. 'And don't you ever scare my friend again,' Eira added before dropping her intense gaze and storming towards her friend, who she guided along the corridor. Elowen looked over her shoulder, with a sympathetic smile.

Oran stood in the corridor breathing heavily, trying to push his rage away.

CHAPTER 17

⋈ COLE

Cole adjusted the flat cap he was wearing, pulling it low over his eyes as he stood in the shadows of a doorway. From his lookout, he had a good view up and down the street and across Regents Park. He had been waiting for two hours, and his legs were starting to cramp.

It was the third night after his escape from the laboratories, and he was due to meet Eira in half an hour.

Her Morse-code note memorised, he'd burnt it at his grandfather's house to be safe. A grid reference with a date and time. He'd come early to stake out the location.

Despite his intentions, he had remained at his grandfather's house, recovering from his injuries, and planning his next move. He hadn't heard from Major Stone since his first night, so he didn't have anywhere else to go. He was lucky that there had been enough tinned food left at the house, and the cold water still worked, though he couldn't heat it. He had found some of his grandfather's old clothes in the back of the wardrobe, musty and smelling of pipe-smoke, but still functional.

Cole rubbed the scar on his cheek and rested his hand on the gun in his waistband. His wound had healed enough that he had removed the dressing. It was still sore, and if he stretched too far, he could feel the skin pulling tight, but he would be able to remove the stitches in a couple of days.

Throbbing headaches had started clouding his mind, making it difficult to sleep. Even when he did sleep, he was plagued with dreams of the fire. This, combined with the fact that there had been radio silence from Major Stone, had put him in an irritable mood.

He had vital information for their cause, and the longer he remained in the capital, the more likely it was that he would be rearrested. The thought scared him more than he wanted to admit. The phone he had stolen from the agent had provided new information on the supply chain concerning the manufacture of the weapons they used to spread the virus. He was carrying the biggest breakthrough in the fight against the Dark in more than a decade.

All he needed was his tablet and the encrypted link to the League, and he could give them the intel, once he proved he wasn't infected.

From the shadow of the covered doorway, he studied the street for the umpteenth time. This was the most direct route to Regent's Canal, and he hoped that he would catch Eira on her way to Macclesfield Bridge.

Blowing out through his nose he pushed off from the chipped doorway. Crouching, one hand on his gun, Cole ran across Prince Albert Road, making for the skeletal trees flanking the bank leading to the canal footpath.

He wasn't familiar with the canal paths, or this part of London, so was curious as to Eira's rendezvous location. Cole slipped through the undergrowth, watching his footing on the roots, and trying not to make a sound. He turned his borrowed flat cap backwards on his head, keeping his unruly hair out of his eyes, wisps of raven-black curls visible around the nape of his neck.

Pausing, he held the gun loosely in his hands and surveyed his location, using his black eye to scan for any hidden danger.

Five minutes until his meeting, and there was no one else around. He wasn't sure that Eira would be able to see him hidden in the brambles, but it was dangerous to wait out in the open under the bridge.

Making his mind up, Cole headed towards the railings under the bridge, quietly vaulting over them and landing on the other side. It was much darker under the bridge, and he cursed his senses as they adjusted to the blackness.

Cole leant against the thick iron column, his back to the murky water so that he could view the pathway in both directions.

169

Glancing at his grandfather's watch in the limited moonlight, he saw that it was 20:00 hours, the time that he was supposed to meet Eira. Nervous tension settled in his gut. What would he do if she didn't show? He desperately needed his tablet, but in all honesty, he was more longing to see her. Even the confusion of her lying about his scar couldn't dampen that desire.

He felt the pressure building in his head as the familiar ache increased. Massaging his temples, he closed his eyes as the fog eased.

Raising his head, his black eye picked up the movement of a shadowy figure under the lower arch of the bridge. What he'd originally assumed to be dumped rubbish was actually a tramp, huddled under layers of blankets.

Great!

Cole pretended he hadn't seen the movement and continued watching the path. *Where was Eira?*

'Duw ou ave light, ma'e?' The Irish accent stirred memories in him and made his heart clench. Tagger was Irish too. Cole was reminded of another reason he needed to see Eira — he wanted to track the movements of his friends.

'Nope sorry, mate, I don't smoke.'

Cole went back to scanning the dark surroundings hoping that his brusque tone had warned the tramp that he wasn't in a conversational mood. How long should he wait? But he knew it wasn't even a question — he would wait all night for her, despite the danger it put him in.

He cursed to himself. He hadn't even considered that she wouldn't turn up.

'Ou ait or sumeon, ma'e?' said the tramp.

Cole glared at him before turning away again.

'Ou ait or da 'olden-aired wuman viv da urple oots?'

Cole looked back at him, confused. 'Pardon?'

'Is ou 'awk? Diff'nt eyes, lack an lue, eather acket wit,' the tramp paused to take a deep sniff, 'mells of moke and pice.'

Cole stepped forward cautiously, resting his hand on his gun. Up close, he saw that the tramp's body was swaddled under a mountain of patterned blankets. It was hard to define his proportions. A wispy beard sprouted from a pockmarked face which was lost under a large beanie hat. A spark flared as the tramp lit a cigar, the flame reflected in his amber eyes. He blew the aromatic smoke lazily in Cole's direction.

'Ou eed tu ay lood ax tu enter.' *Blood tax? To enter where?*

Cole, waving his hand in front of his face to disperse the smoke, was lost for words. It transported him back to days spent with his grandfather, helping him in the garden he so loved to tend.

'R ou eaf, ma'e? Is ou 'awk? Da erson ightingale sed?'

Cole was finding it hard to comprehend what this Irish tramp was saying. Who was Nightingale? The description he gave sounded a lot like Eira, but he couldn't be certain.

Cole's instincts were telling him to pull out his gun, point it at the tramp's face, and demand answers. But he kept control of himself, even as his headache pulsed.

'Ou eed tu ee our ightingale, shee uld fix dat ead ma'e.'

Nightingale was a doctor. That was too much of a coincidence. Eira must be this Nightingale that he was referring to. It wasn't the first time she had lied about her name.

Cole straightened and considered the risks. He was desperate.

'I am Hawk, and I'm here to meet Nightingale.'

'Ike I sed, shee in' ide. Ou eed tu ay lood ax. If ou're outhorised you can nter. If no, ou an wim viv da rish.'

The tramp smiled, his wide mouth full of rotten yellow teeth as he puffed on his cigar. Shrugging, Cole decided that it would be worth going along with this if it meant that he got to see Eira again.

He picked up a rock from the floor, keeping his gun angled towards the pile of blankets, and pressed it into his palm until a bead of blood welled. He looked back at the tramp who indicated the wall that he was leaning against. Feeling foolish, he pressed his injured hand to the wall, wondering what he would do if the tramp turned out to be crazy.

As he stared, the wall vanished in front of him. There was no other way to describe it. One moment it was solid beneath his palm, then suddenly, his hand was hovering in the air. He looked at the tramp who simply smirked, blowing rings of smoke into the still night air.

Cole took a shaky breath, angled the gun in front of him, and took a hesitant step forward through the open void. A tight, twisting staircase, lit by glass orbs floating above his head, descended into the gloom. As his second foot met his first on the landing, the wall behind him reappeared. Cole touched a hand to its cool surface, solid once more.

He turned back and took a deep breath, steeling himself to enter the unknown.

Cole gulped and started down the steps, one hand on the wall for stability, his gun angled straight ahead. The stairs felt like they wound on forever, but he soon heard noises below. It sounded like singing or chanting maybe. Whatever it was, it wasn't a voice he recognised. Then a bright light blazed in front of him, dazzling after the dimness of the stairwell.

Cole came around the corner and ground to a halt, his breath catching in his lungs.

The space was vast, with a high vaulted ceiling and arched brick columns climbing to the roof, lit by globules of light suspended from the vaults, glowing like a thousand stars. He took in the glittering floor and the sparkling bar set to one side. It reminded him of the swanky bars that used to dot the streets in the East End, glittering with mirrors, and upholstered in deep-purple. An assortment of luxury furniture and booths occupied the space around the centre of a large dance floor. A mezzanine walkway surrounded the dance floor, secured with ornate gold railings.

But it was the occupants who shocked Cole the most. As his brain played catch-up with what he was seeing, it started providing the names of the creatures: trolls, dwarfs, gnomes. But many he couldn't distinguish. Most were humanoid in shape, though distinctly different to humans.

Myths.

His black eye was almost blinded by the glowing light emanating from most of the beings present.

It was then that he realised what his eye was picking up.

Magic.

172

Cole took a deep breath to calm his racing heart and tucked his gun into the back of his waistband. He knew that a gun wouldn't protect him from these beings, but it at least made him feel a bit safer.

Every head in the room turned in his direction, and he felt rooted to the spot.

He straightened, holding his hands in front of him. 'I'm here to see Nightingale.' His voice sounded small and weak, and he knew that they could probably smell his fear from across the room.

The mass of Myths simply shrugged and turned back to their conversations.

He felt a tug on his trouser leg. Glancing down, he saw a tiny being clad in leaves, her stick-like arms grasping his shin. He bent down to stare at the creature who scrambled onto his hand without invitation.

A sprite.

The tiny being had sparkling eyes and ragged butterfly wings, fluttering in excitement. It pointed across the dance floor to a shadowed alcove.

Cole gulped before heading in the direction that the creature was pointing. He tried his best to move through the crowd without drawing attention to himself, but it was difficult when he kept tripping over a hoof or standing on a paw.

He finally reached the corner, where he found a booth and table surrounded by plush chairs. The booth was in shadow, but he could make out the shape of a body. Closing his normal eye and opening his black eye, he looked back at the table. Pain seared through his head, and he clamped his eye shut again, but not before he caught sight of a pair of purple Doc Martens, making his heart flip.

Eira.

'I'm pleased and shocked to see you here, Captain.' Her soothing voice washed over him. 'I know this is all strange and you must have lots of questions.'

The forgotten creature in his hand took hold of his sleeve and swung herself down, landing on his trouser leg. She scuttled down his leg and disappeared into the shadows.

'Thank you, little one,' Eira said. Cole glanced down as the sprite reappeared with a glossy cherry within its claws. Eira leant forward, her face still in shadow, but her perfect body moving into the light. She was wearing a Run-DMC T-shirt under a military-style jacket; Cole was staggered that she would even listen to rap.

Tentatively, he stepped closer, trying to form a question through his confusion.

'Sorry for the welcome party, humans aren't normally invited to the Underground.'

Humans.

But Eira was obviously comfortable here, so something wasn't adding up.

'You're bleeding,' she said, suddenly appearing at his side.

Cole's breath was knocked from him. Now that she was standing in the light, he was able to appreciate her fully. She looked the same as before, but somehow different. Her hair was twined in a braid which flowed like molten copper and gold down her slim back. But it was her ears which drew his eye. They were pointed at the tips, perfectly suited to her fine cheekbones.

A memory came to the forefront of Cole's mind. He had seen her with rounded ears before he was arrested.

Cole shook his head, trying to clear the fog and throbbing pain which had started to build within his mind. He could only come up with one question: How?

Then Eira took his hand. Her hands were so gentle, smooth, and warm, and he could have sworn he felt himself relax at her touch. Then he gasped. His palm started to itch, and he looked down to see his skin fusing back together, no sign of the cut from earlier.

Cole snapped his head up and met her green eyes, losing himself in their tranquillity and depth.

'Cole, you're here to fully understand what I am.'

He went to answer, but the pain in his head exploded. He slammed a hand to his left temple, squeezing his black eye shut tightly. He felt like his head was splitting in two. He dropped to his knees, his hand still clutching Eira's.

He heard a rough voice that sounded like water over pebbles, but couldn't make out what was being said. But Eira seemed to understand. She knelt, her knee brushing his as she took his other hand. Drowsiness swept through him, and he felt suddenly languid. It wasn't unsettling. It was like being carried away by a calm river. Cole didn't fight the sleep as it flowed through his body, and he sagged in a stone grip.

‖‖ EIRA

Eira struggled to comprehend what had just happened. She had been an anxious bag of nerves meeting the captain in a Myth stronghold. She had chosen the rendezvous point on a whim. It was the first place that came to mind when she found the secret pocket containing his ID card, and she had no way of contacting him to give him an alternative address.

Oran had quite bluntly pointed out that inviting a human to a gathering of immortals would be like plating him up for supper. He had been partially right, but she was still pissed off at the gargoyle, so she didn't want to take his advice.

Cole, you're here to fully understand what I am.

What I am.

Those words had come from nowhere. But they were true. She needed him to see her for what she truly was to be able to fully trust him. He worked with the League who were notorious for taking a neutral ground, but neutral wasn't what she needed.

She held enough authority and respect within the Myth network that asking for a human to be given permission to gain access to the Underground was a request taken seriously instead of simply laughed off. She now owed some favours.

'Eira, put him to sleep, now!' Oran's words rang out, and Eira didn't hesitate. But peering down, she saw that Cole was no longer on the floor in front of her.

Luckily, the club was so packed that none of the other creatures had seen the incident.

'Oran, what in hell is going on?' She hissed in Elven, guessing that Oran had grabbed Cole and thrown his invisibility over them both.

'I'll explain in a moment. Can you take us somewhere more private?' His breath tickled her ear as he spoke. He was closer than she had expected.

Straightening, she stalked to the back of the vast central room, hoping that Oran was following her. There were several intersecting tunnels which fed directly into the club. Eira chose one and sauntered between various Myths in different forms of undress, trying to look casual.

The Underground club was notorious for ignoring the laws on interspecies mingling. Many scandals had risen from the club, but if it allowed the Myths to enjoy more freedom than they could above, then what was the harm?

Eira turned down a tunnel she knew well. The globule lights flashed on as she advanced. Every time she saw them, she was impressed at the unique combination of magic and technology that had been used to create them. Stopping in a discreet alcove, she folded her arms and waited for Oran to reappear.

Their honest conversation on the roof that morning was all but forgotten by them both since the argument that followed. She could understand why he was upset, but he had no right to explode the way he did. He had scared Elowen, and it had taken a lot of self-control for Eira not to cower as well. He was right that she shouldn't have taken his blood without his permission, but it was too unique an opportunity to turn down. Eira didn't know why Oran couldn't understand her need to stop this virus.

Eira knew that he had been there, watching her throughout the day as she went about her work. She couldn't see him, but her power had flared on numerous occasions when he had been too close.

He had appeared around lunchtime, requesting the details of the building's security, and asking if his biometrics could be added to the entry scanners. She had been too tired to argue and hoped that if Oran was otherwise occupied, she might be able to get a hold on her magic and its unusual reaction to him.

Eira thought Oran had forgotten about their meeting with the captain, but he had appeared in the basement of the Nightingale near the Myth tunnels. Her hint about asking her friends for advice about his inability to turn to stone was too tempting for Oran to risk missing.

'What's going on, Oran?' Eira repeated her question, tapping her foot on the concrete floor, as Oran appeared in front of her, Cole held easily in his arms.

Oran had found some clothes, and Eira was glad not to have the distraction of his body for this conversation. Madam Scudamore had found him a large sweatshirt and had cut holes in it to accommodate his wings. He wore it now, his staff strapped across his broad back with her scarf still wrapped around the hilt like a treasured talisman.

His eyes looked weary as he calmed his breathing. Eira knew the toll that being underground was taking on him. It had taken a lot of courage to overcome his claustrophobia and come down with her. Oran's shoulders were taut, his eyes darting around the curved tunnel. He flared a ball of light to hover above his head.

Eira curled her fingers against her folded arms, resisting the impulse to reach for Oran and help relieve his stress.

'The captain is still infected with the virus. His eye is black.'

'Yes, I know. I told you that he was still partially infected. But as far as we could tell from analysis, he has full control of his mind. He's shown no signs of being under the Dark's control.'

Guilt settled like a knot in her stomach. If she had only left the opal on his flesh for a couple more minutes, he wouldn't have that black eye. Eira looked at the sleeping captain, his face relaxed in slumber. His flat cap was on backwards, his midnight-black hair curling around the nape of his neck. She was suddenly reminded of the picture she had been shown of him with his friends, a bright smile on his face.

'I'm aware of that,' Oran tutted, gently flaring his wings as he shifted position. His claws scratched the hard floor. 'I don't know, Eira. I'm picking up a magical pulse from him, the same way I do with Myths. The only explanation is that the virus has a magical aspect. It would make sense with its ability to spread and hold the host. I just can't tell what type of magic it is.'

He looked confused, staring hard at Cole as if he could force himself to understand what was going on.

'It also looked like his head was causing him pain. Maybe that's the virus spreading through him?' Oran added.

Eira searched his open face, reading everything. The unease that he might be wrong, guilt that he had even raised the subject. Eira approached and grasped Oran's pale arm supporting Cole's back. Her magic momentarily flared and sought his vast power.

'Okay, Light Bringer, I hear you. Let's go and get some answers from friends of mine,' Eira said, her own unease growing.

Eira turned and, glancing behind her, stalked down the tunnel, knowing that Oran had turned invisible once again. It seemed to help keep his claustrophobia at bay as well, so she wasn't complaining. His globule of light floated in front of her, lighting the way.

'The captain's important to you, isn't he?' Oran's hushed tone bounced around the tunnel.

'He holds the key to some very important information.'

'Why is it so important?'

'Do you need me to answer that?' Eira glanced to her side, raising her eyebrows.

He didn't answer, instead asking, 'What are you not telling Elowen about Nora's death?'

'You're too perceptive, Light Bringer. And since we're talking civilly to one another, I'm assuming it means that I've been forgiven?' Eira smiled, knowing he was still a little annoyed at her.

'I had every right to be angry. You might not grasp the importance of blood and how it can be used as a weapon, but blood holds secrets; it's the key to their future.'

'The virus has been spreading unchecked within London and, from what you've said, other major cities in the country, for the past decade,' Eira answered earnestly. 'No one knows anything about it, how to combat it, or even why they've only targeted humans so far. Your blood, combined with the information from Cole, could be the missing piece we need to work this out.'

'But why you, Eira?' Oran whispered into the dark.

'Why not?' she countered.

Oran was silent.

It wasn't a question that she could answer. All she knew was that the only thing she had left from her mother obviously played some part in it all, and she wanted to know why.

But am I worthy of the task?

'I also regret the way I reacted. I'm sorry that I scared Elowen. We gargoyles sometimes snap before we think about the consequences.' Oran sounded contrite.

That was all Eira needed to hear from him. The tension eased from her shoulders, and she felt her body relax. She didn't like fighting with him. Oran grunted, the echo reverberating off the tunnel, shifting his weight.

'So why are you still here, Oran?' It was a question that had been nagging at her. He had a wife, a clan, and a life back home, so why had he remained after he told her that he wouldn't be kidnapping her?

Long minutes passed and Eira thought that he wasn't going to answer.

'When you've figured out why you're taking on this impossible task, I'll let you know why I'm here. How about that?'

Fair enough, Eira thought.

They reached a bend in the ever-winding tunnel. It was a nice change to be travelling with Oran's light. She usually walked the tunnels in the dark, and when she had first started using them, she had gotten desperately lost on more than one occasion. One time, she had been found by Franklin and the triplets, who had taught her to read the waymarkers.

'So, back to my first question?' Oran prompted.

'You're persistent,' Eira said with a small chuckle.

The sound of Oran's answering laugh made her smile.

'Nora was a nurse at the Wallflower. She was a pain in my backside and made my life difficult there. Nevertheless, a life is a life. The Dark had no way of linking Cole's unit to the clinic. Moyra and I made sure of that.' Eira shrugged, making her braid swing behind her. 'When the Dark showed up, they said that they were searching all the clinics in London for the injured rebel survivors. I've been here for two years, and they've never done that before. They usually leave the clinics alone. It was suspicious, and when Moyra reached out to the other clinics, they said that they hadn't been visited. This confirmed to us that they had been tipped off. Nora wasn't at the clinic on the day that the Dark turned up. And then they came after me...'

Eira sighed, feeling better for having spoken to someone about it, even if she couldn't see the other person's reaction to her words.

'I've gone undetected in this city for a long time. I had a fake identity. The flat was in another false name. Like you said, I am very good at hiding my power's glow. So…'

'So, you think Nora tipped them off and then paid the price?'

'I know none of it makes any sense. Why would they kill her?' Eira said, exasperated. Holding her hands in the air, she chewed on her bottom lip, turning it all over in her mind. 'I didn't want to worry Elowen. She's all new to the magic world. She was there when I treated Cole, and my powers were unguarded. It's been a lot for her to take in, and her protection is my top priority.'

'You're a good friend, Eira, and it does make sense. You need to trust your instincts because, from what I've seen, they're usually right.'

Eira was grateful for his reassurance.

'You don't have to face this alone,' Oran continued, surprising her.

They finally reached a fork in the tunnels and followed the path that led to a sheer wall face. Looking over her shoulder towards where she thought Oran was, she knocked on the wall. Three quick taps.

The wall faded, revealing a large, rusty, iron-studded door with a hatch. Two glinting eyes, mostly hidden within the folds of a hood, appeared and studied Eira's face. The eyes glanced to her side, looking around for the other presence it could sense.

'Oran, you need to make yourself visible, they won't let us in until you do. They know that you're here.'

Oran dropped his cloaking magic at the same time as his orb dispersed, casting the tunnel into sudden darkness. Eira knew Oran could see perfectly well with his night vision, but it took her eyes a few extra seconds to adjust.

He stood there, as still as a lethal predator, his magnificent wings flared slightly in the confined space, Cole's body hanging limply in his strong arms. He did indeed look like a demon from the depths of hell. The glowing eyes widened from inside the hood, and the cloak fluttered as they took a deep sniff of the air. Catching the eye of the guard, she spoke aloud, signing with her hands at the same time: 'He's with me. He's not a threat, don't worry.'

The face disappeared for a second before the door creaked open to reveal a room filled with a warm, inviting glow. Eira glanced over her shoulder to make sure Oran was following before stepping into the room.

The space was cavernous, the decor a combination of medieval torture chamber and high-tech laboratory. The triplets had commandeered a disused train tunnel for their many experiments.

The triplets were known as the Alchemists within the Myth network. They were scientists, engineers, and inventors. They had been able to combine many human high-tech creations with magic to turn them into useful weapons and tools for the Myths. The Incognito was one of their most successful experiments.

Eira proceeded into the Alchemists' workshop, dodging all manner of objects: bottled organic matter, half a car engine which looked like it was being pumped full of river water, a suspended clock — disbelievingly like the face of Big Ben — which chimed backwards at an ever-increasing speed. It made Eira feel nauseous just watching it. Oran appeared unfazed as he manoeuvred around the random assortment of objects scattered throughout their workshop.

Eira led them to the back of the room where the station platform still stood. On the upper deck, stood three miniature beds pushed against the curved tile wall, two neatly made. The back wall was covered with a huge contraption which consisted mainly of screens and buttons. A reclining chair was placed in the middle.

Oran arched a white eyebrow, stopping short of the raised platform, shifting Cole's weight to a more comfortable position. Sparks flew from a welding gun held by a small figure on a playground swing, working on something that they couldn't quite see. He was bent forward, a welding mask covering his face, and thick gloves on his hands.

Eira waited patiently for the figure to notice their presence as he finished his work. When he spotted them, he tugged on a rope and lowered the swing to the floor.

The ages of the Alchemists were unknown, but Eira would hazard a guess that they had been around since the first elves traversed the earth.

181

'Oran please meet Isambard,' Eira said, gesturing at the squat figure pulling up the welding mask from his wrinkled face. 'The one next to the computer is Isaac.'

Another figure turned around, raising his hand in greeting, his face fully concealed by his hood.

'And Darwin is...' Eira peered into the gloom. 'In bed!' she finished as a snore reverberated in the room.

'They refused to give me their names, so I named them myself. Well, either that or they've forgotten them. They're—'

'Gnomes,' Oran interrupted.

Eira looked back at him, shocked. He certainly knew his mythical creatures. He had known that Madam Scudamore was a poltergeist, and he easily identified the creatures in front of him. She had so much to learn.

Isambard waddled up to his sleeping brother and kicked him in the gut, causing the poor gnome to roll out of bed with a startled grunt.

They wore medieval style robes with drawstring belts and leather sandals covering their large feet. Eira had never seen Isaac's face, while the other two rarely wore hoods around her. Their skin was green and wrinkled, and their hooked noses were covered in warts. Their ears drooped past their chin, giving them an almost comical look. But their eyes were piercing and could see through even the most complex of lies.

'They can't talk, so I sign to them,' Eira explained as Darwin approached signing something with his hands. He opened his mouth, revealing the empty space within.

Eira was unsure if they had been born without a tongue or if they had been later removed.

'Darwin wants to know what level of Hell I found you at?' Eira grinned.

Oran sniggered.

Isaac walked slowly towards Eira. He reached up to her waist and barely up to Oran's thigh. His toad-coloured hands moved rapidly in front of his robes.

Eira had taught herself many languages and was fluent in most of the human tongues, including her mother's ancestral language – Gaelic. She had then proceeded to learning Elven from Etta and had taught herself sign language one bleak Scottish winter.

Her eyes easily followed Isaac's rapid gestures, and she was shocked at what the gnome told her.

Turning to Oran, Eira said, 'It appears this little spook' – she gestured to Isaac – 'hacked into the CCTV feed during our escape from the flat and managed to record most of the Dark's movements during our flight into Westminster Abbey.'

Oran tilted his head to one side, curious.

'Did Franklin ask you to monitor us?' Eira signed, knowing that the triplets didn't usually interfere with the world above. Isaac nodded once. At least she knew that he was safe. From her back pocket, Eira produced a micro stick.

'Please can you put the recordings onto this for me?' she asked Isaac, holding it out towards him.

Isaac grabbed the stick and waddled back to his chair.

Eira knelt so that she was level with Darwin. Isambard approached.

'I can't explain everything right now,' she spoke out loud at the same time as she signed the words, so that Oran could follow. 'We were attacked by the Dark's agents. Oran was shot with these.' Eira produced the black bullets from her pocket. 'We need to know what these are made from. What their chemical compound is, and if there's anything magical in them.'

She placed the bullets on Darwin's open palm.

'This is a human called Cole. He was infected with the virus.'

Both gnomes stepped back in fright.

'It is fine. He's no longer infected.'

'How?' Darwin signed.

Eira chose to ignore the Alchemist's question.

'We need to check him though. Scan his brain to see if he is fully clear of the virus, just to be sure.' Eira indicated the chair. 'Can you help us?'

CHAPTER 18

‖‖ EIRA

Oran lowered Cole carefully onto the chair, supporting his head. He rotated his shoulders, working out the tightness in his forearms. He had been quiet throughout the introductions to the triplets, letting Eira take the lead.

Eira looked at Oran, a question in her eyes as he stepped back, his pale eyes analysing everything. She suddenly felt chilled to the bone. What would happen if Cole was still infected with the virus, and they had inadvertently led the Dark to the Myth's tunnels? She wrapped her arms around her waist and watched as Isaac fitted a headset to Cole's temples.

The hooded gnome rotated back to his bank of computers and started pressing buttons.

'I'm sure I'm wrong,' Oran muttered, obviously sensing her unease. His shoulder brushed her arm in comfort. Eira clamped down on her power as it flared, expanding towards their link. Was he aware of how her power malfunctioned around him? Eira gulped, trying to work the stiffness from her own arms.

The monitor sparked to life behind Isaac, revealing a 3D scan of Cole's brain, more sophisticated than the technology they had at the Wallflower. Moyra would give her right arm to get her hands on this kit.

The brain scans of Cole's friends suddenly came back to her. She remembered them so clearly: the black mass expanding through their neural pathways, rotting everything in its wake.

Eira stepped onto the platform to get a better look at the screen. She examined the image, sorting through her knowledge of the human brain, trying to find any sign of the virus.

'What are we looking at?' enquired Oran, his breath blowing across her cheek. She had been so focused on the picture in front of her that she hadn't noticed him move.

'It's a scan of Cole's brain.'

Oran looked puzzled. Eira wondered how primitive the kingdom of the gargoyles was, surely they had some technology. The Myths in the city had taken full advantage of human technological advancement, combining it with magic with some intriguing results.

Eira pointed to the right side of the image.

'If you cut open his head you would see these tissues and veins that make up his brain.'

'I've shattered skulls before and they certainly don't look like that,' Oran stated frankly.

Eira held in her splutter. Despite her trust in him, it was disconcerting to hear him talk about such things so calmly.

Eira asked Isaac's permission for her to rotate the image so that they could view it from another angle.

'This is the skull from the front. You can see the holes where the eyes, nose and mouth are,' Eira pointed out. 'A normal brain should be free of any mass or obstruction. Like his right-hand side. This is Cole's left eye, his infected side. Can you see the difference?'

Oran leant forward, his pale eyes roaming over the screen. He nodded, drawing back. 'The left-hand side has a black mass central from his eye socket spreading into his brain. It looks like the black mass which was on my thigh.' He touched his thigh, lifting his clawed foot for emphasis.

Eira nodded. 'Isaac, can you please bring up two files dated six days ago on the micro stick I gave you?'

The full-body scans of Flint and Tagger appeared on the screen.

'These were taken from Cole's comrades who were fully infected. They are not as sophisticated as this 3D scan, but you get the gist. The virus spreads everywhere, controlling all motor functions and cognitive abilities.' Eira gulped. 'We never took a scan of Cole; he was too unwell for the procedure at the time. I wish I had as I'd be able to tell if the virus had spread.'

Oran was silent as she turned to look at him. His alabaster skin seemed to have grown even paler, and his eyes were wide.

'How far had it spread in my body?'

'It was only on the surface for you, spreading across your flesh from the entry wound. Where the bullet had penetrated deeper into your body, your magic was keeping it at bay. How much longer it could have withstood the fight, I don't know. Hence why I needed your blood to examine it closely.'

Oran nodded.

'Where your attacks both differ from Cole's friends is the way in which the virus entered the system. His comrades had no visible entry wounds on them, and they appeared to be in no pain. It simply looked like they were asleep. I think they inhaled the virus, and it took effect much quicker. Cole had a punctured lung from an entry wound made by a serrated dagger, and his body was better able to fight it off as well.' Looking into his eyes, she asked, 'Do you understand now?'

Oran nodded, turning his face away. 'Can you remove the virus like you did with me?'

'I don't know.' Eira sighed, her hand instinctively wrapping around her necklace.

She felt a tug on her trousers and glanced down at Darwin who signed, 'How?'

Could she trust them enough to tell them the truth? She looked at Oran. He was the first hybrid she had ever met. His power equalled, if not excelled hers. But his motives were unknown, his master's views seemed backwards, political ideology based on power not the needs of everyone.

Eira felt Oran's eyes on her, and she bit her bottom lip, deliberating. He knew that she wasn't telling him the whole truth.

You do not have to face this alone.

'How were you able to remove the virus from me, Eira? Why do you hesitate now?' Oran had shifted to stand in front of her. He towered over her, his wings blotting out the light.

Eira exhaled.

She glanced at Cole. His face was relaxed in sleep, but there were deep shadows under his eyes. He looked thinner than when she had last seen him, his skin tauter and paler. The events of the last week had taken their toll.

Cole had looked at her face, her exposed ears, in wonder. Not fear or disgust, but wonder.

'This is what stops the virus. It somehow draws it out when in contact with someone who is infected.'

Eira had removed her necklace without even registering. Her eyes settled on the sleeping human beside her, and she knew she was doing the right thing. Only when the cool chain was removed from her hand did she look up at Oran again.

Oran cradled the necklace within his large palm, the opal bright against his white skin. With his other hand he tentatively picked up the silver chain and held it up so that the opal spun slowly.

'It used to be my mother's,' Eira added quietly. His gaze snapped to hers. Anticipating his next question, Eira said, 'I don't know where she got it from, but she always wore it. It's the only item I have of hers.'

Oran's eyes softened, his lips parting as he ran his spare hand down her arm. Nothing more, just a comforting gesture to let her know that he understood.

'Do you know what the markings mean?' Oran enquired, head cocked to one side as he studied the necklace.

Eira shook her head.

'I've never seen the design before, it's definitely not gargoyle markings. They could be elven, but my knowledge of them is pretty rusty.' Oran laid the opal gently back in her palm. 'Why is the same marking on the captain's cheek?' he asked, grinning.

Eira sniggered, pushing him away. He didn't even budge with the impact. She glanced down at the two gnomes, who gestured for the necklace.

She handed it to Darwin, who brought it up to his eye to inspect more closely. Isambard leaned forward as well, pulling a magnifying glass from his pocket.

Oran and Eira waited patiently for their observations.

Isambard shook his head, shrugging. Darwin signed to Eira, 'Not sure.'

'Even they don't know,' she sighed, turning to Oran.

Oran looked concerned but didn't elaborate.

Eira squared her shoulders. 'Can you all step back and give me a little space?' she said, butterflies swarming her stomach.

Both gnomes stepped back towards their brother who had spun around on the chair to watch. Oran didn't move, just folded his arms, and stared down at Cole.

Eira blew out her cheeks and pulled up the sleeves of her military jacket, flexing her hands. Carefully, she placed the opal on Cole's left temple, making sure the markings were against her palm, so she didn't give him another scar.

The opal heated, and energy pulsed through the room, making everyone's ears ring. The triplets clamped their hands over their ears, and Oran rocked back on his clawed feet, wings spread to stop himself falling over.

With a yelp, Eira dropped the opal, the heat becoming unbearable in her palm. It didn't make sense. She had last used the opal over twenty-four hours ago, which gave it enough time to reset.

She bent down and clutched the chain, picking the opal up from the floor, where it spun, glinting in the light from the monitors.

Eira stared at Oran, confused. But the gargoyle wasn't looking at her. He was staring down at Cole, whose eyes were wide open. He was clutching the arms of the chair, his mouth open in a silent scream.

X COLE

For a heartbeat, Cole was transported back to the chair within the Dark's laboratories. His mind cycled through his escape, the days spent in relative comfort in his grandfather's house, and the unbelievable events of the evening. He could feel the pressure on his head from the headset and knew that the Dark was playing some sick trick on him.

He clasped the chair's arms until his hands turned white and his nails dug into the leather. He took short, sharp breaths to calm his racing heart.

The creature standing in front of Cole did not fit into any of the categories of Myth that he knew. The only word that came to mind was "demon". Its hulking, white body loomed over him, leathery wings spread wide. As he stepped closer, Cole heard the scrape of talons on the floor, and he knew that the creature had claws.

Then the creature spoke, its voice, rough and quiet, stirring his memory.

The reply, in a language he didn't understand, was soft and melodious.

188

Cole turned his attention to the side, catching sight of the woman standing next to him. His instincts were telling him not to take his eyes off the unknown creature, but he couldn't drag his eyes away from Eira, her copper hair falling over her forehead, and her cheeks flushed.

Eira straightened, an object spinning from her fingers, an object he had seen before within the recesses of his mind. She bit her bottom lip, and it turned white from the pressure. Her movements were slow and measured to not panic him.

'You're safe here, Cole. We mean you no harm.' She held her hand out towards him in a placating gesture.

The creature in front growled a remark. Eira responded without taking her eyes from his, her necklace wrapped around her slender fingers. Her response had been direct, guarded.

'Cole, I know that you're probably freaking out right now. This meeting hasn't gone how I had planned it, and I apologise for the actions we took. But we did it with the best intentions.'

Cole opened his mouth to reply, shifting his gaze between the woman he thought he knew and the unknown demon.

You are here, Cole, to fully understand what I am.

The words played on repeat in Cole's head.

'This is Oran.' Eira gestured to the creature in front of him, who looked like he wanted to tear the place apart. He was seething, anger rolling off him in waves. 'He might look big and scary, but he's a big softy really. He's a hybrid like me. Part-gargoyle, part-elf. Trust me, he isn't angry at you, despite what his glare might be telling you. It's me that he's pissed at.'

Eira gritted her teeth, turning to stare at the gargoyle-elf. She followed it up with another remark in the strange dialect they were using, and it seemed to do the trick as Oran blew out his cheeks, stepping back and putting his hands on his hips. He looked less intense.

Hybrid.

Cole's brain finally caught up as he uttered, 'Hybrid? What do you mean, Doc?' His voice was scratchy from days of misuse.

What I am.

But he already knew the answer before she replied.

'I'm half-human, half-elf.'

'But I saw your ears before,' Cole said, pointing at his own ears. He went to pull his flat cap off, but the headset stopped him. A figure appeared in his peripheral vision, reaching towards his head.

'These are the Alchemists. Darwin, Isambard' – Eira indicated the two creatures next to her – 'and this is Isaac.' The figure closest to him gave a small wave, his face lost in his cloak. 'They're gnomes,' she added for clarity.

Cole knew about gnomes. But these three looked ancient, older than he had ever thought gnomes could be. 'Why are they glowing?'

Eira's surprised gaze slid to the gargoyle momentarily before dipping back to his. Oran twisted, approaching once more, his large frame filling the space. Cole tried not to shrink back in the chair.

'Can you describe the glow, Cole? Can you see it with both eyes or only with one?'

'Just the black one.' Cole indicated his left eye. 'I can only see in shadow from this eye. Sometimes, I can see through solid objects. Most people, humans I mean, have a grey line around them. Since coming here, the others back at the club ... they had an intense glow around them. Just like ... like these guys,' Cole finished, gesturing feebly at the gnomes.

Eira's eyes narrowed, and she looked at Oran who had stilled, tipping his head to the side.

'You two don't glow though,' he added, looking directly at Eira.

'Can you see this?' the gargoyle asked, his voice sharp with command.

Cole looked directly at Oran then screwed his eyes shut with a hiss. Oran's silhouette had flared with blinding white light. He risked opening his normal eye a crack, relieved to see Oran's normal form.

Oran nodded once to Eira, whose eyes had gone wide with astonishment. Oran spoke again in the language Cole didn't understand, dipping his head once and tucking his wings in tight. He growled under his breath and stalked further into the tunnel-like space.

Eira turned to the shocked gnomes, holding a silent conversation through signs. They quickly turned and walked off, leaving Cole and Eira alone.

She pulled up a chair and settled next to Cole's head, taking a deep breath, and preparing herself for the conversation.

'I know that you probably have loads of questions. In time, I … we,' she corrected herself, 'will answer them all. This is a situation we've both found ourselves in, and we have a common enemy.' She watched him, trying to gauge his reaction, but his face was unreadable. 'Have you been having headaches? Any blackouts since I last saw you?' What happened with the Dark when you were arrested?

Picking up on her unasked question, Cole answered, 'You want to know if I've been reinfected and if I'm compromised?'

She didn't answer, just kept her eyes locked on his.

'They didn't get the chance,' Cole continued. 'I killed him, Doc, the agent. I had no other option. I killed him in self-defence.'

He clasped his shaking hands together as images of the lab flashed back into his mind. Warm hands encased his as the doctor gently pulled them from his lap.

'It hasn't been easy these last few days, has it, Captain? You won't even believe my story. It involved walking statues and a visit to a historic monument.'

Cole half-smiled at that. 'I've been getting headaches, Doc. They've been getting increasingly worse over the last few days. The pain is mostly in my temples like a fog filling my brain.'

Eira nodded, her hands still holding his. 'My gargoyle friend thinks that the virus is still within you. That's why I put you to sleep. If they can access your mind, they can see this.' Eira pulled back, gesturing to the space around them.

She slowly rotated his chair so that he faced the large screen behind.

'Your scan shows that the virus is still dormant in your left eye, extending towards the left side of your brain. That's why you have access to some of the agent's abilities. My issue is that we didn't take a scan after you recovered from the virus, so I can't tell if it has spread since then. It's obviously having some effect though since you're getting headaches.'

Cole looked at the three-dimensional image and then glanced towards the scans of Flint and Tagger still on the screen. He shuddered.

'My normal way of extracting the virus has proved not to be working,' Eira said, her hand fiddling with something in her pocket that he couldn't see. 'The gnomes have hinted at a way that we might be able to lock the virus down to that part of your brain, halting its progression if it is indeed spreading. It would mean you will always have your black eye and some of the agent's abilities, but the headaches would stop.'

Cole nodded slowly. 'So, you think they wouldn't be able to access my mind?' he asked, gesturing to his temple.

'Let me show you.' Eira rolled up her sleeve, exposing her pale forearm which immediately prickled with gooseflesh in the cold. 'What Oran demonstrated was his vast amount of power. I imagine what he showed you was only a fraction of his true power.' She smirked at that. 'You can identify a magic-user by their glow. That's what you can see with your black eye. It's someone's power potential. The triplets have a small amount of power and have no reason to hide it living down here. But those of us who live above need to blend in, so we've learnt to shield or glamour our power and hide our glow.'

As Eira spoke her forearm began to glow, a soft light illuminating her flesh. As quickly as it appeared, the light disappeared.

'It is one of the first things you learn when your magic develops – how to hide it,' Eira said sadly. 'To appear fully human, I have had to hide every magical part of me.'

Cole remembered the cut on his hand mending itself just before he blacked out, and the warmth he had felt spreading through him. 'My broken arm, you fixed that?'

Eira nodded. Her eyes were focused on his, trying to convey the honesty of her words. Cole had completely underestimated this female in front of him. It was obvious that she was a good doctor, but the fact that she was doing it *and* risking her life in the process, showed just how selfless she was.

'I want to try the same thing on the virus inside you, basically, put up a shield around it to protect your mind. You'll be able to use your eye without any problems, it will just limit the possibility of it growing.'

Cole couldn't think of a response. He was overwhelmed by everything that he had learnt today, and his brain couldn't keep up. And on top of that, he was no closer to rescuing his friends or reaching Major Stone. He wondered if Eira had forgotten about the tablet in the chaos of the last few days.

Eira read his silence as hesitance, and added, 'It won't hurt, and you won't even be aware that the shield is there. It'll be maintained by your body's energy.'

Cole nodded slowly. Was he honestly contemplating going along with this? He didn't know the doctor, not really. She had concealed her identity, hidden who she truly was. But he knew deep down that it didn't change the way he felt about her.

Eira's earlier words echoed in his mind. She had obviously expected him to react badly. Maybe she had had that reaction from other humans? He knew that a lot of people were fearful of magic-users, but that was usually because they didn't understand them.

Cole exhaled. 'Okay, Doc, do your worst!' He even managed a small smile which made Eira relax her tight shoulders. 'But you must promise that you won't knock me out. I need to know what's going on.'

Eira nodded as she rose, pushing the chair back towards the computer.

Cole tried to relax as she moved to the side of his head. He gripped the chair arms in reaction, breathing through his nose. It was like visiting the dentist, that butterfly feeling of knowing something was about to happen, coupled with the fear that it might hurt.

Eira's warm hand rested against the left side of his face, and he couldn't help looking at her. Her eyes were closed, her forehead wrinkled in concentration. He noticed a dusting of freckles across her nose, and he was distracted by tracing them with his eyes. After a while he could feel her power relaxing him, and his hands slackened at his side as the tension in his chest eased.

'Isn't that better? I promise it won't hurt,' Eira whispered, smiling gently at him.

Cole felt his own mouth answering hers with a smile she couldn't see.

From the corner of his black eye, he saw a white light — her magic released in its true form. It was comforting, soothing, and utterly amazing. It took his breath away. Cole forced himself to keep his eyes open, to observe the doctor at work throughout the process.

Eira removed her hand from the side of his head, leaving it chilled where her comforting warmth had once been. His head felt less fuzzy, but other than that, he felt no changes within himself.

'If you look there' — she pointed to where his eye socket met his brain on the screen — 'I've put the shield here.' She drew a circle on the screen with her finger around the virus.

Eira extracted the headset from around his forehead and set it back on the monitor. Then she removed something from the keyboard and casually dropped it into her back pocket.

Cole removed the flat cap from his head, shaking out his hair. It immediately fell over his eyes, obscuring his vision for a second, before he pushed it back. He felt Eira's eyes on him, and looked up to find her staring intently at him.

'I like that look,' she said, indicating the backwards hat.

Cole could have sworn she licked her bottom lip, but it was so quick he wasn't sure.

'I never meant for that to happen.' Eira reached out, skimming her fingers over the scar on his cheek. She quickly pulled her hand away, and turned her back to him, busying herself with something on the desk.

So, she was to blame.

Cole sat and watched as one of the gnomes reappeared from the shadows, and Eira slid something to him with a hand gesture.

'Well, Hawk, are you coming?'

CHAPTER 19

ORAN

The journey through the tunnels had been an uncomfortable one in many ways for Oran. Firstly, his claustrophobia had made it hard to concentrate. Secondly, his rage was burning inside him, consuming all rational thought. As soon as he was out of the lab, he cloaked himself with his invisibility, not wanting to talk to anyone. To his great shock, it seemed the captain was to accompany them back to the Nightingale. Oran had waited, hidden, only for Eira to walk out like she had forgotten he was there describing the tunnels and their uses to Cole, completely oblivious to the fact that she might be feeding the enemy all the information needed to infiltrate the place.

Oran was fed up with everyone having the same reaction towards him. The human, Cole, seemed decent enough, but he represented everything that made his skin crawl.

Arriving at the gatehouse, Oran observed as Eira entered the small living room and collapsed in one of the rolled-button armchairs beside the fire that seemed to never go out. The poltergeist and the other human were nowhere to be seen. Cole had been directed to the spare room, and was now sleeping soundly, Eira's magic taking effect again despite the captain's protests.

Oran wondered where he would be sleeping since the human had taken his bed.

Eira, sensing his presence, said to the room, 'If we're going to have this out, I'd like to at least be able to see you.'

She sounded tired and deflated as she stretched her long legs in front of the fire, toeing off her purple boots. Some of Oran's anger subsided. He knew he needed to keep calm so as not to explode like last time.

'And if you're going to start lecturing me about having another vulnerable human in our mix, you can go and sleep on the roof with Oswald.'

Oran couldn't help the snigger that escaped him.

'All I was going to say was that you're very good at collecting strays.' Oran sat down on the armchair opposite her and dropped his invisibility, making Eira retract her legs with a yelp.

She stuck her tongue out at him before asking, 'Are you one of those strays, Oran?'

Oran huffed, smiling again.

'He has nowhere else to go, and if the Dark arrest him again, the danger of them locating the club, the triplets...' Eira let out a groan, sliding a hand across her face. 'I couldn't risk it.'

'I'm not here to judge,' Oran commented, holding up his hands. 'But yes, it was stupid to meet him at the club.'

'You're not helping!' Eira complained, burying her face in her arms, leaving only her pointy ears sticking out. 'I only wanted to show him who I was. The world I came from.'

Her voice was distant. He understood that desire. Hiding who you truly are eats away at the soul.

'I think he took it well. He didn't run out of the room screaming. Even when he saw me, he was scared but wasn't going to run. But maybe the club was a step too far?' Oran attempted.

'I wanted to gauge his reaction. It was part of a plan.'

'And what plan was that?' Oran raised an eyebrow.

Eira reluctantly sat up and, curling her feet to the side, rested an elbow on the arm of the chair with her face in her hand.

'I'm certain that Cole is part of a rebel group called the League. They're mainly made up of military and police personnel who escaped the Dark when they first took control of the government and other powerful organisations.'

Oran nodded, urging her to continue.

'They only do low-level stuff at present, but they're better organised than other rebel groups. They have access to a lot of resources. But ... they've made no attempts to help the Myths in this fight. I wanted to see Cole's reaction firsthand.'

Not so naive then.

'And what was your opinion?'

'What, before you made me knock him out?' Eira's mouth twisted, and her eyes twinkled as she shifted to look at him. 'He passed, in my view. If he had turned and fled, or even fought, it wouldn't have worked. He basically put his weapon away and was there to negotiate, which shows he will be useful in the future. Whatever you might think, I had it under control.'

'You mean with the trolls?'

Eira raised an eyebrow.

'You need to remember that I'm pretty observant. Maybe next time fill me in? I might be able to help improve your strategy. I do have over a hundred years of experience.'

Eira nodded, accepting his advice for a change. He was impressed with her efforts, even if the plan had been high-risk.

'Do you care to divulge your future plans?' Oran enquired tentatively.

Eira gulped, chewing her bottom lip as she dropped her eyes from his. Oran attempted a different route.

'Eira, where is your necklace?' His voice held enough command that Eira looked up.

'You're not having it, Light Bringer,' Eira replied in a steely tone.

She'd obviously got the wrong impression.

But her anger had stirred his rage again, and he bristled at the emotion flooding his veins. Before he had a chance to think, his fangs were out, and a low growl rumbled from his throat.

'You have no right to it, and you certainly won't be taking it to your father.'

Lunar, did she really think that little of him?

He knew he was risking scaring her off when he told her that the power surge felt by his father was the same one that emanated from the necklace.

He was overwhelmed by the scent of her conflicting emotions, and felt a slight tug on his power. Oran caught his breath, flinching, the anger subsiding like a tidal wave. He had been too weak before, too wrapped up in his own pain to notice the hole, the slight dent in his armour.

Eira's face was set like stone, her breathing ragged as she glared at him, waiting for his rebuke.

Did she realise what she could do?

Oran sought it, the slight pinprick she had made within his defences, so small that if he wasn't attuned to tracing power, he would have missed it. Instead of blocking the connection, he sent his shimmering moonlight towards the opening, guiding it to seek like he did when tracking.

Eira physically shot up from the armchair, eyes wide.

Oh, she knew!

Oran brushed his magic against her vast well of power, then quickly grabbed hold of her power and drew on her reserves. Eira gasped, her face going pale.

Oran still sat, his body tense as Eira's power expelled into his. His wide eyes locked with hers. Her power was like a drug, calming and tranquil, like taking a swim in a moonlit pond.

'You did that, didn't you?' Eira spat out, resting a hand across her heart.

Oran could only nod under the effects of her magic's influence, closing his eyes. Eira paused, then attacked like a striking cobra.

She sprang on the link between them and grappled with his power, drawing on his starlight, shaping and infusing it with hers, controlling it easily. Oran snapped his eyes open. If anyone had entered the room, they would have just seen them both rigid, staring intently at each other.

'We can continue this power-play all night, or we can call a stalemate and talk about it like grownups.'

Oran broke the connection with a sigh. Eira followed, slumping on the armchair with a groan.

'How did you know?' she asked.

'The triplets,' he replied, his chest heaving from the exertion of their battle. 'How long have you known?'

'I wasn't aware immediately. Is it something I've done or caused to happen?'

Eira said it with so much sadness and pain in her tone that Oran knelt in front of the armchair and gently pulled her hands away from her face. Tears tracked down her cheeks, catching on her chin and dropping onto her T-shirt.

How had he been so angry at her when she didn't even know what she was doing?

'I affected your ability to turn to stone, didn't I?' Eira sniffed.

She was quick. Oran weighed up his options. He could lie to make her feel better, but if she ever found out, she would be heartbroken. He knew he had to tell her the truth, even though it would hurt her.

He simply nodded, catching one of her tears with his fingertip.

'When you first grabbed me after the explosion, I was curious as to how you were cloaking us. I found the link and followed the trail to your power; I must have pushed without realising. I honestly didn't know that I could do that, and then, with all the confusion at the abbey…'

Eira suddenly sat bolt upright, eyes wide. Oran pulled back, his eyes steady on her face.

'I used your power to…' Eira trailed off.

'To do what, Eira?' Oran queried, tilting his head to the side.

'I can only use my power when I am physically connected with someone, flesh to flesh. I've never been able to push my power outside of myself.' Eira pushed her hands out to demonstrate, resting her palms on his chest. 'But you can. I saw you do it with the shield that protected us at the flat, and then again with the stone statues.'

Oran nodded in agreement. His power allowed him to extend his magic away from himself, but the further away it was, the harder it was to control. But if he funnelled it into something like his staff or a Heart Stone, it became easier to wield.

'When you were bleeding, you left a trail right to the portal. I was worried that the agents would follow it and find us. I didn't even think, I just reacted. I sent my power out in front of me and made your blood seep into the stone floor. But I must have used your power to do that … or at least a combination of our powers.'

Eira finished, a mixture of disbelief and excitement crossing her face. She withdrew her hands from his chest and rested them against her own like she was trying to hold her power in.

Oran stilled, trying to recall what she had described; as he had stated before, the night of the abbey was hazy and confusing. Drawing in a sharp breath, he tensed, eyes widening as he turned to Eira.

'I remember the strange sensation of my power being pulled as I entered the portal. I thought it was the aftereffects of my power release, and the sunrise causing my stone shift.' Oran shook his head, disbelieving.

'But that doesn't explain how I was able to block your stone shift.'

Eira used his words and echoed his thought process. The despair on her face was enough for Oran to know this is what was causing her the most anguish.

'When you were seeing to the captain, I asked the triplets about the loss of my stone shift like you suggested,' Oran sniggered. 'It took a lot of hand gesturing and some role playing, but I managed to get them to understand. They simply pointed to you and wrote this: *Bloodstream*.'

Oran produced a folded piece of paper from his pocket and handed it to Eira, who stared at the italic script. 'I have only heard it whispered from the ones who survived the war. A legend, a deep secret lost to time,'

'*Bloodstream,*' Eira whispered, standing up. Oran stood as well, his large frame casting a long shadow from the fire. He looked down at Eira who was wringing her hands, padding up and down on the herringbone floor.

'Tell me what you know,' Oran said.

Eira paused her pacing and then whispered, 'I recognise the term. I read it in a footnote in a history book based on the high races and their involvement in the war. It means sharing power through blood. But it shouldn't be possible. We haven't done that, and we're different species. I think it is an elven term.'

'From what I know,' Oran said, 'it was only ever done in the war by the elves. It wasn't a mutual thing. Only one party, the stronger of the two, should be able to draw on the other's power. It usually drains the weaker of their magic entirely, which is why it was only ever done as a last resort in times of conflict.'

'None of that makes sense, Oran!'

Eira gritted her teeth, throwing her arms out in exasperation.

'Well, let's look at the facts,' Oran stated calmly. 'One — we do share the same heritage, we're both half-elf. Two — we must be equal in power and strength if we can both draw from each other. Three — we're both half-illumini, or hybrids as you call it.' Oran shrugged, three fingers raised. 'Since our gifts are unique, it might be making the process different, meaning we can draw on each other's power instead of just draining them.'

'Doesn't this terrify you?'

'Slightly, but I think it answers a lot of what I have been feeling towards you.'

'Which is?' Eira stared him down, hands on hips, and an eyebrow raised.

Oran felt the flush of embarrassment. If he had the ability to, he would have blushed. Instead, he cleared his throat and, avoiding her eyes, looked above her head to the opposite panelled wall.

Sighing, he said finally, 'I've been feeling an overwhelming need to protect you. I can sense almost all your emotions, particularly when you are distressed. You seem to make me mad at the slightest thing… I've only ever felt that way towards Echo.'

He finally dropped his gaze to Eira, who was biting her bottom lip.

Eira replied, 'I've been feeling the same things. It is like I've always known you.'

Dropping back into the armchair, Oran said, 'We'll have to test this new connection and figure the rest out as we go.'

'Does this mean you are sticking around, Light Bringer?'

It seemed that he was.

CHAPTER 20

ORAN

The wind was chilly this high up, and he had to dig his claws into the stone to keep from being blown over. Oran was still filled with wonder every time he saw daylight. Though he hadn't seen a clear sunrise yet, he was hoping he would soon.

Did this mean he had stopped regretting the loss of his stone shift?

It was complicated. He didn't miss the effects of being turned to stone, but he worried what it would mean to his clan and his mate. Did it make him less of a gargoyle?

He did miss the regenerative sleep though. Turning to stone was much easier than laying on a bed, tossing and turning, willing his brain to be quiet long enough for him to fall asleep. Eira had given him her bedroom with the larger bed, hoping that would help, but so far it hadn't made a difference.

He didn't like that she was sharing a room with the captain, but Eira said that he was being old-fashioned.

He smiled to himself as he monitored the street below his perch, the day's light filtered by his aviation goggles. Oran wore his scaled armour over the silver knitted top, polished clean and smelling fresh. Madam Scudamore had done an excellent job.

The limited sleep Oran had gotten the night before wasn't restful, and he had woken that morning to thoughts of his connection to Eira, and what it meant.

A Bloodstream.

Doesn't this terrify you?
Eira's words.

If he was honest, he was relieved because it explained his feelings towards her. What scared him was how easily he had accepted the outcome.

How was he going to explain this to Callan and the rest of the clan? It might mean he would have to finally come clean as to his elven heritage. The thought filled him with dread, but it might finally make him feel whole.

Did it make Eira part of the Crescent Clan? Oran knew their established Bloodstream link couldn't be broken easily – only upon one of their deaths. He had withheld this information from Eira and the effects it would have on the other if such a situation were to occur. The soul-crushing grief would be similar to the feeling of losing a soulmate.

Oran gritted his teeth and shook the thoughts from his head. One step at a time.

Refocusing, he watched Eira and Cole cross the street, approaching the glazed building in front of him. The captain wore his flat cap low on his head, obscuring his eyes. Eira had a band around her pointed ears, her hair worn loose for a change, cascading down her back in uneven curls.

When Eira had outlined her plans to make an antidote for the virus using the power from the opal, he was excited. But he tried to tamp down his optimism, not wanting to feel disappointed if the crazy plan didn't work. He should be taking the necklace to his real father, and for the hundredth time, he questioned why he hadn't done it. Was it his Bloodstream bond to Eira that was stopping him?

Cole had sat and listened to the plan without comment. He'd filled in the gaps, telling them about his escape from the Dark, and his subsequent stay in his grandfather's house.

With his information and Eira's power, they had a chance to put a stop to the Dark's dictatorship.

Cole had then openly laid out his views, which were as crazy as Eira's, and his own ambitions to save his friends. They both knew what they needed to do, and Oran wasn't sure where he fitted in with it all.

So why am I still here?

Oran knew the answer to that too. It had stirred within him as he watched Eira and Elowen making their rounds at the Nightingale. A human and half-breed completely at ease in each other's company, selflessly helping the less fortunate. Not to gain power, wealth, or status, but simply doing it because they cared, risking themselves in the process.

It felt like a void was slowly being filled inside him, and he knew that he wanted to work towards creating harmony between all races.

This morning was the easy part of their plan — a personal matter that Eira needed to take care of — but it wasn't without risk.

Oran was most concerned about the location. They were in central London, surrounded by high-rises, and close to the Dark's bank, used to launder money and help them gain even more influence. The security was mostly automated, but the whining of the drones was ever present.

Oran could see the spires of St Paul's Cathedral in the distance and the shadow of the Shard's sharp profile across the Thames. It brought a shiver to his spine to think about what the captain had said was located under its foundations.

Below, humans still worked, hurrying around in tattered suits with uneasy expressions. They weren't under the virus's influence as far as he could tell, which made the whole situation even worse. Humans knew what the Dark was doing to their own people, but they chose to turn a blind eye to it in exchange for a fat pay cheque. At least the mass of humans allowed Cole and Eira to blend in.

Oran glanced at the digital watch on his arm. Like all the technology he had witnessed this past week, it was alien to him. At least the watch was simple compared to the phone which Eira had tried to force onto him. The watch simply counted down the hour they had between drone patrols. Oran needed to make it inside or risk being caught.

He glanced across to the opposite building, seeing Oswald perched on the gutter. With a thought, Oran sent a command to the chimera, asking him for a report on what he could see. Oswald's answering thought told him that everything was clear.

An idea then occurred to Oran, and before he could overthink it, he acted.

He sent a thought down through the bond.

Your hair looks lovely down.

There was a pause where he watched with delight as Eira stopped just outside the building, turning her head from side to side. Cole halted beside her, instantly alert for danger.

Oran? He heard her ask, directly into his head.

Well, this is going to be a far simpler way to communicate.

Since Oran had refused the phone, he had suggested that they should tug on the other's power if there was danger or a threat. This way would be far quicker and clearer.

This is very strange.

Eira proceeded into the bank, a dumbfounded Cole behind her, clearly not understanding why she had hesitated.

Chuckling to himself, he checked in once more with Oswald before sweeping his magic and consciousness towards the building, seeking the stone statues within.

This aspect of his power still took his breath away. He divided his consciousness into many fragments, pushing them towards the five large statues within.

Guiding his moonbeam magic to inhabit all five, he focused his attention on the middle one. The statues were Egyptian in appearance, seeming to depict pharaohs and their deities.

He opened the eyes of the one in the middle, allowing Oran to watch the scene in front of them, behind a white film.

The lobby of the nameless private bank was swanky; large, polished travertine tiles graced the floor, extending to the glass facade and sleek automatic doors. The reception desk was made from solid black glass, sleek and intimidating like a black wave cresting from the floor.

The juxtaposition between the grandeur in this space compared to the poverty across London was staggering. He could see that Cole had noticed it too. He swept his eyes around the room, his jaw set, **and teeth gritted. Cole's eyes rested on the** centre statue briefly.

Oran had wanted to accompany Eira into the bank, but Eira had refused, not wanting to risk him getting caught. They had agreed that Eira and Cole would gain entry to the vaults, and that Oran would join them by force if necessary.

Watching him, Oran was impressed with Cole. He was hyper-aware of his surroundings, whilst still looking casual.

Eira confidently approached the main desk, her purple boots squeaking on the glossy floor. She asked the attendant if she could see her safe deposit box, producing a key from the folds of her fitted grey dress which showed off all her curves. The attendant, who wore a fine tailored suit, pushed a pair of glasses up the bridge of his nose, and curtly enquired, **'Number?'**

'2567,' Eira replied, a forced smile on her face. Oran spotted the slight shake of her hand as she clasped the key, but the **attendant didn't seem to notice.**

'Name?'

'Eira Mackay.' It was a risk to use her real name.

The attendant nodded, swiping something on his screen. Cole played the role of bodyguard well, head lowered, monitoring their surroundings. It was the slight raise of his head and hand gesture to the side which caught Oran's attention.

Oh, he was well trained.

The foyer was deserted until the squeaking shoes of another attendant appeared in the direction Cole had indicated. He was tall, broad-shouldered, and seemed to be wearing a suit two sizes too big for his frame. He was well presented but seemed not to fit the job role. Oran could make out a mop of strawberry-blonde hair as the man stopped abruptly behind the chair, his hands clasped behind his back.

'Blood for entry,' the first attendant drawled in a bored tone. The second risk. Eira couldn't lie on this one to gain entry.

'Oh, Raymond, we don't have to worry about that for Miss Mackay. I will take it from here; you are dismissed.'

Surprise flickered through Oran, and he found it hard to remain still within the statue. Eira hid her shock well as she glanced at the newcomer.

'It's protocol, Simon. Every customer must...'

Simon, the new attendant, cut Raymond a quelling look. He stuttered something before jumping up from the chair and hurrying away.

'Miss Mackay, this way please.' Simon gestured with a slight bow as if nothing had occurred between himself and his colleague.

Eira sauntered to the side of the reception desk, curiosity gracing her face. Cole fell into step behind her, head snapping up quickly when he grew level with the statue. Raising the eyebrow above his black eye, he pointed backwards to the attendant left behind.

Oran made the eyes of the statue blink once. He understood his meaning.

That was intense and confusing, Eira said into his head.

Oran slowly stretched his consciousness and commanded the statues to rise if there was a threat. The man left behind paced up and down behind the counter, wringing his hands. He seemed to be contemplating something.

Oran, roosting on the high-rise, risked slipping into Oswald's mind to observe the outside from his vantage point, but all seemed clear.

Manipulating his hold on the Sphinx statue, he eased the creature's limbs free of the stone plinth they were attached to. Just in case. The attendant still paced, hands shaking by his sides, unaware that the statues behind him had risen to life. How humans functioned with such dull instincts he didn't know.

Fully slipping back into his own body with a deep sigh, Oran twisted his watch, activating the screen. He had thirty minutes before the next drone patrol. As a precaution, he sent a command to Oswald who alighted next to him on the stone ledge, rumbling with a growl as he monitored the street below.

A movement in the back of Oran's mind caught his attention. His fragmented consciousness had detected a problem. Oran dived back into the awareness of the Sphinx. The attendant was now sitting at the counter, his hand tapping at the computer keys.

Oran reacted, his attuned senses propelling him into action. He fully extracted the heavy statue from the plinth, directing the other statues to do the same.

The attendant's hand jerked, a slight movement below the desk. The bulky statue was cumbersome as it staggered towards the human. Hearing the clattering, the attendant finally looked up, his face paling in horror as the statue loomed over him. The Sphinx brought its stone fist down and connected with the human's face, knocking his glasses off his nose.

The monitor on the desk flashed as something loaded and then beeped once as it depowered and went into safe mode.

Lunar.

Oran didn't hesitate, sending a large burst of power into the five statues, activating them with commands on how to proceed.

Oran you need to get inside now. Eira's voice was frantic in his head.

How was she aware of the situation in the foyer?

Back in his own body, Oran dug his claws onto the ledge and pushed off, plummeting headfirst towards the ground, wrapping himself in his invisibility. Oswald followed close behind.

His stomach surged with the drop. Adrenalin pumped through his veins, and he grinned, loving the way the wind whipped his hair around his face. He slammed onto the pavement as humans scattered in terror. Snapping his wings behind his back, Oswald landed on his shoulder, instantly becoming invisible too.

The familiar whine of approaching drones caught Oran's attention. He propelled himself into action, running towards the glass doors of the building, throwing a shield over himself at the last second. He smashed through in a rain of shining glass, skidding to a stop, claws gouging elongated marks in the shiny floor.

He took in the scene.

The five Egyptian statues, eyes glowing, were in defensive positions, spaced out along the glass facade. How was he going to defend a penetrable substance? Even if the glass by some miracle was bulletproof, it wouldn't last under heavy fire. He could always increase the stability with a shield but that would take a huge amount of energy to maintain.

And if the agents used the bullets encased with the virus…

Oran shuddered at the thought.

The best thing he could do was find Eira and Cole and defend themselves from there.

Eira I'm in. Where—

A grinding sound made Oran pause and drop into a defensive crouch, his fangs bared in a growl, crescent-moon dagger in hand as the light began to fade.

Well, that solved one problem.

Pushing his goggles up onto his forehead, and dropping his invisibility, he took off at a run towards where he'd last seen Eira.

||| EIRA

Cole cocked his pistol and took aim at the attendant's chest. Eira noticed that his hands were steady, but his breathing was rapid, and his heart rate accelerated. He didn't want to take a life unless it was necessary. At some point on the journey to the vaults, he had rotated his flat cap backwards. Eira stared at him, wanting to run her fingers through the curls on the back of his neck.

Shaking the thought from her head, Eira focused. The attendant had his arms slightly raised but gave no impression that he was frightened. His scent was bland, muted even for a human. His hair, so similar to her tone, was cropped short, and he had a square jaw and strong nose. He looked to be in his mid-forties, but it was hard to be exact. It was his eyes which captivated Eira: they were blue, not the startling diamond-blue of Cole's, but pastel sky-blue, almost like developing storm clouds. He was slightly hunched but still tall, his suit ill-fitting, too large for his form. His eyes were alert, fully locked onto Cole. Separating them was a small white table with a long metal box on top.

Eira's box, her mother's safe. She had been so close to opening it after all this time, but then the siren had sounded, alerting them all to a situation. That was when Cole had drawn his gun without hesitation.

'How did you know we have a friend outside?' Eira demanded.

Tell your friend outside that if he wants to live, he needs to come into the bank, now. She repeated his words in her head.

This was a trap, it had to be.

Eira had communicated to Oran to come inside anyway. They needed him.

Cole's smoke and spice scent washed over her as he angled himself in front of her, trying to push her body behind his. Eira was touched, but she could take care of herself.

The silly, grey corded dress that Madam Scudamore had insisted that she wear, would make fighting difficult, but the slits up the side and stretchy fabric allowed for some movement. A blade was in her hand in an instant, and Cole eyed it warily.

Eira smirked back, twirling it expertly in her fingers.

Cole wore his trademark leather jacket but had switched his leather trousers for fitted jeans which highlighted his narrow waist and long legs.

The attendant moved his hand slightly, drawing Eira's attention back to him.

Cole raised his gun. 'I think you owe the lady an explanation.' His tone was firm; he was taking no nonsense.

They were in the bank vaults deep underground, in a square room lined with safety deposit boxes. It was shiny and glossy just like upstairs, and brightly lit with fluorescent bulbs. Why her mother had chosen this particular bank was beyond Eira, and she wasn't even sure how she could have afforded it. The nerves and excitement she had felt about opening the box had been washed away by the fear of what was about to happen.

'Let me show you,' answered the attendant. His voice was so deep that it took Eira by surprise.

He moved his hand across to his left arm, pushing the shirt sleeve up to reveal a tattoo on his inner forearm.

Eira drew back further from Cole, gasping as she brought her hand to her mouth. Cole risked a sideways glance at her, momentarily taking his eyes off the male in front of him.

The symbol on the stranger's arm was a mark she would recognise anywhere. It was a symbol of her childhood, her family. Images flashed through her mind: colouring in the symbol with felt tip pens; wearing a purple T-shirt with the mark on; the purple flag flying high, emblazoned with the symbol.

A half-sun on its side with three lines descending from the top. Gold on a purple background.

The symbol of her mother's political party.

The symbol of a hope that died with her mother on the day of her assassination.

This stranger must have known her mother.

'If I don't activate the shutters, we will be overrun by agents,' the stranger stated calmly, indicating to the screens behind them.

Eira placed a hand on Cole's shoulder, turning to look at the screen. The cameras showed the foyer and street outside.

Five statues stood sentry at the windows their eyes glowing. A suited man lay behind the counter unconscious, glasses knocked across the floor. The automatic doors suddenly smashed, and deep grooves appeared on the floor.

Oran.

Eira flicked her gaze to the other screen. She gasped as a dozen drones flew down the street, followed by two blacked-out armoured trucks.

Eira spun around, her attention back on the attendant. 'Fine, do what you must. But do it quickly.'

He walked briskly to the main console and tapped a few buttons. Cole followed his movement, keeping his gun trained on him.

Oran's voice floated faintly through her mind. *Eira I'm inside. Where—*

The foyer was plunged into darkness as shutters came down. Then Oran materialised, white wings spreading behind his broad back. Oswald was perched on his shoulder. He had a pearlescent dagger in his hand, and looked dangerous as he stalked forward. He really was magnificent.

Follow the stairs down, we're in the vaults, Eira replied.

Movement on the screen outside snagged her attention. Agents in black military gear had surrounded the bank.

'Right, you'd better start explaining yourself,' Eira snarled, glaring at the man in front of them.

Cole still had his gun trained on the man's chest, and Eira stepped closer to stand beside him.

'Who are you, and why do you have that symbol on your arm?' Cole's eyes slid to hers briefly before flicking back to the stranger.

The attendant watched her, his eyes darkening to rain-cloud grey, his hands slack at his sides.

'I'm known as Storm, and I was one of the leading members of the party. I helped smuggle you out of London when your mother was killed.'

Cole gasped, lowering his gun ever so slightly.

Eira kept her face neutral, her heart hammering like a trapped moth inside her ribcage. She flicked through her blurry memories of the escape from London. There had been so many different people, most of their faces fogged by the grief and stress of the incident. He might have been there; his voice definitely sounded familiar.

'That's not widely known by many but still doesn't prove anything. What were Rosalind Mackay's exact words to the new members who swore fealty to her cause?' she demanded.

'She said, "To stand equal alongside the few, was to rise into a new future where one day we might be free".'

Eira nodded, closing her eyes for a second. She didn't know what to say. This stranger in front of her had been part of her mother's campaign to bring equal rights to hybrids. A dream inspired by her daughter.

A rippling tension suddenly grew within her body, straining down the Bloodstream as she felt Oran's wrath snap between them. He was warning her that he was ready to unleash himself. Eira pushed back like she had in the gatehouse, sending her power along the bond to calm him, instead of drawing on his, shouting *STOP* straight into his head.

Oran suddenly appeared in the doorway, curved daggers in hand, lips pulled back to reveal his deadly teeth, and Oswald hissing on his shoulder. His huge wings flared as he charged into the room.

Eira felt his power wash over her, overwhelming her mind and her eyes. His starlight burst from him, quickly filling the room.

Oran's power splintered and drew back together in front of Eira and Cole. He didn't attack, just held a shimmering shield in front of them for protection.

He dipped his head in acknowledgement to Eira, then locked eyes with the attendant, rage obvious on his face as he glowered at the stranger.

He has magic, Oran spoke inside Eira's head.

Eira was still reeling from everything that had happened in the past few minutes, and Oran's statement only added to that.

'What?' she blurted out loud before she could stop herself. Cole was shielding her entirely. He looked at her with a question in his eyes at her outburst.

Eira shook her head. She glanced at Oran standing protectively at her other side. *What do you mean he has magic?*

He isn't human, that's for sure. His scent is all wrong. He has a very strong glamour. Who is he?

Eira scrutinised the stranger. She knew there had been others, hybrids and Myths who had been supportive of her mother's cause.

He knew my mother when she was alive. He was part of her movement for equal rights for hybrids. He also helped get me out of London as a child when my mother was assassinated by the Dark.

Of course, Oran didn't know about that part of her history. She refused to look at his face, not ready to see the sympathy and sadness there. She didn't want his compassion.

Before Oran could reply, Eira said, 'How did you know we had a friend outside? You're not fully human, are you?'

Storm's stare was intense. He hadn't flinched once, not at Oran's arrival or the sparkling shield in front of him. Definitely not human. No human would be able to stay calm at the display of such power.

'I have my ways and means. Who I am and what I am are not important at the moment. What I have, on the other hand, is extremely significant, and I promised your mother that I would give it to you. She was very important to me, and I've stayed here to protect her legacy, waiting for you to turn up.'

Eira was lost for words. How was she supposed to react to that statement? It was all too much for her to process. It sparked questions about certain aspects of her mother's life which didn't make sense. She had come here for answers, and she only seemed to be getting more questions.

Oran sniffed the air, his nostrils flaring, trying to ascertain the stranger's scent. His eyes grew wide, the whites swirling like mist. Storm — *Simon* — snapped his attention to Oran. Thunderclouds seemed to roll in his eyes as his pupils dilated.

What is it, Oran?

Oran stood stone-still, seeming to brace himself for impact.

Oran, Eira repeated, placing a hand on his bicep.

Oran shook himself and stepped away from her side. He dropped the shield, his magic raining like falling stars onto the floor.

'Oran, what is it?' Eira pleaded out loud.

'Nothing, Eira. It can wait.'

The gargoyle folded his arms, sheathed his daggers, and strolled to the back of the vault, where he stood with one clawed foot propped against the wall, Oswald still on his shoulder. It looked so casual that Eira almost laughed. Cole observed the whole scenario with a look of confusion on his face, but he had lowered his pistol. Not completely but enough to be unguarded.

Eira narrowed her eyes at Oran. Shrugging, she sheathed her own dagger under her dress. She knew the gargoyle well enough to trust his insight, but she was intrigued by his sudden change of demeanour.

'Right, Miss Mackay, we're pressed for time, so if you wouldn't mind,' Storm said, indicating the metal box on the table.

A glance at the monitors behind her showed the agents shooting at the metal shutters, which were withstanding the impact without much damage. But it was only a matter of time.

Cole held his gun loosely in his hand, but he still stood in front of her protectively.

Eira extracted the key from the folds of her dress. She was shocked that such a small thing could hold so much hope.

Inserting the key in the lock, it clicked, and Eira exhaled. Glancing at Cole, he nodded his reassurance and placed his warm hand on her back. She took a deep breath and lifted the lid.

What she saw was unexpected.

With shaking hands, she reached in and extracted the envelope with her name written on it in her mother's neat script. Eira looked at the envelope for a long moment, tracing her mother's writing. Like her voice and her smell, her writing, had been forgotten to time.

Eira held the envelope to her chest, expelling a shuddering breath. She felt Cole's fingers stroking her back in comfort. She would read the letter privately, in her own time.

Without looking at Cole, she instead held Storm's eyes. His strawberry-blonde hair was scraped back from his face showing his high forehead and his mouth set in a grim line. His eyes were filled with such sadness and regret that Eira was convinced he had known her mother well. Storm gestured to the other items in the metal box.

Cradling the envelope under her armpit, Eira reached in and extracted the sword her mother had left her. It was exquisite. The rounded pommel was metallic, the colour changing depending on how the light played on it, like oil on water. On the rounded stone, there was an engraving of a sun in outline.

Eira clutched the sword tightly, and her whole arm vibrated with the power of it. She could have sworn a spark momentarily lit the stone on the end.

A sharp intake of breath made Eira glance around at Oran who had positioned himself near her right shoulder. Eira sensed his power flowing along the bond. Her power merged with his as she allowed it to be shaped and guided to his will. It was strange to give control to another, but she trusted Oran completely.

Cole tensed, sensing the sudden shift in her body.

Eira placed a hand on the sheath and drew the blade in a long sweep. The blade was almost dark-blue, reminding her of Cole's hair in certain lights. It was well-balanced, more a short sword than a broadsword, and Eira was confident that she could use it. There appeared to be a crack straight up the centre of the blade. As she angled it, she saw that the pommel and grip were also split. Maybe it was broken.

Her power seemed to swell as Oran explored the blade with his seeking magic.

What's your assessment, Light Bringer?

Oran gulped, hands slack at his side.

It's old. Ancient in fact. It has some kind of stored power. I think it splits in two. It's obviously been forged by magic.

Eira turned to Storm for answers. His face was sorrowful, making him appear older. He briefly glanced back at the box and raised his hand to point out another object inside.

Reaching in, Eira picked up a dagger that matched the sword, its power radiating through her as soon as she touched it.

'These are known as the Skye blades,' Storm said, his tone strong but quiet. 'Many have sought them. Only someone true of heart, someone selfless, can wield them to their true strength and power. The bearer must win their trust and form an unbreakable bond with them.'

Storm held up a long finger as Eira opened her mouth to ask a question.

'Listen carefully, this is the most important piece of information I have to share. These swords will turn the tide in the upcoming war. They must not — I repeat, *must not* — fall into the wrong hands. They have been given to you, Eira, because you hold the key to the future survival of the high races. Your unbreakable bond with another must unite the high races and finally fulfil your mother's dreams.'

Storm finished, dropping his hand to the table. His pale blue eyes were clear, un-fogged, like a weight had been lifted. Even his stance was different. The use of her name had caught Eira off guard. She stood there, too many questions and emotions flickering through her mind. Oran had retracted his power from their link without Eira even noticing. She felt oddly empty without his magic's warmth.

Unbreakable bond. Did he mean her bond with Oran? Eira thought as she turned to question the gargoyle, but the look on his face made her hesitate. He looked as thunderstruck as she felt.

Cole whistled. 'Well, that was a destiny speech if ever I've heard one.' He smiled at her, a dimple appearing in his cheek.

Despite herself Eira snorted. She knew Cole was trying to break the tension filling the room.

'Storm, or Simon, or whoever you are. You may or may not have known my mother and helped me in the past. But I have no interest in destiny and powerful swords. I'm a doctor not a warrior.'

She sheathed the weapons and went to place them back in the box. Oran's hand shot out, quick as lightning, and grabbed her wrist. Eira turned to him, eyebrows raised.

But before the gargoyle could speak, Storm said, 'Aren't you already trying to change fate with another gift from your mother?'

The sharp inhale of breath which lodged in Eira's throat made her eyes sting and her ears ring. How did he know so much? She felt her own power swelling, forcing itself to the surface, ready to defend herself if needed.

'Who gave my mother these weapons?' Her words were sharp, spat at the stranger in front of her.

'Your father gave them to her to pass down to his daughter.'

Eira's knees nearly buckled, and her head span. If it wasn't for the reassuring presence of the two males either side of her, she would have collapsed.

'What do you mean, my father? He disappeared when I was two years old,' Eira hissed.

Oran's head suddenly jerked, his whole body going taut. Eira glanced at the screens to see the agents breaking through one of the metal shutters. The animated statues staggered into action, defending their posts. Eira knew the strength and control it took for Oran to maintain contact with them and, without thinking, her power sped down the open connection, buffering him with her own strength.

He grunted, eyes closed.

They watched as one statue was blown to dust by an agent wielding a semi-automatic.

'You need to go now. This way.' Storm pointed to the opened vault door. He glanced at the metal box, where Eira was still poised to drop the weapons.

Take them, Eira, Oran pleaded in her mind.

Not thinking twice, Eira spun away from the box, gripping both the sword and the dagger in her hands. The envelope was still tucked tightly under her arm.

Storm beckoned from the open door. Cole, pistol in both hands, went first, Eira behind him, with Oran bringing up the rear.

The attendant led them to the main corridor and took them deeper into the bank, away from the advancing agents. He set a demanding pace which had them all jogging to keep up. It seemed that all the staff were hiding, as they didn't bump into anyone along the way.

Most of the statue connections have been broken, Oran warned inside her mind.

She looked back over her shoulder and was shocked to find that he had disappeared. His faint scent of sea salt drifted to her on the next turn, so Eira knew he was close.

They descended a flight of stairs into a darker, more disused part of the bank. Here the vaults were thick and impenetrable, and Eira wondered what kind of treasures were stored within these confines.

Cole slowed, his breathing becoming more strained. Eira clutched his arm and sent a burst of power into him. Given the extent of his injuries, he was doing a good job keeping up with their supernatural pace.

Storm finally came to an abrupt halt near a tiled wall between two vaults. To Eira's great relief, she spotted a circle with an arrow inside, located discreetly in the bottom corner. A portal.

In the semi-darkness, Storm scored his hand and applied it to the waymarker. If she hadn't believed that he was magical in some way before, this confirmed it.

Oran stepped forward and ducked into the tunnel as soon as the door swung open. Oswald flapped into the dark behind him. Cole braced his hand on the door frame, clutching his chest and gasping for breath.

Eira hesitated, her hands full of the gifts bestowed upon her by her mother. A complete shock but finally a conclusion to two years of cowardice towards the unknown.

She looked at Storm who waited in the doorway.

'Aren't you coming too?' Eira asked, concerned for his safety once the agents arrived.

'Don't worry, I have my own exit strategy.'

Eira turned to follow the others into the gloom when a hand wrapped around her wrist. She looked around to find Storm staring at her, his eyes bright in his shadowed face.

'Your mother was a great woman. She would be proud of you.'

She felt a sudden heat on her wrist and gasped, trying to pull free from his calloused fingers, but his grip was tight. After a few seconds, he released her.

'If you ever need me, hold onto the mark and think of the sun.'

Glancing at her wrist, she saw an outline of a sun, the same symbol as on the blades she carried. It looked as if it had been branded onto her skin, and the fact that it wasn't healing told her that it was magical.

Eira snapped her head upwards, but Storm had gone, leaving the corridor deserted. She traced her fingers over the marking, and they came away sticky with his blood. In the faint light, it appeared to be blue.

CHAPTER 21

⋈ COLE

Cole manoeuvred the tray to rest on one arm and used his spare hand to lightly tap on the door.

Why am I knocking on my own bedroom door?

The room he was sharing with Eira. They were in separate beds, but it was still strange.

This whole situation was strange and, for the umpteenth time, he questioned his logic and sanity.

They had returned to the gatehouse via the tunnels, in silence, exhaustion and the overwhelming amount of information weighing heavy on their shoulders. Eira had excused herself and had not been seen since. Oran had disappeared in his astonishing way. Neither hybrid appeared for dinner.

Cole had settled himself by the fire in the living room to give Eira the space that she needed to process everything that had happened. His wound was aching from the exertion. His second attempt to contact Major Stone via the encrypted network on his tablet had been met with silence. Elowen had joined him after her shift at the Nightingale and had invited him to dinner.

Cole admitted it was a relief to have another human within their weird group. Elowen was much better acclimatised to this strange new world he found himself in and seemed to take everything in her stride. Cole was curious, but much of it was terrifying and had made him realise how limited his abilities were in comparison.

The poltergeist, Madam Scudamore, had forcefully insisted that he take dinner up to Eira, and, not wanting to get on the bad side of the matronly ghost, he had agreed.

No sound came from behind the door, so he took a deep breath, and gently pushed it open.

The room was dark, the red velvet curtains drawn. He knew the room layout well enough to enter and close the door behind him with a foot. He cleared his throat, assessing the bedroom with his black eye. He picked out her silhouette on the floor between the twin beds, her outline a shade of grey. Cole knew that she would be glowing with a silvery light if she dropped her glamour. How powerful was she? Oran's power had been blinding, and if he was right, she could at least match him.

'For my feeble human eyes, would you mind switching on a light?' he asked jokingly.

He heard shuffling in the dark and then a soft bedside light was switched on.

Eira sat on the floor, her back to one of the single beds. She wore only her dark Run-DMC T-shirt — a stark contrast to her long pale legs stretched out in front of her. Cole's eyes roamed along her creamy white thighs, and he swallowed hastily, averting his gaze.

Clearing his throat again, he said hoarsely, 'Madam Scudamore thought you might like something to eat.' He held the tray out in front of him.

Eira turned to him. She had tied her hair into a messy bun on top of her head, and unruly curls fell against her forehead. Her pointed ears peeked out from beneath her curls, making her elegant neck look even longer. Again, Cole found his eyes wandering along the exposed lines of her neck, and he licked his bottom lip, gulping again.

When his eyes finally locked onto hers, he noticed that they were red-rimmed from crying. An open envelope and folded letter were discarded beside her, and her new sword was unceremoniously dumped by the foot of her bed.

For the first time in his life, he didn't know what to say. He hesitated like an idiot, then stumbled into action. He gently set the tray down beside Eira, avoiding her sad gaze.

'It's risotto. That ghost is a mean cook.'

Eira just gazed at the tray, her expression so hollow that it pulled at his heart. Stiffly, she pulled the tray onto her lap and started spooning the steaming, creamy rice into her mouth.

Cole turned, removing his leather jacket and hanging it on the footboard of the bed, his tablet in hand. *Should I leave?*

Running his fingers through his messy hair which flopped over his eyes, Cole paused on his way to the door. Before he could regret the action, he slid to the floor, leaning against the opposite bed so that he was facing Eira.

Her eyes shifted to him as she blew on a spoonful of rice. Cole noticed a mark on the underside of her forearm that looked like the sun. Drawing his knees up, he rested his elbows on them, still holding his tablet. 'Elowen was worried about you.'

Eira's eyes widened slightly. 'Did you fill her in?'

Cole shook his head, his hair obscuring his vision once again as he looked down at the floor, twisting the tablet between his hands. 'Oran didn't show up for dinner either. There's no telling where he is with those skills of his. He could be in this room.'

Eira's mouth twitched, some colour returning to her high cheeks.

'He's on the roof of the Nightingale, taking his new role as Head of Security very seriously.'

Cole gaped at her, stunned, before his mouth twisted into a smile. 'How do you know that?'

Eira tapped the side of her nose, eyes glinting for a moment before the sorrow set in again. Maybe it was a hybrid sense, an immortal's ability, but they seemed to communicate without speaking. He was adamant that back at the bank there were long intermissions of time where they seemed to be discussing stuff without speaking.

Cole was too scared to ask. It would be another superpower he didn't have, another reason he felt that he didn't belong here. A lonely mortal pretending to be something he wasn't. He knew he was only part of this new super-team because he possessed something that they needed.

The information and the means to accomplish their goals. Access to the League's resources. And he was even failing at that.

'Any reply?' Eira enquired, pointing at the tablet with her spoon.

'Nope,' Cole answered, blowing out his cheeks, deflated.

Cole laid his palm on the screen, activating the device with his biometrics. He could just rock up at headquarters and pay the price of admission. The intel he carried could be a bargaining chip for any disciplinary Major Stone dished out.

But to do that was completely out of character for him, not to mention reckless.

Nimbly scrolling through his stored music, Cole selected a Fugees classic, chucking the tablet onto the bed behind him, and leaning back to rest his head against the mattress. As the opening chords to 'Killing Me Softly With His Song' started to swell within him, he tried to ease his tension. Swaying his hand and tapping his foot to the beat, Cole drifted, trying to forget for a moment, the situation he found himself in.

Cole's heart ached for this woman. The doctor who had saved his life twice, despite the risk to herself.

He spoke without registering what he was saying. 'I grew up in a council block in Peckham. As you can imagine, we weren't well off. My father could never hold down a job. He was quick to anger, and the alcohol didn't help. He abused my mother. My father would take his temper out on us both, but my mother took the brunt of it.' Cole gulped, shutting his eyes.

'I would skip school and go to the one person who actually cared about me, my grandfather. When he died, everything went to shit. My mother turned to drugs, trying to numb the grief and the pain of my father's fists.'

The song's melody poured over Cole as the lyrics resonated within him, helping him to work through the memories he was discussing.

'I used to avoid going home after school or wherever I had bunked off to. I used to hide at my grandfather's empty house.' Cole sniggered. 'My parents were too lazy and intoxicated to sell it for the money. I'm glad they never did; they would only have squandered it all on drugs and alcohol. Anyway, I was fourteen, it was raining, and there was no food left at my grandfather's, so my stomach had eventually sent me home. I remember being soaked to the bone. I never owned a coat.'

Cole tensed at the memory, screwing his eyes up tight before exhaling and forcing himself to continue. It was important that Eira knew he understood her grief.

'I remember the flat being dimly lit. All I wanted was to go and get some food from the kitchen. My mother appeared at the top of the stairs. She was in her nightie, her strap was falling down her shoulder. I remember thinking it was odd but not uncommon for her to be in her nightdress in the middle of the day. She reached towards me and then ... she fell down the stairs. She landed right at my feet.'

Cole screwed up his face, wiping his hands across his eyes.

'They'd been arguing as usual. My father pushed her, and he was so out of it that he didn't even know what he'd done.'

Cole exhaled a long sigh, finally opening his eyes to stare at the exposed beams on the ceiling above him as the last words of the song drifted away.

'I'm telling you this because I know how you feel. To watch a parent die and be powerless to stop it. To keep doubting yourself about whether there was something you could have done to stop it. When you finally accept it, the grief doesn't go away, but you become more able to deal with it.' Cole rested his hand on his chest, close to his heart.

Eira had been quiet throughout his monologue. He knew that if he had looked at her, he wouldn't have been able to get the words out, but now he turned towards her, gazing at her properly.

Tears left trails down her cheeks. She made no move to wipe them away. Her eyes were fully locked on his, moving slightly, searching his face.

Cole hastily gathered himself up, his long legs catching as he twisted closer to Eira, slinging an arm around her slim shoulders. He leant back against the bed and drew her in close.

'I'm such an idiot. I didn't mean to make you cry. I just... I don't know. I was trying to..." He was rambling, knowing he was probably making it worse, but he couldn't stop himself.

Another Fugees song started to play: 'Ready or Not'. So inappropriate, but Cole found he couldn't move from where he clung to her. Eira stirred, sniffing, wiping the tears with the back of her hand. She didn't shift away from him. Cole hesitated, but then he rested his chin on the top of her head, rubbing her shoulder, trying to soothe the sadness away.

'You know, don't you? I saw it on your face at the bank,' Eira said quietly, her voice vibrating against his chest.

Cole wanted to deny it, but Eira was too observant for that.

'Your mother is a legend in our rebel circles. Not so much within the League, but when I was starting out, her assassination was mentioned. Not in detail, but enough. Many of her old party members were rumoured to have died or gone into hiding. But she started the fight against the Dark's oppression. We have a lot to thank her for.'

They were both quiet for a long moment.

Cole continued hesitantly, 'I guessed you were there. There was never any mention of a daughter, you know. But from your reaction, I put a few pieces together. I'm sorry if I've guessed wrong, and if my story brought back some memories. I just, I don't know... I want you to know that I understand that feeling, and if you want to talk, I'm here.'

Cole fell quiet, listening to Eira's steady breathing and the music in the background, unsure if he had made it worse or better.

'I was there,' Eira whispered.

Cole held his breath, waiting for her to continue.

'I know that feeling well, it eats you up inside.' She sounded bitter.

Eira twisted from his arms, putting the tray on the floor, the sudden loss of her body heat making him shudder. Cole laid his arm along the mattress. She brought her knees up to her chest resting them within her T-shirt and placed what appeared to be a torn photograph on his lap.

Cole raised the pieces to the light. The background was green and leafy, a park perhaps. One half showed a woman with brown curly hair, clutching a toddler who resembled Eira. The cheeky toddler was sticking out her tongue. The other half was a male turned slightly from the camera, his arm in the photo from taking it. His hair was long, almost white-blonde, some parts braided. His elven ears were distinguishable and so were his intense green eyes. Eira's eyes. What made Cole choke was the way he looked at Eira and her mother. There was so much love in his gaze, but sorrow was written plainly there too.

'I've never known my father. He disappeared not long after this photo was taken. My mother refused to tell me why he disappeared, or even tell me his name. I used to resent her for it.'

Eira gulped.

'The envelope included this photo which matches the half I have. There's also a letter which doesn't make any sense. I'm starting to think I didn't know my mother at all. Her aims, her goals. Why I have these damn weapons.'

Eira shrugged, throwing her hands in the air, deflated. She rested her head back against his arm to look at the ceiling. Carefully moving the photos aside, Cole laid his head back too. They both stayed there for a long time, their even breaths filling the space between them.

Finally, Eira spoke. 'Hawk?'

'Yeah?' Cole twisted his head towards her, meeting her gaze, relieved to see a glint back in her eyes.

'I like your music choice.'

⫼ EIRA

There was so much blood coating her hands and the front of her clothes, Eira could taste the coppery tang on the tip of her tongue. Still, she couldn't staunch the flow. Her powers weren't working, she couldn't heal the open wound under her hands.

Then a figure loomed over her. His white teeth flashed as he stared at her, ignoring the rain pelting around him. She was petrified, her body frozen as the stranger in the black glasses reached down to her. He grinned a wicked smile which stretched his mutilated ear and the hideous scar on the side of his neck.

Eira, wake up! a voice shouted inside her head.

The scream burnt Eira's throat as she pulled herself awake from the twisted nightmare. For a moment she was lost, unsure where she was, her own scream ringing in her ears. Her eyes wouldn't open, and she was trapped, twisted in the bed sheets.

Warm, soft hands gently surrounded her, drawing her in. The mattress dipped as a body pressed in next to her. Eira, reeling from the dream, started to shake.

'It's okay. It was only a dream,' a calming voice said in the dark, hands stroking her shoulder.

Eira, are you ok?

A familiar power rumbled inside her, concern and anger flowing through their connection.

Eira thought she could smell sea salt and a mixture of smoke and cinnamon. She knew those smells.

She snapped her eyes open, quickly coming back to reality.

'Hawk? Oran?' Eira choked out, her voice strained and rough from the scream that had torn from her throat.

'Just me, Doc. Unless he's here too?' The weight near her shifted as Cole looked around the room.

Eira peered up into Cole's face. He had managed to squeeze onto the narrow bed and sat up against the headboard, an arm clutched around her, gently stroking her bare arm. Comforting her like he had before.

Eira was still lying on her side, her head resting almost against his chest. Through the fogginess in her brain, she noted that he was topless. Glancing down, she saw that he was wearing pyjama bottoms slung low on his hips. Despite everything else that she was feeling, Eira felt a blush rising in her cheeks. She was only wearing her T-shirt. Looking down, she saw that she was tangled in the quilt, a bare leg sticking out in the dark.

She knew that Cole wouldn't be able to see anything, but she still untangled the quilt and covered herself more fully, laying back against his shoulder. Cole tensed with her movement, his hand stopping his calming strokes, thinking that she was pulling away. But something about his warmth and scent made her remain.

Eira was shuddering uncontrollably, and his presence was helping ease the regret and sadness tied to the dream.

Cole's hands swept lightly down her shoulder again. 'My nightmares have returned since the whole mind extraction thing,' he whispered.

Sea salt drifted to her in the room's stillness.

Oran.

The door looked like it was ajar even though she was sure that Cole had closed it.

She recalled his command in her mind to wake up, right before she screamed. *Was he there?*

Eira tentatively pushed a kernel of her power towards their link, not wanting to disturb him if he was asleep. Oran was still struggling with the change to his sleeping pattern.

Oran, are you in my room?

Still no answer.

'Do you want me to get you a drink?' Cole asked, his breath rustling her hair.

Eira shook her head and then, remembering that he wouldn't see her, she answered, 'Nope, I'm honestly fine.'

Still the scent of sea salt hung in the air. She could feel her power pulling and shifting, telling her that Oran was nearby.

The Bloodstream flared, and a globule of light appeared floating above her hand. Eira sat bolt upright, staring at the soft white light. As she moved her hand, it moved too.

She glanced at Cole who leant forward, his hand on the mattress on the other side of her, his stunned face lit from below. His black hair glowed almost blue in the light.

Eira looked up, scanning the room with all her senses. The sea salt scent had faded.

Oran are you in my room? she shouted down the bond. Her anger at Oran, and Cole's comfort, had dispersed the nightmare.

Nowhere nearby. But you did wake me.

Are you doing this?

Mostly you, just with a push from me.

Care to explain?

Light might make you feel safer.

He repeated the words she had used when trying to help him with his claustrophobia in the tunnels.

We start training tomorrow.

Oran withdrew from their link and the light faltered, winking out. The room appeared even darker as her eyes readjusted to the gloom. Cole's increased breathing mirrored her own as they sat in the dark.

'I didn't think light was your superpower, more of a...' Cole left the sentence hanging as she felt him shift, scanning the dark.

'Superpower?' Eira queried, tilting her head to look at him.

Cole sighed and fell back against the headboard. 'That's what I call them. You know, like in the comics. All the superheroes have them.'

Eira snorted. 'Comics?' At Cole's confused look, she continued, 'I had a very sheltered childhood.' She saw the shock on Cole's face before he schooled his expression, remembering how good her vision was.

'Comics use a sequence of illustrations to tell a story. Characters normally speak with speech bubbles. There are some classics out there. Batman and Superman were my favourites as a kid.' Sadness filled his eyes as he thought of his childhood, his mouth pulling into a thin line.

Eira rested back against his shoulder. 'What would be my superhero name then?'

She sensed the grin that swept his face as he tightened his arm around her. 'Oh, I don't know... Super Healer or Doctor Magnificent!' Cole swept his hand grandly through the darkness.

Eira spluttered with laughter. 'What would Oran's be?' She sniggered, hoping that he wasn't within earshot. 'He does call himself Light Bringer,' Eira added.

'That fits, since Batman is already taken.' Cole shrugged.

'Oh, I have it! How about... Demon Invisible or Sneaking Bat?'

They both sniggered in the dark.

CHAPTER 22

⦀ EIRA

Eira woke to the warmth surrounding her, comforting and solid. She fluttered her eyelids open to a mop of black curly hair and steady breathing.

Cole.

In her bed.

Then she recalled the nightmare, Cole's comfort, and something about comics. Eira smiled as she remembered their last conversation. *How had I fallen asleep?* She rarely slept after the nightmare reliving her **mother's** murder. It sometimes twisted like it had last night, so that **she had her powers and couldn't do** anything to save her.

Eira gulped, stopping her flow of thoughts.

She raised her head from Cole's shoulder. In the night, he had slipped down onto the pillow, taking her with him. His head was turned to the side facing her, his raven-black hair obscuring an eye and his forehead. He looked so peaceful.

Eira found herself watching him, hands twitching to move the hair from his face. She recalled his words last night. Cole held his own grief, his own turmoil over his **mother's** death. Some of his personality made sense to her now. His quiet resolve, his determination to help others, and his loyalty.

Placing a hand on the mattress, she eased herself up within the narrow space between Cole and the wall. His exposed chest and healing scar snagged her attention. The wound was pink, neatly knitted back together, and she could see that it was time to remove the stitches. Eira gently laid a finger on his chest, tracing it from his pectoral to his stomach where his hand lay splayed across his belly button. Cole shifted under her touch but did not wake. The arm with which he'd been holding her groped in the empty space trying to find her. He tucked his arm under his head and rolled onto his side. Eira nimbly moved out of his way, slipping to the end of the bed.

Slipping on a pair of jeans she had worn a few days ago, not wanting to disturb the sleeping captain, she padded to the window. With the light starting to filter through the curtains, she guessed it was a couple of hours before dawn. Turning to exit the room, Eira paused. Her **mother's** letter and family photograph were on the chest of drawers. She was certain that she had left them on the floor. *Maybe Cole had placed them there?* The door was half-open.

Then Eira remembered the scent of sea salt. Oran.

Had he been in her room and lied about it?

Eira picked up the envelope, stuffing the contents back inside, irritation spiking. If she could find the gargoyle, she would take it up with him. Then she remembered his other words last night.

We start training tomorrow. For what?

Placing her mother's letter in her bag, Eira sighed. She was even more confused than she had been before.

Feeling restless, she tiptoed to the door, pausing to look over her shoulder at the sleeping captain. Debating storming into Oran's room, she hesitated. She knew that he was finding it hard to sleep at night, so waking him would lead to a full-blown quarrel.

Exhaling, Eira crept down the narrow stairs in the dimness.

The fire in the hearth, kept lit by Madam Scudamore, was the only light in the open-plan living area. Strolling to the kitchen, Eira wasn't surprised to see the ghost. As far as she knew, she never slept. Her feet floated inches above the floor as she moved a pan onto the ancient stove.

When Eira had first bought the house, the poltergeist had unnerved her with her sternness, but she had quickly become accustomed to it. Now Eira respected and secretly admired the ghost. To be bound to a house for five hundred years, much of that spent alone, she understood why she could be dismissive at times.

'So, over the stunning gargoyle you chose the skinny human?' Madam Scudamore asked, amber eyes sparkling with mischief.

Nothing happened in this house without her knowing. *Maybe she moved my* **mother's** *letter?* Their pact on Eira signing the deed for the house was that the ghost never interfered with her privacy, so Eira was certain that she hadn't. Sticking her nose into her business was allowed, but she couldn't meddle.

'I haven't chosen anyone,' Eira said hotly, putting her hands on her hips.

'Mm-hmm,' Madam Scudamore tutted, turning back to the stove.

Ignoring the ghost, her annoyance growing, she went to her work area. Opening and shutting cupboards more loudly than she normally would, Eira extracted the beakers and test tubes she needed for the experiment.

Allowing the methodology of her work to calm her, Eira first used a drop of Oran's infected blood, sucking it up with a pipette and placing it onto a slide. Tongue out in concentration, she angled the coverslip over the bottom slide and sealed it shut. Slipping the slide under her microscope, she angled her head to the viewing lens and had an initial look.

Leaning back, biting her lower lip, Eira considered what she could see; Oran's blood was different to any she had encountered before. It was pitch-black, for a start. Flecks of metallic silver glinted within it, showing his elven heritage. Her blood had them too. She needed more blood samples from different sources, but what she really needed was a sample of the virus before it had entered anyone's bloodstream.

Eira sighed, knowing how difficult it would be to get that.

A shudder swept through her as her flesh prickled. She turned to find Madam Scudamore's hand floating through her shoulder in what would have been a squeeze of comfort from anyone but a ghost. As a poltergeist, unlike other types of ghosts, she could move material items, but nothing made of flesh. That was why having her around was ideal for sneaking into shops to procure certain items where a blood tax was needed for entry. She couldn't stray far from the gatehouse, but as her master, Eira could give her certain privileges, and leaving the house was one of them.

The ghost's mouth was turned down, her eyes forlorn. She obviously understood enough of what was happening within the gatehouse to offer support.

A plate of steaming scrambled eggs and toast was placed on the counter beside Eira. She nodded her thanks, grateful for the care the ghost was showing. Her heart snagged, thinking of her aunt and how she used to take care of her too. She wondered if the tiny stone nightingale had made it to Scotland yet.

231

Despite the uneasiness settling in her, Eira shovelled the welcome food into her mouth. Over the next hour, as dawn broke over the horizon, Eira set up her next experiment to extract Oran's blood from the virus. Closing the lid of the centrifuge, Eira stretched out the tense muscles of her back, the temptation to send her own magic to ease the pain making her sigh. She needed to reserve her power for the day ahead.

'The human has risen,' Madam Scudamore's voice brought Eira back to the present. Lost in her work, she had forgotten the ghost was there. Cleaning her hands, Eira nodded to the housekeeper who had a bemused smile on her face, eyes twinkling in acknowledgment.

Making a quick exit, Eira approached the hidden door to the Nightingale, swiping up her purple Doc Martens from where she had chucked them the day before.

Why was she hiding from Cole? It wasn't like anything had happened. They had shared a bed, nothing more. *Or am I being naive?* Eira blew out her cheeks, slipping on her favourite pair of shoes in the comfort of the isolated corridor.

Eira went in search of her friend. It didn't take her long to find Elowen on the ground floor of the clinic. Unlike the disrepair of the Wallflower, Eira had spared no expense refurbishing the abandoned building into a clean, sterile hospital with some of the latest technology. It wasn't as sophisticated as the triplets' gadgets, but it was enough to get by. Obtaining supplies was almost impossible, but the Myth network had been large donors and benefactors to her cause.

They couldn't understand why she spent so much of her time at the Wallflower when she had her own hospital. She couldn't find the words to explain that she wanted to — *needed to* — help humans as well as Myths.

Eira had trained a team of Myths to oversee the patients. Her staff ranged from gnomes to tiny sprites. She never refused any species and gave them roles suited to their skillset or magical ability. None of them possessed her incredible power, but treating Myths was easier than humans since they healed a lot quicker. She was still called in from time to time, but it was only for emergencies.

As she sauntered through the clinic, she was met by nods from those she knew. To see an elf within their mix — even though she was only half-elf, and many were not aware she owned the premises — was unheard of. She was the only one of elven descent within her hospital, and sometimes new patients were suspicious of her. The elves had all but abandoned the lower classes within the city to their fate, closing their boundaries, and sealing themselves off from the mortal world. Most of them blamed the elves for the Myths' exposure and involvement in World War II.

Eira entered a room to find Elowen bent over a bed, examining a dwarf with a bottle opener on his chubby toe. Human objects caused a high percentage of the admittance to the clinic.

Elowen tutted, drawing air through her teeth as she placed her hands on her hips and stared at the dwarf, who seemed to sink into the bed further. 'Humpty, I have told you time and time again that bottle openers are not to be used as toenail clippers.'

The poor dwarf only nodded, his great, dirty-blonde beard wagging in time.

Eira stifled a grin. Elowen had settled in far more quickly than she had expected. The patients didn't seem to mind being treated by a human, but that might have been because Elowen made it hard not to like her. She, like Cole, had easily accepted the magical world and the dynamic range of characters within it. *Well, at least I hope Cole has.*

Elowen flicked her brown eyes to her, thick with makeup as usual. Eira had refused Elowen's request to wear her uniform and had insisted she dress as she was, her true self.

'Now, Humpty, you consider my advice whilst I get the Vaseline.' The obedient dwarf nodded once more, propping his hands on his round belly.

Elowen rolled her eyes, but Eira could see her friend's concern as she joined her.

'I was worried last night, Eira.'

Elowen was aware that Eira had finally opened her mother's keep-safe box. She didn't know who her mother was, or the circumstances surrounding her death, but she knew enough that Eira let the grief show on her face.

'That bad?' Elowen asked gently. 'I would have come to your room to comfort you, but we had a group of injured imps to take care of.'

Elowen had opted to live in a room at the clinic, much to Eira's protest. She wanted to be nearby in case she was needed. Eira suspected she was throwing herself into work to distract herself from thoughts of the Wallflower, Nora's death, and the increasing agent threat.

Eira needed to tell her friend something, so she said, 'It opened up more questions than answers to be honest.' It was true, but it certainly wasn't the full truth.

I finally know what my father looks like, and I am not sure that I want to, Eira thought but didn't say out loud.

Elowen squeezed Eira's shoulder like Madam Scudamore had, and, turning back around, gestured for her to follow. It seemed that she knew Eira needed a distraction too.

It was late afternoon when Oran contacted Eira. She had assisted Elowen on her rounds, quietly obeying her orders. The routine of helping others eased some of Eira's uncertainty. The cases she saw had been simple and treatable through non-magical methods. Even though she had hardly touched her magic, Eira still felt exhausted from being on her feet for most of the day with only a cheese sandwich as a snack.

Third floor. Come and find us. Oran's words through their bond were quick and to the point.

Eira stepped into the lift, pressing the button for the third floor. Her irritation flared on the slow ascent, prickling at the fact that he had so rudely summoned her.

The lift doors opened, and Eira walked down the narrow corridor to the large room at the back, following the sound of music. She stepped into the room and stopped, shocked.

All the blinds were shut, but there were dozens of globules of light floating near the ceiling.

The sound of bass vibrated the room. If Eira wasn't mistaken, it was Tupac.

The smell was the next thing that reached her, and it was so powerful it made her eyes water. Her heightened senses detected the underlying salt of Oran's scent and spice of Cole's before she rounded the corner.

Knowing that Oran had detected her as soon as the lift doors opened, she stood in the doorway and watched Cole, who was unaware of her presence.

He had been inventive with the building materials left behind from the work done previously on the Nightingale and created an obstacle course. As Eira watched, leaning against the doorframe, Cole ran, knees up to his chest, over a ladder laid on the floor. Squatting at the end, his back muscles rippled with strain as he held the position. Raising, he brought a knee up to his chest and rotated it back down, repeating the process with his other.

Turning to run back down the ladder, his breathing laboured, Cole caught Eira watching him. Colour crept into his already flushed cheeks as his eyes met hers and swept down again, his black hair obscuring them.

Eira twitched a smile as heat spread through her cheeks too. Embarrassed, she dropped her gaze to the floor. Her whole body felt too heavy, too tight, as she felt his eyes on her again.

Trying to control the feeling heating her body, Eira bit her bottom lip and risked a glance up. Cole stood, hands on hips, at the beginning of his ladder-run, slowing his breathing as sweat poured down his bare chest and a smile played on his lips.

Oran was the more muscular of the two. His body was thick with corded muscles, and his chest was rock solid. Cole, on the other hand, was slimmer, slight of shoulder and hips, athletic in an understated way. Firm toned muscle still graced his body, but he couldn't match Oran's strength.

A huge thud vibrated across the floor. Breaking their stare-off, Eira snapped her head up in time to see Oran stepping away from a giant stone column he had just set down.

The gargoyle was topless as well, his alabaster skin glinting with a sheen of sweat, his raised star constellations moving up and down with his heavy breathing. Oran flared his wings to their full width, flapping them once before tucking them against his back and rolling his shoulders. He really was a magnificent sight. He had tied his long mohawk at the base of his neck, his braids and trinkets ringing as he swivelled his neck, highlighting his chiselled jaw.

'Would one of you care to explain why I have a gym and half a church in my clinic?' Eira asked, folding her arms.

Cole sauntered over, using his T-shirt to mop the sweat from his neck, and gave a cheeky grin which made Eira feel hot all over again. What the hell was happening to her emotions today?

'Training,' came Oran's reply from across the room.

He had lined up six familiar stone columns in a grid of three by two. Moving closer to them, Cole trailing after her, she noted the strain on the gargoyle's face. He looked tired. Hauling six granite pillars would do that to even the strongest immortal, but it was more than that. He was weary, and his eyes were distant and closed off.

'Please tell me they are not from where I think they're from?'

A sparkle flared in those misted eyes before the shadow crept back into place.

'Oh, Oran, you didn't? How is the roof even being supported? Do you know how old that church is?'

Eira was secretly impressed that he had the strength to move them from their resting place, the historic church opposite, let alone fly them up and into the building.

'Great St Bart's is a medieval monument. It was commissioned in 1123. They are sacred grounds, the structure is listed,' Eira lectured, hands on hips.

His eyes still twinkled as he folded his arms and winked, radiating smugness.

Explain.

Training. Oran's reply.

Eira ground her teeth and threw her hands in the air, exasperated, turning to Cole who was watching their exchange, a slight smile on his lips.

Hands raised, Cole said, 'I just want to get back in shape, and whilst Batman over there was being a strong man shifting the pillars, I thought I'd do a workout.'

Eira's eyes softened. Of course, he would feel like that; he had talked about her and Oran having superpowers last night, so of course he would feel the need to train. Guilt and regret knotted her stomach. If only she had fully healed his wound, he wouldn't feel inadequate. Could I heal it now? Erase it like it never happened?

'The columns have suitable replacements,' Oran reassured her.

Eira raised an eyebrow. 'What do you need them for?'

'All in good time.' Switching to Elven, Oran said, 'Bloodstreams normally work one way, the stronger participant taking power from the weaker, generally to increase their own power. Ours seems to work differently. We can each draw from the other, intensifying our own power. It appears, as you have demonstrated, that you can harness my power. I would like to see if I can use your power as well.'

Eira nodded, remembering the glowing orb she had created last night. A thought occurred to her. 'So, might I be able to turn invisible as well?' Eira asked, speaking fluently in the ancient language.

'That took me a decade to master, so let's start with the basics,' Oran answered, chuckling.

'How about combining our powers like I did at the abbey?'

Oran nodded and shrugged his great shoulders as he stepped back, claws clipping on the concrete floor.

A shuffling sound drew Eira's attention away from their conversation. Cole had pulled on his T-shirt and was stalking out of the room, his shoulders tight.

'Hawk, wait!' Eira called.

The look of disappointment that greeted her when he turned was enough to make her feel guilty for isolating him. She held out a hand, pleading with him to wait. Angling her body to Oran, she said in the mortal tongue, 'Why are we speaking in Elven? Hawk has the right to know what we're saying.'

Cole's eyes widened as he stopped in the doorway, curiosity sparking in his blue eye.

'This connection isn't something to spread around, Eira. It's sacred. We have this for the rest of our existence. It can't be undone,' Oran replied steadily in Elven, a bite to his voice.

Eira widened her eyes in surprise at that, but what had she expected? Still, she pushed, irritated that they hadn't discussed this before. She kept her arm stretched towards Cole, but her full glare was targeted at Oran.

'Cole is part of this. He's already suspicious. What harm is there in telling him?' she almost snarled in Elven.

She felt her power surge, inflating to fill her body. Her power was normally so calm and steady, it was unusual for her to feel it writhing inside her the way it was.

'He is a means to an end. He's mortal, a human, that's all.' Oran's voice was like ice, dismissive.

Eira sucked in a sharp breath. 'You know that isn't true.'

They were still speaking Elven, and Eira was glad of it.

'You mean you've chosen.'

He was the second person to say that today.

Rage filled Eira, and she drew sharply on his magic. The gargoyle rocked on his hind legs, a flash of surprise crossing his face before he schooled his expression.

'Now give me the power to heal myself,' Oran demanded through gritted teeth as he sliced his crescent-shaped blade against his forearm.

Eira stilled. His movements were lightning quick as he slashed again, further up. Black blood welled in the cuts, a stark contrast to his ivory skin. Slowly, it began to run down his arm to his palm where it fell in droplets to the floor.

Eira stepped forward, flooded by her instinct to help him, but Oran moved back. The desire to protect and help Oran overcame her though, and her power flowed along their bond. Then she halted.

'You'll heal quickly enough on your own.' She folded her arms across her chest. A movement in her peripheral vision caught her eye. Cole quietly stepped to her side, watching.

'The bond will force your hand, Eira; the need to protect the other is overwhelming. Now, give me your power, so I can heal myself.' Oran drew the blade along his arm again.

Eira pursed her lips. 'Not until we tell Cole.'

Oran moved the dagger up further, angling it against his neck.

'You wouldn't dare!' Eira shouted, her eyes wide.

She propelled herself at Oran, but he took another stride back. The challenge in his eyes was enough to make Eira pause. He would do it just to prove a point. Depending on where and how deeply he cut, the wound could be serious, even for an immortal.

Eira watched as Oran flexed his fingers, sweeping the dagger from below his ear across his throat.

She sprang towards the gargoyle to wrestle the blade from his hand, but Oran was quicker, flying into the air with his neck sliced open, black blood dribbling down his chest.

Snarling, he set the blade to the other side of his neck as he hovered in the air. Eira gritted her teeth, her power swelling to an uncontrollable crescendo. She simply let go, and her magic naturally flowed along the Bloodstream, filling Oran with her power. Eira shuddered as the magic drained from her.

Cole gasped. The cuts on Oran's body sealed shut. He landed on the hard floor, his mouth set to a grim line, but his eyes shining with pride. Eira placed her palms on her knees, ragged breaths heaving in her chest. *Had this all been a test? Training, as Oran had stated?*

A seed of anger crept back in, and she was just about to yell at him when Oran started talking.

'Captain, what you've just witnessed is called a Bloodstream. Eira and I can pull on each other's power to give each other strength, as well as use the other's power themselves.'

Eira's head shot up, face full of surprise. She was stunned into silence.

'As you can imagine, we're only beginning to understand the implications of this. It is a rare bond that hasn't been seen in centuries, and never between those of different species.'

Oran's stare was piercing, but Cole didn't flinch as he stared back, processing the information.

This was a test, wasn't it? Eira spoke silently to Oran.

Oran shut his eyes, weariness crossing his face again.

You seem to use the bond when you have high emotions, he replied.

Like when I'm angry at you?

Oran nodded. *But you showed restraint under pressure. We need to learn a balance, to take too much power from the other could be devastating, to give too much could result in a major blowout. You also showed that you could hold back on giving power until it was necessary. We need to trust one another.*

Eira was stunned. Did she trust the gargoyle, with her life, and with her magic? But how had the Bloodstream even been created? She was worried it had been caused by her power, but she hadn't thought it possible. She dropped her gaze and sucked on her bottom lip, guilt clouding her thoughts.

So, I must learn to control my emotions?

Oran didn't reply but his silence was enough.

What causes your emotional trigger?

There was a long pause where Eira thought he wouldn't answer.

My trigger is something more dangerous than rage.

What could be more dangerous than anger?

What you said about Cole being a means to an end. Did you truly mean it? She had to know.

If you need to ask, you don't know me very well.

'You're doing it again, aren't you? That secret way of speaking to each other.' Cole's voice interrupted their internal conversation.

'It seems we can communicate telepathically through our bond,' Oran clarified.

Cole whistled, scraping his fingers through his hair which flopped back over his forehead. 'Superpowers indeed,' he mused.

A ghost of a smile tugged on Eira's lips as she remembered their conversation from the night before.

'Eira is adamant that you need to know about this, and I trust her judgement.'

Eira gasped in surprise. Even though Oran had questioned her before, Eira comprehended it was to get a reaction. She really had underestimated his motives. Guilt flooded her. He was right, she hadn't trusted him, but she vowed then that she wouldn't make that mistake again.

'What I don't trust,' Oran said, 'is the other immortals in this game we now find ourselves tied up in. I'm worried that they will use our bond for their own gain. Most likely with force. I'm tired of being a pawn in their power-plays. Today we decide our own fates.'

Oran's voice was fierce, full of passion and determination.

'What I suggest is an oath which will forbid us to discuss our Bloodstream with anyone outside of the three of us. You can think about it of course, but if you ever try to speak about it in front of others, you will be stopped and forget what you were going to say. I have similar bindings with Nelka and Callan.'

Eira was curious as to what those bindings might be. She looked at Cole, his eyes wide and his mouth open. Eira caught his eye, and he flashed her one of his handsome half-grins which melted her heart. She knew his answer.

She inhaled, preparing for another question, but Oran held up a long finger for her to wait.

'I have authority to offer protection to other gargoyles seeking safety on the clan's behalf. As you're not a gargoyle, I would probably be exiled for even suggesting it. So, I can't offer that kind of safety, but I can offer my personal guardianship which will extend to Nelka and any members of her family. So, in a backwards way, you would both have the protection of the clan. I can tie it into the oath.'

Eira's throat was clogged with emotion, but she rushed to Oran, throwing her arms around the gargoyle's waist, her head barely reaching his lower chest. Staggering backwards, Oran gently patted her back.

Thank you, she said through their bond.

Oran's words echoed in her mind. *You do not have to do this alone.*

Did this mean they stood a chance? Suddenly feeling self-conscious, Eira eased back, her eyes blurring.

Cole, who had watched the whole exchange with a bemused smile, shrugged. 'What do we need to do for this oath thing?'

'Simply present your arm and my magic will do the rest. There will be a mark on your flesh.' Oran indicated the crescent moons beside his eyes.

Cole confidently extended his left arm. Eira raised her left arm then slipped it behind her back, remembering the sun mark already there. She presented her right arm instead. Oran gathered both their wrists in his large hands, bending, he looked them both in the eye.

'Do you both submit to this oath, which is a promise that will hold you until Lunar takes you?' His gaze was mesmerising, his swirling white eyes commanding.

Cole glanced across at Eira, unease spreading across his face. He gulped, nodded once, and with a steady voice replied, 'I submit,' without removing his eyes from hers. Without realising, she grasped Cole's spare hand, squeezing it once.

Eira repeated, 'I submit,' looking at Cole.

This was more than just a bonding of a secret, it was something more, a possible future, a way out of the segregation between their races. If they could work together, maybe there would be hope for others. Excitement spread through her at the thought of the future they could build together.

Warmth enveloped her wrist. It wasn't the blazing heat she had felt when Storm marked her; this was gentle, a caress. She watched as Oran's palm glowed with his starlight, his closed eyes creased in the corners as he concentrated. Eira could have sworn the music playing in the background, the distant traffic, the clinic itself, paused as their agreement was made. The world held its breath, hope kindled for a better future.

The sensation ceased as abruptly as it had begun. Oran released their wrists, straightening, tucking his wings around his shoulders. Eira knew what she would find when she looked at her inner forearm: a crescent moon embossed into her skin.

Cole glanced at his own arm, turning it over. He raised an eyebrow, head tilted to the side. 'I don't feel any different, do you?'

Eira felt no different, but everything had changed for her in that moment. She glanced down and noted that her hand was still clasped in Cole's, a connection that felt entirely natural.

CHAPTER 23

ORAN

Oran, perched on the roof of the Nightingale, traced the new marking on his forearm. Like Cole and Eira's, it was the shape of a crescent moon, the symbol of his clan. He would be exiled for unofficially making them part of his clan if anyone were to find out. Callan's temper was explosive at the best of times, so he dared not think about his reaction to what Oran had done. He only hoped that, given his status, his relationship to Callan's daughter, and the current issue of the virus's potential to infect immortals, he might be able to talk him round. He needed the clan's support if their plans were to succeed.

How could I not protect Eira?

He had been right beside her through her nightmare the other night, seeing and feeling everything that she did. After that, he was even more intent on protecting her and keeping her safe as her ... what? How to describe their relationship? *Am I a friend? Partner?* They were connected, whether they wanted to be or not. Oran couldn't bring himself to tell Eira that he'd had a brief snapshot of her mind when she relived her mother's death. It was too private, too personal. But if he had accidentally done it to her, could she do the same to him? Oran hoped not.

The days following their oath had settled into a comfortable routine. Oran would practice with Eira or watch her doing her rounds at the Nightingale. Cole had introduced a shooting range, running track, and rope climb to their training. Oran knew the human felt undermined by his and Eira's abilities and was making up for his mortal disadvantage by practicing hard. Oran had to hand it to Cole, he was dedicated.

Oran sighed and his gaze drifted to the stagnant, grey clouds as the mist fell, soaking him. He had stopped wearing the suncream, his pale skin having grown acclimatised to the sun. He still wore aviation goggles, but more for comfort than necessity.

A nudge alerted him to Oswald's presence. The chimera butted his hand, seeking attention, his flat face crumpled and twisted to the side as Oran scratched him behind the ear. Oswald rumbled with contentment. He gave Oran security, a constant reminder of his life before he had embarked on this mission. He was surprised his father hadn't been in contact. Oran had sent several messages to Nelka and the clan giving them reassurance, but he had been cowardly and hadn't attempted to do the same to his father.

Oran stood, needing to fly to clear the thoughts tumbling in his head. He flared his wings, enjoying the breeze and light rain on them as he rolled his shoulders.

He had not taken the binding oath with Cole and Eira lightly. He understood its importance. Why his biological father never bound him in that way he wasn't sure. He had much more severe forms of doing so than an oath.

Oran needed to ensure that their bond would be hidden from the high races. He didn't want Eira bound to a higher authority the way he was. Bringing Cole into the oath had not been part of the plan, but the fury on Eira's face at his exclusion was enough to convince him. He knew that if he left Cole out, he would have lost Eira's trust in the process. What he didn't understand was why keeping her trust was so important. He knew he should just return home to Lunula, forget about the Bloodstream and this virus, but he couldn't. No matter how hard he tried, he physically couldn't leave. The bond was too strong. But it wasn't only that keeping him at the gatehouse. He was ready to take control of his own life, and to not let himself be used anymore. He needed to establish his own path, a new future for his children, where discrimination was a forgotten word.

Oran launched skywards, enjoying the familiar rush as his wings flared behind him, holding him still in the sky. He disappeared most mornings to fly and scout, keeping track of the Dark's movements. Power-sharing with Eira was starting to take its toll, draining his magic reserves. Oran knew the simple answer. He needed to sleep, but he was finding it tough adjusting to resting in a bed at night, instead of turning to stone. He knew that Eira was aware of his struggles, but he was too proud to ask for help.

Alighting on the open window in the corridor leading to their training room, Oran paused, picking up on the racket that Cole called music.

Scenting that they were both in the room, Oran made himself invisible. He drifted closer to the open door, watching.

Cole sat on a stool amongst the makeshift obstacle course, facing Eira, whose back was to the doorway. She was wearing leggings and a cropped vest, her feet bare. It was common in his clan for females to have their bodies exposed, so it wasn't a shock for him to see the creamy expanse of her back. Her head was bent slightly as she manipulated something against the captain's exposed chest.

Oran edged into the room to observe Eira cutting away his stitches. Cole gritted his teeth as Eira gently snipped and pulled the fine threads out with long-handled tweezers. The background music changed to a song without the heavy bass, a slow melody. Cole grinned, his eyes dancing across Eira's face. Eira looked up, her lips twitching as her eyes searched his face. Cole ran his knuckles down Eira's spine, his thumb trailing behind. It was such a tender gesture that Oran went to leave the room, embarrassed that he was intruding.

Eira had chosen and she wasn't even aware.

I know you're there, came Eira's voice in his head, laced with amusement.

How?

Your power flares down the bond when we're close to one another, and I'm attuned to your scent by now.

Oran was silent; he would have to be more vigilant in blocking their link. Eira couldn't do it yet, but he had figured out how, his century of knowledge, and his other bindings helping with the process. He must make this part of their training once Eira had mastered her emotions.

Nelka is the only other one who can detect my presence.

Eira was quiet as she finished with the captain's stitches.

You were in my room the other night.

Oran paused, contemplating how to answer. He had come to check on her after her nightmare had woken him. The nightmare still haunted his own dreams. Seeing Cole comforting her, his arms wrapped around her, had stopped Oran in his tracks.

You said you wouldn't be sharing a bed with the captain, he replied.

Eira's head jerked, her eyes darting around the room, trying to locate him. Her cheeks flamed red.

I'm putting a lock on the door. Eira clicked her tongue, huffing.

'Batman is in the room, isn't he?' Cole asked. His arm naturally rested on her lower back but neither of them seemed to be aware of the contact.

'Yes, Sneaking Bat has made an invisible appearance. Is he going to grace us with his presence?' The last part was louder.

Cole sniggered.

Oran dropped his camouflage, his wings wrapped around his shoulders as he leant against the wall nearest the stone columns. He didn't want them to know how close he had been to their intimacy.

'Sneaking Bat? Is that a new code name?' Oran asked, nonchalantly inspecting his nails.

Eira snorted, trying not to laugh. Cole's mouth twitched but he held himself together.

'Yes, that's your new code name, and I'm apparently Super Healer.'

Eira turned back to Cole, her expression becoming professional once more. Slipping back into doctor mode, even though her patient had an arm around her waist, idly drawing circles on her exposed flesh, she said, 'Stitches all out, Hawk. The wound has healed well.'

Eira sucked on her bottom lip. Oran knew she was weighing something up in her mind.

Taking a deep breath, she added, 'With the virus contained, I think I can heal your wound and erase the scar.'

Eira moved a hand to Cole's scar, ready to summon her power. Cole gently grabbed her hand, lowering it to his knee.

'I don't want to forget this scar, what it means. The people I've lost and am fighting for. The people I have met because of it. I wear it proudly.'

Well said, brave mortal, Oran thought.

Eira held Cole's gaze for what felt like an eternity.

Oran raised his head to the ceiling, his heart aching for connection with another. His soul cried out for Neika. Oran ground his teeth, the broken sleep and strain on his power was making it hard to focus.

He cleared his throat. Eira spun around, her face dazed. She shook her head, stepping out of Cole's embrace; the look of longing on Cole's face was clear.

246

The next few hours passed in a blur of frustration and endless patience. Both could draw power from one another easily without much concentration. Their types of power enabled them to manage the flow and amount they took from one another without over-drawing and emptying the other's resources. It helped that their power reserves were vast.

Using each other's powers was where the challenge lay. The effect that Eira's power had on Oran was all-consuming, it numbed his senses, and he found it hard to concentrate when trying to heal himself; his sleep deprivation wasn't helping. Oran could see the positives of having healing magic when in battle, but he could never be a healer.

Eira was far better at blending their powers — she had mastered a basic shield and light globule within the first day of training. She naturally fed her own power into his without being aware, one reason why Oran left their connection open. But despite her competence with other aspects of his power, Eira struggled to manipulate stone.

Her rage had subsided, but frustration had taken over. Eira groaned, throwing her hands in the air, exasperated. For the last half an hour she had been trying to manipulate a rock, turning it from round to square. All she had managed was eroding the surface, which was at least a step up from the previous day.

'Why do I need to know how to do this? Isn't manipulating your moonlight enough?'

Oran, perched on an empty stool, his lids hooded with exhaustion, replied, 'It is enough, Eira, like it's enough that I can heal myself using your power, but if we are ever going to completely blend our powers, you must learn concentration with my power, and this is the way to do it. All new things are difficult to begin with. Have patience.'

Eira puffed out her cheeks, exhaling her frustration. Oran smirked, not bothering to open his eyes. The muffled gunshots from Cole could be heard in the silence that developed between them. He was practicing in his makeshift gun-range, and it seemed he was a pretty good shot. Oran much preferred his staff or blades to a gun, but he understood the importance of them to a mortal. Being able to inflict damage from a distance without being in peril.

He suddenly felt alertness sweep his body and, opening his eyes, he saw Eira standing in front of him, her foot tapping.

'Falling asleep on the job, Light Bringer?' she asked with a smile.

I know you haven't been sleeping, she said in his head when he didn't reply. *I could...*

I know you could, he answered, cutting her off.

Oran growled, pushing himself to his feet. He prowled past her to the edge of Cole's firing range. Cole paused, sensing the tension, and pulled off the ear defenders, placing them around his neck. Head tilted to one side, he cleared his hair away from his black eye and looked at them both in question. Oran felt like storming out, flying away from their concerned looks.

'Fight me for it then.'

Oran whipped around to Eira.

'Fight me for my help. If I win, you let me help you sleep until you can manage it on your own.'

His jaw dropped in surprise. He couldn't believe she was suggesting this, but the look on her face was fierce and determined. He must have finally fallen asleep, and this was a weird dream. Shaking his head, Oran gulped, touching the tip of his pointy ear. Not a dream, because in his dreams, he didn't have these ears.

'You do know that I'm one of the most lethal warriors in my clan? I've trained in combat since I was six years old, both on the ground and in the air.'

'So, you won't have a problem beating me then.'

He didn't understand. He was huge compared to her, and she was a healer not a fighter. But then he remembered how easily she had handled the daggers in the abbey. Maybe she could fight.

'First to draw blood. Two rules. One, no magic or draining one another's power, and two, definitely no invisibility tricks.'

She sauntered past him, eyebrows raised as she pointed to him in challenge. Oran glanced at Cole for support, but he only shrugged, his gaze following Eira as she padded across the room to her sword. He looked intrigued, concerned but bemused.

Oran shrugged, drawing out his staff. Taking a fighting stance, he unfolded his wings from his shoulders, flapping them once before snapping them tightly against his back.

Eira took position a few metres away, drawing her new sword from the sheath. He could have sworn that a pulse vibrated down the bond. The Skye blade sucked in the light, muted purple and blue in the presence of his orbs lighting the room. Oran noted that Cole had moved to lean against the wall, giving himself a better view of the fight.

Eira held her blade loosely in one hand at her side, her feet together, her guard completely open.

'Are you sure you know how to use that?'

In the space of time that it took Oran to taunt her, Eira struck. She closed the space between them in two leaps, bringing the sword down in an arc to slash at his side. Caught off-guard, Oran parried the move, rotating his staff vertically and stepping back to keep his balance. A dull thud sounded as the short sword glanced off his staff, vibrating his arm. Oran twisted his staff upwards to knock into Eira's face, removing a hand from the grip, but she had already pivoted out of range, and his staff met thin air. He brought it up to his shoulder, spinning it around his neck and back down in defence.

Oran couldn't help himself; he crouched, baring his teeth and snarling. Eira's grin was wicked as she stood in front of him. She didn't hesitate and struck again, this time striking towards his other side, where he easily countered the attack, her sword scraping along the staff. Oran used his strength to propel Eira backwards. She kept her footing, bending low, twisting on the spot, and thrusting the sword up towards his thigh. The sound of metal on wood reverberated through the room as her sword met the staff. Eira grinned, her eyes lit with excitement. Oran stepped back, pivoting his weight onto his back foot. Like a ballerina, Eira rose on her toes and thrust at his chest, but Oran brought his staff up, deflecting the blow.

Again and again, Eira used her agility to thrust and sweep her sword, trying to gain an opening, pushing Oran back. She was far more skilled than he had given her credit for.

He was enjoying the thrill of a fight with an opponent who was well matched without any tricks; he was so used to using his magic to his advantage, it felt good to have a simple spar.

Oran smirked and sprang in the air, using his claws to propel himself off the floor. He somersaulted, head over feet, and landed behind Eira, his wings flaring to counter his landing. He vaguely heard a gasp which must have been Cole.

'Who trained you? From what age?' he asked, breathing heavily.

'An elf named Pyke. I started training at twelve. Not as early as you, but I made up for it.'

The elf part surprised him.

Oran rotated his staff in a figure-eight, one-handed, flipping it across his knuckles and back to his palm just for the fun of it. He nimbly spun it into his other hand. He started to circle, waiting for Eira to attack, but she didn't. Cole had stepped from the wall, his eyes flickering between them both.

'Are you going to admit you need my help and draw a line under this fight, or are you going to show me your spinning tricks all day?' Eira jeered.

Oran smiled, a snarl escaping. 'If you're this good with one blade, how are you with two?'

He deftly twisted his staff, breaking it apart and activating the hidden spike on the other end. Eira's eyes widened in surprise as Oran rushed at her.

My turn.

Eira twisted her blade in defence as he slammed both parts of his staff against the sword, throwing his weight behind it. She gritted her teeth with the effort of holding him off, knees slightly bent. Oran removed one section of staff from the blade and thrust downwards towards her side. The ebony wood met metal with a loud grinding sound. He looked down in surprise to find Eira had miraculously split her sword in half, deflecting the blow.

He had wondered if it could do that, and now his suspicions were confirmed. There were only a handful of magical weapons in existence that could, his staff being one of them.

Knowing she didn't have the strength to hold him, Eira sprung backwards, using Oran's weight to make him stagger, but his wings held him up. She freely windmilled both swords in her hands, eyebrows arched, grinning in challenge.

Oran launched forward, swinging the separate parts of the staff in different directions. Eira mirrored his moves with her swords, parrying them both. Then she moved out of his reach before he could apply his weight to the attack. She was forever on the move, never seeking the advantage, only deflecting. Like a dancer never wanting to be held. The fight continued as Oran's frustration grew, exhaustion weighing on his shoulders. Cole's face was a blur as they continued their chase.

He had always been taught to attack, swift and brutal, to kill an opponent quickly and effectively using strength and bulk. Nelka and Gaia, who were taught by the same masters, never lasted this long against him.

Oran halted in the middle of the room, a thought suddenly occurring to him. Sunrise elves.

Eira either didn't hear his thought, or simply wanted to take advantage of his hesitation. Instead of defending, she sped towards him, bare feet slapping on the floor. Oran instantly lifted his staff, slotting the sections back together with an efficient twist as he braced his feet apart, aiming the staff horizontally to take Eira's impact. If this had been a fight to the death, he simply would have thrown his staff at her like he had the agent in the flying craft.

Eira, swords in both hands, a look of determination on her face, winked as she suddenly dropped to the floor, momentum carrying her beneath the staff, and sliding between his clawed feet. Oran felt warmth seeping from his ankle. He glanced down to see her honey hair disappear behind his legs. To his astonishment, his right ankle was bleeding from a slice near his shin. His wound quickly healed as his power naturally absorbed hers.

Oran turned to Eira, watching her gasp for breath as she knelt on the floor. Cole stood at the edge of their sparring circle looking stunned, his gaze darted to Oran as he snapped out of his stupor and jogged over to Eira. He knelt in front of her, hands soothing her shoulders in gentle swipes. Oran was surprised Eira had let him approach. The primal energy flooding through her would be enough to make her edgy.

'You were trained by a Sunrise elf, weren't you?'

Oran watched as Cole presented his hand, hauling Eira to her feet. She turned, confusion lighting her face as she swept her hair back. Cole stepped away, keeping quiet. He always let Eira have space, lead when she wanted to, and offer comfort when required. It was like he was in tune with her needs.

'I'm not sure where Pyke comes from,' she said. 'He's old, I know that. He remained throughout my teenage years to train me in his fighting technique. I mastered different weapons and hand to hand combat under his guidance. He never talked much about his past.'

Oran nodded, sheathing the staff along his spine. 'Are his ears punctured with star shapes?' he asked, indicating his own ears.

'Yes,' Eira breathed. 'As a child, I was always fascinated that I could see the light through his ears. Do you know him?'

'I know of him.' Oran shook his head in disbelief but continued, 'Pyke comes from a brotherhood of elves called Sunrise. Since long before anyone can remember, they have been the gargoyles' protectors by day. They are an elite force trained to take on opponents with their speed and agility. They don't immediately attack but look for opportunity, reading their opponents strengths and weaknesses. They're specialists in deception. There are not many left these days, only a small special task force remains at the keep, protecting Callan when he rests during the day. It is the only inter-species alliance existing today.'

Eira blinked slowly, processing his words.

Oran continued, 'I've sparred with a few, so I'm aware of their techniques. Your skillset is astonishing, Eira. That blade suits your fighting style. It's almost as if it was made for you.'

Eira looked at him, sadness and regret filling her eyes, but she still didn't say anything.

Oran shrugged. 'You won, so I'll accept your help.'

Eira simply nodded, looking anything but pleased with herself. Cole caught his attention; he had retrieved his tablet. The captain nodded once before stating, 'The League have replied.'

CHAPTER 24

⫿⫿ EIRA

Her heart still hammering, Eira tried to focus on what Cole was saying, but her head felt fuzzy. The sparring match with Oran had been intense. Knowing his pride wouldn't allow him to ask her for help, she had orchestrated the fight, and Oran was a worthy opponent, but she hadn't been prepared for his strength. If Oran had been at full capacity, Eira knew she would have struggled. But she had engineered the outcome she had wanted and had lost the tension and frustration which had been building within her the last few days.

Looking at the males in front of her, she didn't register their words or expressions. She was in a daze.

Oran had known Pyke or was at least aware of him. Sunrise elf. Defender of the gargoyles. She should be excited that she had finally found a coexistence between two races, but suspicion outweighed the delight. Why had she been trained by such a skilled weapons master? Had they planned for this? And then she had been given the swords. Nothing made sense anymore.

'I need to go,' Eira said in a flat voice.

Eira headed for the door, hearing footsteps behind her, she didn't turn as she entered the corridor. A warm hand wrapped around her waist, turning her gently. She looked up into mismatched eyes that searched her face. Cole was so close his breath tickled her cheek. His hands rested on her exposed hips, and heat swept through her body at his touch.

Eira was new to whatever this was. Since her nightmare, he had been a reassuring presence with gentle touches, caresses so natural that Eira knew he wasn't even aware of what he was doing. Eira had allowed it, knowing that Cole needed the comfort as much as she did. Since reading her mother's letter she had felt unhinged, questioning everything she had ever known.

'What's wrong, Doc?' he asked.

Eira liked the nickname, it felt personal. She had started calling him Hawk, suspecting only close friends called him that. Like her, he had allowed it.

253

'Nothing,' she muttered, stepping out of his hold.

His hands dropped to his sides. Cole's mouth twisted into a smile which sent butterflies leaping inside her stomach.

'You just kicked Oran's ass with your super-ninja moves and you haven't even gloated about it.'

Eira knew that he was trying to lighten the mood and make her smile. 'I did that for his own benefit.'

'Still, I've never seen a fight like that. You were both incredible. Your skill with that sword was mesmerising.'

Eira's anger spiked, and her eyes flared. 'You mean my deception? That's what Oran said.'

Cole reached forward, hand catching her wrist and sliding down to her palm. 'He didn't mean it that way, and you know it.'

Eira did, but she wasn't ready to back down.

'Come on, Eira, this is what we have been waiting for: a reply. We need your input,'

'Do you? All you need is Oran's help to reach your goal and then my necklace. You don't need me.'

Eira yanked her hand from his grip.

Cole tilted his head, his mouth a thin line, his jaw tight. Disappointment crossed his handsome face, letting Eira know that she had gone too far.

'You know that isn't true, Doc. This was your plan,' Cole stated coolly.

It was true, but everything was so confusing right now. Her past seemed like it had been twisted, manipulated to get her to where she was now.

'I need to think, Hawk,' Eira said, turning to go.

She knew that Cole would normally give her space, but they had been skirting around their feelings all week, and it seemed like Cole was ready to push.

'Come on, Eira. Let's talk this through,' Cole pleaded, hand catching hers again.

Eira whirled on him, eyes blazing. Her pulse spiked, and she clenched her spare hand. 'You do not need my help on this one. When you've achieved your goal, you'll have what you want, and then you'll go back to the League.'

Eira hadn't meant to say that out loud, and she raised her hand to her mouth as if she could push the words back in. Cole stared at her, eyes wide in surprise. He took a sharp breath. Eira spun around and ran down the corridor to the stairs, not wanting to wait for the lift and see the hurt on his face.

The stairs were a blur as she thundered down them.

Eira didn't pause as she slammed her hand against the biometric reader on the hidden door and entered the stillness and quiet of the gatehouse. Crossing the living room with a curt nod to Madam Scudamore, she ran up the stairs, taking them two at a time. Throwing open the door to her room, she clicked it shut behind her. Only then did Eira hesitate, resting her back against the door.

She scanned their room. They might sleep in separate beds, but the belongings scattered throughout were merged, shared. They were both untidy; clothes lay scattered everywhere, her hairbrush was on his bed, his flat cap hanging off her bedpost, a dismantled gun sitting on top of the adjoining chest of drawers. Madam Scudamore would rip her hair out if she was allowed in here. Tears prickled her eyes, and Eira closed them, pinching the bridge of her nose. She took a steady breath.

Eira knew she would find no solace in here with the risk of Cole coming to find her. She knew that Oran would feel her distress through the bond and hoped that he would give her the space she needed.

Retrieving her boots from under the bed, Eira pulled on a pair of semi-clean socks. She really needed to get on top of the washing. She looked around for her leather jacket before remembering it had been lost in the blaze at her apartment. Tears threatening to consume her again, Eira spied Cole's beloved leather jacket on his bedpost.

Without a second thought, she grabbed it, stuffing her arms inside the worn fabric. The smell of spice immediately surrounded her. This was a bad idea. She nearly removed the jacket but couldn't bring her body to see it through.

Needing to keep busy, Eira retraced her steps back downstairs as quickly as she had ascended them.

'Is the house on fire?' Madam Scudamore called as Eira flew past. Taking the stairs to the basement at the same speed, Eira didn't slow until she entered the chill and darkness of the Myth tunnels.

Her feet guiding her, bend after bend, Eira let her mind settle, her pulse regulate. Questions still swirled in her head, but she was able to work through them.

She knew she couldn't answer the questions that had arisen from her mother's letter without returning to Scotland. Or finding her father, something which filled her with trepidation. At least she knew what he looked like now. She should show Oran the photo and ask if he recognised him. But Eira hesitated at the idea. He was so closed off about his elven heritage, she didn't want to upset him.

The sword was her next dilemma. *The bearer must win their trust, form an unbreakable bond with them. Someone true of heart.* Wielding the sword had been exhilarating, explosive. They had been so well-balanced, and it had fit perfectly in her hands. Eira had promised herself that she wouldn't use them, but the temptation was too strong to resist.

But these things were impossible until she had completed her current task. She needed to find a pure strain of the virus to help her make an antidote.

Feet echoing in the damp tunnel, Eira relied on her night vision, wishing her gargoyle protector was with her for his light. She then remembered and reached for his magic, trying to create a globule of her own, but she was met with a stone wall.

Staggering, Eira leant against a curved arch. *Am I too far away?* She tried again, panicking that she couldn't reach the moonlight and stardust which had become so familiar to her. Had Oran worked out how to break the connection? He said it was permanent, irreversible. Her eyes narrowed. That gargoyle had some explaining to do when she returned. In her heart, she knew that he had sealed the bond to give her space, but she was still angry that she wasn't able to draw on his reassuring power.

Which left the Cole problem — at least this one was manageable. It was obvious how he felt. *But what do I truly feel?* Her sheltered life meant she had no experience with relationships, romantic or platonic.

Sighing, Eira neared the tunnel with the illusion masking the Alchemists' workshop. She rapped on the door three times, and it immediately swung open for her. Stepping over the threshold, Eira let her eyes adjust to the brightness.

She was greeted by Darwin, who grabbed her hand and pulled her towards the platform at the back, his excitement obvious.

'Hey, slow down there.'

But the gnome didn't slow, leading her around their living space to the monitors at the back. Eira found herself sat in the task chair, the triplets surrounding her, their hands signing rapidly.

'Hey, slow down, one at a time. I can't understand when you all speak at once,' Eira said, holding her hands up.

Isambard elbowed his brothers out of the way, taking charge for once. Pushing to the front, staring at her wide-eyed, Isambard carefully laid three objects in Eira's cupped palms. One was her opal necklace, glowing softly in the artificial light. The other two objects were simple bracelets made from titanium. Eira flipped the bangles and saw a small white opal attached to each.

Eira looked up with a gasp. Had they done it? Isambard, guessing her question, signed: 'Maybe.'

With the three of them signing, gesturing, and showing her drawings, slowing them down at times and asking questions, she was finally able to establish what they had created.

Eira held out her hands finally, halting the Alchemists. 'Right, so let me get this straight.' She held up her necklace. 'This is constructed from a material you've never seen before? It's neither natural nor man-made, but it contains ancient powerful magic within the opal?'

Darwin nodded, his large ears wobbling with the gesture. He held up his three stumpy fingers.

'And you think that the three lines on it are elven? Based on that picture?'

Eira indicated the faded parchment they had presented to her. Yellowed with age, it was hard to see the three tall figures in silhouette upon the crest of the hill, the central one taller than the others. They did indeed look like the symbol on her opal, but it was a tenuous link. They suspected it was elven because of the text below which read: *At the beginning there were three.* Eira snapped a photo of the image with her phone, not wanting to disappoint the triplets.

'So, what about the bullets I gave you?' she asked, indicating the plastic tray with the dust and fragments of the cracked shells.

'The outer case is easy to define. It's magnetite which is an iron ore, one of the most magnetic of all the naturally occurring minerals on Earth,' Isaac signed to her.

He demonstrated by setting a magnet near the tray, the fragments of the bullet flying straight at it.

'The virus is harder to define. It appears to be a combination of ancient magic, technology, and some kind of organic matter — probably blood — which is hard to separate. The magic is dark.'

Eira nodded, watching their hands form the signs as they gestured excitedly.

'The most important discovery was that, when cracked open, the virus doesn't escape. It seems to only be triggered by contact with flesh or blood, and uses the organic matter to spread, multiply, and take over the host,' they signed.

Eira was struggling to keep up with their rapid hand movements, but she caught enough to understand what they were saying. She remembered Cole's description of his attack, especially the gas that was first thrown into the warehouse. She shuddered to think of how quickly the virus could spread in gaseous form. She had read about the gas chambers used during the war on mortals and immortals alike.

It raised one question: who was the controlling force behind the virus?

The brothers continued signing, excited to share what they had found out. 'We've taken fragments of the virus-infected bullet and set them in a casement, as close to the genetic makeup of the one on your necklace as possible.' They held up the bracelets, an opal shining on each one.

'They need to be charged with magic to activate them. We think that by pouring your healing magic into them, they will be able to work in the same way as your necklace and extract the virus from a victim.'

'And protect the wearer from being infected too?' Eira asked.

Darwin nodded, grinning.

'I don't even know what to say. Thank you so much! This is more than I ever expected. The only problem is that the virus repels my magic; it doesn't seem to have any effect on it.'

Isambard stepped forward and tapped a yellowed nail against the crescent moon on the inside of her forearm.

She had to use the Bloodstream. Knowing she wouldn't be able
to discuss it with them, she just nodded her understanding.

CHAPTER 25

X COLE

Cole bent, fishing out what appeared to be a dirty sock from under his bed. He lobbed it into the nearly full laundry basket in the corner of the room. He had spent the last few hours sorting and tidying their room since they were both as messy as each other. It had made him laugh to begin with, but now it was just adding to his annoyance.

His music selection reflected his current mood: dark and moody. Eminem ft. Dido's 'Stan' started playing, filling the room.

Cole sighed, straightening as he sat on the edge of the bed. He should feel lighter, more at ease now that the League had finally deemed him worthy of a reply. But the confrontation with Eira had muddied the water.

When you've achieved your goal, you'll have what you want. You'll just go back to the League.

Eira's words reverberated in his head as he mulled them over yet again. Is that what she was worried about? He knew there was more to it, her **mother's** letter being the main catalyst. Despite his oversharing, she had not sought his counsel and had instead disappeared. Cole knew better than anyone that sometimes grief could only be worked out on your own, but he could sense that it had built up so much within Eira that she was a ticking time-bomb.

Cole braced his exposed arms on his knees, his sweater pulled up to his elbows, and traced a finger over the crescent moon. *I submit.* When he said that, he had meant it with regards to the oath, but also to Eira. He knew he was overthinking her motives for disappearing, but he couldn't help it.

As Oran had stated, they were a team.

Only, they weren't acting like one, disappearing and keeping secrets when plans finally had to be made. The meeting was in forty-eight hours, and his team members were nowhere to be found.

Oran had vanished too when Cole returned to the training room after pursuing Eira. Not knowing what to do, Cole had headed back to the gatehouse. Madam Scudamore told him that Eira had sped through like the house was on fire. At least that meant he wouldn't have to confront her whilst she was in a bad mood. It had given him time to think.

The door latch clicked, and Cole bolted to his feet, hoping it would be Eira. He still felt like a guest, but it was clearly their room based on the amount of stuff they had acquired in the last week. Eira opened the door, pausing in the entryway when she saw him.

Walking in, she pushed the door closed behind her and leant against it, her gaze flickering to his and then sweeping the room. Eminem still played through the speakers, the angry beat thumping on his eardrums. He bent to grab his tablet and turned the music off, savouring the silence that followed. He waited, hoping that she would speak first. He didn't want to argue with her, but he also knew that they needed to get things out in the open.

He glanced down at his feet, letting his hair fall over his eyes, nerves rattling through him. He had never been this way around women before, but Eira was different.

Cole risked a glance. Eira was studying her feet too, her purple boots crossed at the ankles.

'You cleaned up,' she said quietly, indicating the clean room.

Cole shrugged. He had done well given the state of the room. The clean clothes were in the chest of drawers, and the dirty ones in a pile ready to be washed. He had even made the beds. Eira glanced at her bag and the sword propped against it. They were the only things that he hadn't touched.

'I was looking for something,' Cole answered.

Amusement crinkled her eyes; she knew exactly what he was looking for.

'Where have you been?' Cole asked carefully.

'Sorry I ran off with your jacket,' Eira said, shrugging out of it.

Cole stepped forward, raising his hand to stop her. 'Leave it on. It suits you.'

She pulled his leather jacket back up her arms. Cole's lips quirked into a small smile, his cheeks suddenly flushed with embarrassment. *Why did I say that?* He lowered his hand, looking at the door instead of at her.

'What's happening, Cole?'

The use of his first name made Cole flick his head up. He had become accustomed to Eira using his nickname, and the change was an unwelcome jolt. Eira was before him, her intense green eyes searching his face. His breathing hitched and his insides turned to lava as he became aware of how close they were.

'What's happening, Cole?' Eira repeated. He should tease her, shrug it off, but his tongue had turned to stone and his throat felt like it was filled with gravel. He gulped.

Eira tentatively raised a hand and swept his unruly hair back from his face, gently running her fingers through it. Cole let his hands fall slack at his sides. His breath caught in his chest as she moved her hand to his cheek, tracing the scar she had placed there.

Cole closed his eyes and inhaled. 'It can be nothing or it can be everything, Eira,' he said huskily.

The sweet smell that Cole associated with her washed over him, mixed with the old pipe smoke from the jacket. Her warm hand stroked his cheek, sending flames down his spine.

Cole opened his eyes.

Eira's eyes were filled with sincerity, capturing Cole entirely.

'I've never done anything like this before. I'm so mixed up right now.' Eira leant forward, resting her forehead against his. Cole took a deep breath, inhaling her heady scent.

He lifted his hands and rested them on her narrow hips and smiled as she returned the gesture.

'So, talk to me, Eira. Tell me about it,' Cole whispered, his breath tickling her cheek.

She closed her eyes and pulled her bottom lip into her mouth, something he had noticed she did when she was thinking. 'Everything I thought I knew, everything about my mother and her death, and my life after, seems to be a fabrication. The swords, my training, the whole...'

Eira sighed and laid her head against his shoulder, and Cole's arms instinctively wrapped around her, pulling her close. Having her in his arms felt so natural.

'Break it down, start from the beginning. What's unsettling you the most?'

Eira was quiet for a moment.

'As you know, my mother was the head of the Equal Rise party who were campaigning for equality for hybrids. They were legal, did things above board before the Dark came into power. I know they had support from Myths and hybrids, and they sometimes crossed the line, but it was always for the greater good. I don't remember Storm — the escape from London was a blur — but he knows too much about me and my mother. And he was powerful enough that Oran backed down in their standoff. I think Oran sensed something that he isn't sharing.'

Eira exhaled a long breath, holding up her right wrist. Cole saw an outline of a sun raised there, a counterpart to the moon on the other one.

'Storm branded me with this and said that if I ever needed help, I could just hold the mark and think of the sun.'

'Between us we have a full set,' Cole chuckled.

Eira's mouth twitched, and Cole's heart fluttered in response.

'It's making me question if some members of my mother's party are still alive, and if so, why they never sought me. And who arranged for me to live on my family's island? Were Etta and Pyke brought in by someone to train me up for something greater? Do my aunt and uncle know more and, if they do, why haven't they told me?'

Cole pulled back, looking directly at her, eyes wide. 'You were brought up on an island?'

'That's what you've taken from that?' Eira accused jokingly, pinching his side.

'Ouch,' Cole protested, rubbing at his side. 'But I am curious. What was it like growing up on an island? What did you even do?'

Eira paused, thinking. 'I read a lot. History, medical journals, mythology, romance.' The last word was said so quietly against his chest that Cole almost didn't hear her. 'Anything I could get Etta to bring from the mainland. We had a TV, but the signal was pretty dodgy. When I wasn't learning or fighting, I used to bake, garden with my aunt, explore the island, and swim in the sea.'

Eira went silent, wistful longing filling her face.

'Right, we're going to have a movie night for our first date,' Cole said. 'You've got a lot of catching up to do.'

Eira tensed, and Cole felt his confidence waver.

'We're doing this then?' she whispered.

'Yeah, I believe we are. I mean...' — he pulled back from her slightly, indicating their bodies pressed together — '... it seems as though we've already decided.'

Eira's laugh rumbled through his chest, warming him from the inside.

'We'll take it slowly and do it right, Doc. You lead if you need to, there's no pressure. But you have to talk to me,' Cole said seriously. And with that, he leant forward and placed a featherlight kiss on her neck.

Eira stilled against him, but she didn't flinch, and when Cole pulled away, a shy smile graced her face.

'But we've gone off topic. Tell me more about the island.'

Eira cleared her throat, hands fisting in his jumper. 'Right. Yes, the island.' She sniggered then continued, 'It's not like some tropical paradise with palm trees and white sand. And yes, I do know about places like that before you ask,' she added at the cheeky grin that crossed Cole's face.

'It's in Scotland. I am bound not to reveal its location to you for my family's safety with what happened to my mother. But as you can imagine, it is cold and barren in the winter but spectacular in the summer. Spring is always my favourite — I love watching the heather and wildflowers blooming on the hills. And the wildlife there is amazing: terns, puffins, seals. The water's always cold, but it is a nice way to cool down in the warmer months.'

Eira's eyes had a far-off look, as if she were back on the island, watching the sea break on the shore.

'It's been so long since I was last there. I miss it. And my family.' Coming back to herself, Eira gave him a small smile. 'I'll take you there one day, if you like?'

'I'd like that,' Cole uttered, heart twisting with hope. They remained silent for a long moment.

'I think all your questions are valid and worth considering; I would never dismiss your instincts. But be wary and only ask the people you trust. I agree that we know nothing about Storm, but he seemed sincere and did help us escape when he could have handed us over to the Dark. Speaking from experience, I'd try not to question everything about your past at once. It'll twist you up and send you down a road you might not want to go down. Your past has shaped you, but it doesn't define you. You're filled with love and kindness, and from what you've said, I think you got that from your family growing up. Use that kindness and focus on the now.'

Cole knew he wasn't the best at giving advice, but he wanted to help Eira see things clearly. His mind was drawn back to the night of the fire, one small action that changed his life. The memory swamped him, and he could almost taste the smoke on his tongue. Who was he to give advice when he had done that?

He felt a comforting warmth as Eira's hand gently cupped his face and turned it towards her. He saw the understanding there, the compassion and the acceptance, and the memory faded until he could breathe freely again.

'Oh, Cole,' she whispered. But then wrinkled her nose and her eyes crinkled at the corners.

'Batman's talking to you, isn't he?'

Eira nodded. 'How do you know?'

'Your face gets all irritated, like you've smelt something bad.' This time she poked him in the chest playfully, making Cole huff.

'His timings might get a little annoying,' Cole sniggered.

The bond Eira shared with the gargoyle was hard to come to terms with and, in moments like this, he almost resented it. But he knew that it was important, both to her, and to their overall goal. So, he had to just strap in for the ride.

CHAPTER 26

||| EIRA

Eira felt elated despite everything that was going on. Cole had held her so carefully, his warmth calming the worry inside her and melting her heart. The small amount she knew about relationships had been gleaned from novels, and midnight imaginings on cold winter nights.

She was dating. The thought sent a nervous thrill shooting down her spine as she exited their bedroom. Eira felt like running to Elowen and giggling like a love-sick teenager experiencing their first crush.

She glanced back at Cole as she hoisted the laundry basket onto her hip. He swept his dark curls from his face and grinned at her, the heated look making her insides tighten. His hair had been as soft as she had imagined, and she loved running her fingers through it.

Everything had changed in that moment. No, it had changed when he had uttered the words to seal their oath. It was in that moment that he gave in to his feelings for her. Now she just needed to do the same.

Sharing her fears with someone had helped to clear her crowded mind. Cole was right — she couldn't change the past, only accept it and be the instigator of her own fate. Eira knew he had been speaking from experience, and it made the advice even more poignant.

We'll take it slowly and do it right.

Those words had meant the world to her. Eira wasn't naive, she knew that she wouldn't be his first partner. But she could tell that there was something different between them. Special. Something that he maybe hadn't had before.

'Stop looking at me like that,' Eira said, stepping into the narrow stairway, conscious of Cole behind her.

'I like the view.'

Eira tutted, smiling to herself. She could tell from his tone that he had a smug smirk on his face.

Eira still wore his jacket, its heady scent making it hard to concentrate. She swallowed, trying to clear her mind — she was about to have an important conversation, and she needed to focus.

Entering the fire-lit living room, Eira glanced around. Madam Scudamore had drawn the rich, crimson curtains which meant it was dark outside. Enticed to the brightness of the kitchen, Eira carried her basket through, following the sound of clattering pans, her stomach growling with the welcoming aroma.

Oran's scent greeted her before she saw him, and she pushed at their bond. Still blocked. She stopped, her senses on high alert to something being off. Cole was a solid presence behind her, placing a hand on her lower back, his touch gentle and soothing.

Letting out a deep breath, Eira stepped into the small kitchen. Madam Scudamore was at her usual place near the stove, her back as straight as a rod. The tension in the room was palpable, and Eira's body tensed in response. Where was the gargoyle?

She turned and saw him languishing at the table, noisily eating a bowl of soup. Oran had his head bent, his small horns on show and his wings wrapped around his shoulders. He had no weapons on him, which Eira took to be a good sign. She had beaten him fairly, but Eira wasn't sure that he would hold up his end of the bargain.

He didn't look up, just carried on eating, dipping a hunk of bread into his soup. He was clearly angry and worked up about something. Cole skirted around her and headed to the other side of the table, a cheeky smile on his face that he was trying to hide.

Sighing, Eira stepped forward and placed the laundry basket in the far corner. Turning to Madam Scudamore, she put on an overly cheery voice and said, 'That smells amazing.' Eira walked around Cole, taking the seat nearest him.

'Leek and Stilton soup. I believe one of your favourites,' the housekeeper replied stiffly, placing bowls in front of them both.

'Thank you,' Cole said cheerily with a smile at the poltergeist who simply tightened her lips and turned away. Blowing on her spoon, Eira tried her best to eat the soup, waiting for Oran to break the tension. Pushing down her rising irritation, Eira dunked the warm homemade bread into the steaming liquid.

Glancing up, she saw the housekeeper disappearing from the room, the laundry in tow.

267

'You trust me, don't you, Eira?' Oran spoke in Elven, his voice a rumble from the other end of the table. Eira turned to him. His head was bowed, and he stared intently at the food in front of him.

'Yes.' *I'm trying to.*

Oran nodded.

'Why is the bond blocked? What happened?' Worry was building in Eira's chest.

He shook his head, seemingly lost for words. Taking a deep, shuddering breath, he finally spoke in English. 'What you're about to witness is a gargoyle trait. I hate it, but it's necessary. I need you and the captain not to freak out. Sit perfectly still and don't break eye contact with me. Especially you, Cole,' Oran said.

Eira glanced at Cole, who shrugged, placing his spoon in the bowl. He squared his shoulders, bracing his elbows on the table, and her heart leapt. He was so willing to accept her world.

'Are you ready?' Oran's tense voice rang through the room.

Eira nodded, forgetting that he wasn't looking. 'Yes.'

Oran's head shot up. Eira shuddered, scraping her chair back on instinct. She wanted to turn to Cole, throw her body in front of his to protect him, but she remembered her promise and held herself in her seat. A hand found her knee and squeezed, and she relaxed slightly.

Oran's eyes were wide, luminous in the light, and fully dilated like an animal. The swirling mists that were usually present in his eyes were missing, replaced by a deep black void. His fangs were fully extended, and a growl ripped from his throat. She was a cornered animal, with no way to escape, and her instincts were urging her to fight.

Trust me. She remembered the words he had spoken and tried to remain calm.

'Eira, I'm going to open our bond. You'll be flooded by my emotions, but I need you to reassure me and calm my instincts.'

Was he joking?

Oran opened the floodgates to the bond. Eira tensed, her breath catching as his power poured into her. But there was something else there too. Something so raw and primal that it made the hairs on her arms raise. Her magic instantly surged forward, wrapping around the conflicting feeling, soothing, and calming as it went.

He sighed as it worked, his entire body shuddering. But his gaze was locked on Cole, unwavering.

Cole stared back, appearing unfazed. But Eira knew better. She squeezed his hand that still rested on her knee, and he was clammy with sweat. Without thinking, she funnelled some of her power into Cole, soothing his fear.

'Within my clan, when a female accepts a male's advances, the eldest member of their family must challenge the suitor. It would seem that this instinct has surfaced with regards to you, Eira,' Oran hissed. He looked to be slowly regaining control with Eira's help. Although his eyes were still black, they had lost the predatory glint.

'But we're not family. We are...' Eira hesitated. *What are we?*

Oran tensed at her words. Gulping, Eira stood up, trying to diffuse the tension. Continuing to sooth Oran's primal rage with her magic, she approached him tentatively.

Eira sat on the edge of the table and gently turned Oran's face to look at her. He resisted at first, his mouth set in a stubborn line, but he finally relented, and Eira could see the sadness and guilt there. At the other end of the table, Cole released a drawn-out sigh.

'What happened when Nelka accepted your advances?' she asked.

Oran's mouth twitched slightly. 'Callan would have fought me to the death if Nelka hadn't stepped in. Like you have.'

White started to spread slowly around his irises, bringing him back to himself.

'What happened?'

'I couldn't fight back without risking killing him. Callan's a great warrior, and he's like a father to me.' Oran gulped, more whiteness flooding his eyes at the memory. 'He had me pinned to the keep wall with his stone powers. I wasn't in too much danger as I could shield against him with my light, but it was getting dangerous for others and the surrounding buildings. I just needed to ride out his primal instincts.' Oran let out a small chuckle. 'Echo stepped between us, straight into danger like it was nothing. Like you, she used some of her power to soothe the chief.'

Oran closed his eyes and when he opened them again, they were clear, the swirling mists captivating.

'Echo projected her power and declared to all, "He is mine, I choose Oran Light Bringer as my mate, my Starlight, my everything." I'll hear those words until the day Lunar takes me.'

Eira finally let out the breath she had been holding in. Oran's sadness now flowed down the bond.

'You're my protector, Oran. You've been that way since you shattered my window and saved me.' Eira laid her palm on his bicep, closing her eyes. 'I fully trust you, Light Bringer, with this and any future challenges we might face. We're a team and we need to start acting like one. All of us.'

Eira opened her eyes and saw Oran looking at her with a mixture of respect and admiration. She turned to face Cole, who was staring at them both.

'And just to clear things up, I do accept Cole's advances. I don't know where it'll lead, but I'm willing to find out.'

So many emotions flitted across Cole's face that Eira couldn't tell what he was feeling. But then he turned to her with a wide smile, and she knew she had said the right thing.

'Is that why you disappeared, Oran?' Cole asked. 'Or were you scared that I might have kicked your ass like my girlfriend did?'

Eira knew that it was Cole's way of claiming her back, and she couldn't help but grin at him.

A squeal from the doorway had everyone whipping around in their seats. Elowen clapped her hands, bouncing on the balls of her feet with excitement, vibrating on the spot with untapped glee.

'You and the captain,' she said, gesturing between them both. 'Finally!'

Eira rolled her eyes. 'Did everyone know?'

'Oh yes we did,' a voice echoed as Madam Scudamore floated through the floor. 'Is it safe to come back now? There was far too much testosterone flying around in here for my taste!'

Oran huffed and picked up his bowl.

Eira sat back down, hoping her soup hadn't gone cold. Cole squeezed her knee before tucking into his.

'Did I also hear that you' – Elowen pointed to Eira with her spoon – 'kicked that one's ass.' She gestured at Oran, an impressed look on her face.

'Oh yeah, you should have seen her,' Cole answered.

Oran threw his head back and laughed, the deep bass rumbling around the room.

ORAN

'That was superb, Madam Scudamore,' Oran declared as he mopped up the last of his soup with a chunk of bread.

Madam Scudamore gave a small nod as she sat at the table with them.

Thanks to Eira, he had managed to master the torrent of emotions flooding him, and he felt much more like himself. The rage had come on so suddenly that he'd had to leave or risk killing the human. He had known what it was, had been on the receiving end before and witnessed the effect on other gargoyle males. The key was for the female to step in and declare her acceptance of the advances, putting a stop to the fighting before it could get too dangerous.

Oran was glad that he had Eira's powers soothing him through their bond — he wasn't sure he would have been able to control himself if not. He had hoped that by putting some distance between them, he would be able to get a hold on his emotions, but it hadn't helped. He only decided to return home when he felt a spark through the bond. A spark of joy and hope from Eira. That was what had convinced him to risk coming back.

Oran looked at Eira now. The light that had been extinguished in her eyes since the heist was back, and she looked happy and relaxed.

To say you nearly killed Hawk would be an understatement, Eira said in his head.

I said that you'd chosen, didn't I? I was right.

Eira stuck out her tongue. *Will you let me help you later?*

I keep my word.

He nodded once in Eira's direction, understanding her motives.

'I visited our mutual friends today,' Eira said.

Elowen stilled, her spoon halfway to her mouth. 'Do you want me to go?'

'Of course not. This concerns you too. You as well, Jemima,' Eira said, giving the poltergeist a stern look as she floated away from the table. The ghost arched an eyebrow but didn't protest.

'A wise person told me today,' Eira started, glancing at Cole, 'to trust my instincts and the people I know. We're a dysfunctional family, but we have to start working as a team.'

Elowen grinned from ear to ear, happy to finally be included, and even Madam Scudamore looked shocked. Oran crossed his arms and raised an eyebrow at Cole who simply shrugged. Oran was interested to see how Eira would explain it all, knowing that Elowen didn't know the full story.

Eira took a breath. 'Our friends managed to decipher the ingredients in the virus. The outer shell is magnetite, but the inside is more difficult. There's organic matter — probably blood — powerful and dark ancient magic, and some tech fusing it all together. A toxic combination. The important factor is that it isn't activated when opened. It seems to only work when it comes into contact with flesh or blood, which we kind of already knew since it spreads through the bloodstream.'

Do you recognise the ancient magic part? They said it felt like night.

Sounds familiar, but I can't put my finger on it.

Eira glanced in his direction. Cole had his arm on the table, forearm up, his moon marking on show, and Eira's fingers absentmindedly ran over it again and again.

'Magnetite is magnetic, isn't it?' Cole enquired.

'Yep, it sure is.'

'We might be able to use that to our advantage,' Cole muttered, looking thoughtful.

'So, there's no cure apart from your necklace?' Elowen asked.

'Yes, it appears to be the only cure until I have the resources to create an antidote.'

'And what did they say about the necklace?' Oran asked.

'They couldn't identify it without smashing it open. The only thing they could tell me is that it's an ancient artefact.'

They think it's elven, Eira told him through the bond.

Watching her fingers on Cole's arm, he could see that the tapping and stroking she was doing wasn't random. She was communicating with him.

What makes them say that?

'So, your necklace acts like the virus? Something encased in a shell activated by organic matter,' Elowen stated. Oran was impressed with how easily she was keeping up with the conversation.

'Yes, something like that. But I think what we can discern is that the virus is manufactured, it's made by combining magic and technology. My necklace seems to be purely magic. It somehow has the power to defeat the virus even though the necklace appears to have come first.'

Or the virus is something ancient manipulated for ill-gain, Oran supplied, still watching Eira's fingers.

Is that even possible?

Oran raised an eyebrow in her direction, giving a small shrug.

'Madam Scudamore, in all your centuries have you ever heard of a powerful artefact capable of healing?' Eira asked.

The ghost startled, unused to being included. 'Less of the old, missy,' she teased, a fake scowl on her face, before continuing, 'Not to my knowledge.'

Eira nodded, unsurprised. 'This is where I need your help, please.'

She reached into her back pocket and extracted a slip of paper, handing it to the poltergeist across the table. Oran remembered that, of all the spirits they could command, they could manipulate solid matter.

The ghost scanned the list. 'It's a long list. I might not be able to locate them all.'

'Please try your best. As your guardian, I give you permission to leave the house to locate the items on the list and return when you have exhausted all avenues.'

The housekeeper nodded, a grin on her face as she descended through the floor. 'I'll make a start once I've done all that washing your new courtship gave me.'

They all sniggered.

Books for research, Eira said down the bond, anticipating Oran's question. Her long fingers traced a sequence on Cole's bare flesh. How she was keeping track of who she was communicating with, Oran didn't know.

'Our friends also made these.'

Eira slid her phone onto the table, metal bracelets wrapped around it. Oran stretched out a hand and grabbed them, pulling them towards him. The bracelets contained a small opal, black veins barely visible beneath the hard shell.

Oran shot Eira a questioning look.

Look at the phone too.

Oran was aware that Elowen and Cole were distracted, looking at another bracelet that Eira had placed in front of them. Oran took a moment to study the picture of an ancient manuscript: three figures on a hilltop, an elven inscription below. His breath caught in his throat. He automatically traced the pointed outline of one of his ears.

You recognise it, don't you?

A fable, a legend that's all.

Eira was about to push, but Cole interrupted. 'What are these?' he asked, twiddling the bracelet between his fingers.

'Our friends took a small chip from the bullet with the virus and used the genetics from my opal to make a temporary solution to our problem. The wearer should be protected from the virus, and it should be able to cure the infected.'

Elowen looked up in wonder. 'Well, that's incredible.'

Eira simply nodded.

It needs to be charged with your power, doesn't it? Oran guessed.

Eira's eyes shuttered. She lightly tapped on Cole's moon embossing before replying. *My magic won't work on its own. It needs to be a combination of both mine and yours.*

'We need some live bait then.' Cole flashed a wicked smile at them all.

'Elowen, this is where I need your help,' Eira said. 'Once we have established that the bracelets work and we have the means to produce more, we will need to dish them out to any Myth willing to have them. We need to explain it in such a way that they understand it's life or death, and I think you'll be able to convince them.'

Elowen grinned, a flush spreading over her cheeks. 'I'll do my best, Doctor.' Then her face fell. 'What about humans?'

'Once we know it's safe, we can start supplying them to humans, when we can make more... That's if I can't find an antidote sooner. This is where we need to tread carefully.' Eira's eyes darted to Oran.

She reached forward and grasped her friend's hand. 'Don't worry, I haven't forgotten humanity.'

'How will you test them?' enquired Elowen.

'That's for me to worry about,' Oran replied in an authoritative tone.

Elowen inhaled. 'I'll draw up a list of who we have in at the moment and a schedule of how it can be done.' She rose with a spring in her step, turning to Eira who silently mouthed thank you.

When Elowen had gone, Eira groaned, throwing her upper body over the table, arms spread in front of her. 'That was difficult having three conversations simultaneously in my own head,' Eira muttered, her voice muffled by the wooden tabletop.

Oran huffed a chuckle, and Cole rubbed her back.

As Eira flashed Cole a tired smile, Oran rose, placing the bracelet on his wrist, worried that he was intruding.

I'm not finished with you yet. She lifted her hand and pointed at him as she spoke into his head. Oran remained still. She turned to Cole, slipping the bracelet around his wrist, and giving his hand a squeeze, then turned and walked towards Oran.

Cole's gaze tracked Eira as she crossed the room, ushering Oran out in front of her.

'I know you must have so many questions,' Oran said with a yawn, squeezing himself up the narrow staircase.

'They can wait until morning,' Eira said gently.

Relieved to hear that, Oran shoved open the door to his bedroom. The room was completely dark, and Oran suddenly felt awkward.

Not seeming to notice, Eira pushed him into the room and followed him, pulling back the duvet. 'When was the last time you slept properly?'

Oran shrugged. *The day of my injury.*

'How the hell are you still standing?'

Oran tensed, cursing. He had only meant to say that in his own head, but in his tiredness, he had apparently projected it to her as well.

'You've been letting me draw on your power all this time without thinking about the effects. If we were attacked tomorrow, you're our best defence. How well do you think you'd be able to fight as exhausted and drained as you are?' Eira scolded.

Oran knew that Eira was exaggerating. She could certainly hold her own against their enemies; she just needed more confidence in herself.

Stepping forward, Oran sank onto the bed, the mattress indenting with his weight. 'I know the consequences. I've just never had to do it before; I can't turn my mind off.'

'Oran, I understand,' Eira breathed. 'I know that it's my fault that you've lost your stone shift, and I'm so sorry. But I will find a way to fix it, I promise.'

Oran opened his mouth to protest but she pushed on, needing to get this off her chest. 'If this team is going to succeed, you need to trust me. It goes both ways. I trusted you today, even though Cole's life was in danger.'

Oran closed his eyes, guilt washing over him. 'I am truly sorry, Eira. I tried my best to handle it.'

'You don't need to be sorry. We worked through it. As a team. I know it was hard for you, and I appreciate how much effort it must have taken to keep your emotions under control.' She pulled the duvet up under his chin and gently tucked it around him.

Oran's eyes fluttered, and the last thing he heard was a whisper of, 'Sleep well, protector,' before he fell into a deep, dreamless sleep. She didn't even have to touch him to knock him out.

CHAPTER 27

||| EIRA

Eira stared down the barrel of the pistol she held clasped in both hands. She could see the target in the distance: a small piece of plywood with circles descending in size drawn on it. She knew that, under normal circumstances, she would easily be able to hit the bullseye. But these were not normal circumstances. A warm body was wrapped around her, and it was making it hard to concentrate. His spicy scent was overwhelming, and she could feel his heart beating against her back, drawing her attention from the gun in her hand.

Eira stood, legs shoulder-width apart, facing forward. Cole had positioned one leg between hers, his hip angled into her side with his other leg almost wrapped around hers. His long arms enfolded her shoulders and stretched towards the gun she was holding, keeping her in position. But it was the taunting kisses he was applying across her neck and exposed shoulder, that were sending electrical charges down her spine and making her lean into him.

'Is this how you teach all new recruits to hold a gun? If so, I don't think it's very professional.'

Eira felt the smile against her skin as Cole muttered, 'Only the special ones,' before he applied a warm kiss to the place behind her ear, then straightened, resting his head on her shoulder. 'Right, stance good,' he said, pushing closer to her, but trying to get things back on track. 'You can probably see the target with that sharp eyesight of yours, so just angle your sight down the scope and pull the trigger.'

'Is that it?' she asked.

'Yep, not like swordplay where you actually need some skillset,' Cole replied. Eira twitched a smile as he continued and corrected, 'It's harder when you are under pressure, and you need to think and be the one to shoot first. Shooting a flat target is okay for practice, but a real live body...' Cole blew out his cheeks leaving the sentence unfinished.

'You don't always have to shoot to kill. You have the kill zones, they're here...' Cole removed one hand and pressed his fingers to Eira's temple, gliding down the side of her face and neck.

Eira hitched a breath as Cole's steady hand moved to her collarbone, tapping just above her breastbone, and whispered in her ear, 'Chest or heart'. His wicked fingers travelled between her breasts, skimming the opal which was resting there. Eira tried, and failed, to stabilise her racing heart, but the heat continued to spread through her.

Cole rested his hand against her stomach, his fingers drawing lazy circles on her exposed skin. 'Stomach,' he whispered. 'But of course, as a doctor, I would hope you already know where all the body parts are. And with your training, I imagine you also know lots of ways to kill someone.'

Lost for words, Eira just nodded.

'Of course, a well-aimed shot to the knee, shin, or even the shoulder, can stop an enemy long enough to escape. Especially if...' Cole brought his arm back up, his hand encircling hers on the gun.

'... They're under the influence of the Dark and are incapable of thinking for themselves,' Eira finished, tilting her head to look at Cole.

Then she pulled the trigger, their eyes still locked. The impact vibrated along her arms, pushing her back against his solid chest.

'You had no other option than to kill that agent, Cole. He would have done worse to you,' she said, sensing his thoughts.

Cole's eyes shut as he inhaled, his chest expanding against her back. Eira lowered her arms, and Cole placed his against her hips. It seemed to be their favourite resting place.

'There's always a choice, Eira. I should have stabbed to wound him, not to kill him.'

Eira placed a hand on the side of his face, stroking his scar. Cole's eyes were so full of grief and regret that it twisted her stomach. She would do anything not to see that expression on his face.

'In the moment, you took an opportunity. You had just relived some of your worst memories.' She didn't know what they were, but his mother's death must have been amongst them. In time, she would find out and hopefully heal them. 'Next time, will be different. You'll learn, from experience, to react in other ways, especially now that we have a different form of weapon in the bracelets.'

Some of the tension eased from Cole, as he laid his head on her shoulder and wrapped his arms around her tightly. 'Thank you,' he breathed.

Eira grinned, joining her arms around his, the pistol hooked in her palm.

'Please tell me you made that shot without even looking,' Cole whispered onto her neck.

Eira snorted, throwing her head back on his shoulder and chuckling. 'What do you think?'

Cole raised his head, squinting at the target. 'A little off-centre I think.'

'Well, next time you can stop distracting me, and I'll get it dead centre.'

With a sigh, Cole released her and stepped back, the sudden loss of his body heat making Eira shiver. He walked to their drinks stand, an upturned crate. Eira followed, placing the gun on the makeshift shelf across the shooting range. Eira had to admit that Cole was resourceful, creating most of their training area using things he had found lying around.

The shooting range stood in the centre of the workout area, which he had created from leftover plywood sheeting. A couple of ropes hung from the rafters; Eira expected that Oran had helped install these. She had watched Cole's muscles flex as he scaled one easily, hooking his hands over each other, legs twisted around the rope to pull himself to the top. His wound seemed to not be causing him any problems, which pleased her. Eira was surprised that he didn't want it healed, but she understood that, to him, it was armour — a sign of a battle fought and won. The six columns stolen from the church opposite the gatehouse stood sentry to their workout area; Oran still hadn't told them what he planned to use them for.

Eira accepted a cup from Cole, downing the water in one. She had opted to train with him this morning, knowing he needed the distraction; they were both on edge waiting for Oran to return from his mission to obtain an objective they needed. Eira hadn't seen the gargoyle before he left, so hoped he had finally slept. They had been training since dawn and were running out of stamina and ways to fill the time.

Cole sighed for the umpteenth time, glancing to the door as he swept his hair from his face. 'Do you think he's actually here and playing with us?'

Eira snorted. 'I can't sense him or scent him. But then, he might have closed the bond again.'

Eira was tempted to try drawing some of Oran's power, but she knew it was a risk if he needed it.

Cole put his hands on his hips, glanced at the door and then at the exposed ceiling, exhaling. Wanting to take away some of his anxiety, Eira placed her cup back on the table and approached him.

'So, you know how you've been doing a very good job of distracting me...' She wrapped her arms around his waist from behind, hooking her arms through his.

'Um, yeah.'

'Well, I think it's my turn.' Eira kissed his neck, ghosting her lips across his ear, making him tremble.

'So, I'm gone for the whole morning, working hard, and this is what you two have been doing?' came a rumbling voice from the doorway.

Letting his cloaking disappear, Oran leant against the doorframe, arms folded loosely across his chest, Oswald perched happily on his shoulder. A quick sweep of him with her eyes told her that Oran wasn't injured. In fact, he appeared less tense, and he had a smile on his face — something she hadn't seen in a while.

Eira continued her lazy kisses of Cole's neck, forcing herself to not feel embarrassed for being intimate with him. 'Oh, we have been working hard. The captain has been showing me how to shoot a gun with little to no distraction. I was just off-centre apparently.'

Eira grinned into Cole's neck as she heard him chuckle. Oran rolled his eyes and advanced into the room, not looking convinced.

'Is the package secure?' Cole asked, his voice tight. Eira held him tighter, and he wrapped his arms around hers, holding his breath as he waited for the gargoyle's reply.

'The package is secure with no issues,' Oran replied, stalking past. Oswald sprang off his shoulder with a yowl, taking roost in the exposed beams. Cole deflated in Eira's grasp.

Eira sauntered after Oran who sat on a stool at the head of the table spread with papers, his wings tucked in tight. Her eyes narrowed as she scrutinised his face. He did appear rested, but there were creases at the corners of his eyes, and black smudges under them. He still looked a little hollow.

'Did you sleep?' she enquired, hands on hips like a demanding teacher. Oran nodded.

So that was how it was going to go. Sullen gargoyle.

'I have some questions,' she said bluntly.

'The Doc has been holding them in all this time. It's a wonder she hasn't burst,' Cole added, slouching in the chair across from Oran.

Eira jabbed Cole playfully in the ribs, eyes wide with challenge. Cole smirked and grabbed her hand, pulling her onto the chair next to his. 'You're making Light Bringer nervous with all your glaring and poking.'

Oran huffed, a smile spreading across his mouth, his fangs appearing. At least that was a good sign.

Eira stuck her tongue out at Cole. 'As my very rude boyfriend has pointed out, I have been thinking hard.'

Cole jerked, nearly falling off his chair as he stared at Eira, stunned.

'How have you learnt to block the bond? And don't give me any of your "I'm more experienced than you," shit.'

Oran's smile grew as he looked at her. 'We're about to have a meeting with the League which will shape the outcome of our future plans, and *that's* the first question you ask?' he teased.

Eira ground her teeth, exasperated.

'She is determined,' Cole butted in.

Eira nearly growled at him, but she stopped herself, seeing the way he gazed lovingly at her.

'I presume you know how to shield your mind?' Oran's voice drew her attention away from Cole, and Eira nodded. 'It's the same as that, the same as glamouring your power's glow. The same as adding the shield block to the captain's mind. I've only succeeded faster because yes, I am more experienced, and my mental skills are more acute.' He added, 'Try it.'

Oran pushed his power down the bond, sparkling with his moonlight. Eira breathed deeply and thought about fortifications, a strong wall between them. She managed to hold his power at bay for the span of a heartbeat before his starlight flooded through the void.

Eira gritted her teeth, remembering the weeks it had taken her to get to grips with hiding her power's glow, something she did now with ease.

'It takes practice, Eira. I only blocked the bond because my emotions would have overwhelmed you. At the time, you needed a clear head to make a choice. I promise I will keep the bond open until you've figured out how to do it too,' Oran held up his hands in surrender.

Oran would do that. This bond was a burden on them both, an invasion of their privacy. But if he knew she had trespassed into his mind, he might not be so willing.

It's my way of repaying my debt to you for helping me sleep. Thank you.

Try expanding your mind beyond your consciousness, holding it, and then drawing it back in. It's how I practise controlling the stone creatures I create.

Eira nodded, not fully understanding but determined to try.

'Right, next question,' Oran said smugly.

'What made you back off with Storm?'

Oran shifted a talon-tipped shoulder, unfolding his arms. He hadn't expected that. Was he going to answer truthfully?

'I identified him as welkin.'

Eira paused, working through her memories to find out why that word was familiar. Gasping, she blurted, 'From the underground chamber?'

Oran nodded.

Eira turned to Cole. 'When we escaped the abbey, we came through this octagonal chamber. According to Oran, the artwork on the walls depicted the three high races: elves, gargoyles, and welkin. I'll take you there one day; it's beautiful.'

Eira buzzed with excitement at the thought of going back there. To trace the history would be amazing. Looking back at Oran, Eira added, 'But he didn't have wings?'

Oran shrugged, his great wings shifting with the movement. 'All I know is that he had enough authority to make me stand down. He had powerful magic, but he had it well cloaked. He was strong, that was for sure.'

His answer only opened up more questions. How had her mother known such a powerful Myth? Could he be linked to her father as well? Eira might have to consider returning to the bank to find him... But she knew he wouldn't be there if she did. She glanced down at the sun embossed on her wrist and considered reaching out to him.

She looked up to find Oran watching her. He raised an eyebrow in question, but she shook her head.

Oran continued, 'You know the picture you showed me? The fable I mentioned?'

Cole jumped in, 'What picture?'

'It was the only thing I couldn't show you at the time.' Eira slid her phone from her back pocket and handed it to Cole. He studied the faded parchment picture. 'The triplets think it's related to my necklace. The three figures look like the engraving.'

Cole absentmindedly ran his fingers along the three vertical lines on his face. 'What does the writing say?'

'In the beginning there were three,' Eira said.

'Who walked the earth forever young, two a mirror of each other, one who was rare and fair. Together they carried knowledge in their grasp, the hands of eternity around their necks, and a mighty power not yet formed,' Oran recited. 'Every race has their creation stories and that's the elven one.'

Eira tilted her head, not comprehending. It had sparked the image of the elven mural in the room they had just been talking about.

'Have you ever been told how magic is defined and why hybrids are so feared?'

Eira shook her head, a feeling of satisfaction filling her that Oran had finally picked up on her term.

'The high races have pure power which can be categorised into elemental, mind, and time. Gargoyles and welkin lean towards the elemental spectrum, with a few exceptions like Echo. The elves can have a combination of all three, but most have the power of mind. Having the power to manipulate time or see the future is so exceptional that it is rarely seen in any of the races but has been known to manifest in the elves.'

Eira was stunned. Why had Etta never taught her this?

'What about humans?' Cole enquired.

'So, this is where hybrids come in. When the different types of power are combined, the power is intensified. If the right bloodlines are mixed, the power is strong, unique, or if not, it is diluted.' He paused, staring off into the distance. 'That's why I was angry when you took my blood. Blood defines our heritage and, as the virus shows, it might have been the matter used to create something so evil.' Oran looked solemn as he added, 'For us, both our parents were strong magic users.'

Eira chewed her bottom lip looking confused. 'But my mother was mortal.'

'That brings us back to the captain's question. Some mortals hold power even if they can't access it. The high races are fearful of such combinations with humans who have that power. We will always be feared because of what we could be capable of doing.'

Eira gulped, dread filling her. She had never considered her powers like that. A warm hand rested on her knee and the dread receded slightly. Her smile was sad as she met Cole's eyes, conveying her thanks.

'So, your parents were elemental and mind?'

Oran nodded.

'What were mine?' she asked.

'You are a puzzle, Eira. In a good way,' he added with a smile when her face fell. He rested his chin on a pale hand, his white eyes intense. 'I can trace power, but I'm no expert on this. It might take your science to uncover your exact makeup. I suspect that you have mind power to be able to enter a being's flesh and control pain. Then, the rarest of them all, time. I would bet my left wing that you have time in there, to control the healing process as you do.'

Eira sat very still, processing everything he had just said. She was glad for Cole's contact as he traced his thumb over her knee in soothing circles. She took a shuddering breath and whispered, 'So, my mother either held time or mind in her mortal blood?'

Oran's curt nod was enough.

'How does that bring us to the elven fable?' Cole asked. He had been watchful, considerate of their conversation. Eira was starting to see two sides to him, the serious and the playful. They were interlinked and made him who he was, but he used them to suit the situation. Very few people could do that.

'It's said that the first three elves to walk the Earth each had the three different categories of magic. Not much is recorded about them, but your necklace might come from that period.'

Eira looked at her necklace in astonishment. In the silence that followed, Oswald took it upon himself to fly lazily down, planting his bottom on the paper covering the table. Seeking Eira's hand, his podgy face butted it until she scratched behind his ear. They all laughed at the chimera.

Cole handed Eira her phone back, his wolfish grin making her hesitate. Unlocking the device, she glanced up, mouth open.

'What's this?'

'My number,' he replied coyly.

Cole had added a new number to her contacts with the title: Hawk Boyfriend. He looked so smug that Eira couldn't help but grin back. The heaviness that the conversation had caused lifted from her as she stared into his eyes.

'Where's your phone?'

Eira had only seen him use his tablet. He had shown them the agent's stolen phone, but she expected that it had been copied for all the useful information, wiped, and then dumped somewhere.

'It's at basecamp in a locker somewhere. Before you go on a mission, they take your phone. I'll retrieve it tomorrow.'

Eira clocked the use of "they", not "we". Was he detaching himself from the League? She felt a spark of hope settle in her stomach.

'One of the team didn't. The agents who came looking for you showed us photos of you all. That was how they knew what you looked like.'

Oswald flopped onto his back, his paws waggling in the air as he demanded his belly rubbed. Obeying, Eira scratched his hard stone scales as he rumbled in delight.

Cole looked annoyed. 'That shouldn't have happened. Protocol is in place for that very reason unless... Lofty. I bet that idiot sneaked his out. He was forever on it. He was the one who was shooting his mouth off and got us noticed.'

Cole looked like he wanted to break something and, concerned about her knee, Eira encased his hand with hers. As soon as he looked up at her, the anger in his eyes subsided and he relaxed. Wanting to cheer him up, Eira pointed the phone at him.

'Say cheese.' She snapped a photo of Cole, a heart-melting half-smile on his face. It was enough for now.

'So, back to the task at hand,' Oran interjected with a bemused expression. Eira put her phone back in her pocket and looked up. Cole straightened, clearing his throat.

'Right, we know the layout by now – we have been over it enough times.' Cole pointed out the entrance of the League's headquarters on a plan in front of them. 'Here, we will be searched for any weapons. Members will be armed. I'm guessing that they will be on their guard even though I am officially a member; I've been gone too long and have been unable to prove my status. The cameras are here and here,' he said, pointing out different locations as he spoke. 'The meeting is likely to be in the room beneath Oswald's right foot. Again, only cameras, no thermal or pressure sensors. Nothing as sophisticated as the Dark or the triplets. I'm confident that Batman here will go undetected, but he'll be our only line of defence if things go wrong.'

Oran nodded his understanding.

'My biggest concern is this.' He indicated his black eye. 'There's no hiding that I've been infected. Even if I wear my cap, it'll be seen by the members on the floor. They're suspicious at the best of times, and I don't want to give them the wrong impression before we've even met the Major. I could wear a contact lens or something, but that's lying too.' Cole blew out his cheeks, leaning back in his chair.

'My powers do enable me to manipulate my appearance,' Eira said. 'I might be able to hide your eye for an hour or so. It's difficult and takes a lot of power, but it's an option.'

Oran raised an eyebrow. 'I wasn't aware you could do that. You can always draw on my power to feed yours,' he suggested, looking thoughtful.

'That's how you had human ears when the agents came to arrest me, wasn't it?' Eira nodded in answer to Cole's question. 'My other concern is you, Eira.'

Here it comes. Thoughts of their argument came to mind. He wanted to protect her and was going to argue that she should stay here. Eira drew a breath to protest, but Cole continued before she could speak.

'Your surname is too recognisable. You need to use your fake identity from the Wallflower. I'm concerned that there might be members of the Equal Rise within the League, and that puts you in danger.'

Eira looked at Cole in astonishment.

'You need to change your appearance too. They need to associate Doctor Backwater with a completely different person. If they were ever infiltrated, they wouldn't be able to link your appearance to the doctor that went missing at the Wallflower.'

Cole was right. Eira chewed on her own bottom lip. 'I have potions which can completely change my appearance, but the magic renders my powers useless, which I think is a risk if I have to disguise your eye and communicate with Oran. It's either one or the other.'

They all sat there deep in thought as Oswald stretched all four legs and curled up like a housecat, crinkling the papers under him.

'I think Cole's eye is more important as he'll be the one to win their trust,' Oran said. 'It can be combined into the narrative that you can drop the glamour when appropriate. After we've made our point.'

They both nodded. 'I'm sure Elowen can help me disguise my appearance somehow. She's pretty good with makeup,' Eira proposed.

'So, this just leaves these then.' Cole said, sliding his bracelet onto the table.

CHAPTER 28

△ COLE

The flames were mesmerising, the core was blue, spreading to purple and intense orange as they climbed and licked the ceiling of the first floor. Why was no one else scared? They were larking around, swigging from cans, and getting merry on the back of a prank gone wrong.

Then a scream shattered the peaceful night as the smoke became intoxicating. The gang staggered away and dispersed into the night, leaving behind a small, lone figure. The scream pierced the night again, long-drawn-out and pleading.

He approached. A shattering sound, rain crashing down on him, stinging his flesh. The heat was so intense that it made him gag. It felt like his skin was melting.

Then there she was, a stranger, but somehow recognised too. She screamed as she erupted into flames, her hair the same colour as the fire itself. Pointed ears burnt away as he stared into her beautiful green eyes. He was captivated as he stepped towards her.

'You did this, Hawk,' she said. 'You killed the people in that house.'

Cole jolted awake, his eyes immediately scanning the room for danger. He could almost see the flames, taste the smoke at the back of his throat. The room was dark, quiet apart from the gentle breathing next to him. A solid presence against his side.

Eira.

A twisted nightmare of his worst sin, warped with Eira inside the burning house. He took a shaky breath, scraping a hand over his face before curling into her. Her presence was warm and comforting. She hadn't moved from where he had found her, flat against the wall, when he had come back to their room after a shower. She had made sure that Oran was asleep before falling into their bed and passing out into her own deep sleep.

He knew how exhausted Oran and Eira were. They had spent the rest of the afternoon combining their powers to supercharge the bracelets and manipulate his black eye to blue, which had given him double vision. It had taken more power and concentration than either of them had anticipated. Neither had been very talkative at dinner.

Cole had felt like a third wheel most of the afternoon, and the dread and anxiety had slowly crept in as the day progressed, leaving him feeling uneasy and moody.

It was a far cry from the joy and playfulness he had felt that morning, Eira tangled in his arms. Then, he had pinched himself, not trusting that it was all real.

Cole slipped quietly out of bed, doing his best not to wake Eira. He wouldn't be able to sleep now, not with the looming mission and the very real fear the dream had instilled in him. He was giving himself to her, piece by piece, and there was nothing he could do about it. Not that he wanted to stop it.

Cole knew the room well enough that he was able to make it to the door without tripping on anything.

A rush of air made him turn back. His black eye made out the shape of Eira next to him as warm hands met his chest and pushed him against the door. Cole took a sharp breath, his body heating as he felt Eira press against him.

A silken head rested on his shoulder. He automatically encased her waist, a hand winding in her hair. Some of the nightmare subsided with the solidness of her.

'You weren't there,' Eira whispered.

'I was just getting a drink, that's all,' he lied.

A silver-white globule appeared in the dark, floating above the vacant bed.

'Light might make you feel safer,' she said with a smile ghosting her lips.

'Isn't Light Bringer going to complain about you pinching his light without permission?'

'What he doesn't know won't hurt him.'

Cole huffed a laugh into Eira's hair.

'You had a nightmare, didn't you?'

How did she know that? But then Cole seemed to always know when she needed comfort, so of course she was able to sense it too.

Cole sighed and nodded.

'About your mother?'

How could he tell her about his biggest mistake? How he accidently took a life when he was a stupid teenager. Eira hadn't baulked when he told her about the agent, but this was different.

The person he'd killed in the fire had been completely innocent.

'Come on, Hawk, come back to bed. You need your sleep.' Eira pulled away, trying to guide him back to bed.

As her head rose, she stilled, her green eyes meeting his. Her expression softened, and he knew that she could see the raw horror in his face. She leant in and pressed her mouth to his, stepping closer.

The cheeky taunts, feather-light kisses, and tender hugs had been enough. They had started to cement a solid intimacy between them rather than merely a fierce lust. But nothing could have prepared Cole for the jolt of euphoria and pleasure that shot through his body at that first pairing of his lips against hers.

It was a hesitant kiss, a brush of her lips against his to gauge a reaction. It was enough for Cole to take control.

His hand fisted in her hair, and he gently pulled Eira towards him, tilting her head slightly, whilst his other arm embraced her more tightly, aligning their bodies. Eira hooked her arms around the back of his neck as the kiss deepened, pushing him against the door with a rattle of the latch.

It felt so right. He tentatively ran his tongue over her bottom lip, and she shuddered in his hold, her lips parting to him. She mirrored his movements as the kiss turned tender and sweet. A feeling of contentment swept through him. Here with Eira was exactly where he needed to be.

His whole body on fire, Cole tried not to let the kiss explode into something more, even though he trembled with the desire to do exactly that. Knowing his control was slipping, he pulled away, placing one last gentle kiss on her lips before resting his forehead against hers, mingling their breaths.

'Well, that was unexpected.' His voice was rough and deep.

Eira huffed a breath against his lips, apparently unable to articulate her thoughts. She brought both her hands from his neck and cradled his face, thumbs skimming his cheeks, brushing against his scar.

Cole tilted his head and kissed her palm, a soft movement that had Eira smiling.

'That was better than anything I've read in a book,' she

admitted with a grin.

'We're going to ride that?' Eira asked, pointing at the motorbike in front of her.

Cole did a double-take. He knew it was her, but she looked so different. Elowen had worked her gothic magic; Eira's braided hair had been dyed black, and her eyebrows had been darkened. Her eyes were still green, but Elowen had done something with makeup, so that at first glance they seemed brown.

'We sure are,' he said.

'You know how to drive it, don't you?'

Cole advanced on Eira in the dimly lit garage. 'I've been a passenger on this bike since the age of eight. My grandfather taught me how to ride it in the carpark out there. When my mother died, I would take it out at night, enjoying the freedom. Since then, I can promise you I've ridden loads of motorbikes and have a licence to prove it.'

Whilst talking, he had steered Eira towards the Harley Davidson's black-leather seat cushion. She now stood pinned between the bike and his hips.

She looked so attractive in her black, skinny jeans, ripped at the knees, his Tupac T-shirt, and a leather jacket that Madam Scudamore had managed to procure at short notice. It wasn't his leather jacket, but it would do.

Eira gulped as she tilted her head, a lazy smile spreading across her face. 'I think I need to see that licence, Hawk.'

His insides turned to jelly at that smile. Cole spread his hands on her hips. 'Too bad I left it in my other set of leathers. You are just going to have to trust me.'

Grasping her hips, Cole lifted her onto the seat, causing her to shriek in shock. He leant into her, placing his leg between hers. In this position he finally looked down on her.

'Surely you aren't scared of riding a motorbike. Not when I've seen you face off against Oran.'

Cole tickled his nose against hers, sliding a hand behind her neck. Eira's breathing hitched, her body trembling.

'Hawk we don't have time.'

Her complaint was lost to his lips.

This kiss was lazy, seductive, him claiming her. It was Cole's reassurance that last night had happened, that their first kiss had been real. He needed to disperse his anticipation of the next few hours when he would need to act like a stranger around her. He had to convince the League to help them. It seemed that her goals had somehow merged into his goals — Cole's eyes had been opened to the possibility of a different future.

Eira met his demands beat by beat, pressing into him and sliding her tongue into his mouth. She encased her arms around his lower back, fisting his top underneath. Again, something like tranquillity spread through his senses, calming his nerves and the tension that had been building since arriving at his grandfather's house.

As before, Cole withdrew, knowing that they didn't have the time to get carried away yet. They were both breathing heavily, and Eira's lips were swollen.

'I just needed to check that last night had been real, that it wasn't my imagination.'

Eira grinned, her face lit with a cheeky humour. 'That was definitely real, Hawk.'

'Your magic, your power feels like heaven.'

Eira tilted her head back, looking at him questioningly.

'You don't know you're doing it, do you?' Cole chuckled. The look of embarrassment gracing her features was answer enough. 'It calms my very soul. You've used it on me before, haven't you? When I fell and my wound reopened at the clinic.'

'I did,' Eira said coyly.

Cole stepped away and held out a hand to her. 'Ready?' he enquired, tugging Eira to her feet. She nodded, looking as reluctant as he felt. This plan could all go terribly wrong.

Walking to the garage door, Cole heaved it open, sending flakes of rust and peeling paint swirling through the air. He kicked the bike off its stand and wheeled it out to the courtyard. His grandfather's garage was in a shared row, many of them now abandoned. It was just past dawn, so the air was crisp and overcast.

Eira closed the garage behind them, bringing two helmets with her looped over one arm.

'It's chilly out here,' she said, shivering.

'Warmer with me wrapped around you,' Cole couldn't help replying. Eira stuck out her tongue, eyes sparkling with mischief.

Replacing the stand, Cole sat astride the bike and clicked the choke lever. Turning the key in the ignition, he squeezed and held the clutch and then pressed the release button, praying the sleeping beast would work smoothly. A great throaty sound issued from the engine. Cole looked up, grinning, the work he had done on the motorcycle had been worth it. He closed the choke and opened the throttle, leaving the Harley to warm up.

Removing his leg from the chopper, he admired its rough beauty. The leather on the slung seat was worn, cracked with age like his leather jacket, and the once shiny metal now matted.

'My grandfather bought this old gal when he lost his wife suddenly, before I was born. He cared for it so well, I'm not surprised it started first time. I haven't ridden it since I left London when I was sixteen. I should have taken it with me.'

Like Eira's exit from the capital, his own had been rushed and traumatic. With his old gang after him, he didn't have time to take anything apart from the clothes on his back. Luckily, he had been wearing one very special leather jacket.

Eira squeezed his shoulder, handing him a helmet. She placed a metal sphere on the engine, clicking to activate the device.

'Explain how it works again.'

'It's an Incognito, an invention of the Alchemists. It uses magic and tech to create an illusion around the user, a projection of the surroundings. This one, and the ones we use on the Nightingale van, deadens the sound as well. It's as close to invisible as you can get without Oran's powers.'

They had debated using the converted van that the Nightingale used as an ambulance, but Eira didn't want to take it in case it was needed by the hospital. The chopper would be faster and more stylish anyway.

Cole pulled the helmet onto his head, clipping it under his chin, and snapping the visor up. Eira tied a fabric band around her ears and let him help with her helmet as she flipped her long plait down her back. One last quirk of a smile at Eira, he braced his legs either side of the motorcycle, placing his hands on the high handlebars, enjoying the feel of the bike purring beneath him.

'Right, Doc, your turn.'

Eira still seemed apprehensive, but she slung a leg over the other side, one hand on his shoulder. She settled behind him, her thighs braced against his.

'Harleys are more solid and comfortable than other bikes. They don't lean as much into the bends.' Cole clicked his visor shut, muting his surroundings.

'Yeah,' came Eira's muffled voice through the helmet, still not convinced.

Cole hooked the stand back and, bracing the chopper's weight, he let out the throttle. With a mighty rumble, the bike drew forward, coasting out between the garages. Steering it onto the highway he let the throttle off, changed gear, and sped into the city, weaving between the few vehicles he encountered. To his relief, they did appear invisible as the few early risers on the streets didn't even react to the thundering echo of the Harley heading west out of the city.

For the sheer fun of it, and to gauge Eira's reaction, he floored it. Eira's scream was lost on the wind as she threw her arms around his waist, and Cole chuckled, enjoying her close contact and her unease. She was one of the steadiest, most unflappable people he knew, so it was fun to unnerve her.

'Too fast for you, Doc?' Their helmets were mic'd, so it was easy to talk over the roar of the engine.

Her answering jab to the ribs was enough to make him smile again.

Cole easily navigated their way through London, aware of the drones which appeared at intervals en route like swarms of flies in the sky. They were lucky that the heat sensor drones didn't come out until after dark, the reason why they had timed their re-entry into the city wisely.

As they neared the western boundary of the city, the buildings became more dilapidated, some little more than skeletal wrecks coated in ash. Cole swallowed, his dream playing on his mind.

Up ahead, they saw the barriers and checkpoint huts marking the Dark's territory at every major and minor exit into the city. Another reason for the chopper. Cole felt Eira's thighs tighten around his. She took a deep inhale and braced as he changed down a gear and swerved left onto the pavement, which the Dark had carelessly left unobstructed. Cole knew that the major highways were completely barricaded, but minor ones like this were far less problematic. As they raced by the checkpoint, he glanced sideways to double-check that they hadn't been spotted. The agents never even looked their way. Eira relaxed against his back as she let out a breath.

As the last of the damaged city subsided into a blur, and the hue and peace of the countryside streamed past them, Cole started to find the ride exhilarating, especially with his passenger. They kept to the back roads and, after another thirty minutes of silence, Eira said, 'It's probably safe to turn off the Incognito. Just press the top button.'

Cole obeyed, and the rumble of the engine grew louder. Eira, who had loosened her grip after leaving London, looked up at the jewel-coloured leaves in the canopy above. A hazy sun filtered through the yellows and oranges of the trees.

'I haven't been outside of London for two years. I've missed this. The tranquillity of nature, the ever-changing landscape, not having to hide who I am all the time.' Eira spoke so softly that even with the mic, Cole almost didn't hear her.

'When I finally left London and went to train for the police, I had the same reaction. I know London has its parks and waterways, but under the dictatorship of the Dark, it all seems to be in shadow.'

'Why have they not spread out into the countryside, do you think?' she asked.

'Cities have boundaries, easier to control. Shipping and transporting goods are easier.' Cole leant the chopper around a steep bend.

'If they're not stopped, it will spread, I can foresee it. Oran said that they've already spread to places like York, Manchester, and Birmingham.'

Cole nodded, taking in that bit of information.

'How did your team get into London?' Eira enquired.

Cole kicked down a gear and eased the Harley up a steep hill.

'If I said I parachuted from a plane like James Bond, would you believe me?'

'If the League had those kinds of resources, I would be very surprised. And who's James Bond?'

'You don't know who James Bond is?' Cole asked incredulously, but Eira's giggle told him that she was joking.

'James Bond is one of my uncle's favourites. He only watches the Sean Connery ones because of the Scottish connection. We used to stay up late watching them on repeat, much to my aunt's annoyance.'

Cole could just imagine a teenaged Eira sat on the floor, watching the classic car chases and fake explosions on an old-school TV.

'You still owe me that date by the way. Movie night?' She poked him in the ribs again.

'Hey, less of the beating up your boyfriend while he can't defend himself, and I'll think about the movie night,' Cole teased.

Eira's answer was a squeeze, which settled the debate. 'Seriously, how did you get into London with all those checkpoints?'

'How did you?' he threw back at her.

Cole tensed expecting another jab to the ribs. Teasing and banter had always been part of his personality; he had used it as a front to survive his grief and loneliness at first, but it had gradually become ingrained. He was so relieved that Eira seemed to give back as good as she got.

'As I was a registered medic, it was easier. They were in desperate need of help, so all it took was one of my potions to dilute my elven genetics and change my ears, a fake identity, and entrance was easy.'

Cole whistled. 'I wish it had been like that for us,'

He navigated through a sleepy hamlet before he continued.

'It took a few months of prep, but Lofty was able to hack the checkpoint system. We had fake identifications, but unlike some people, we couldn't change our blood. Over a week, we took it in turns to enter one at a time, whilst Lofty fed a fake blood and ID into the system. It was nerve-racking. If we'd been caught, our police or military records would have flagged us to be turned straight away. We pretended to be bank workers ironically.'

'Well, now we know all we need is an invisible motorcycle,' Eira joked. When he didn't answer, she continued, 'What was Lofty like?'

A loaded question, but Cole understood why she had asked.

'He was the best hacker and computer whiz I've ever known, apart from Isaac maybe.' Eira laughed at that. 'If it wasn't for him, we would never have found out what the Dark was up to.'

Cole paused, watching the hedges blur as he twisted with the never-ending road.

'But he was never a team player. He could be sullen at the best of times, shouting his mouth off the next. We all put up with him because finding a reliable hacker was hard. As it turned out, he wasn't that reliable. If he hadn't gotten drunk, Tag and Flint would still be here, and Sam wouldn't have been killed. None of this would have happened.'

'A wise person once told me the past shapes you, but it doesn't define you, Hawk. If the Dark didn't find out about your mission, we would never have found a way to defeat them. We would never have even met.'

Cole's insides twisted with butterflies at her words. 'I really wish I wasn't driving this motorbike.'

'Oh, yeah?'

'I just want to kiss you all over again.' Eira's thighs tightening around his told him that she wanted that too. Cole turned right into a nondescript entrance flanked by two low bricked columns, no signage or identification.

'We're here,' he said, his voice tight.

CHAPTER 29

⋉ COLE

Eira extracted her arms from around Cole's waist, placing them behind her. The sudden loss of her warmth was like being doused with cold water.

Cole had explained that they would be clocked on entry, and a doctor wrapped around his waist would lead to far too many questions. His heart fluttered, the anxiety building.

'Do you remember before you were arrested, I acted mean to you?'

Cole huffed. 'I sure do. I was taken aback at your sudden change to sassy doctor.'

Eira sniggered over the mic. 'It helped calm my nerves to pretend to be different for a while. It helped me deal with the situation.'

Cole nodded his helmeted head as he eased the chopper along the gravelled drive.

The sweeping drive was long, meandering through a small, wooded area before emerging at a bend next to an ornamental lake. The sight of it still took his breath away. Eira's breath hitched, and Cole imagined the wonder on her face seeing it for the first time.

A large stone-built mansion appeared on the crest of an incline, with views over the lake. Two wings extended from the main building, forming an H. The ornate chimneys pierced the overcast sky, smoke pouring from them. But it was the main entrance that took centre stage, with its protruding, sandstone oriel window above the steps leading to a thick dark-wood door.

'What is this place? I never imagined it like this. I should have asked more questions,' Eira said, a hint of wonder in her voice.

'For the history buff in you, it's seventeenth-century, which I believe is Jacobean. Welcome to Bramshill House. You should see the great hall. It's got ninety-two coats-of-arms. It was a police training academy; I trained here at sixteen, and just never left.'

'How have the Dark not located it?'

'It has been spread around that it's abandoned and burnt out. Pictures leaked on the internet, news articles, anything we could do to stop them looking. I think the Dark are too lazy and arrogant to look beyond their urban borders.'

'Fair enough.'

Cole coasted the chopper through what used to be the stable block. It all looked abandoned, but he knew better.

Eira took a deep breath, risking one more question as they approached the main entrance to the house. 'When Tag and Flint were captured, how was this place not found in their minds?'

'Chain of command. I was the only one who knew about it. We trained and lived elsewhere, which is why I was the golden egg. If they had been able to read my mind fully...' Cole was unable to finish that sentence. Instead, he continued, 'Tag and Flint knew the risks. They gave their lives so I could protect this place. That's why I am so surprised they've allowed me to return and bring someone with me.'

Eira didn't have a chance to reply, as Cole pulled up to the steps, stopping the bike and kicking down the stand.

Eira climbed nimbly off, removing her helmet and swinging her dark hair free. She was the distraction. She made a show of staring at the stoic mansion, sweeping her eyes over the arched turreted front, whilst Cole scooped the Incognito into his hidden pocket.

Heaving a leg over the motorcycle, helmet still on, Cole looked at the place where he had trained and lived for six years. It still felt like home. It had been his first haven after the death of his mother and the conflict from the gang he had fallen into.

Eira swaggered up to him, swinging her hips invitingly, and briefly placed her hand on his shoulder. He pressed his hands into his pockets to stop himself from reaching for her.

'It's beautiful, Captain,' Eira said loudly.

'Yes, very grand, wait until you see inside, Doctor,' he replied, taking off his own helmet. He turned towards the camera he knew was set up above the door, making sure it caught him.

They hadn't been able to change his eye from black to blue, much to Eira's frustration, but Oran had placed a glint of his light on Cole's eye, making it appear blue. As long as nobody looked too closely.

Placing his helmet on the chopper, Cole removed the flat cap from his back pocket and pulled it on.

Eira was behind him, waiting to follow his lead. Risking one last glance at her, Cole set his features into a neutral expression and stalked up the grand staircase.

They were greeted at the top by two armed mercenaries in camouflage gear standing either side of the archway. Cole stepped forward, unsure what Major Stone's tactics would be.

He crossed the threshold without an issue, and carried on into the opulent entrance hall, sensing Eira behind him. The walls were fully panelled with a flagstone floor. Upholstered benches flanked the entrance, and an impressive chandelier was suspended from the ceiling. It felt like a scaled-up version of the gatehouse.

'See, Doctor, very grand,' Cole said, spreading his hands wide.

Eira smiled, eyes twinkling. She crossed her arms in front of her, tapping twice with her fingers against her arm. The Morse code had been a genius idea when they needed to communicate, but in situations like this, they had created a simplified version for ease.

A door opened somewhere in the building, and the sound of clicking heels approached them. Cole turned, watching the figure approach. A woman in a grey skirt-suit and stilettos, a notepad in her hand, stepped into the brightly lit entrance hall. Her brown hair was pulled back into a side-knot which showed off her pearl earrings; she pushed her black glasses up onto the bridge of her nose as she approached, flanked by two mercenaries with automatics.

For a moment, Cole wished he could speak straight into Eira's mind like Oran could. He wanted to warn her about the spikiness of this woman. Meet Moneypenny... You see, I am James Bond.

'Welcome back, Captain Hawkins,' the lady said curtly.

'Hey, Janet,' he replied, flashing one of his charming smiles.

'And this is the doctor, is it?' she sneered, her lips curling.

'Yes, the doctor. Doctor Emma Backwater, please meet Janet the secretary.'

Janet pursed her lips, looking Eira up and down. Eira just stared her directly in the face, unmoved by the scrutiny. She plastered a pleasant smile on her face and stepped forward, extending her hand.

'Pleased to meet you.'

Janet stared at the outstretched hand in front of her, a look of mild disgust on her face.

Eira shrugged, letting her hand fall to her side. Cole stepped forward, a snide look on his face as he addressed the secretary again. 'We're here to see Major Stone. Take us to him.' He had to force himself to add, 'Please.'

Janet raised an eyebrow. 'You know the procedure, Captain Hawkins. You've been gone a long time, and we will need to conduct a thorough search of you both.' Her eyes flickered to Eira for a second, but then focused back on him.

Sensing the rage building in Cole, Eira stepped forward, lightly brushing her finger over his hand. 'Of course, Janet, anything to speed up the process.' She stepped forward, raising her arms. Cole gritted his teeth and followed suit, keeping his gaze on the floor to avoid watching the mercenary putting his hands on Eira's body.

Satisfied that Eira wasn't carrying anything threatening, the mercenary moved towards Cole. He stood stock-still, praying that they wouldn't find the Incognito in his pocket. The mercenary tapped his own head, indicating Cole's cap. Lifting it off his head, he handed it to him. The soldier made a show of feeling around the edges before handing it back.

'Right, this way please,' Janet said, gesturing down the corridor. Cole glanced at Eira and rolled his eyes at the secretary's back.

Cole proceeded first, placing his hat back on his head, Eira behind him, with the heavily-armed mercenaries bringing up the rear. Cole barely registered their surroundings, having walked the panelled corridors a thousand times, but Eira made a good show of appearing interested in the architecture of the grand house. He knew she was bursting with questions about its history.

Janet took a left, and Cole let out a sigh of relief. They were going to the meeting room in which he had told Oran to hide.

Janet unlocked the panelled mahogany door, holding it open for them to enter first. Cole turned left into the room, Eira going right. She made a discreet L with her finger indicating that Oran was to the left.

'The Major will be with you shortly,' Janet stated, and without another glance in their direction, she walked out, closing and locking the door behind her.

Eira raised an eyebrow, taking in the large room. Set at the back of the mansion, it overlooked the expansive courtyard gardens. Arched windows were dressed in fleur-de-lys-patterned, gold-silk curtains that blended with the pale sunflower walls, the dark exposed-timber floor a stark contrast. It was a sunny room, one of Cole's favourites. Major Stone held most of his meetings here, preferring the natural light. A large mahogany table with seating for eight people sat in the centre of the room near a white-marble fireplace.

Eira placed her hands behind her back and strolled along the wall, stopping every now and then to scrutinise an oil painting. Cole followed her, approaching the head of the table. He pulled out a chair and sat down, propping his long legs on the tabletop, and leant back, folding his arms behind his head. Eira positioned herself to his right, drumming her fingers on the surface, her middle finger flicking to the seat opposite her.

They waited for what felt like an age, neither of them talking or moving. Cole guessed that Major Stone was watching them through a camera, waiting for a reaction. But he wouldn't get one.

Eventually, the door unlocked, and three figures walked in, all in military uniform. Two males and one female. Major Rick Stone stood at the front and stared down the table at Cole. He was stocky, his buzz-cut hair peppered with grey, and his nose twisted from having been broken too many times. He raised a large, wrinkled hand and stroked his moustache. 'Captain Hawkins, alive and well.'

Cole's body was tense with the need to stand to attention and salute, but he forced himself to stay seated, giving a mock salute without even looking at Major Stone. This man didn't deserve his respect right now. He had left him in enemy territory for two weeks.

Major Stone's nose flared, eyes darkening at the obvious disrespect. The other two high-ranking officials glanced between Major Stone and Cole nervously. Cole didn't know either of them. The woman had blonde hair pulled into a tight knot, her short stature dwarfed beside Major Stone. The man was tall and broad, and he kept his hands clasped behind his back.

Major Stone cleared his throat and turned his attention to Eira, who he knew was trying not to snigger. 'You must be the doctor.'

'Yes, Major Stone, I'm the doctor. Please call me Emma.'

Her pleasantries seemed to disperse the atmosphere as Major Stone sat at the head of the table, his generals taking seats either side of him.

'This is General Kay.' He indicated the woman to his left. 'And General Bolton.' A gesture to his right.

Cole nodded his acknowledgment. Eira smiled at them both, clasping her hands together, her elbows on the table.

The tense atmosphere resurfaced as both parties waited for the other to make the first move. Cole's apprehension had somehow been left at the door; he could sit here all day.

'So, Captain Hawkins, you have intel?' General Kay said, breaking the silence.

'Yes, I do.'

'Which is?' she tried again.

'First, what I want to know is why I was left in the centre of London for nearly two weeks without any contact or rescue attempt?' Cole stated bitterly.

'You said it yourself, Hawk, you might have been compromised and had no way of proving it,' Major Stone said sternly, crossing his arms. Cole had kept his face tilted downward since Major Stone had walked in, keeping his eyes in shadow under his cap.

'But you knew I was already compromised, didn't you, Major?' The ice in Cole's voice surprised him.

The two generals shifted, pulling in sharp gasps. Cole rotated his flat cap on his head and raised his head, staring straight at Major Stone. The shock on the generals' faces told him that Oran had dropped the illusion.

Major Stone placed both forearms on the table, outwardly unsurprised.

'If you knew I was compromised, Major, why risk my visit?'

Major Stone swallowed. 'Because of the intel you have gained, and because of her.' The major didn't glance at Eira, but it was obvious who he was speaking about.

'Oh yes," Cole said. "We know that you went to Doctor Moyra Watts but were disappointed that she wouldn't give up any information.'

Major Stone's sharp intake of breath was the only evidence of his surprise.

'You see, the Doc over here is one of Doctor Watts's most valuable assets. Not only did she save my life, stop the virus within me, and is on the way to producing a cure, but she is also very highly respected and protected because of those capabilities. So, I guess I was just spoilt goods until I could bring her to you, right?'

The tension in the room was palpable.

'Was I that expendable? Like Tagger and Flint? Left to rot at the hands of the Dark?'

Major Stone's gaze was piercing, threatening. Cole leant forward, a challenge in his eyes.

Eira cleared her throat, drawing Major Stone's attention to her. 'We know that the League gives resources and funding to the Wallflower, for which we are truly grateful. We also know how close you and Doctor Watts are.' Eira's voice seemed to calm hostilities on both sides. 'We know that Doctor Watts contacted you when three of your members were admitted to her clinic,' she continued. 'Two of which, you organised to be transferred elsewhere, so that when they rose infected, it wouldn't lead back to the clinic. But Captain Hawkins was the oddity, he was the highest risk if turned. And now, only partially infected, he might still become a problem. You were willing to take that risk though and move him from the clinic, isn't that right? But the Dark came first. Moyra didn't have time to contact you and had to make the difficult decision to either let him be arrested or compromise the safety of her clinic,' Eira concluded.

The temperature in the room seemed to drop with Major Stone's icy gaze. 'How do you know this? Are you a detective as well as a doctor?'

No denial then.

'No, I'm not. I'm just very persuasive when it comes to my demonstrations. Moyra told us everything when I showed her what I can do.' Major Stone's eyes grew wide. 'Oh yes, all the information we fed you is true, we really do hold the key to removing the virus from a host. Care for a demonstration?'

Eira pursed her lips, her own eyes narrowed with the challenge. The two generals looked stunned, eyes darting around. Major Stone sat rigid.

Whilst Eira held their attention, Cole had removed the Incognito from his jacket. He now fisted it in one hand.

'Unlike you, Major, I do not leave friends behind.'

Cole slammed the small orb onto the table at the same time as Oran removed his hand from the body that he had been shielding. All three members of the League jumped to their feet, fear and anger clear on their faces.

'Now, I suggest you stay behind me. He will wake soon, and we don't want him to give away this location, do we?' Cole said with a smirk.

They moved hesitantly, not taking their eyes off the table as they stepped behind Cole.

Cole activated the Incognito. 'This will shield us from him. I swear that he will not be able to see or hear us.'

No one answered.

Cole had said that they needed live bait for this plan. It could have been anyone, but he needed it to be his friend. The one who had given his life for his survival. Luckily, Oran had been able to intercept him with little trouble.

James Tagger was dressed in an immaculate black suit, his chin resting limply against his chest, ginger hair falling over his face.

At a subtle signal from Cole, Oran released Tagger from his enforced slumber. The man's head flew up, his black-void eyes darting from side to side. He immediately tried to stand, but the gargoyle had bound his hands and feet to the chair. He started to moan and pant as he tried to break free.

Cole kept his cool, not letting the sight of his friend in distress affect him. Visibly, at least. Inside, his throat was burning with bile, and it was all he could do not to react. It was a necessary evil. Major Stone needed to see the effects of the virus up close. The League members shrank away, their hands flying to their weapons.

Without further ceremony, Cole reached under the table and placed his bracelet on Tagger's wrist. The effect was immediate, Tagger's body shook, and his mouth opened in a silent scream. His eyes widened with the strain, and he fought against the restraints. Cole watched in astonishment as the black veins tracing his friend's body receded.

Cole risked a glance at Eira, the women who had made this possible. She had been watching him, not Tagger. Worry creased her beautiful face, but she softened when she caught his eye.

Finally, Tagger stopped convulsing and looked around the room with green eyes, all trace of the virus gone. Cole turned to Major Stone, who nodded once, something like grim acceptance gracing his face. Cole took that as a sign of approval to drop their protection, so he deactivated the orb, sliding it across to Eira.

Tagger physically jumped, staring around in bewilderment. His face, normally so full of humour and joy, was pale and slack. He gulped, licking his lips. 'Hawk is that you?' he croaked.

'Sure is mate.' Cole's own voice hitched with emotion. 'Welcome back.' Tagger took them all in. Then his gaze settled on Eira.

'Who's the babe in black?'

‖‖‖ EIRA

Eira watched as James Tagger came around from what must have been an extremely traumatic dream of slavery. She almost choked with laughter at his first words, but Cole didn't have the same restraint, letting out a bark of laughter. He had been instrumental in coming up with the plan and connecting Moyra to Major Stone had been the ultimate golden nugget, the ace up their sleeve.

I like him, came Oran's voice in her head.

Eira had to agree, the other man was indeed very likeable. But the delight he brought to Cole's face was the main reason she liked him.

This has all been most entertaining. An insight into human behaviour. Oran almost sounded bored. She could picture him leaning against the wall, picking at his nails.

What would the gargoyles have done in this situation?

Oh, there would definitely have been bloodshed.

Eira quirked a smirk, no one taking any notice of her as they stared at Tagger.

You were right to have chosen the captain for this. He's good at negotiating.

Before Eira could reply, Cole's voice brought her back to the conversation.

'Tag, this is Doctor Backwater. She saved my life, and now yours.'

The Irishman wolf-whistled, his eyes sparkling as they swept Eira's form. 'Are you sure, mate? She looks nothing like any doctor I've ever seen. She's hot!'

Eira sniggered.

'I can promise you that she is a doctor,' Cole bit out. Eira angled her head at his tone. Was he trying to lay claim to her without saying it out loud?

But Tagger seemed to understand. He grinned, looking between the two of them subtly before turning away.

'Well, Doctor, it appears I owe you a thank you for getting me out of that hellhole. Now, can someone get these off?'

Cole stood, grasping his friend's neck, and placing his forehead against his. 'It's good to have you back, Tag.' Raw emotion coated his words, and Eira resisted the urge to comfort him, to touch his hand and sooth him.

Cole released Tagger's bonds, removing the bracelet at the same time. Tagger rotated his wrists, working the tightness from them. He looked down at himself. 'I need some new clothes and a pint.'

'All in good time, mate.' Cole reached down and pulled his friend to his feet.

Eira, the only one left sitting, eased her feet onto the table as Cole had done, looking calm and in control.

Cole turned to Major Stone, all humour gone from his face. 'This is what we've come to bargain with. A way to expel the virus from a host. But without your help we can't produce more.'

Cole handed the bracelet to him; Major Stone turned it around in his hand.

'A gift to show our good intentions.'

'But—' Eira blurted as she took her feet off the table. 'Captain, that's yours.' For your protection.

'I know, Doc, but it's a gesture of goodwill.' Cole glanced at her, eyes wide, willing her to understand.

'I presume that Flint was the other demonstration?' Major Stone asked.

Cole nodded. 'He's safe and well.'

'I would expect nothing else, Captain.' The respect on Major Stone's face was clear. He turned to his generals. 'You are dismissed.'

'But...' started General Kay.

'I said, dismissed,' Major Stone replied in a tone that held no room for arguments.

They both saluted and marched from the room, shutting the door behind them.

'Right, I'd like to hear your plan.'

'*Our* plan,' replied Cole in an even voice, 'is to strike the serpent at its head.'

Somehow the plan they had come up with had become important to them all. It was Oran who had suggested the wider plan, the architect behind its creation. Not all of it had been worked out yet — the stone columns in the training room came to mind — but their intentions were the same, merged.

'You speak like you have a team, Captain. But all I see is the doctor. Have you left the League to pursue your own goals?' Major Stone enquired coldly.

Eira was so fed up with being called the doctor that it took all her self-control not to fly at Major Stone and punch him in the face. She braced her hands on the table, watching the exchange. Tagger stepped forward next to Cole.

Cole's jaw locked, a tendon in his neck pulsing, hands clenched at his side. 'I'm still very much part of the League, Major. The goals of the League are my own goals, as they always have been.'

Eira wasn't surprised by Cole's reply — she knew they had to keep Major Stone on side, but disappointment still gripped her.

'Good to hear it, Captain. After we've talked tactics and heard Tagger's report, you can take the doctor back to London and return to brief your new team.'

With that he stalked to the other end of the table, then turned and saluted. 'That's an order, Captain Hawkins.'

Cole saluted back rigidly, glancing at Eira with devastation in his eyes.

Eira's breath hitched, and she had to blink back tears. What else had she expected? But the scent of sea salt wrapped around her, and she knew her protector was with her.

CHAPTER 30

ORAN

'Oran, release him now!' Eira cried, digging her nails into his bicep, nearly drawing blood.

Oran had Cole pinned to the trunk of an oak tree, his forearm at his throat. If he really wanted to hurt him, Cole would have been dead on first impact. His eyes were wide as he grabbed at Oran's arm, trying to find purchase.

'What is this about, Oran? We've been through this. I like him, Oran, I like him a lot, and would prefer him whole. Don't make me...'

Eira sounded panicked. He could feel her magic seeping through the bond, trying to calm him. His eyes snapped to hers at her comment.

Oran had been entertained by the humans' exchange — it was eye-opening to watch negotiations without snarling, fighting, or drawing blood. What had infuriated him was Eira's disappointment and sadness, her deflation. As the meeting had proceeded, she had become more withdrawn. He knew that the dismissal of Major Stone had been a part of it, but it was Cole agreeing to leave her in London that had really hurt. Her pain had seeped through the bond, combining with his own emotions.

Oran had launched at Cole without thinking the instant he climbed off the bike. His nerves were frayed. The regenerative sleep Eira had lulled him into had helped, but he was still on edge. He knew what he needed.

Nelka, his Echo. His Starlight.

Oran loosened his hold on Cole's throat, turning to Eira, snarling.

'Oran, please don't make me knock you out.'

He could tell from the look on her face that she would do it without hesitation, and he could already feel her magic cooling his rage.

With one last frustrated growl, he withdrew, letting Cole drop to the leaf-strewn ground. Cole bent forward, sucking in heaving gasps of air. Eira ran to his side, kneeling in the dirt, stroking his hair from his face, and Oran knew she was using her magic to take away his pain.

'I'm fine, Doc. Honestly, I'm fine,' Cole panted, leaning back against the tree and grasping Eira's hand.

Oran's hands shook, and he stared at them, trying to keep his rage under control. Running them through his mohawk, he lifted his head to the blazing, crimson sky above, shutting his sensitive eyes to the intense light.

'Oran, what's going on? Have you spent too much power?'

Eira's shadow fell over him. Why was she not shouting at him for nearly harming her mate? No, he wasn't her mate yet.

Oran looked into her eyes, and the concern on her face was nearly too much. With her hair dyed black, she reminded him so much of Neika. He swallowed, hesitating, before saying, 'I felt your anguish, your disappointment, at the meeting.'

Eira's eyebrows knitted together in confusion. 'But we won, Oran. The Major is going to help us.'

'He means what you felt about the Major's orders.' Cole's clear voice came from behind her as he stood up and walked towards them. 'I know because I felt the same way too,' he continued.

Eira turned abruptly, eyes searching Cole's face. He lifted a hand, cupping the back of her neck, and rested his forehead against hers.

'I'm not going anywhere, Doc. We'll find a way around it. It was bad enough leaving Tag there, but I won't ever leave you.'

Strong words, Captain.

Eira closed her eyes, bracing her hands on his hips, breathing him in. She swallowed, nodding, lost for words.

'We're a team, Oran, and you too.' Cole looked at him.

Oran staggered back. No one had ever said that to him, apart from Neika. It was always an order, or a challenge. An unfamiliar feeling settled in his chest.

'You played a blinder by the way, Batman. Great timing on making Tag appear. I wish I could have recorded their reactions.'

Cole chuckled, and Oran was shocked that he hadn't attacked him for his behaviour, or at least shouted at him. He had just brushed his overreaction off, like it was normal to be slammed into a tree.

Oran backed up. This was how it felt to be accepted. To be understood.

His movement caught Eira's attention. She looked at him again with alarm on her face. 'Oran?' She tilted her head, approaching him.

Oran what's wrong?

Oran inhaled, panicked.

Please don't, Eira begged, reading his intentions.

'Why do you feel you must go? Your emotions were amplified because of mine, that's all. This Bloodstream affects us both. But we're getting there.' Eira held out her hand to him.

'Because I...'

Oran stumbled over his words, the mix of emotions in his head overwhelming him. He was a member of a clan, the Keystone to that clan, but he was ignoring their orders to return. He was a soulmate to a gargoyle he adored, but he hadn't returned home to admit to the one he loved that he had lost the ability to turn to stone. He was part of this new team, where he had an endless pool of magic, and access to power he had never used before. It was mind-bending. But he was afraid to commit. He was a spare part in this trio where Eira and Cole's affections for one another left him with such heartache and longing for his own soulmate. And, adding to that, the fact that his real father hadn't reached out to him felt like a knife in his chest.

Oran closed his eyes, pinching the bridge of his nose. A warm hand threaded into his and gripped his forearm. He clasped Eira tightly.

'Because I know how you feel, Oran. I've been there – not able to fit in, questioning who I am. You need to know that I accept you for what and who you are. Yes, you have a temper, you're overprotective, and don't even get me started on your choice of pet who's shredded at least two of Cole's socks,' Eira whispered.

'I was wondering why I could only find a few,' Cole sniggered.

Oran huffed a laugh, opening his eyes. 'How do you know I feel like that? That I'm so confused?'

Eira bit her bottom lip and looked at the floor. 'I feel your emotions the same way that you feel mine. I don't know if it is the bond developing, but it used to be only glimpses or flashes, but now I get whole images.'

Eira closed her eyes, a tear running down a cheek. She quickly swiped it away, smudging her makeup.

Shuddering a sigh, she ploughed on. 'I can describe Nelka even though I've never met her. I know the respect and loyalty you feel towards Callan, and the fear and confusion you feel towards your real father. How you're imprisoned by orders and tradition, responsibilities that you can't shy away from. You're in physical pain because your clan has been tugging at your bonds and you've ignored it. All to stay here with us. And whilst I'm glad you're here, that's the part I don't understand.'

Eira tilted her head waiting for his rebuke, his challenge, his rage. He could feel it under the surface of her power, but it didn't explode the way he thought it would.

Oran was still. Even Nelka couldn't read him that well, which could only mean one thing. Her power was merging with his, increasing her ability to use mind magic. And that scared him.

Oran gulped, but he still couldn't find the right words. Then a thunderbolt of fear spiked in him. Did she know? Was she aware of why their bond was so strong and unique? Would she reject him if she knew the truth?

With a jolt, Oran withdrew his hand. He snapped his wings out and launched himself into the air pulling his goggles over his eyes. He didn't even feel the branches scratching and pulling at his skin as he shot straight through the canopy.

Eira's scream of Oran! projected loudly within his mind and was lost in the beat of his mighty wings. He wanted to close off the bond, but he had made a promise to keep it open.

Spiralling higher, Oran flew in a random direction. The clouds drifted between his talons like spider-silk. He broke through the cloud barrier, the air so thin his heaving breaths fogged in front of him as he hovered on the spot. Up here, he felt like he was in another world, the cloud a soft floor you could almost walk on, illuminated red and orange by the setting sun.

As the sun descended and dusk broke, bringing Lunar's rising, Oran bellowed to the heavens, his arms outstretched. He roared his frustration to the crescent moon until his voice went hoarse.

For the first time since finding out he was half-illumini, he was at a loss for what to do, where to go. Eira was right about everything she'd said. But he didn't know where to even begin to get his feelings straight.

It was so quiet up here. Maybe he should just stay suspended here forever. The only sound was the thud of his wings and his deep breathing. Until it wasn't. He strained his ears, trying to pick up on the approaching sound. A sound like windchimes in a cave met his ears, and his heart flipped.

Putting the aviator goggles on his head, he kicked out with his legs, wings flaring as he propelled himself forward, tracking the sound. He sped through the dark-blue sky, stars twinkling to life as the night unfolded, riding the breeze to help him gain speed. The windchimes grew louder, filling his soul with a rumble so primal and raw he almost sobbed with relief.

Oran spotted a crumbled folly on a hillock, ringed by a small grove of birch trees, their silver bark ghostly-white in the gloom. The sound became a melody, a calling audible to him alone. With a grin on his face, Oran turned invisible as he free-fell toward the outer border of the thicket. Alighting on the packed earth, he wrapped his wings around his shoulders, suddenly nervous.

The sound on the ground was intense, rolling and echoing across the hill, reverberating in the tower ahead. Oran picked his way through the white trunks, naturally not making a sound, like a predator stalking its prey. As he neared the folly, he didn't dare breathe.

A soundwave like a whisper spread from the folly, washing over his body like a wave cresting on the beach. He inhaled deeply. A sound like bells, a chuckle, followed the tempo of the melody. Oran staggered forward like a blind man in the dark and the sound washed over him again.

Oran lost all sense of self as he stumbled forward, arms outstretched until he collided with soft flesh. Kneeling, he peppered kisses over her swollen stomach. Something so treasured and important to him, he questioned why he had abandoned them.

'You have been missing for half Lunar's rotation and you go straight for the babe, Oran Light Bringer?' the musical voice tutted, speaking in Gork. Oran grinned onto her belly, tenderly stroking the surface. A hand, clawed at the tips, caught his mohawk and yanked his head back. Even though he was invisible, she always knew where he was. Oran closed his eyes, allowing himself a moment of reflection before he dropped his camouflage,

313

fluttering his eyes open at the same time to behold something beautiful.

His Echo. His Starlight. His soulmate. Nelka.

She stood, hands on hips, in a pose so reminiscent of Eira that he grinned. Her round belly swelled under her fighting leathers. Scaled armour like his own adorned her full breasts, shoulders, and hips. Oran swore that Nelka's belly had grown in the two weeks that he'd been away. Like him, she had clawed hind legs, but she was petite and slim for a gargoyle. Oran's eyes swept along her taupe forearms, the colour of a pebbled beach, up to her shoulders each adorned with metal, crescent-shaped shoulder pads. Her membrane wings flared, and he took in their indigo hue, matching her hair and nails.

Finally, he rested his gaze on her face, and her beauty took his breath away. She had sharp features, but they softened when she smiled, which she did often. She was like a gust of night-kissed air, so wild and carefree that he had become lost in her the day she had freed him from the trunk. Her eyes were so dark that they shone like onyx in the moonlight. Crescent-shaped engravings either side of her eyes crinkled as she narrowed her eyes at him, her long nose flaring.

Within a heartbeat, Nelka had Oran pinned by the neck against the side wall, her braided hair swinging with the movement, the trinkets jingling. Oran let her propel him backwards, completely at her mercy.

Nelka sniffed him, head tilted to the side so Oran could see her profile, her rounded ear pierced along the ridge, and small horns on show.

'You smell like another,' she spat, fangs bared. 'Like honey or nectar. No jasmine.' She snapped her full attention back to him. 'Explain. I felt you almost die, and then you sent me cryptic messages via your stone creatures.'

Nelka wasn't angry, she was pleading. Oran had never seen her like this before, and it broke his heart that he had been the one to cause it.

Nelka removed her hand and Oran sagged to the floor, bringing his legs up and bowing his head.

Running a finger along his pairing mark, he spoke to the root-infested floor, knowing that if he looked at Nelka, he would falter, stumble, and close up. Oran needed to get it all out, the confusion and the apprehension he was feeling. Despite what he had told Eira and Cole, his pairing bond and mating with Nelka gave him a certain privilege over their sworn oath, akin to talking to himself, so he wouldn't be betraying them. He didn't hold back; it had always been this way between them.

As his lips moved, beginning with why his father had sent him to London in the first place, it became easier, the weight peeling off his shoulders in layers. Oran told Nelka how he had found a female, so young but so determined and spirited. How the Dark had chased them through London, their barricade in the abbey, and how he got shot and infected. He told her about Cole and his team, and how they fitted into the story. About the Alchemists and what they could do. Eira's necklace and how they forged a Bloodstream bond between them. He told her of the effects of the bond, how it made him feel and how it was developing, how it terrified him also. The sworn oath between the three of them, and how dangerous it could be if others found out. He glossed over the bank heist, but even talked about how Eira had kicked his ass in a duel, and who had trained her. He tried to explain the primal rage he had felt, the need to protect her as she accepted the captain's advances. He ended with their meeting with the League and how he had slammed Cole into a tree, joking that now he knew how he felt.

Taking a shuddering breath, Oran finished, 'The worst thing of all, though, is that through the Bloodstream I've lost my stone shift. I can be awake during the day. It feels so weird but so inspiring. You should see the sunrises, Echo. They're breathtaking.'

At some point, whilst he had been talking, Nelka had moved. She knelt and sat between his outstretched legs, her pregnant tummy pressing against him. He dropped his hand to the bump, marvelling at the fact that they had created life. After five devastating miscarriages, it was finally happening. The joy it had brought him in finally knowing he would be a father, a better one than his real father had ever been. As he caressed his mate's bump, he felt a flutter, a pulse so faint he almost missed it.

Oran's head flew up, eyes sparkling as he locked eyes with his Echo, who had been quiet throughout his exchange, never interrupting, as steadfast as usual. Her eyes said it all, the love they shared was unbreakable, even if he was now linked to another female. He knew Nelka would put a positive spin on it and work around it. She lifted his head, wiping the tears which he didn't even know were falling.

'When I felt you wounded,' she said, 'my own heart stopped. I couldn't breathe. My right wing went numb. I couldn't fly, and my thigh throbbed. I wanted to find you, but I didn't know where you were, Oran. I was so scared. That night was one of the worst of my existence. When I woke and received your nightingale, I was so relieved.'

Oran titled his head, kissing her palm. 'I regret putting you through that, you, and the babe. I love you, Echo, my Starlight.'

Her smile was thin and fragile. Oran had never seen her so sad. He had put her through too much. 'I'll never leave you or the babe again.'

Could he risk his pregnant mate coming back with him to London to fulfil his bargain with Eira? He couldn't leave either of them; it felt like he was being pulled in two different directions.

'I understand, Oran, I really do.' Nelka stroked the side of his face.

Nelka placed her slender wrist in his pale hand, forearm up to the sky. A crescent moon was already embossed there, marking the oath she had sworn to protect his identity as half-illumini. Oran's moonlight flared silver in the night. Two crescent moons appeared interlocked, binding Nelka into the Bloodstream pack and her silence on everything they had just discussed.

Oran inhaled Nelka's scent. She rose onto her knees, gently pulled his face to hers and kissed him. It was like a shooting star, moonlight on a millpond, like coming home. It was so tender and brief that his body begged for more. She bit into his bottom lip before withdrawing, so he knew that she was still annoyed.

Oran sucked blood from his lip, knowing that it was the least he deserved.

'The chief is here, Oran. That's why I intercepted you. I never imagined that any of this could happen or was even possible. You have a sworn Bloodstream now, and it needs to be protected above all else. You were right to bind the truth, hide it from others. But you also have responsibilities to the clan, the chief, us. There's upheaval within our clan and others. We need our Keystone. But I also understand that you're needed back in London.'

316

Oran dropped his head, the reprieve he had felt on unloading his mind to Nelka overtaken by the dread of facing Callan. Soft hands lifted his face, cupping his cheeks, and tracing his crescent moon engravings. He peered into the face he knew so well, eyes bright with determination.

'It is time he knew, Starlight,' Nelka said. 'I have what you requested, but you need to face him before I can help you.'

They flew, hand in hand, over dark fields, and scattered forests, riding the thermals in the light of the obscured crescent moon. Protected by Oran's invisibility, they were unseen by the sleeping mortals. Like phantoms, they glided until the land ended, the smell of salt filled their nostrils, and the sound of waves crashing on the rocks soothed Oran's tension. Lunula, the main stronghold of the Crescent Clan, was located by the sea, so it made sense that Callan would want to meet somewhere familiar. Oran had first learnt to fly by jumping from a cliff just like these, catching an updrift, and riding it until he could control his wings.

Nelka led them in a dive over the cliff, swirling towards the thrashing, black water. Oran dropped their invisibility and mirrored her movements as she hovered to scan the jagged rockface, before diving towards it. Oran followed her, marvelling at her agility, and landed next to her on an outcropping halfway up the cliff face.

He snapped his wings in tight and directed his attention to the shadowy recesses of a cave. Nelka stood at his side, the rock beneath their feet trembling, stones and gravel bouncing loose and tumbling into the ocean below.

'I told you not to find our Keystone. He was mine,' the voice reverberated around the cave, vibrating in Oran's very soul. The sound was like rolling thunder, rocks cascading down a hillside.

Oran clenched his hands into fists, resisting the instinct to pull out his staff. Nelka placed a hand in his, a united front always.

'A Keystone is the central summit to our clan,' the voice continued, 'the piece holding us together. When that's missing, we all crumble. The two Springers cannot hold the responsibility alone. Especially when one is with fledging.'

Callan referred to the chain of command within the clan — Oran, the Keystone at the top, then Gaia and Neika underneath him as the Springers.

The plateau rumbled as scraping footsteps echoed inside the cave, and Callan's huge form emerged into the moonlight. Darker than his daughter, he was stouter than Oran, built like an ox. Like many of the elder gargoyles he preferred to be bare-chested, the embossing and traditions of his clan on full display across his rippling muscles. A black pebble, suspended on a leather thong around his neck, pulsed navy in the moonlight. His night-dark wings splayed as he stepped forward on clawed feet, wide nostrils flaring as he puffed out steam. Callan tossed his head as if ready to charge them with his large, scaled spiral horns.

'Light Bringer, where have you been to cause your Starlight to suffer so? Your clan was left wondering whether you were dead or alive.'

He spoke with anger, but Oran could see the fear on his face as well. His own anger subsided.

Oran stood firm, his voice steady as he replied, 'I've been assisting someone — one like me — to fight a situation that we have ignored for too long.'

Surprise flickered in Callan's amber eyes as he dipped his head, his black braid falling over his shoulders. The darkness behind him stirred. Oran wasn't surprised to see Gaia emerge from the darkness.

Echo and Ebony.

The sisters' nicknames. Gaia, like her sister, had their mother's indigo hue, but that was where the similarities ended. She had a stronger build, her father's darker colouring, small, scaled horns protruding from her forehead. Her powers to manipulate the night allowed her to be a stealthy assassin. Where her sister shone with starlight and enjoyment, Gaia was sullen and withdrawn. She rarely smiled and preferred her own company.

Oran noticed that she seemed more hollow than normal. In fact, she looked uncomfortable.

'State plainly, Keystone, what you're referring to,' Callan thundered, the cave shaking with his voice.

Neika squeezed his hand in encouragement. It was now or never. Glancing at her, Oran inhaled, rising to his full height as he stared Callan down.

'Come on, Chief. You've always known, or at least had suspicions about my heritage. You know I'm half-illumini.'

Oran flinched as he spoke aloud the words that he had held within himself for a decade. This was who he was, and he was daring anyone to have an issue with it. He finally accepted that he was different. It had taken a determined, selfless doctor to make him see it, but now that he had, he wasn't going to let go of it.

Nelka wound her other arm over her bump and hooked it around his elbow. Oran knew that if he looked at her, he would see pride shining from her face.

The ground shook once more as Callan drew on his magic. Oran threw a shimmering shield around himself and Nelka, palm outstretched as his light pulsed outwards.

The rock cracked, shifting and twisting underneath them. It swelled behind Callan, creating a small, raised seat. The chief sat down with a drawn-out sigh, looking suddenly ancient. Gaia, not knowing how to react, placed a clawed hand on his shoulder.

That was unexpected.

Oran exchanged a glance with Nelka, eyebrow arched.

'How long have you known, son?'

Callan rarely called him that, even though he knew he was his real father, regardless of biology.

'A decade, Pa.' Oran's own voice was thick with emotion, all formalities now forgotten.

Callan deflated, placing his head in his hands. He shook and the ground replied in kind. 'I presume you know as well, Echo?' Callan raised his amber eyes to them both.

Nelka simply nodded, watching her father.

'Why didn't you come to me?'

'I was scared that you'd reject me. Being half-species is a threat to the clan,' Oran whispered. 'I've always known that I was different, but I just thought my differences were a gift from Lunar.'

Callan huffed, shock clear on his face.

'I would never, ever do that to you, son. If I thought you were a threat, Hella and I would have killed you as a babe when we first held you in our arms.'

The name of Callan's dead mate sent a wave of sadness through Oran. She had been a mother to him, and to know that they both accepted him was a balm to his soul.

'Who told you?' This was important.

'He did,' Callan spat, steam pouring from his nostrils.

Oran knew who he referred to: his biological father.

'When you were found, we requested his counsel. We were still on good terms then. Ambrose identified what you are. He said you would be strong, fearless. A bridge between the two races. That Lunar's light would shine from the dark within you, and that you would be the first to walk in the light. He said that he would return for you when you had matured, but he never did.'

Oran buckled against Nelka, his eyes darting across her face, needing her comfort. She placed a hand against his cheek and Oran relaxed, his breathing becoming less laboured.

Oran didn't know what was worse, that Ambrose knew he was alive as a babe, and decided not to take him in, or that he hadn't come back for him. The rejection was too much. Callan's words were true; he was the first to walk in the light in some way.

'I don't know why he never came back, or why he decided to tell you when he did, but we're grateful to have you. You will always be my son and you will always be welcome in this clan.'

His rumbling voice was closure, a thick rough hand rested heavily on Oran's shoulder, squeezing once. The contact alone was unheard of, but the words spoken were what mattered. Oran felt all the weight he had been carrying for a decade lift from him. As Oran opened his eyes, Callan returned to his stone seat.

'I know why he did it, Pa. It's a power-play, an entrapment to further his end goals. He sent me to London, and like a fool, I blindly obeyed. I tracked what he sought and found it. But she is under my protection now, and I will not give her up.'

Oran spoke with a strength he didn't feel at that moment.

Gaia turned towards him, darkness rippling around her feet like mist. 'What have you found, brother?'

It was the first time she had spoken, and her voice was rough and strained. Oran licked his lips, holding back his own questions; now was not the time to enquire.

'The mortal term is hybrid. She is half-elf, half-human. Her powers are equal to mine in strength. She's as defiant as Echo.'

Oran grinned, squeezing his mate's hand.

'What are her powers?'

'She can heal. I have never seen a combination of powers like it. She saved my life.'

320

'And now you owe her for that?' Callan's question was loaded with suspicion.

'Oh, that debt has already been repaid. I saved hers first.'

'So, you haven't returned to the clan because you've been … what? Protecting this hybrid? Is that more important than your pregnant mate? Your duties?' Venom coated Callan's words, all signs of affection gone.

'This female sounds like she's capable of protecting herself, Pa,' Nelka said. 'But her cause, what she is working towards, is just. We've stood by for too long and it's about time we gave aid.'

Oran stared at Nelka, pride swelling inside him at her words.

'You trust your mate in this matter?' Callan asked darkly.

'I do, Chief,' Nelka said immediately.

Callan stood. The rock floor rumbled as he advanced towards them. 'And what might this hybrid's cause be? What has been so important that you have been rejecting your duties, your clan, and your family?'

Oran stood his ground, wings flaring against the wind whipping up from the crashing waves below.

'She has the ability to stop the virus claiming humanity. To stop humans from becoming slaves to the Dark. We've known about this threat for too long, have stood by and done nothing to stop it. It isn't only dangerous to mortals. It almost consumed me. Before long, the Dark will grow tired of mortals and will move onto magic-users. And then none of us will be safe.'

Oran looked to Gaia for support, knowing that she had seen the virus's effects. She stood there, tight-lipped, her face a stony mask.

Callan had stopped and was staring at Oran. He didn't seem to notice the tremors running through the stone around him. 'I forbid you to get involved in this matter,' he said, his voice dangerously quiet.

'Why must we stand by when innocents are suffering?' Nelka countered.

Callan flinched, turning his eyes to her. 'I swore an oath to Ambrose that we would not get involved. After what happened during the war, we will never involve ourselves in human conflict again.'

Oran was taken aback. Ambrose had been the driving force behind giving aid to the humans during the war. What had changed?

'Unlike you, I have sworn no such oath. I will not stand by and watch this happen,' Oran stated, pushing his shoulders back.

'You are sworn to me, to this clan,' Callan growled. The walls of the cave shook, and cracks splintered along the floor. 'You will return to Crescent Bay, and you will not become involved in this matter. That is an order. Is that understood?'

Oran grimaced, fangs bared. He would not roll over in this.

'No.' The sound was a feral grunt.

Callan slammed a clawed foot on the floor, indenting the rock. Steam billowed from his nostrils as he leant forward, hands clenched into fists, wings flared. Gaia sank back into the shadows.

'You will obey, even if I have to force you, son.' There was pain in his voice at the thought.

As the bindings took hold of Oran, tying him to Callan's will, he crouched over Nelka, who hissed with his pain, his wings protecting her and the life she carried. The pain was so acute, that it blurred his vision. For the past week, Callan's demands for him to return had been muted, nothing more than a nagging pressure at the edges of his mind, easy to ignore. Now it was like a hurricane, brutal and direct. All he had to do was submit to it and the pain would stop. The pain that his Starlight was feeling would ease.

Oran strengthened his shield, encasing him and Nelka as the ceiling rained hard rock upon them, pelting his protective covering.

Oran gritted his teeth, fists screwed tight against his thighs. I will not submit. That one thought took shape in his mind as he forced his will against Callan's order.

He would not submit to another's will, not in a situation as important as this. He would protect those he loved.

Oran started to rise against the pressure pushing him to surrender, his whole body shaking. He opened his eyes, and moonlight shone from them, the raised marks at his temples glowing.

'I. Will. Not. Submit.' The words came out in a growl.

His power surged through the cave. Images swirled in his mind: Nelka's tender face, her belly expanding with the new life they'd created; Eira's determined expression as she stared him down; Cole's knuckles as he traced along Eira's exposed back, his thumb trailing her spine, the look he had given her in that moment.

Oran would only submit to those he was growing to love, to care for. He respected and loved Callan like a father, but on this, his chief was wrong.

I accept you for what you are and who you are. Eira's words.

His power filled the cave, pushing Callan and Gaia back towards the shadowy recesses. The chief braced his feet, head angled, wings tucked in towards the expanding light explosion cresting over him.

Oran sank onto the plateau on all fours, wings sagging at his side. His chest heaved. He had never expelled that much power in one blast before. Dizziness gripped him. Oran tilted his head to Nelka who knelt beside him, concern and sadness shining in her eyes. Closing his eyes, he nearly collapsed, but suddenly he felt power flowing through him once again, strengthening him and pushing back the dizziness.

Eira.

Somehow, she had been able to share her power with him, despite the distance between them.

A large rough hand rested on his shoulder, and Oran braced himself for the rage that he knew was coming.

'You're ready, son, to become Chief. With that will and power, and with the heart to defend and protect, you will make a formidable leader.'

CHAPTER 31

||| EIRA

Eira stretched her bare feet out towards the ever-burning fire, wiggling her toes. She sighed, tongue stuck out in concentration as she scribbled another name off her list. Slamming the notebook on her lap, she threw her head back against the orange upholstered armchair.

It had been over twelve hours since Oran left. She knew he could take care of himself, so she wasn't worried about him getting hurt. It was the fear that he might not return which gripped her, that he would leave them whilst they still needed him. Despite her efforts, she had come to rely on him and Cole, and not having one of them around was disconcerting.

Closing her eyes, she extended her mind along the bond, practising the way Oran had instructed. It had become easier to expand her mind with Oran gone, and she knew that she was subconsciously seeking his presence all the time.

Eira had felt him in the small hours of the morning when the words, *I will not submit,* had thundered in her head, jolting her awake. A massive surge of power had followed. She had felt his pain, his determination and resilience, faint due to the distance between them. But at least he had shown himself. Cole had stirred, his legs tangled between hers, hand around her waist clutching her to him like his life depended on it. Eira had pushed her magic into him, soothing him back to sleep. It wasn't that she didn't want him to know, she just needed a moment to sort through the jumble of emotions overwhelming her. Then she had felt Oran's magic falter, and without thinking, she poured her magic down the bond, aiding him.

That had been hours ago, and she hadn't felt anything since. Apprehension was gnawing at her bones.

Eira exhaled, exhausted from the lack of sleep and the long shift that she had put in at the Nightingale to distract herself. Cole didn't come to find her at the clinic, and his absence at lunch was surprising. Eira knew that he had a lot to organise with Flint, but when he still didn't show at dinner, she became concerned. She'd sent him a quick text message, but he hadn't replied.

She dozed off in the armchair, the warmth of the fire lulling her to sleep. Eira woke to the smell of cinnamon and soap. She kept her eyes closed, pretending to be asleep, her heart fluttering with anticipation.

Cole's nose brushed the bridge of hers, his breath tickling her cheek. Her chest heaved, the tightness easing in his presence.

'I'm sorry, Doc. I didn't switch my phone on until now. I forgot I had it back to be honest.'

Eyes still closed, Eira smiled as his nose traced further down hers and he placed a tender kiss on her lips. She drew a hand around the back of his neck, running her fingers through his damp hair.

Eira pushed up and, catching his bottom lip between her teeth, she bit down, making Cole gasp. She ran her tongue over the bite, her magic healing it quickly before she slipped her tongue into his mouth. It was an odd way to kiss as she was upside down, but she still enjoyed it. Eira set the pace of this kiss, needing his presence after his absence all day. Long minutes passed as they lost themselves to each other, but then Cole chuckled against her lips and pulled back. 'As much as I'm enjoying this kiss, I might spill your hot chocolate all over you.'

Eira opened her eyes to Cole's dazzling, blue eye sparkling with humour. Extracting both hands from around his neck, she sat up, a red flush creeping into her cheeks. Cole reluctantly stepped away from her, but it gave her a chance to take him in. His unruly hair was damp from the shower, falling over his black eye as he quirked a smile down at her. He wore loose-fitting jogging bottoms and her Run-DMC T-shirt, which was tight across his athletic physique. He had a steaming mug in each hand, the sweet smell of chocolate wafting from them.

'Since you've pinched my T-shirt yet again, I thought I might borrow yours.' His eyebrows lifted in challenge. Eira narrowed her eyes, smiling back. She had taken a liking to his Tupac T-shirt and was indeed wearing it now. She self-consciously pulled it further down her thighs, remembering that it was the only thing she was wearing. Cole's breath hitched as he followed her movement.

Shaking his head, he moved around to the armchair.

Instead of sitting by her, Cole threw a long leg over her head making Eira automatically duck. Taking advantage of her bending forward, he slid behind her onto the chair, and Eira found herself nestled between his long legs, one slung over the arm and the other pressed against hers. She felt all flushed again.

She settled against his chest, a feeling of peace stealing over her. Cole offered her the mug and folded his arm around her waist.

Eira wrapped her hands around the mug, letting the warmth seep into her. She sighed, tipping her head back against Cole's shoulder, his spare hand caressing her thigh.

'He'll come back, Eira. He might be a sullen bat, but he's steadfastly loyal with all his oath and honour crap,' Cole said after a while, easily reading Eira's worries.

'I felt him last night. The connection was faint, but he shouted in my head so loudly it was like he was next to me. He was in distress, standing up to someone or something. But I haven't heard anything since.' Eira bit her bottom lip, trying to stop it trembling.

Cole slid a hand up her neck, caressing the patch of skin just behind her ear. She closed her eyes, letting him comfort her.

'Why didn't you wake me?' he asked softly.

'You kind of did wake, but…' She winced and trailed off.

'Oh no, you didn't use those superpowers on me, did you, Doc? No wonder I found it so hard to wake up this morning. I was offended when you weren't there,' Cole said seriously.

Eira opened one eye, catching the sarcasm in his voice, but still needing to check. The side of his mouth quirked upwards, a dimple appearing.

'Is that why you sulked for the rest of the day and ignored my messages?' she asked, grinning at him.

'Ouch, Doc, you wound me!' He nuzzled the side of her neck with his nose, running his fingers to the tips of her pointed ear. Eira shivered at the contact. 'Have I told you how much I love these?'

Cole stroked up the side of her ear again, and Eira arched her back in his grip — his touch felt amazing, but it was almost too sensitive. Cole huffed against her neck, loving the way she reacted to him.

He pulled away, swallowing the last of his hot chocolate and setting the mug on the floor. Left wanting more, Eira cleared her throat and set her own mug on the paper-strewn floor.

'What are you doing?' Cole enquired picking up a sheet of paper, squinting to read it.

'I'm cross-referencing the agent names from the information you stole with the military records.'

Cole went still. He turned to her, impressed. 'You're trying to work out who's running the Dark?'

'Yeah.'

Cole whistled long and low. 'My smart beautiful doctor. Why didn't I think of that?'

Eira's face went red, unused to the praise. Sliding back behind her, Cole stroked a hand down her exposed shoulder like it was the most natural thing in the world to call her beautiful and then touch her tenderly. She was new to all this. In most of the books she had read, couples would just move straight onto the physical contact, without spending time building the relationship first. But this was different. Special. Every day was a new experience, a new bit of information learnt about him. And every day, she fell for him a little more.

'How far have you got?' Cole asked.

Eira swallowed. Reaching forward she pulled a record book onto her lap and showed him an entry.

'Do I have to ask how you got these highly classified records? Or shall I just presume it was a certain ghost?' Cole teased, resting his chin on her shoulder.

Eira chuckled. 'Madam Scudamore struck gold to be honest. She couldn't get many police records, but I've made a good start. I'm working backwards from the last conversion which we know was Flint and Tag. We know there have been more, but that was where our information started. The Dark are surprisingly good record keepers, they even use first and last names. You wouldn't believe how many Smiths there are.'

Cole snorted, sweeping a hand up to tuck a stray curl behind a pointed ear. Most of the dye had washed out, so only the tips were black.

'You're working on the assumption that the further back we go, the less conversions there'll be, so we might be able to establish the ringleader? The first person was infected a decade ago, though.'

'I know it'll take time, but we don't really have any other options. The latest records show the grunts, privates, lieutenants, and the uniforms on the street. And I've already found a few captains,' Eira said, showing Cole an entry cross-referenced against the Dark's database. 'Madam Scudamore has gone to see if she can find some parliamentary records for me, as we know they were the first to be turned.'

'I'm so proud of that clever brain of yours. I know we're taking the direct approach with what we are about to do, but you've considered the larger picture, how we can strike at the top and end this.'

Cole rained kisses down her neck, sucking her skin until she tipped her head to the side, moaning. His other hand encircled her waist, drawing her into his lap.

'You haven't been the only clever one today, my beautiful Doc. I've solved a problem too,' Cole said, his breath tickling her neck. Eira had all but forgotten that he'd been out for the day, her mind so muddled from his attention.

'Oh yeah?' she breathed, her body straining for more kisses.

'I've solved my return to the League dilemma.'

Eira turned so fast that Cole jolted. One minute she had her back against him, kisses being applied to her neck, the next she was facing him, legs straddling his lap, holding his face. The look of shock slid from Cole's face as a seductive grin spread across his lips.

'I forget how fast you are. I must say I like this new view.'

Warm hands slid up her exposed knees and her skin heated. She felt both hot and cold. His hands caressed her thighs, taunting her with his light touches. A sharp breath escaped Eira as she looked down at her compromising position and the sensitive area she was sitting on.

Knowing she was embarrassed, Cole stopped his hands, leant forward, and kissed her. 'It's alright, Doc. We don't have to do anything you aren't comfortable with. I was only teasing.'

The fact that Cole was still willing to take things slowly, even with the position they were in, filled Eira with warmth. And she made up her mind.

She pushed forward, pressing her body against Cole's and kissing him hard. His hands glided further up her thighs, and her magic swirled through her, filling her with desire.

Cole met her demands, sweeping his tongue into her mouth. Eira looped her hands around the back of his neck as the kiss became lazy, consuming. His hands moved up her ribcage, drawing circles on her flesh. His mouth remained on hers as his hand travelled across her chest until her breast was a warm weight in his palm. He squeezed gently, his fingers stroking the sensitive skin. Eira shuddered, moaning against his lips as she arched into his touch. She opened her eyes to find Cole watching her, a sexy smile on his face.

Suddenly not feeling embarrassed, Eira leant her head against his forehead, both catching their breaths.

'Now you are the one doing the distracting. I've lost my train of thought.' His voice was ragged, his lips swollen from their kiss. He flicked her nipple one last time before withdrawing his hand from under her T-shirt. Setting his arms either side of her hips, he drew her in for a hug, bracing her fully against his chest. 'That was unexpected.'

'Yeah,' was all Eira could manage. She should be nervous. It was the first time she'd ever done something like that. But with Cole it felt so right, so normal. The fact that he had stopped, knowing that she craved more, made her want him even more. She didn't know if it was consideration, or a ploy to leave her hanging, but it no longer mattered.

Gathering her thoughts, Eira laid her head on his shoulder, arms outstretched, drawing patterns on the cushion. 'What were you saying before I so rudely interrupted you? Something about solving a certain problem?'

Cole laughed, the rumble vibrating against her chest. 'I took the old gal,' he said, and Eira smiled, knowing he was referring to his chopper, 'to see Flint, to fill him in on yesterday's meeting, and to ask a favour.'

Cole took a deep breath. Eira knew that leaving Tagger with the League had been hard for him. That he would rather have them close. She recalled their exchange as he clasped his best friend by the neck and whispered in his ear that nothing was as it seemed, and that he needed someone he trusted to be his eyes and ears there. Tagger had nodded once, and that was that. But they hadn't told either of them about her, Oran, or the world Cole now inhabited. That might have been a step too far.

Cole continued, 'I took Ben to the Wallflower.'

Eira leant back, looking at Cole, her eyebrows bunched together in confusion.

'Moyra was surprised to see us again after the whole demonstration thing, but she listened.'

'What did you say?' Eira breathed.

'The truth. As close to it as I could get anyway.'

Eira inhaled.

'I told her a doctor had saved my life, one of her doctors in fact. That she had captured my heart, and that I didn't want to be parted from her. I told her how clever, selfless, and determined that doctor was. How that doctor liked me a lot too, and in all the chaos of our situation, I wanted a chance to see where it went.'

Eira couldn't breathe. She licked her lips, eyes darting across his handsome face. Raising a hand, she traced the three vertical marks on Cole's cheek. He closed his eyes at the contact, turning his head to kiss her palm. They didn't need words at that moment.

'I could kiss you all over again,' Eira said softly as a grin blossomed on his lips at the memory of the bike ride where he had stated just that. 'So, what did she say?' she asked, not fully understanding his plan.

Cole's eyes danced with amusement. 'She said that I must've lost my marbles to think I stood a chance with that particular doctor.' Eira went to poke him, but he grabbed her hand, grinning. 'I know all your moves now, Doc.'

'Do you, now? I could have you doubled over on the floor crying if I wanted,' Eira threatened.

Cole raised an eyebrow in challenge, his smirk telling her that he might want to experience that. Clearing his throat, Cole continued, 'I think she understood. I think she and Major Stone are closer than we expected. She knows how it feels to be separated from the ones she cares about; she didn't say as much, but her expression said it all. Anyway, I wanted to use her relationship with Major Stone to our advantage. I asked if she would pretend that the threat to her and the clinic had escalated and that she needed my — and Flint's — protection because two agents had gone missing. I suggested waiting a few days, so that it didn't arouse suspicion. In the meantime, I'm stringing the

Major along that I'm on a stakeout, gathering information on the Dark's incoming shipments. I mean, that is kind of true anyway.'

Eira was lost for words. It was a risky plan, but it was achievable. 'You think the Major will fall for it? I don't think he fully trusts you.'

'Only time will tell.' Cole shrugged. 'I know I've lost his trust. That's why I left Tag there. The Major must understand how much I care about James and Ben — he knows the risk it took to get them out. So, he's the one with the upper hand right now, or so he thinks, at least. He'll be working on him as we speak, trying to understand my motives. But Tag's very good at twisting the truth.'

Eira smiled, remembering Tagger's reaction to her. She liked him already. She expected that Tagger knew about Cole's attraction to her and hoped that he would be loyal and protect their secret.

'Now who's the clever one?' Eira asked, planting a kiss on Cole's forehead. His answering grin was enough to melt her heart.

Eira stiffened suddenly as her power spiked. She was on her feet in an instant. Cole jumped up beside her, shouting her name as she flew through the hidden door. Her body answered the call in her head before she was able to articulate words.

Eira raced up the stairs two at a time, her bare feet slapping against the concrete. She rounded the corner into the third-floor corridor, speeding past the window she had left open to welcome Oran back.

Her power drove her forward as she burst through the door into their training room. She could sense him there, but she needed to see him with her own eyes.

Eira ground to a halt in the doorway, taking in the sight of him. He looked different somehow. He was leaning against one of the pillars, his body relaxed, an arm wrapped behind it. He wore the same scaled armour, his ivory wings wrapped over his shoulders, talons hooked against his collarbone. His staff peeked out from behind his back, her peacock scarf braided around the shaft, and his pearlescent curved blades glinted on his thighs.

But it was his face that looked so different from how he had been the last few days. The furrows on his forehead had smoothed out, and there was a light in his eyes again. He looked calm and composed. Happy. His mouth parted in a grin when he saw her, his fangs poking out slightly.

Eira bounded across the room and threw herself at him, wrapping her arms around his waist.

'Steady there, you're going to knock me over!' Oran laughed, his voice the sound of water over stone. He circled her waist with his arm and held her close.

'I felt you shout in my head. I could tell that you were fighting someone, and I felt your power and defiance. I was so scared, I didn't know what to do. I've been so worried, Oran,' Eira said in a rush.

'It's okay, Eira, I'm here now,' Oran muttered, rubbing her back.

Jogging footsteps came from the corridor. Eira turned, one arm looped around Oran, needing his touch to reassure her that he was still there. Cole rounded the corner, his cheeks flushed.

'Didn't take you as long as I expected,' Eira mused.

'I opted for the lift, didn't want to strain my human legs and heart,' Cole shot back, striding into the room. 'Good to have you back, Batman. This one's been beside herself.'

Cole grasped Oran's arm, which had been around Eira's back.

'Good to be back,' Oran said. And from the look in his eyes, Eira knew that he meant it.

'What happened, Oran? I understand that you needed space after slamming me into the tree, which, by the way, I'm not holding any grudges about,' Cole said with a smile. 'But Doc here felt that were in trouble.'

'I did have an unexpected encounter,' Oran stated, but didn't elaborate. 'Thanks for the power boost, by the way. I needed it.'

'You're welcome,' Eira said, pulling away from Oran, eyes narrowed as she searched his face. 'Your crescent moons are missing.' She reached up to brush two fingers across the now smooth skin next to his eyes. 'And your eyes are more silver.'

Oran opened his mouth to reply, but a different voice answered – a voice like wind chimes. 'Oran, Light Bringer is now destined to be clan chief. He bends to no one's will but his own.'

Eira flinched in surprise, hands cupped to her mouth. Cole sprang back, clutching his chest. Oran brought his arm out from behind the stone column, a huge grin on his face as he raised his hand. Eira and Cole gasped again as a stunning female appeared in the space next to him.

'Echo,' Eira whispered. 'No sorry, I mean, Nelka.'

She staggered, clutching Cole's shoulder, while Cole shook his head in astonishment. They'd gotten used to Oran's inhuman beauty, but Nelka was a demon goddess. Radiant, beautiful, and dangerous.

Oran's rumbling laughter spread through the room. 'That was so worth it,' he choked out, bracing his hands on his thighs.

Nelka cocked her head to one side, taking them both in. Eira knew from Oran's memories that she was beautiful, but she shone with a wild light in person. Her black eyes were quick and perceptive, but so full of life and starlight that they were hard to look away from.

Nelka advanced towards them, and Eira dropped her eyes from her mesmerising face to her form, inhaling a sharp breath as she saw a swollen stomach peeking out from behind the indigo wings that she had wrapped around herself.

'Oh, Oran,' Eira whispered, looking at her gargoyle protector. He stood frozen, raw emotion on his face as he gazed at his mate.

In a heartbeat, Nelka had them both captured in a hug, an arm slung over each of their shoulders, her pregnant bump between them. It was like being hugged by the wind – it was the only way Eira could describe it. Completely caught off-guard, Eira stood still, not knowing what else to do. Nelka spoke, but Eira didn't understand what she was saying.

'Echo says thank you for saving my life. She's overcome with emotion at the moment,' Oran said from afar.

She knows about the Bloodstream, doesn't she?

With our soul bond, it was like speaking to myself, so yes, she has been tied into the agreement.

What else does she know?

Eira peered around his mate's braided indigo hair at Oran; his eyes were intense.

Everything, he finally replied.

Eira inhaled as Nelka finally let them both go. Cole remained where he was, a look of such wonder on his face that Eira poked him in the ribs, drawing his attention away. He grunted, catching her hand, and placing a kiss on her palm. He might have just been hugged by a demon goddess, but he was still hers.

Oran led Nelka to a stool where she sat, one hand on her bump. Oswald suddenly appeared from the rafters, landing at Nelka's feet and winding in and out of her legs like a housecat. She spoke to the little beast in her mother tongue as she scratched his ear.

'Where are your manners, Doc? I'll go and get our new guest some refreshments,' Cole said brightly. Giving Eira a kiss on the cheek and squeezing her hand reassuringly, he jogged out of the training room. Eira knew that Cole wanted to give them a moment, and that he probably needed a moment to himself to adjust as well.

Eira looked at the two of them, suddenly feeling awkward. Oran loomed over his mate protectively, a hand rubbing her shoulder. Was this why he seemed so much happier? More complete?

Blowing out her cheeks, Eira sat on the spare chair next to Nelka. Feeling uneasy and not sure what to do next, she sat on her hands.

Would you stop fidgeting?

I don't know how to act.

Just be yourself. She already likes you.

Please speak first, I need a moment.

Oran snorted, folding his arms. 'When I flew away, Nelka found me the way she always does. We talked.'

'I basically had him pinned against the wall by his throat,' Nelka added seriously, rubbing her bump. Oran rolled his eyes.

Eira leant forward, eyeing her. 'You had *that* pinned against a wall?' Apparently, her slight frame hid a lot of strength.

'Oh, he might be big and scary, but he's no match for a female scorned.'

Eira huffed a laugh. 'Cole will be pleased that you got a taste of your own medicine,' she said.

Oran stroked the back of Nelka's head. The look he gave his mate was so affectionate, that Eira realised how hard it must have been for him to watch her and Cole together over the past week.

'I let you, Starlight. I deserved it,' he said.

Nelka tutted, rolling her eyes.

'Anyway, after our … reunion, Echo said the chief was looking for me. Which was inevitable as I'd ignored his orders for too long,' Oran trailed off, falling silent.

'When Oran learnt about his real heritage, we struck a bargain that he would tell Pa in his own time. Last night was the right time to tell him. It went better than planned. It seemed that the chief already knew,' Nelka continued for him.

Eira glanced at Oran, knowing what it meant to him, that Callan had always known and raised him anyway.

It turned out my real father knew about me from a babe. He was meant to come back for me when I was older, but again, he never did. Oran said through the bond, unable to speak it out loud as sadness clouded his eyes.

I'm sorry, Oran. I really am.

Oran nodded, glancing at Nelka who reached up, catching his hand, understanding his sadness.

Why tell me?

Because you need to know.

Eira tried to catch his eye, but Oran had eyes only for his mate.

They were interrupted by Cole entering the room carrying a tray laden with snacks. He presented it to Nelka first and said, 'I'm not sure what gargoyles like to eat, but Batman over there has eaten everything we've put in front of him, so I hope you're the same. Everyone likes hot chocolate anyway.'

In that moment, Eira's heart swelled even further for Cole. To be confronted by two immortals who could probably kill him with one swipe, and be able to act so normally, was a commendation to him. Maybe other humans could do the same?

Nelka's eyes lit up, and she accepted a steaming mug and a biscuit with a nod. Oran grabbed his own mug as Cole set the tray on the floor. He then spread his long body on the floor with a grin at Eira as he wedged a biscuit in his mouth.

'What've I missed?' Cole asked.

'Well, Nelka here slammed Oran against a wall,' Eira said, eyes shining with amusement.

'Did she indeed? I need some tips for next time,' Cole stated, waving a biscuit in Nelka's direction. Nelka smirked and raised her mug at him in salute, winking.

'So, what happened next?' Eira enquired, looking at Nelka.

Oran picked up the story. 'I told him about you.' Eira's sharp intake of breath was enough for Oran to hurriedly correct himself. 'Not about the Bloodstream, your name, or your appearance. Nothing that puts you in danger, I promise.'

Eira sat back. *I trust you.*

I know. Oran blinked in her direction.

'We told him about the wider cause,' Nelka said. 'Hinted that we wanted to bring the Dark down, and that you have the means to achieve that. We stressed the importance of saving innocent lives. We even talked about how the virus would eventually infect magic-users.'

'Do you believe that?' Eira asked her directly, needing to know where she stood.

'Yes,' Nelka stated without hesitation. Eira let out a breath.

'Callan made a bargain with my father that he would never become involved in human affairs again,' Oran's voice was cold, hard.

The more Eira learnt about Oran's real father, the more she disliked him.

'Do you remember what I told you about my markings? That most were ornamental but that some hold bargains or oaths sworn to others? The crescent moons either side of our eyes hold our chief's commands. If we refuse, he has the power to force his will onto us.'

Eira's pulse raced, sitting up straight in her chair. She remembered the words that Oran had shouted. *I will not submit.* 'You refused, didn't you?'

Oran nodded once, eyes closing.

'Oran challenged the chief, refusing to bend to his will. This meant that he was able to break his sworn oaths,' Nelka concluded.

Eira leant forward, bracing her hands on her knees.

Cole whistled, looking impressed. 'Has that ever happened before?' he asked.

'Not for a few centuries, at least. A chief normally hands the command to his next in line when the time is right. It's done without conflict. Pa has been in charge of our clan for as long as anyone can remember. Our arch, our hierarchy, is always a tripod. A Keystone and two Springers,' Nelka said, drawing a triangle in the air. 'Oran at the top, and then myself and Gaia, my sister, at the bottom. We form the chief's support, his inner circle.'

'So, one of you three would inherit the clan when Callan thought the time was right?' Eira queried, trying to keep up.

Oran paced behind Nelka, placing his hands on her shoulders, stroking along her collarbone.

'He has never indicated who the heir would be. I certainly didn't expect or want the position,' Oran said. 'I am not blood, or even a full gargoyle,' he added quietly.

Eira gasped as his words settled in her. Nelka's earlier words also rang clear in her mind. Cole swore.

Why? Eira asked silently to Oran. *Why did you not bend?*

Oran didn't answer. He watched her from over his mate's shoulder. His eyes burned with determination.

I accept what I am and who I am. A healer once told me that.

'Since I can remember, I've always been beholden to someone else's will. Callan's, my fathers. Never my own. I've been used as an instrument for tracking, for spying, for death. I rarely questioned my orders, only doing so a couple of times.' Oran looked at Eira, continuing in her head: *I'd started to question the way things were long before this, but then I met you. You've shown me that there's a different way.*

'Callan is a just ruler, fair and loyal, and he's a good father to me. But on this he was wrong. I reacted in the moment...' Oran faltered.

Nelka glanced up at her mate, the love they shared shining in her eyes. '"*You're ready, son, to become the chief. With that will and power, but with the heart to defend and protect, you will make a formidable leader.*" That's what Pa said.'

Throughout the exchange, Eira had watched Oran, the words shared down their bond almost bringing tears to her eyes.

Do you want this?

Oran was still, frozen in the moment.

I don't know, he answered honestly.

Eira knew how it felt to have destiny creep up behind you like a shadow in the dark. Cole's hand rested on her knee, drawing circles on her bare flesh. Eira smiled to herself, loving that he always knew when she needed comfort.

'So, do we have to start calling you Chief Oran now?' Cole quipped, grinning cheekily.

337

Oran rolled his eyes, the tension easing from his shoulders.

'That's all changed now that I have free will. Callan is still chief. He will keep the peace like nothing is amiss until I return to claim the stone throne. That is the **bargain we struck.'**

Eira released **a breath. She didn't know what this meant for** their Bloodstream. A thrill went through her as she thought about it. Not only was she bonded to a kick-ass warrior, but he was now to become Chief too.

Nelka shifted, and her bump jolted. Oran immediately bent down in front of her, caressing her stomach and pushing Oswald out the way. He spoke low, comforting words in their mother tongue, removing the mug from her hand.

'It's alright, Starlight, stop fussing. The babe only moved, that's all,' Nelka said, so that Eira and Cole could understand.

Eira leaned forward, her professional training getting the better of her. 'How far along are you?'

'A little **over eight full Lunar rotations.'**

Oran corrected, 'A little over seven months. The gargoyle calendar is in moon rotations which is twenty-nine days, making our months shorter than yours. Females have the same gestation period **as humans.'**

'May I?' Eira asked, lifting her hand. 'My magic won't hurt, and I can check that the baby is healthy.'

Nelka looked to Oran, who nodded his reassurance. She lifted her leathers, exposing her round belly. Oran traced her movements, a look of longing on his face.

Eira rubbed her hands together to warm them up, then placed them gently on **Nelka's bump. She closed her eyes, sending her** healing magic into the bump, her palms glowing. She had done this plenty of times on human mothers. The first difference was **Nelka's flesh which, like Oran's,** was thicker and tougher than a human. It was always a miracle viewing new life in this way, and still took her breath away.

Withdrawing her magic, Eira opened her eyes. The expectant gargoyles were watching her, the concern all new parents experienced clearly showing on their faces.

'All is fine. She's developing well and has a steady heartbeat. **She's in a good position with all limbs and wings attached.'** Eira smiled at that last remark. It was an odd experience to see a foetus with wings.

Oran's face went slack, and Nelka's eyes filled with tears.

Worried she'd done something wrong, Eira pulled back, glancing at Cole, who shrugged.

Oran gulped, shaking his head. 'A girl?' he enquired.

Eira slapped a hand to her mouth. 'Sorry, I thought you would know... The technology these days...' She trailed off, shaking her head. 'Of course, you don't have the technology. Can't any of your healers tell? I'm so sorry, both of you.'

Oran reached out and grasped Eira's hand, his face filled with wonder. 'No one can do what you can do, Eira. It's a miracle we've waited so long for.'

We've had so many losses.

Eira's own tears threatened to spill. For whatever reason, she looked across to Cole who had been following the exchange closely. He too looked overcome, a wistful smile on his face.

Eira inhaled deeply. Before she could change her mind, she guided Oran's hand to his mate's stomach, spreading his palm. She flicked her gaze to Nelka, who appeared confused. Eira splayed her own hand on top of Oran's pale one.

Send your power down the bond.

Oran didn't hesitate. As his moonlight flowed through her, Eira threaded her power with his and showed him what she could feel, the new life growing in Nelka's womb. After everything he had done for her, this was a gift that she could give him. Eira felt Oran's hand spasm as he inhaled.

You can see everything. Her tiny feet, arms, her wings. It's incredible, he whispered through the bond.

I think she even has horns.

I can feel her heartbeat.

All too soon, Eira retracted her hand.

Tears streamed down Oran's face, and his spare hand grasped Nelka's. She was also crying.

'Th-thank you,' Oran stuttered, voice hoarse.

'I have technology downstairs which can show you a physical image of her. It's called an ultrasound.'

Nelka reached for Eira's hand and squeezed it, the tears free-falling down her face.

'My pleasure,' she said to them. Standing, she left them both to their joy as Oran bent and kissed the swollen bump. Eira turned to Cole who stood, his own eyes large with tears. He grasped her hand, and Eira gently wiped his tears away.

'You're amazing. Amazing,' he whispered.

CHAPTER 32

ORAN

'This is your plan for the columns?' Eira asked, staring at Oran with her hands on her hips.

Oran sniggered to himself, once again reminded of how similar she was to Nelka. 'Are you ever going to stop questioning me?'

'Maybe. If you ever stop coming up with impossible ideas.'

She raised an eyebrow, crossing her arms in front of her.

The sun had just set, and they were all gathered in the training room. The previous evening, they'd created a new routine which allowed Nelka to participate — they would sleep later, and rise later, meaning that they would be awake when Nelka wasn't in her stone shift.

Oran was sleeping better than he had in weeks, the warmth of his mate cradled in his arms lulling him to slumber. The only disconcerting thing was waking to find her stiff and hard beside him, turned to stone for the day.

Now, Oran mirrored Eira's pose, folding his own arms over his bare chest. 'If we don't give it a go, we'll never make any progress.'

Eira huffed.

Oran suppressed a smirk. He had much to thank the doctor for, so he could be patient. Being able to experience his unborn babe's presence was a miracle he would never forget. It was like she had been wrapped up in his starlight, glowing as their combined powers traced her small body, her heartbeat. *She...* Oran thrilled. The thought of it nearly had him rushing over to Echo and begging to do it again.

The doctor had made good her promise and, the following evening, had shown Nelka a photograph taken from a machine that Eira had rubbed along her stomach. It was blurred, nothing like how he had felt her inside, but it had made Nelka so overjoyed that she cried all over again.

Oran looked at his mate, taking in the mischief in her eyes as she watched Cole assemble the guns he had commandeered from the League. He had explained the process to Nelka, who had watched with wide eyes having never seen a gun close up before. Catching her eye, he shook his head, sighing.

Eira chewed her bottom lip, her eyes roaming over the columns. She seemed nervous.

Oran stepped into her line of sight, his shadow swamping her. Placing his hands on her shoulders so she had to look up, he asked 'What's wrong?'

Eira sighed. He'd never seen her look uncertain before.

You can do this.

What if I can't?

Then we find another way.

But this is a solid plan, I don't want to mess it up.

'Show me how you normally manipulate your features. Start with your ears,' Oran said, stepping back.

Eira rolled her eyes like a sulky fledgling and then closed them, exhaling. Oran watched as her pointy eyes reduced in size and became rounded. She opened her eyes again, gritting her teeth like she had an irritation, then exhaled and let go of her power, allowing her ears to return to normal.

'How long can you maintain the effect for?'

'A couple of hours, four at most. I did it when the Dark raided the clinic, but it used up a lot of my power.'

Oran nodded. 'Can you maintain it for longer if I feed you my power? Like we did with Cole's eye?'

Eira had taken genetics, an impression from Cole's other eye, and blended it with his light to create an illusion to cover his black eye. She snorted now. 'What, like a battery?'

Oran tilted his head in confusion. Whilst he was learning a lot of their phrases, there were some that still stumped him.

'Never mind,' she added, noting the look of confusion on his face.

'Explain.'

'A battery is something that stores electric power. It's used in mortal objects, like Hawk's chopper. It gives them the power needed to operate.'

Oran clicked his fingers so suddenly that everyone looked at him. Cole paused, a section of a gun in his hand, and Nelka sauntered over to them.

'Heart Stones,' he said, directing his statement to Nelka. She nodded once and disappeared.

Eira looked up at him, eyebrows raised like he had gone insane. Oran ran his hand through his mohawk, trying to get the idea straight in his head. Could they risk testing it? Nelka had only brought six Heart Stones with her. They were rare and sacred to the gargoyles, so he had to tread carefully.

'Your manipulation of stone using my power didn't work. Would you agree?'

'Yes, I would.'

'But you can create a globule or shield of light and shape it to your will without even thinking.'

To prove that she could, Eira held out her palm and an orb of moonlight appeared.

'I can heal myself using your power,' he continued. 'I haven't tried to heal anyone else, but I think I would be able to.'

'Are you just listing what we can and can't do with the bond?' Eira said tartly.

Oran mock-snarled at her, making her smile. 'So, my new plan...' he began.

'A bunch of stone creatures terrorising the streets would be enough of a distraction for anyone,' Eira interrupted, throwing her hands in the air. 'Can't we just stick with that plan?'

'It's not enough, Eira, for what we're planning now. We need time. We need to empty their base with a true misdirection. Give them something they are desperate to retrieve,' Oran pushed back.

'But what you are proposing is unachievable. I can't make a statue look realistic, even if you can carve one to look human. I can only manipulate something which is alive. Something that's organic,' Eira argued, blowing her cheeks out.

'How about when you combine my elemental power into the mix? You already did it at the abbey when you used stone to soak up organic matter,' Oran rebuked. 'My first thought was that I could carve the stone first and then you can add the likeness, the flesh. But the process needs to be done at the same time.'

Nelka entered the room, a black pouch in her hands. Cole, who had been peering down the barrel of a gun, dropped his gaze, watching the commotion.

Eira stilled, her breath catching. Oran could see her logical brain analysing what he had suggested, which made her special;

she could combine science with magic, the likely with the unlikely.

Giving her time to fully understand his meaning, Oran watched Cole place ear defenders over his ears and bring a large gun to his shoulder. Looking down the scope, Oran saw Nelka turn next to Cole, her attention focused on the target at the end of the room. As Cole went to pull the trigger, Nelka sucked in a deep magic-infused breath. The instant Cole fired, she pushed the breath from her mouth sharply, her lips a tight circle.

The target shook with the impact of two missiles, the noise filling the room.

The captain tore off his ear defenders and stared at the target in confusion. He glanced down at his gun, checking it over for any malfunction, shaking his head when he couldn't find any. He walked to the target.

Oran glanced at Eira who stood with her bottom lip caught between her teeth, her cheeks pink with the effort of restraining her laughter.

'I think you were off-centre, Captain,' Nelka stated coolly, sauntering up to stand next to Cole at the target. One hole was right on the bullseye, the other slightly to the left. 'You'll find that this one,' – she pointed at the hole in the centre – 'was mine.'

Cole glanced up in astonishment, his mouth dropping open.

Eira doubled over, spluttering with laughter. 'Hawk, your face is a picture right now!' she laughed.

Instead of getting angry or frustrated, Cole turned and smirked at Nelka, an impressed look on his face. 'Now that's a superpower I wish I had.'

Nelka performed a mock bow, stopping short when her stomach got in the way, grinning back at Cole with a glint in her eye.

Walking back to Oran, she dropped a bag into his hand and sat against the wall, stretching her clawed feet out in front of her.

Oran drew his attention back to Eira who, having managed to get her giggles under control, was staring at Cole with a look of wonder on her face. Oran cleared his throat and she turned, looking at him expectantly.

Oran beckoned for Cole to join them, then bent and picked up a sizable rock from the pile they had accumulated over the past few days. He chucked it to Eira who caught it easily in one hand.

Cole halted by Eira's side, sweeping his night-black hair from his face, eyebrows bunched in confusion.

Test my theory.

Eira huffed and gave him a disapproving look.

You know his features better,' it will make it easier. Capture something.

Eira sighed again, then with an apologetic look at the captain, she took his hand in hers, the rock in her other hand, and nodded at Oran, who fed his power to her.

Oran moved closer, his attention on the rock. He could feel his power flowing towards Eira, twisting and mingling so that it was hard to tell where one started and the other ended.

The rock began to shudder and glow with a silvery-white light. Oran pushed his will into the process, giving the instructions but letting Eira control it. The rock shone brighter before snuffing out with a shake.

Eira glanced at the rock in her palm and let out a strangled choke, dropping it. Oran's hand shot out and caught it before it smashed on the floor. He straightened, glancing up at Eira, who clung to Cole, a look of horror on her face.

Oran turned his palm over and stared at the creation of their combined magic. Even knowing what to expect, he was shocked at the perfection of the rendering.

Around the edges the rock was grey and gritty, but in the centre, there sat an eye. It was an exact replica of Cole's bright-blue eye, the surrounding flesh matching his skin tone perfectly. The only thing missing was the twinkle of life shining out.

Nelka approached the group and gasped at the creation in his hand. The eye quickly disappeared, returning the rock to its dark colour once more. He wasn't sure if it was Eira's shock, or their inability to maintain the magic that had caused it to drop, but he felt the drain on his power.

'That was incredible and creepy at the same time,' Cole stated. 'Is this the new plan then?'

Oran looked at Eira, pressed tightly against Cole's side.

Why are you scared? he asked.

We just turned stone into flesh. Don't you think that's at least a little bit creepy?

Oran shrugged. *I think the amazing outweighs the strange. It's never been done before.* He dropped the test stone back onto the pile without a second thought.

'Even if you use the Heart Stones for the statues' movements,' Nelka said, gesturing to the columns, 'neither of you can maintain the perception with one statue, let alone six.'

'Heart Stones. What are they?' Eira enquired in a quiet voice.

'Here, I'll show you.'

Oran pulled a rounded pebble from the bag that Nelka had given him. As he turned it around, they saw veins of orange and red twisting beneath the surface.

'In the abbey, it used up a lot of my power and concentration to maintain all the active statues at once, even though much of the energy was being directed through my staff. A Heart Stone is like the battery you mentioned, it maintains and strengthens my power.'

Oran reached out with his mind to Oswald who was perched in his regular spot in the rafters. The little beast spread his membrane wings and flapped down to land on his shoulder. Oran raised a hand, glowing silver with his moonlight; the light flickered and almost spurted out as Oran studied his own hand in disbelief. His light was normally white, but now it was silver, pearlescent.

Your eyes have changed as well, Eira said in his head.

He looked up from his hand to Eira, then to Nelka.

Nelka spoke gently in their mother tongue. 'It could be Eira's influence, or the fact that you're now to become Chief intensifying your power.' Nelka approached and laid a hand on his cheek. 'Your eyes now look like the surface of Lunar herself. You truly are a gift from her, my Starlight.'

Oran squared his shoulders at her words and continued moving his glowing hand toward Oswald's chest. The stone melted away from his touch to reveal a pebble suspended in the chimera's chest, glowing a flaming orange.

'This makes Oswald appear alive and gives him his energy. It draws from my power in small quantities. It's like what we call a spout in a bathing chamber, when the water is left on.'

'A tap,' Cole chuckled. 'Your power slowly leaks from you.'

'How many of these Heart Stones can you maintain?' Eira asked.

'I controlled ten creatures in the clan wars,' Oran replied, removing his hand from Oswald, and watching as the beast's scales reappeared.

'There were clan wars?' Cole asked, surprised.

'There is always bloodshed between the clans,' Nelka replied, dismissing Cole's comment with a wave and placing a hand on her swollen belly.

'So, controlling six figures shouldn't be a problem then?' Eira asked hopefully.

'Not a problem for me alone, and if we combine our magic, it will be even easier. Like Echo said, it's maintaining the organic illusion that's the problem.'

Eira nodded. 'You want to tie that element into the Heart Stone as well, don't you?'

'Exactly.'

Nelka twisted her head to Oran, considering. 'It would burn through the Heart Stone so rapidly that it wouldn't last long.'

'That's why timing is essential. But we need to test it to see if it even works first.' Oran tossed the Heart Stone in the air, watching it glint as it fell back into his palm.

'You're going to waste one of our sacred stones on a test?' Nelka gasped. Placing her hands on her hips, she flared her wings and stared at him. 'You're going to burn through them all, aren't you?'

'I sure am. I will not let the Dark take them. There's no safe way to get the stones back when the Dark falls for the bait, so I'd rather sacrifice them.'

Nelka took a deep breath, and Oran knew that she was preparing to argue.

'I know what you are about to say. I respect and agree with your opinion, Starlight. I don't suggest this lightly. More Heart Stones were wasted in the War and within the clan conflicts, for far less important causes. If we don't do this, we won't have a way to draw the snakes from the nest.'

Nelka sighed, sliding a hand over her face, her body sagging at his words. Oran placed a hand on her shoulder and squeezed. When she raised her head, she looked regretful but resigned.

'I never win an argument against you! I suppose there's a first time for everything,' Oran joked, nudging Echo in the side. She snarled in return, a grin spreading across her face.

'What are Heart Stones made from?' Eira asked.

'Dead gargoyle souls,' Nelka replied nonchalantly.

Eira looked horrified, and Oran sighed heavily, crossing his arms over his chest.

'It is not as simple as that. Nelka didn't have to say it so bluntly.' He stared down at his mate, who shrugged, unrepentant. 'When Lunar takes a gargoyle, their soul becomes embedded in their Heart Stone which is inside them.'

Eira stepped away from Cole, staring at Oran in shock. 'So, Nelka's right. We're going to activate our decoys with dead gargoyle souls?'

'These...' – Oran held up the pebble between his thumb and finger – '... are not gargoyles such as Nelka or I. I would never be so wasteful. Loved ones' Heart Stones are sacred, and they're treasured for eternity. Families protect their Heart Stones with their lives.'

Oran recalled the one Callan wore around his neck, the soul of his beloved Hella. He pinched the bridge of his nose, closing his eyes as memories of her overwhelmed him. He missed her so much.

'These are lesser gargoyles. Creatures of stone like chimeras and thorks. Their souls are no less important than the gargoyles, but we don't really have any other option.'

His statement was met by silence. Nelka and Eira did not seem happy about the idea, but Cole shrugged, knowing that sacrifices were sometimes necessary.

Do you have a Heart Stone, being a hybrid?

Eira's sudden question jolted Oran from his reprieve.

I'm not sure. I hope so.

He glanced at Eira, who pursed her lips and didn't reply.

'Right, we go forward with the plan then. Are we all agreed?' Cole demanded, moving the debate on.

'Yep, I suppose,' Eira said quietly, hugging her arms around her waist.

Nelka nodded sharply, still looking displeased.

'So, who will be the decoys then? I presume I'll be one of them since I'm a wanted fugitive,' Cole sniggered, trying to break the tension. Looking at Oran, he continued, 'What about you?'

'Not sure that's a good idea, Captain. I was detected by the heat-seeker drones, even though I should have only been perceptible as a blur. I'm hoping that I destroyed all the ones I encountered, so there shouldn't have been any remaining that saw my true form. I still don't think it would be a good idea to walk a gargoyle through the middle of London right now.'

Cole nodded, agreeing with his logic.

Nelka was quiet. Oran turned to her, unfolding a wing to wrap around her. He bent forward, leaning his forehead against hers. 'I'm sorry, Starlight, for suggesting we use our sacred stones to do this,' Oran whispered in Gork, tucking a stray strand of indigo hair behind her ear.

'I know, Starlight,' she replied, laying her hands against his bare chest, tracing one of his markings.

'One of the statues, our duplicates, has to be me,' Eira said softly. 'And the others should be Flint and Tagger.'

CHAPTER 33

||| EIRA

Cole's sharp intake of breath behind her told her that he didn't agree with that idea.

Eira glanced at Oran. *Do you agree?* she asked.

Yes. Oran blinked once.

Eira sucked in a breath and turned to Cole. If she had her gargoyle protector on side, they could resolve this.

This evening had been uncomfortable, and Eira was exhausted. The rock that she had sculpted into Cole's eye had sent shivers up her spine, and the thought of activating it with the soul of a dead gargoyle was macabre and sickening.

But what other option did they have? Their first plan, like Oran had concluded, wouldn't give them enough attention; the Dark wouldn't respond in force to stone creatures roaming London. They would know it was faked. They needed a larger, more realistic distraction, to keep the Dark busy while they snuck in. Doppelgangers of themselves would draw the Dark out en masse.

She squared her shoulders ready to face the captain. Eira sighed at the stubborn set of Cole's jaw. 'I understand that you're worried about me being in danger, but we don't have a choice. Who else is there? We need as many as we can get. Oran agrees, don't you?' she asked, turning to where Oran had been standing. But the room was empty.

Thanks for the support. A chuckle was the only reply she received.

'It's not that I don't agree, Doc, I'm just uncomfortable with the idea. Have you thought through the implications?'

Huh? She hadn't expected that. Sure, he wanted to protect her, he also knew that she could look after herself.

'If we use you as bait, the agents will come flooding out. When they arrested me, they said that I'd brought them the 'golden egg' or something like that. It seemed they were already looking for you before they even accessed my memories.'

Eira tilted her head, confused. 'What happened?'

'After I killed – you know – there was an image of you on the screen, glowing, with your necklace in hand. It was from a memory I didn't even remember making. I wiped it from their system, so they don't have it anymore. I might have also destroyed the whole console at the same time.'

Eira stepped forward and wrapped her arms around him. 'You were protecting me even then,' she said gently, pressing a kiss to his cheek.

Cole smiled against her neck, pulling her closer. 'What I'm trying to say is that the Dark were already suspicious of you. The evidence has been removed, but there might still be agents aware of the orders to capture you.' Cole pulled back to stare into her eyes. 'If you do this, you'll have to hide. You won't be able to stroll down the street or walk back into the Wallflower to work.'

'I can't do that anyway, not fully,' Eira concluded, gesturing at her ears.

Cole nodded, understanding her meaning. Eira knew that he hated the fact that she had to hide as much as she did.

'We'll be fugitives together then,' Cole joked.

What about after? They hadn't discussed that part. It would be risky to stay in London, but they had so much to do there that they couldn't leave straight away.

'Have you thought this through?' Cole said seriously. 'All the hosts are linked, so one glance at the fake you, and they'll instantly register you as the doctor who disappeared. You know they won't stop until they've captured you. There could be other consequences too.'

Eira jolted back, understanding his meaning. She could be putting the people she loved in danger. She'd seen the implications of that first-hand, when she had watched her mother die for standing up for what she believed was right.

Eira pulled out of Cole's arms, ready to run. She needed to get away. She needed to think. But before she could leave, Cole grabbed her wrist and held her to him.

'No, you don't, Doc, not this time. We need to talk about this.'

Eira bit back her retort, trying to calm the defensiveness that rose in her whenever she felt trapped.

'No, I haven't, Hawk. I haven't thought about the implications, or my safety, or even the safety of the people around me.' She closed her eyes and took a deep breath. 'And what about your safety, Cole?'

'I'm already a wanted criminal,' he said, flashing her a smile that didn't reach his eyes. 'I've been running since my mother's death. From myself, from the gang, from the fire. I found a moment's reprieve with the Police Academy and then I became swept up in the League, which put me in danger again. I'm fed up with running and hiding too.'

What did he mean? She didn't know anything about a fire or a gang.

'My identity, my life, it's already forfeit, Eira. I just don't want the same for you. If you do this and expose yourself as the figurehead to this campaign, you'll be in danger.'

'I'm capable of protecting myself, Hawk. I do know the implications of my exposure. I've been protected by others my entire life. Now, I'm finally getting to experience life, and you're questioning my judgement, my choices.'

Tears threatened to fall as she spoke. Cole tried to gather her to him, but Eira stood her ground. His face twisted with sorrow, and it nearly broke her. She knew that he wasn't trying to question her choices, and that he was looking out for her, but she'd had enough of that.

'Why do you want this, Hawk? Why are you even involved in this?' she spat. Why do you want me? she thought.

The words came rushing out in a torrent of emotion like floodgates being opened. 'This whole thing is a mess. You got what you wanted, you got your friends back. Yet you're still pursuing this as if it's what you want. How are you so calm about everything? I'm bonded to a gargoyle who has so much power it's mind-blowing. Did you see what we could do? We turned rock into flesh, and you didn't even freak. He's destined to be clan Chief, and I have no idea where I fit into that. His mate just blew a sound wave like a bullet from her mouth, and you laughed about it. Shrugged it off like it was nothing. I can put people to sleep like that.' She clicked her fingers. 'I can save people's lives with a touch, and I could probably kill you in one move. But you're only...'

Eira trailed off, realising she'd gone too far. She could see the hurt and anger simmering in Cole's eyes.

He released her hand, his eyes narrowed as he stepped away from her. 'A human, a weak mortal. That's what you were going to say, weren't you? Because my reflexes are slower, I fire a gun instead of using a blade or staff. Because I can be easily killed or infected. Because I'm a liability.' Cole threw his arms in the air, scowling. 'I know I haven't got any superpowers, and I know that I owe Oran for getting my friends back, because without him, I wouldn't have stood a chance.'

Cole stopped, his hands balled into fists at his sides.

'If we are being honest, then yes, hell yes, I'm jealous of Oran. What man wouldn't be? Have you seen his rippling muscles, his strength, his skill with a weapon? The hold he has on you. The insane way you two communicate. God, Doc, the bat nearly killed me twice, and I haven't complained. But, Eira, have you realised how you fixed him, made him whole? Without him you wouldn't be who you are now, and he wouldn't be who he is. God, he defied his chief to return, not just for you, but because he wants to make a difference. Like we all do.'

He sighed. 'I accepted these...' Cole pointed to his black eye and twisted his wrist to show his moon embossing. 'I accepted this...' He raised his shirt, exposing his scar. 'Why is it so hard for you to understand that a human has accepted you too? Isn't this what you have always wanted, a coexistence between the races? Since my mother died, I've been running, ricocheting from one scenario to another. The only decent decision I ever made was joining the police. The second, was remaining here, Eira. Not just for you, but because of the importance of our cause. I've never felt as accepted as I do here with the random family that we've created.

'I only wanted to be certain that once we do this, you know that there's no going back to that hidden life ... for any of us.' Cole reached out a hand and then dropped it by his side. 'You need to think beyond the now. And yes, I have dreamed of that future. If I hadn't, what's the point of any of this?'

Cole turned and stalked away from her without a second glance as tears streamed down her face. She remained frozen there for a long time, replaying his words in her head, and came to a realisation. That the man who had just walked out the door was the one thing she wanted most in the world.

✗ COLE

Cole tipped the drained spaghetti into the sauce and jabbed it roughly with a spoon. His damp hair fell into his eyes, and he pushed it back with a sigh, leaning his forehead against the wall cupboard, and screwing his eyes shut.

The chords of a song began from his tablet. He preferred old school hip hop and rap, but had stumbled upon a more modern song which fitted his current mood. 'Anxiety' by the Black Eyed Peas. He forced his mind to shut down.

On leaving Eira, he had stomped upstairs to the bathroom, hoping a cold shower would cool his mood. No such luck. Knowing that Eira would be in their bedroom, he'd headed downstairs, hoping that doing something mechanical would help calm the storm in his stomach.

That was not how he had imagined things to go. He'd had everything planned: a romantic meal of spaghetti Bolognese and a movie. He'd wanted to do something special for their first date. After begging Elowen and Madam Scudamore for some privacy, he'd left a note on the bed for Eira to find. She should have spotted it by now.

Dropping the spoon into the pan, Cole gritted his teeth. Slamming his palm against the cupboard door, one, twice, he shouted, 'Idiot, idiot, idiot.'

He'd said too much, bared too much of his soul, and he was worried that it had damaged things beyond repair. He'd never fallen as hard or as quickly for someone as he had Eira. Being with her, and with the others they had gathered around them, was the happiest he had ever been. He cared for them all, but the way he felt about Eira was overwhelming, all-consuming.

He knew that she could take care of herself, admired her for it in fact, but it didn't stop him from wanting to protect her. He had only wanted to make sure she understood the implications of what she was planning to do.

Cole turned, having made up his mind to go and smooth things over with her, but stopped short.

Eira stood near the divider wearing the figure-hugging, grey cord dress she had worn to the bank, and her favourite purple boots. Cole's heart flipped as he spotted that she was wearing his leather jacket too, her hair unbound in loose curls over her shoulders.

Eira held a note and a navy-blue knitted top in her hands. He glanced down at himself and almost covered his torso, a red flush creeping into his cheeks. In his haste and frustration, he'd stormed downstairs without a top on. She had gone to such efforts, and he felt underdressed, standing here in only his jogging bottoms.

A small smile twisted her lips, but her eyes were solemn as she raised the note for him to see. 'I have an invitation to a date.'

'I didn't mean to tell you what to do…' Cole began at the same time as Eira spoke.

'I've never dreamed of a future because…'

They stopped, sniggering. Then they both moved, closing the distance between them, Cole scraping his hip on the table in his rush to get to her.

Her sweet scent and the ancient smoky smell of his leather jacket flooded his senses, wrapping around him, and filling him with a sense of coming home. Cole rested his forehead against hers, a gesture they had become accustomed to.

'You're so damn beautiful,' he whispered, tucking her curly hair behind a pointed ear.

He inhaled, ready to apologise and beg her forgiveness, but Eira placed a slender finger on his lips, her eyes gentle. He wrapped his hands around her hips, waiting for her to speak.

Eira gulped. 'I've never dreamt of a future because no one has ever asked me what I wanted. Yes, the steps I've made to get here today have been my own, but they've been through reactions to situations, or trying to find information about my father. It's always been about survival. I know that you were only challenging my choices earlier, and it wasn't you trying to control me, but it reminded me that I'm finally fully experiencing life, and it's scary.' Eira exhaled, her breath tickling his cheek before she continued. 'Like you, I don't want to make the same mistake as my parents. My mother was careless and put herself in the firing line. I don't want my decisions to put the people I care about in danger either, especially you, Cole.'

Her words were like music to his ears. Cole stepped forward, pressing her back against the wall and kissing her. She returned his kiss eagerly, parting her lips to give him better access. He had never before experienced the feelings that Eira stirred in him, and he knew he was falling in love with her.

A hissing sound snagged his attention, and he quickly pulled away, turning towards the stove. In his frustration, he had cranked the heat too high, and the tomato sauce had bubbled over, spilling onto the counter.

'That's our dinner date ruined then.' Eira giggled behind him. 'Madam Scudamore is going to be furious! And she already doesn't like me.'

Warm hands slowly turned him, sliding over his lower back until he stared into her gorgeous green eyes. Eira lifted a slender finger and traced his hideous scar from his pectoral to his stomach, burning a trail of fire in its wake. Lifting a hand, Eira interlaced her fingers with his and tugged on his hand, her head tilted in invitation.

Cole caught his breath, licking his lower lip. 'But, Doc, I thought...' his voice trailed off as Eira's words vibrated in his head. Her choice.

'I want to experience all of life, Hawk.'

CHAPTER 34

||| EIRA

Oran's nostrils flared as Eira strolled into the training room, a small smile on her face.

When she spotted him leaning against the columns again, she asked, 'You're not going to make another member of your clan appear, are you?'

He'd spoken into her mind that morning, telling her that she had an hour to get ready and come to the training room. Eira had reluctantly unwound herself from Cole's naked body, ignoring his demands for her to return to bed.

Heat flushed her cheeks as she thought about what they had done last night, and the way it had made her feel. Cole had been tender and attentive, and it was so much more than anything she had read about in her books. It felt like a joining, a union, between them.

You've mated with the captain, Oran said bluntly.

Taken aback, Eira replied out loud, 'How do you know? You couldn't feel it, could you? Through the bond?'

Oran suppressed a laugh as she felt her cheeks warm.

'Remember our bond is mostly emotion. Although you were the one who mentioned layered imagery,' Oran replied.

So, he did remember that conversation.

'Believe me, I was busy myself last night. I didn't have time to worry about whether you and Cole were mating.'

'Why do you keep calling it that? It makes us sound like animals,' Eira blurted in disbelief.

'Isn't that what we are?' Oran asked, raising a silver-white eyebrow. 'What's the mortal term for it then?'

'I don't even want to go there,' Eira stated, waving her arms in front of her.

'It's only natural.'

'Still feels wrong discussing it.'

Oran chuckled at that, unfolding his arms, and stepping forward.

'As long as you took precautions, Eira, because of, you know, what could come from mating. I should know. I finally have one on the way.' Oran shrugged.

Eira's face heated again as she took a sharp intake of breath. 'I might be naive to all this, but I do know how it works,' she huffed, exasperated. 'I am not discussing this with you. It's like…'

'Like what?' Oran smirked.

Eira threw her hands in the air. 'I don't know! Like discussing it with a family member or something. I know we're bonded, but I don't want to talk about it. But I will tell you that I have a potion that prevents anything like that.'

Oran grinned, relishing her discomfort.

'How do you know, anyway?' Eira pushed, needing to know.

'Your scent is mingled with Cole's. It was how Echo knew I'd been bonded to another. That was the reason she threw me against the wall. Your scent is interlaced with mine as well.'

'Great, so you've both claimed me!'

Oran sniggered, moving even closer. She tried to imagine her new scent. Oran smelled like sea salt, and Cole smelled like spice and smoke. She couldn't imagine them smelling good all mixed together.

Another thought occurred to her. 'Can other Myths smell that my scent has changed? Does it mean I can be linked to you? It might put Cole in danger.'

'They would need to know you and be able to identify your scent in the first place to do that. I can promise you, it's a very subtle change. Only kin, and the ones you're bonded to, will ever be able to identify it. Cole isn't in danger, and he won't be able to tell the difference in your scent.'

'Does that mean I'm bonded to him now?'

'You've only mated with him. It would take a fusing of your souls and hearts to be fully bonded.'

'Is that a gargoyle thing?'

'Most of the high races have some form of connection process between mates. Ours is a sacred ritual in our temple. Before you ask, I'm soul-bonded to Nelka.'

'What does that mean then?'

'We've committed our souls to one another. It's deeper than just love or a simple mating bond, which is the same as a human's wedding ceremony. That's only words. A soul-bonding goes further. We feel each other's pain and are attuned to the other's emotions. If one of us was to stop existing, it would be like having our own souls ripped out. You only soul-bond with another if you connect deeply.'

Eira shivered at the thought of losing someone you were that connected to. Would the same thing happen to them because of the Bloodstream if one of them were to die? 'Has a soul-bond ever been made with a mortal?' She needed to know.

'I'm not sure. Don't forget, it's forbidden to merge our genetics with mortals or other races. Look at the results.' Oran grinned, gesturing to himself. 'Lifespan would be the first problem if a mortal and immortal were to soul-bond.'

Eira felt suddenly deflated.

Oran saw her sadness and placed a hand on her shoulder. 'If you and Cole soul-bonded, I don't know what would happen.'

'Since I'm half-human, I might have the lifespan of a mortal,' Eira said with hope.

'You're definitely immortal. You couldn't be as powerful as you are and be mortal.'

'So, our Bloodstream is similar but different to a soul-bond?' Eira said to change the subject.

'I don't know much about Bloodstreams, but they're normally a connection made by blood for a short period of time. Ours is unique; it has been shaped by our powers. We feel each other's emotions but not physical pain.'

Eira nodded, remembering the turmoil she felt from his mind the other night.

'The bond is developing every day.' He opened his palm, and a globule of moonlight appeared, swirling silver and white, his eyes lit the same colour. 'Your mind powers have developed – you would never have been able to contact me at such a distance before. Have you been practising?'

Eira nodded. 'When you disappeared, I was trying to find you. I expanded my mind and pushed my power out.'

'Good,' Oran said, placing a hand back on her shoulder with a serious look on his face. 'I know you can shield your mind from others. From now on, I think you should shield Cole's as well. Other immortals might seek a way to control him or gain memories which could be used against you both. Our oath will be a form of protection, but it's better to give him as much protection as we can.'

'He said that he thinks of us as a family,' Eira found herself stating.

Oran went still, emotion flickering across his face too quickly for her to read. 'I suppose we are, a dysfunctional one at that.' He smiled, fangs fully on show. He seized her chin in his calloused palm, running a thumb along her jawline. 'Promise me you will do as I've asked.'

'I promise.'

'Right, now to the reason I asked you here,' he said quickly, pulling a Heart Stone from his pocket and walking to one of the columns. His hand glowed and the column's surface expanded and divided at his touch. Oran placed the stone inside, retracting his hand and letting the surface seal shut, returning to normal.

'You're right about who the columns should be turned into. Has Cole agreed? I know it was a problem for him yesterday.'

Eira gulped, still uneasy about the process and fearful of what their combined magic could do. But she couldn't think of another way to lure out the Dark.

'All issues have been resolved, I promise you,' Eira said. Last night, they hadn't talked, needing only the physical contact instead. But Cole was collecting Tagger as they spoke, so he must have accepted it.

'How about Nelka?'

Oran's smug grin was answer enough.

'I presume we're going to test this crazy theory of yours now, without any distractions from our other halves?'

'Exactly.'

Eira cast her eyes over the stationary columns and bit her lip. 'There's no one for me to copy.' But then she understood. 'You want me to copy myself?' Oran nodded. 'I'll go get a mirror then. This is going to be weird.'

Eira turned to go, but Oran reached out and grabbed her wrist. 'Use my mind, my perception of you.'

Eira recoiled slightly, her hand threaded around Oran's on reflex. 'But that's a complete invasion of your privacy. I can't even do that,' Eira said, horrified.

'We both know that isn't true. I've trespassed too, Eira.' She flinched again, drawing a sharp breath as her heart hammered, but

Oran continued. 'I saw your dream reliving your mother's assassination.'

His tone was understanding, and she realised she wasn't in trouble for accidentally straying into his mind.

She chewed her bottom lip, knowing she couldn't deny it.

'When you were unconscious and I healed your wound, I went too far, too far down the bond, I think. It was so raw, so open back then. I only glimpsed layered images from your childhood, your first flight, training,' Eira whispered, stumbling over herself as she smiled. 'Nelka rescuing you from the chest. You, invisible, watching Nelka at a party, and her spotting you.'

Oran sniggered. 'I was an outsider, as you can imagine. I was infatuated by Nelka and used to use my invisibility to watch from afar, observing. Of course, her power enabled her to track me. She has slammed me against a wall more times than I can count for following her. But she gave me life, enjoyment, a purpose.'

'You're not mad?' Eira had to ask.

Oran shook his head. 'This is how the bond works, we trust each other. I just didn't realise it until you told me so.'

I accept who you are and what you are, Oran recited in her head.

'But, Oran, I could do all kinds of things without knowing.'

'Believe me, I know you could.' *But I trust you.*

She stared at him, shocked. 'If it's any reassurance, you opened your mind to me when we were testing the theory on the rock. I think this is how it needs to work. I couldn't have shaped the rock without you guiding me.'

Oran tugged Eira to the column nearest her. With his spare hand he splayed her fingers on the surface, laying his palm on top.

I'm simply going to open a viewing hole in my mind using the bond and let our magic do the rest, he told her, nodding in encouragement.

Eira inhaled, planting her feet more firmly on the floor.

Oran channelled his moonlight into the Bloodstream, and his vast power flowed into Eira, a sensation that was familiar but overwhelming. She closed her eyes as she always did when concentrating. She inhaled and split her magic, flowing one large part towards the column, and funnelling a small trickle into Oran's mind. There was no resistance, and she was able to enter easily.

What she saw and felt took Eira's breath away, jolting her whole body. It felt physical like something she could hold and grasp, and she knew she could manipulate his mind if she really wanted to.

Oran opened his eyes, and Eira saw what he saw. She was a passenger in his head. She nearly pulled back in shock but forced herself to concentrate.

His vision was sharp, able to take in so much more than her eyes did. If she looked closely, she could even see the dust particles floating around the room.

Stop freaking out. Breathe. Oran's instruction vibrated in her own head and his, making Eira jump.

It's so weird.

I know, but you need to concentrate. Just relax.

Oran squeezed her hand. She released a breath and tried to do as he requested.

Look at me, Eira.

Eira turned her body to Oran, her own eyes closed. Through Oran's eyes, she took everything in and gave herself to the magic. Her palm glowed, heating slightly as their combined power created their first Frankenstein. Eira could only see herself in Oran's view, but she heard the crack of stone, and the air filling with dust. The drain on her power was immense, but as soon as it flowed out, Oran's power was there to refill it. As she was finishing, Oran said, *Round the ears.*

Were they at the face already? Eira rounded the ears on the statue, humbled that Oran was protecting that part of her.

Open your eyes to me.

Eira shook her head, knowing how disorientating it would be, but Oran squeezed her arm, urgent now. They were using a vast amount of power and needed to end this. She snapped her eyes open and stared at their creation. She saw how Oran had defined her eyes, the vivid green, a slight silver tint to the pupil. His impression, his emotions, flowed through her in that moment as their eyes connected. It wasn't formed into words but was enough that Eira knew exactly what he was thinking.

Brave, so like Echo, defiant, accepting. Trust. Love.

Distracted by Oran's raw emotions, her knees buckled slightly. His strong grip kept her upright.

Eira you can withdraw from my mind but keep looking at me. I need you to maintain the render, so that I can bind it to the Heart Stone.

Eira withdrew her power from his mind, retreating down the Bloodstream, sighing as she became whole again. She gritted her teeth as weakness overcame her, but pushed on, maintaining her concentration. From the corner of her eye, she saw Oran's palm leaving hers and a beam of moonlight flare up, almost blinding her. Eira screwed her eyes tightly shut, their connection suddenly shattering.

Breathing through her nose, Eira glanced up at Oran, who had bent over her in the moment, their hands still linked, his membrane wing encasing her side, blocking the view of the column. Oran's chest heaved as he scooped her under the arms and brought her to her feet, then slowly lowered his wing.

The room was filled with dust, catching in the sunlight, and creating a haze. Eira looked down at herself, noting that she was covered in it too. As the stone dust settled, they beheld their creation.

They both gasped, unable to believe their eyes. Eira placed her hands over her mouth as she took in the figure before her.

It was a mirror-image of her, the only difference being the rounded ears. She hadn't expected it to be so life-like. The flesh matched her shade perfectly, and they had somehow managed to capture the different shades in her hair, the copper, and the blonde shimmering in the light.

Oran stepped forward, his claws clicking on the floor. He reached out a hand and ran a finger along the arm.

'It feels like flesh, but it's cold,' his voice was hoarse. Oran's expression was as conflicted as she felt.

To my knowledge, this has never been done before.

It's incredible, but so freaky.

You were amazing, Eira.

'Shall we activate it?' Eira asked, not knowing how to respond to Oran's praise.

Oran nodded, his legs shaking slightly. They'd both used too much power. Oran closed his eyes, wrapping his wings around his shoulders. The Eira statue shuddered and then advanced, so smoothly that Eira staggered back all over again. The eyes weren't quite right with Oran's moonlight behind them, but from a distance, it appeared so real. Oran gave the statue instructions, making it walk, run, and jump around the room. He even made it sit on a chair.

'Why isn't it more like Oswald?' she asked.

'I've given control to Oswald, so his personality has developed over the decades. I won't be giving control to these creations,' Oran said roughly.

That eased some of Eira's worry.

'So, do we just wait for it to explode? It seems like such a waste?'

Oran nodded, taking the stone Eira to a far corner where it would cause no damage. 'I'll stay, you can go. Get cleaned up. You must feel as exhausted as I do,' Oran's voice was strained as he sank onto a stool, putting his head in his hands.

Eira turned to go, hesitating. Before she knew what her feet were doing, she had approached the statue. She reached out a tentative hand and touched the shoulder of her creation. It was like touching flesh but without any of the movement or heat of a real person. Intrigued, she sent her magic towards the statue, telling herself it was just flesh.

Her magic felt weak, drained by the process, but it worked. It identified the statue as organic. Statue-Eira sagged, sleeping.

'I've solved our burning through the Heart Stone problem, Oran,' she whispered, her voice weak as she looked at the gargoyle.

He raised his head from his hands, not registering that Eira was still there. Oran glanced from her outstretched hand to the sleeping statue and wonder lit in his face as he understood what she had done.

CHAPTER 35

⋈ COLE

'The Major has allowed us to stay then,' Flint stated as Cole and Tagger strolled into his grandfather's kitchen.

Evidence of the house's new inhabitants was scattered across the laminate worktop; discarded pans sat in the sink, noodle pots and crisp packets littered the farmhouse table in the centre of the room, empty beer bottles were stacked in a neat row along the boarded-up window. Cole sighed at the mess, but he had to admit it was nice that the place was being lived in again.

Flint sat at the table, apparently oblivious to the mess he'd created. His broad frame seemed to fill the room, reminding Cole that it wasn't only Myths who were tough.

'It's a bit early to be on the beers mate,' Tagger said in his thick Irish accent, pulling out a chair and dropping into it.

Flint merely raised the beer in mock salute, the overhead light shining on his bald head.

'I've never seen the Major that agitated before, he must really like Doctor Watts to risk leaving you two here for her protection,' Tagger remarked, stroking his ginger goatee. His eyes still sparkled with humour, something Cole had been worried that he might lose after everything he'd been through.

Flint raised an eyebrow at Cole, a knowing look on his face. Cole rotated the chair opposite him and sat bracing his arms on the back, flicking his unruly hair from his eyes.

Cole had met Tagger halfway between Bramshill House and London. Major Stone had indeed been agitated, worrying about protecting Moyra and the Wallflower. Cole grinned at the thought of Moyra convincing Major Stone of this imagined threat. As soon as he'd seen him, he'd demanded a full report from Cole, who made one up on the spot. Cole had then requested permission to take Tagger with him, saying that he needed his skills as his second-in-command to scope out the Dark's transportation links. It was at least partially true. Major Stone had been so relieved about Cole's report that he acquiesced easily. To make him even more amiable, Cole had handed over four Incognitos, making a display of showing willingness.

'So, Captain, why am I here? I know it's not because you've been missing my pretty face,' Tagger grinned. 'I was enjoying having the Major by the balls.' He held out his hand scrunching his fingers together as though clutching an invisible object. Flint choked on his beer as Cole spluttered with laughter.

'As you're leading the second team on the raid on the Dark's main transportation links, I thought you might want to scope it out.'

'Fair play, mate. What have you found out?'

'We've had it under surveillance over the past week, and they haven't changed their routine. It seems that the same shipments are scheduled at the same times. I'll show you the plans when we get back to base.'

Tagger frowned. 'I thought this was base. And who is "we"?'

On cue, the kitchen door opened, flooding the room with the brisk autumn air. Flint flinched, and Tagger quickly swung his legs from the table, immediately alert. Cole didn't react, knowing he had to remain casual around her in front of his friends. For now, at least.

Eira stood behind him in the dress she'd worn the previous evening. He gritted his teeth, trying to stop his mind wandering to memories of the way she'd shuddered when he had stripped the dress from her body. She was wrapped in a thick bomber jacket against the cold, a bag slung over her shoulder.

Flint and Tagger remained where they were, taking a cue from Cole that they didn't need to worry about her arrival. Eira tugged her hood down, her honey hair curling around her shoulders. The headband was back in place to hide her ears, and Cole wished he could tug it off.

Tagger half stood, recognition flickering across his face.

'Hey, Doc,' Flint said.

As Cole took in her expression, he shot up from his chair, gently clasping the back of her neck. The carefree joy from this morning, when they'd woken up tangled together, had been replaced by tension and strain. She was pale, and there were dark marks under her eyes.

'I'm fine, Hawk, honestly,' she said, wrapping her own hands around his wrists. Her fingers started to tap a sequence. Cole stilled, counting the beats of the secret message.

Oran. Statue. Test. Worked.

Cole couldn't stop his sharp intake of breath. They'd done it without him. But what did he expect? He knew that it was something they needed to do in private, with no distractions, but the thought still irritated him. They hadn't even discussed it properly. After last night, he knew that Eira could see a future for them, but he still wasn't sure what that meant. All he knew was that he was falling in love with her.

Cole took in her exhausted appearance. The test had obviously drained her. And at that moment, he knew exactly who the test-subject had been.

'Oh, Doc.' Cole pulled her close, running his nose along hers, placing a light kiss on her lips.

'Seems the Major isn't the only one who has a thing for doctors,' Tagger said, his annoyance clear.

Cole had forgotten his friends were there, his attention taken up with Eira and her obvious distress. This was not how they'd wanted this conversation to start. He turned to Tagger who was standing, arms folded, one eyebrow raised.

'Ben, can you please get E—' He winced. They both knew her as Emma, but he couldn't bring himself to call her that. It was another lie. 'Can you please get the doctor some water?'

Cole rotated his chair back around and guided Eira to sit down with a hand to the small of her back.

'I'd rather have one of those if you have one going.' Eira pointed at Flint's beer, and Cole arched his eyebrows.

Flint shrugged and went to the ancient fridge in the far corner, its loud hum a constant companion in the room. He extracted a cold beer, cracked the metal top with his hands, and slid it across the worn table to Eira.

'Right,' Tag said, 'I know you hinted that you had a thing for the doctor in the meeting back at the League, and I thought you were punching then. But now I *know* you're punching. Because damn!' He whistled, his eyes raking over Eira appreciatively. 'I presume this is the same raven-haired beauty from the meeting? I was confused then; she isn't your normal type.'

'What is his type then, Tag?' Eira asked, swigging her beer with a glint in her eyes. Cole sat on the edge of the table, arms crossed, his thigh touching Eira's arm as he too waited for his friend's reply.

Tagger's face flushed as he muttered, 'He does normally go for blondes. But you're a redhead, just like me. Maybe I've been his type all along!'

Eira laughed, throwing her head back as Cole threw a bottle cap at his friend. The tension in the room immediately eased, and everyone relaxed.

'Have you boys got any food? Proper food, I mean, not this junk,' she added when Tagger pointed to the open packet of crisps on the table. 'Anything high in protein?'

Cole understood that she needed energy, quickly. He eased off the table, gesturing to Flint to tidy away his rubbish.

Half an hour later they were sitting around the cleared table, tucking into a cheese omelette with spaghetti from the tin. It wasn't much, but at least Cole was able to rustle something up.

'I've missed your cooking, Hawk, even if it is basic. We only got gruel when we were under the influence,' Tagger remarked.

'I second that,' Flint added, reclining back in his chair with a belch.

'Do you remember much from when you were under the influence?' Eira asked, stretching her feet out to rest them on Cole's lap. The colour had returned to her skin, and her easy humour with his friends lifted Cole's heart. He was glad that Eira had risked asking, but he was dreading their answer.

To his surprise, Flint spoke, folding his arms over his broad stomach. 'It's all a hazy dream. Like Tag said, the routine stuff is easy to remember. Y'know, like eating, sleeping, training. But specific details like what we were forced to do are blurry.'

Flint looked confused as he let out a sigh. Tagger nodded in agreement, fear spreading across his face. Cole knew that they would discuss their ordeal with him in their own time, but their evident pain angered him. He wanted to fix it, to make those responsible suffer. Eira caught his eye and nodded, knowing what he was thinking.

Cole bent forward, eyeing both his friends as he said, 'You're both loyal to me, I know that. But I need you to swear that you won't breathe a word of what I'm about to tell you to another

368

living soul. Once I've told you everything, you'll both have a decision to make.' Cole wished he was able to create a binding oath with them the way Oran had.

'Now I'm intrigued,' Tagger smirked. 'I'm game, and you know my loyalty and trust will always rest with you. You were the one who never gave up until we were free.'

Cole's heart swelled.

'Same as the ginger man over there,' Flint added.

Cole gestured to Eira, who reached up and unwound her scarf from her head, pushing her hair back so that her pointy ears were on show.

Pride swelled in him as he watched Eira tilt her chin, looking his friends straight in the eye. Their jaws dropped, shock written across their faces.

'I say it again, mate. How did you manage to pull someone as stunning as her? Sweetheart, with those ears, you look like a goddess.' Tagger shook his head in disbelief.

Flint rumbled with laughter. Eira's shoulders relaxed as she sagged back onto her chair, a look of relief on her face.

Cole quirked a smile at his friends, pleased with their reaction. 'Gentlemen, please meet Doctor Eira Mackay.'

'You are a real doctor then?' Flint asked, finally getting his laughter under control.

Eira bowed her head and grinned. 'Fully trained and qualified.'

Cole glanced at Tagger, who had a pensive look on his face. 'Mackay?' he asked, then clicked his fingers. 'Mackay's Scottish, isn't it? One of the older Gaelic clans?'

Eira nodded, tense.

'But you don't have a Scottish accent?'

'My home is in Scotland, but I never picked up the accent.'

'Okay, mate, let's get serious here. We can all establish that Eira is a hybrid. Half-elf, I suspect?' Tagger gestured towards Eira, who had turned to him in surprise.

'Who says I'm not a full-blooded elf?' she said defensively.

'I have seen and spoken to full-blooded elves in Ireland, and believe me, Cole wouldn't be able to do anything but drool and stare at you if you were.'

Cole choked, a slight blush colouring his cheeks.

Eira stilled. 'I didn't know that any of my kin were left on the far isles,' she whispered.

'They are. They're just very secretive and well-guarded.'

'Why did they speak to you then?' Flint snarked.

'That's a story for another time. But for now, we're here to listen to your story,' Tagger said, sitting back.

Eira looked like she wanted to push for answers, but Cole cleared his throat, drawing the conversation back.

'Eira is a qualified doctor and has saved my life twice. But alongside this, she can do other things too. It's probably better if we just demonstrate.'

Cole laid his forearm on the table, wrist up. Eira interlaced her fingers with his and in a quick fluid motion she sliced three cuts along his arm with her elven dagger and then syphoned his pain away. Tagger and Flint jumped to their feet, reaching for their absent guns.

'I'm a doctor in name and training, but I also have the power to heal.'

Cole felt Eira feed her magic into his body, letting her white light show, so they could witness the miracle of his flesh knitting back together. He knew that they were staring at his arm in awe without even having to look at them.

'Damn,' Tagger muttered, rubbing the back of his head. Flint froze, his wide eyes locked on the glow from Eira's palms.

'When Cole came to the clinic, he had a punctured lung,' she said. 'He was basically inhaling his own blood. Without this healing power, he would have died on the table.'

Eira's face pinched with sadness at the thought, and Cole leaned in, giving her hand a reassuring squeeze. He owed her his life; she now held his heart and soul as well.

'I can do much more than just healing wounds,' Eira stated. This was their only lie. His friends needed to believe that Eira could produce the stone duplicates on her own.

Tagger had sunk onto the chair again, his head in his hands. Flint leaned heavily on the worktop.

'What have you got yourself wrapped up in, Hawk?' Tagger asked wearily as he raised his head.

'Something bigger than us. Something bigger than the League could ever achieve. These are the steps we must take to end this dictatorship. The plan, as I've laid out to the League, is true. It's just that the backup team is a dysfunctional bunch of hybrids and Myths.'

'There are more?' Flint spluttered.

'Sure are. They're my family now, and can be yours too, if you want,' Cole answered, glancing at Eira. Her proud smile told him that she felt the same way.

'Wait until you meet the gargoyles,' Eira giggled.

Tagger let out a strangled noise and nearly fell off his seat all over again.

Cole placed a hand on each of his friend's shoulders. Their heads were covered by hoods to keep the location of the Nightingale a secret. After he and Eira had explained their plan, they'd agreed to join, as Cole knew they would.

Eira had arrived in the Nightingale van, so it was an easy trip across London, hidden within the Incognito's illusion. Night had fallen fast. Cole suspected his friends would have to stay, but first he had to introduce them to the others.

'Right, we're here. Remember your oath not to utter a word to anyone. Especially the Major,' he added. Both hooded figures nodded.

'I'm going to remove your hoods now. I'm right in front of you, and Eira is just behind me. Then you have Oran and Nelka to my left. They're...' Cole released a breath and continued, 'Well, they're quite something. Just remember that you're safe here and try not to freak out.'

Cole removed the black hoods from their heads and stood back to give them space. He watched Tagger, knowing that his reaction would be priceless. Tagger didn't disappoint. His eyes went comically wide, and he stumbled back, clutching his throat. Flint had more control, shaking with the effort it took to keep himself in place.

'Are you shitting me?' Tagger wheezed. 'How are they even real?'

Eira sniggered beside him and answered, 'Believe me, Tag, I can promise you they are as real as any of us. Oran stop doing your predator stare and come meet the new recruits.'

Cole turned to see Oran's lazy grin, his fangs on show. He slowly stepped forward with Nelka trailing behind him. There was a glint of mischief in her eyes too, and Cole hoped she wasn't planning on playing a prank on them. Not yet anyway. They'd both been given clear instructions on how to act. Rule number one had been to wear more clothes, so they were both in their armour.

'Tagger, Flint, this is Oran Light Bringer and his mate Nelka,' Eira said, gesturing to them in turn.

Nelka came to Oran's side, arm resting on her bump, the other resting on his bicep. 'I like the jumpy ginger one, don't you, Starlight? I reckon we should start with him for the feast,' she drawled in her melodic voice, licking her lips and baring her fangs.

Then she lurched forward, startling Tagger so much that he fell backwards onto his ass. Cole slid a hand over his face with an exasperated sigh but couldn't help the grin that followed. He looked to Eira, whose shoulders were shaking with silent laughter. Giving Nelka a pointed stare, he strode to his best friend and heaved him to his feet.

'Nelka is a prankster. You should've seen the stunt she pulled on me the other night. Of them all, she has the superpower I want the most,' Cole muttered, trying to calm his friend down. He heard Nelka draw a sharp breath and whirled on her, hand outstretched. 'Not yet, Nelka, please. It's too soon.'

Nelka winked and went to sit on the nearest stool, a hand idly stroking her bump. Oran waited, silent and rigid. It was unlike him not to make a remark. Cole glanced at the gargoyle and saw the same signs of strain and exhaustion that Eira had shown earlier, and it worried him. They were both clearly drained from making one statue, so making three might be too much.

'Thank you, both,' Oran rumbled. 'I apologise for my mate; she has a wicked sense of humour. I know you're important to Cole, which means that you're important to Eira as well. I promise that although we look scary, we're just as intrigued to meet you as you are to meet us. We don't get to meet many humans.'

Tagger nodded, for once at a loss for words.

Flint seemed a little more relaxed and stepped forward. 'Nice to meet you.'

'Tag, Flint, this way. I'm sure you need a drink after your shock,' Eira teased, leading them to where Nelka sat.

As they followed Eira, Cole grabbed Oran's arm, dragging him to a stop. Oran snarled, flashing his teeth, but Cole stood his ground, staring steadily at the gargoyle. Shock flickered across Oran's face before he grimaced in apology. Seeing that he had control of himself again, Cole released his arm. He needed to ensure that what they were doing was going to be safe for Eira. He wouldn't have her risking herself for this. And though he wouldn't say it out loud, he was worried about Oran as well.

'Are you both strong enough to do this? You look as tired as Eira. We can wait if you need more time,' Cole hissed in an undertone, so those with heightened hearing wouldn't catch his words.

Oran's posture deflated as he sighed. He ran a pale hand through his mohawk. 'It isn't a question of strength, it's about the recovery period afterwards. If we can do it now, it gives us time to recuperate and means we can be at full capacity when needed.'

With that, Oran turned and stalked to the table with the others. Cole let his hands drop to his sides. He hadn't thought about it like that. Major Stone was keeping them in the dark about when the mission would be authorised, so it made sense to be prepared. The team needed to be at their full strength.

Cole followed and sat at the table. Tagger was asking Nelka an endless stream of questions which she seemed happy to answer, and Flint looked content to observe.

Eira turned and said, 'That went better than expected. Nelka only broke one rule.'

Cole sniggered and grabbed her hand, bumping her shoulder with his. They stood together watching the odd mix of creatures in front of them. Warmth spread through him as he looked at his family.

Eira's hand pulsed once in his. It was time. Cole glanced around the training room, noticing that Oran had disappeared. Eira tugged his hand, and he remembered when she had done that the night before, and what it led to. His breath caught, and his pulse quickened. Catching Tagger's eye, he nodded.

Eira led him to a harmless column he knew would be shaped into a mirror image of himself. Cole gulped, suddenly nervous. He hadn't seen Eira's replica, didn't even know where it was, but he was anxious to see one made of himself.

Cole tried to retrace the conversation on the drive over, when Eira had explained the process. If he could remember, maybe it would help him relax. Eira said that she and Oran had opened their minds to each other and combined their power. Oran shaped the form, and Eira rendered the figure, but they had to do it at the same time. They created a loop, like a circuit, between them and the subject to be copied. The creation was then bound to the Heart Stone with a huge spark of light.

That doesn't sound too bad.

Cole flexed his shoulders, breathing evenly like he did when training, trying to stop his racing heart. There was a spark, and a silvery dome encased them.

Cole looked to Eira for an explanation. 'There'll be a lot of dust,' she replied.

'It also gives us some privacy where I can remain visible,' Oran explained, materialising behind the column.

'So, they won't see us?'

'That's the plan. Echo is keeping them occupied, believe me. I think she might have broken rule three,' he joked, crossing his arms over his chest, and leaning against the column. 'Forget I'm here,' he added as he paced behind the column again.

Cole blew out his cheeks and stretched. He glanced at Eira, who had a bemused expression on her face. She approached, her purple boots scraping on the floor, and lifted both hands to slide his leather jacket from his shoulders.

'Are we doing this naked then?' Cole mused, trying to mask his building panic with humour.

Eira's eyes lit up, lips pursed. Pulling his arms out, she flipped his jacket and slid her own arms through the sleeves. Cole's lips twisted into a smug grin. He loved her in his jacket, especially over that dress. He could feel his blood heating and his pulse quickening for a whole different reason as his skin became tight across his chest.

'Believe me, I could render you naked if I wanted to, but I'm not sure you'd want everyone seeing your...' Eira tilted her head with a lopsided grin.

Cole's face flushed. He closed the distance between them, resting his hands on her hips. 'My assets are for your eyes only, Doc,' he purred, his breath caressing her forehead as he leant into her. Eira snorted, poking him in the ribs.

Cole raised a hand to the back of Eira's neck and pulled back to search her face. She still looked weary, but the determination had returned to her eyes.

'Are you sure about doing this now? Both you and Oran look ready to drop.'

Eira threaded a hand through his hair, tugging him to her, their bodies lined up. The kiss she applied to his lips was languid and slow. Cole became aware of her body against his, her breasts pressed against his chest, her leg angled into his groin. This kiss was different to any they'd shared before. It was laced with power, sending shockwaves of pleasure through his body. Cole rocked into Eira with a groan, pushing her back. His hands migrated from her hips to her backside, massaging her ass, and Eira let out a sharp breath, moaning against his lips.

Her power flooded his veins, filling him with euphoria as he gave himself over to her, basking in the vast expanse of her power. He pulled away slightly, feeling another layer, a hidden depth to her magic. He opened his eyes and noticed that he had lifted Eira up to rest against his hips, both hands clasped on her ass, with her legs twined behind his back. He gasped as he realised what was happening. Eira had an arm thrust out towards the column and dust was swirling around them. His black eye focused through the dusty air and he could make out Oran's form in the gloom, head angled away, palm resting on the column over Eira's.

Bloody hell.

They were creating the statue duplicate whilst Eira was ... seducing him. That meant Oran was linked to her emotions through her mind. Cole nearly dropped Eira in shock at the realisation that Oran could feel everything they were feeling. It was Oran's power threaded through hers which he had felt.

Eira glanced down at him through lowered lashes, her jaw tight with strain. Her eyes suddenly opened, and he saw forks of lightning flashing through her green irises.

'You need to understand, Hawk, this is what I am, what I'm becoming. I'm so scared,' Eira whispered. It was an odd sensation to hear her speak out loud but also in his head.

His black eye suddenly flared and Eira glowed with a soft light which radiated throughout her whole body. She had either dropped her glamour purposely, or she was burning through so much power that she no longer had the strength to maintain it. Their combined power seared through Cole, the sensation almost making his knees buckle, and he grabbed onto Eira as he rode the wave.

'This is how it feels when we combine our powers. Doesn't it scare you? It scares me.'

Again, her soothing voice seemed to come from outside and within his head. Cole understood what she was doing. She had completely dropped her guard and was spilling her very essence into him. He wasn't sure if she was doing it through fear or a desperate need for him to see her fully, but he wanted to embrace it all.

Cole dropped one of his hands from her bottom, and her leg slid down his hip. He hooked a stray, dust-coated strand of hair behind her pointed ear, running a thumb down the edge. Eira hummed, leaning into his touch. Cole stroked his hand down the side of her neck and then trailed his knuckles down her spine, and she arched her back, closing her eyes. He kissed her exposed neck.

'There's nothing you could ever do that would scare me, Eira. This is strange, but you, your combined powers, and your link to Oran doesn't scare me. As I said before, it has shaped you and made you who you are today. The woman I've fallen in love with.'

Eira released a shuddering breath and collapsed in his arms. There was a flash of silver-white light, and then Oran was right beside them. He gathered a ball of light in his hands and sent it pulsing towards the column. Cole glanced up and, through the falling dust, saw an exact replica of himself. The bright blue eye opened, and the figure moved forward. Cole flinched, gathering Eira closer to his chest. It was so life-like, it even walked like him. Watching it advance towards them, he was filled with horror.

'Eira did most of that on her own,' Oran muttered, placing a hand on Cole's shoulder. 'I was the sculptor and battery charger. She wouldn't let me in, let me near you. She gave more power than she should have.'

Cole was astonished. 'She said she feared what she could do, what the two of you can do together. I think she was showing me exactly how it felt to have even a fraction of your power.'

Oran nodded, the dust coating his skin making him even paler than usual.

'It's done now,' the gargoyle said, standing.

As he spoke, the shield dispersed, and Cole was left exposed to the wider room. Wiping a hand over his dust-coated face and hair, he lowered his head, and brushed a kiss on Eira's nose. A smile spread across her lips, but her eyes were heavy. She looked exhausted.

'What were you thinking, Eira? You took on too much,' Cole whispered so the others wouldn't hear.

'Oran said to protect you, so I did. I knew you would be embarrassed that he could feel what you were feeling. Anyway, only I know you well enough to create a life rendering.' Eira lifted a hand and traced his scar.

'True, but you've used too much power.'

Eira's eyes fluttered open; they had returned to their normal deep forest-green.

'You said that you're in love with me,' she said with wonder, her face full of joy.

Cole gulped, remembering the words he had spoken as the magic coursed through his body. He bent and lightly kissed her dusty lips. 'I did. And I'm not scared of you either. What you showed me, what you gave me, was incredible,' he sighed. 'I do love you, Eira.'

'That's good, Hawk,' Eira whispered sleepily. 'Because I think I've fallen in love with you too. Now, before you kiss me again, can I have some of your hot chocolate with marshmallows please?'

Cole chuckled and held her closer to his chest, a feeling of acceptance settling there and something like fireworks exploding within his heart.

Cole watched as Oran and Eira sculpted the statue of Tagger, Nelka standing silently beside him. Being involved in the creation of his statue had been an experience he would never forget, and it was made even more unforgettable by the declarations of love. But being able to stand back and watch fully was mind-blowing.

A shimmering shield was still in place to stop the dust filling the room, translucent so that everyone could watch. He was grateful that the shield Oran had created for his statue was opaque. He needed the intimate moment he had shared with Eira to have been private.

I love you.

They had both said it to one another, and he hoped she had said it because she meant it, not because she was exhausted and scared.

Eira stood, arm outstretched, one hand on the column and the other on Tagger's shoulder. It was nothing like their embrace earlier, Cole was pleased to note. Eira had a faint glow around her, flowing from her palm into the stone. He could see that she was really flagging, her magic almost depleted. But she had done Flint's statue, so it was only Tagger left, and then she could rest.

Tagger stood as steady as a rock, even though the tightness around his eyes showed his nerves.

Cole shifted, his leg bouncing with impatience, arms folded loosely over his chest.

'I understand your concerns, Hawk. They've used too much power, and they're heading for burnout,' Nelka whispered, stroking a hand over her swollen belly. Cole glanced sideways at the gargoyle, seeing his concern reflected in her face.

Eira had been in no fit state to continue when she completed his rendering, but after a hot chocolate and a brief pause, she had eased herself from the chair and announced it was Flint's turn. Her body was tense and rigid, and her head sagged forward as if she no longer had the energy to hold it up.

Cole exhaled, scraping his hands through his hair. 'They're running off Oran's reserves, aren't they?'

'Yes, since Eira nearly consumed hers with your sculpture, they're now burning through Oran's pool of power,' Nelka replied with a hint of scorn in her words. She was worried, and she had concerns about the use of the Heart Stones.

Cole watched Tagger's head being sculpted into existence and flinched as ginger hair sprouted from the scalp, growing until it reached the right length. At least it meant they were almost finished.

'How do you feel about this?' Cole asked, gesturing at the moon on his arm.

Nelka glanced at his arm briefly before refocusing on the scene in front of them. She raised her own forearm, tugging up her sleeve. She had three crescent moons embossed there, two interlinked. 'How do *you* feel, Cole?' she countered.

Cole swallowed, gathering his thoughts as he watched Tagger's hooked nose appear on the stone face.

'I'm accepting of the bond, but also insanely jealous of their connection. I've witnessed how much they need each other and how the connection has improved them.'

Now that Cole had said it out loud it sounded odd, and he was worried that he had offended Nelka somehow. He needed reassurance from the only other person who could understand his position.

Nelka was quiet for a long moment, her eyes never leaving Eira. 'Oran needed this bond more than he will ever understand. It means that he has reached his full potential, both in power and acceptance. I fear that, without Eira, he would still be drifting.' Nelka's words were spoken so quietly that Cole had to strain to hear her. 'But yes, Captain, I am slightly jealous that my Starlight is bonded to another female, even though their elven heritage links them.'

Cole nodded, understanding all too well.

'Open your eyes, Tag,' Eira's voice rang out in the room. Tagger snapped his eyes open and met Cole's, looking to him for some reassurance. Cole gave his friend a sympathetic smile, trying to ease his worry.

Cole started forward, Nelka at his elbow. He watched Eira as a flash of light shot towards the statue, filling the chest, and animating it.

Stone-Tagger momentarily opened its eyes before falling asleep. Tagger himself bent forward, placing his hands on his knees, and sucking in deep breaths as the shield faded. Eira immediately sagged and crumpled, every inch of her white from the stone fragments. Cole moved to catch her, but Oran suddenly appeared behind her, holding her under the arms. His chest heaved as he locked eyes with Nelka.

'Hawk,' Nelka said on a sharp intake of breath. But at that moment, Oran's eyes rolled back in his head, and he collapsed backwards, taking Eira with him. Nelka then collapsed where she stood, pitching sidewise. Acting on instinct, Cole leapt forward and caught Nelka, bracing her weight before she hit the floor.

CHAPTER 36

||| EIRA

Eira took a deep shuddering breath as she awoke. The air sawed down her throat, and her lips felt dry and cracked. A warm hand wrapped around hers, and a smile tugged at her lips as the smell of spice and smoke wafted over her.

'Hey, sleepy head. Welcome back.'

Eira's eyes fluttered open to meet Cole's. His dark hair fell across his face, and his mouth was quirked up in the grin that she loved so much. The bedside light was on, casting half his face in shadow.

'Hey,' she croaked, trying to sit up. The covers were tucked in so tightly around her that it was hard to move. Eira was flat on her stomach, and as she tried to move her legs, her muscles locked, a moan escaped her mouth. She sent her power flowing through her joints, easing the cramps in her limbs as she tried to heave herself up.

Cole rose from where he had been sitting on the floor, magazines sliding from his lap. He tugged back the covers, and the sudden cold made Eira pull her exposed knees up to her chest. Cole looked down at her from his vantage point, a lazy grin on his face. 'I do like it when you wear my clothes,' he drawled with a smirk.

Eira peered down at herself as Cole repositioned the pillows behind her on the headboard. She was in his Tupac T-shirt, something she didn't remember changing into. With a hiss, she eased herself back against the headboard, closing her eyes as the room spun. Cole laid the cover back over her and perched beside her. Eira ran her fingers through her hair, tugging on the tangles as she went, grimacing.

'Have some water, Doc.' Cole pushed a cold glass into her hand.

Eira cracked an eye open. 'This brings back memories of when I looked after you. I just hope I'm not sick all over you.'

Cole sniggered. 'If I remember rightly, I wasn't actually sick on you. You were too quick for that.'

Eira slowly drank the cool liquid, sinking back into the pillows as the water soothed the rawness in her throat. 'How long have I been out?'

'This is the third night.'

Eira started, lifting her head so quickly that dark spots appeared in her vision. *I've been asleep for three days?* She'd never used her power to this level of exhaustion. A thought occurred to her and had her pushing forward, trying to shake the covers off and stand up.

'Hey easy, Eira,' Cole said gently, guiding her back onto the bed.

'Oran,' she croaked.

Oran! she shouted in her head as panic set in. The link between them felt faint, and she tugged on it but got no response. She fidgeted, fighting the covers, and Cole, to find the gargoyle. Wherever he was.

Cole cupped her face in his hands. 'He's fine, Eira. He collapsed right after you did. He's safe with Nelka across the hall. Since you've just woken up, he'll probably be stirring soon too. You both burned through a huge amount of power.'

Eira stopped shifting when she saw the sincerity in his eyes and relaxed.

'Now I don't play the overprotective boyfriend often, but you need to let me look after you for a bit. You need some food, and probably a shower. Your hair looks like a bird's nest.' He ran his hand through her hair, sending up a cloud of dust.

Eira smacked him away, but he easily caught her hand and brought it to his mouth with a tender kiss.

'Do I smell chocolate or am I dreaming?' Her stomach rumbled as she spoke, and Cole chuckled.

He reached to the chest of drawers and pulled down a tray of food to place on her lap. She grinned as she saw the cheese toastie and the still-steaming hot chocolate with marshmallows.

'How did you know I would wake up?'

'You haven't moved at all over the past two days, but about an hour ago you started shifting around and groaning, so I figured that was a good sign.'

Eira reached out and squeezed his hand. 'Thank you for watching over me, Hawk.'

Cole gulped, attempting to smooth her hair again. 'I was worried about you. You looked like you were in a coma or something.'

'It was a regeneration sleep to allow my powers to replenish. I've never burnt out like that before.'

Cole withdrew his hand. 'You have done it before. It was after you made my eye on the stone.'

Eira nodded, remembering. 'Yeah, but that was simply through using too much power over a longer period of time. This was more like a flood of power leaving my body all at once.'

'Oran said you needed to do it now, so that you had time to recover, but I didn't know it would be this bad.'

'What happened?' Eira asked, biting into the cheese toastie.

'You and Oran collapsed, and then Nelka fainted as well.'

Eira stared at him wide-eyed. 'Is she okay? The baby?'

'As far as I can tell she and the baby are fine. I'm sure she would appreciate you checking her over though.' Cole shifted further onto the bed, bracing an arm on the other side of her lap. 'Oran was behind you, wasn't he? Keeping you up?'

A flush crept into Eira's cheeks, remembering why Oran had had to support her. She'd been careless and impulsive in her need for Cole to understand how she was feeling, why she was scared, and her desire to have his body pressed to hers.

'I used up too much power in your statue's creation. It wasn't evenly spread. I blocked and filtered Oran's power to limit his involvement because I was trying to spare you from Oran seeing your emotions and your mind,' Eira whispered, suddenly not hungry. She looked at the tray, unable to make eye contact with Cole. 'It meant that Oran had to spend his power on the next two creations. We should have listened to you and stopped. But I just wanted to get the whole process finished.'

Cole lifted her chin, his blue eye glinting with understanding.

'I know that neither of you enjoyed the process. It was pretty crazy to watch.' He smiled to show that he was teasing, before continuing, 'I think even if the power had been evenly spread out, you would've both been severely weakened, and this would still have occurred. You've achieved something never done before, something which should be physically impossible. And you did it to save people, to change the future.'

Eira swallowed, trying to accept his words but guilt still clawed at her gut. She picked up her hot chocolate, letting the sweet, warm smell calm her.

Cole, sensing that she didn't want to talk about it anymore, changed the subject. 'So, Nelka shouted a warning before Oran collapsed. Luckily, I was next to her and caught her before she hit the floor. She came around quite quickly but was weak. It was like she knew Oran was going to collapse?' Cole said, a question in his voice.

'They have a soul-bond,' Eira explained, blowing on the mug.

'Right. And what does that mean, exactly?' Cole pinched a marshmallow from her mug with a smirk.

'It's something most of the high races have, in some form. It's when two beings mate and form a deep connection. Oran called it a spark. They fuse their hearts and souls. He said they can feel each other's pain – she must have collapsed because Oran did.'

Cole had stilled, a crust from her cheese toastie halfway to his mouth. He swallowed and then continued to pick at her leftovers. 'How did they know they had the spark?'

Eira shrugged, slurping her hot chocolate, knowing what was going through his head because she was thinking the same thing. She waited a heartbeat to see if he would broach the subject but when he didn't, she joked, 'How did you move Oran?'

Cole's face twisted into a smirk even though his eyes remained distant. 'I carried him, of course.'

Eira rolled her eyes and quipped, 'Flint did it, didn't he?'

Cole chuckled. 'We weren't sure what to do. All the immortals were unconscious, and it was just us mortals left to deal with you all. I got Nelka settled in their room when she woke up, and then I picked you up with Flint, and we carried you here. The three of us together couldn't shift Oran, so I went to the Nightingale for some advice. Elowen convinced a couple of bridge trolls to carry him to his room.' The look on his face at the mention of the bridge trolls was comical, and Eira couldn't contain her laughter. 'What? They're quite something! I assume it was a bridge troll that directed me to the nightclub?'

'Yes, most bridge trolls have an ancient power which allows them to shift and assume the form of a human. Many masquerade as tramps since the Dark pays no attention to the vulnerable. They can glamour their power like most of us. In London they act as the keepers of the entrances to the underground network. They are bound to their bridges, the way Madam Scudamore is linked to this house. It's odd that you were able to find two in the Nightingale.'

'I think Elowen pulled them from the tunnels actually,' Cole corrected.

'Oh, that means they're protectors of the tunnels then, easier for them to move around as they're linked to it all. I'm surprised they listened to Elowen though. They don't usually get involved in the affairs of others.' But Elowen did seem to have a way with the Myths that put them at ease and made them like her.

Eira shrugged, placing her mug back on the tray. The hot chocolate had given her the settling warmth and energy she needed.

'I apologise for allowing the trolls into our home.' Cole's tone was low, ashamed. 'And Tag and Flint saw the gatehouse. I know how well you guard the place.'

Eira's gaze flitted to him, seeing his eyes staring at the tray. *Our home.*

'Hawk, you don't have to apologise for looking after the wellbeing of our family. It was out of your control, and you made the right decision.' Eira interlaced her fingers with his, turning his hand upwards so she could trace her thumb across his palm. 'Our home is protected. I trust Flint and Tag; they still don't know the exact location, and I'm on good terms with the leader of the bridge trolls. They've helped me out a few times now, so I think I owe them.'

Cole bent forward, placing his forehead against hers. She loved when he did that. '*Our* home,' he mused, his breath ghosting over her face.

Eira threaded a hand around his neck. 'You said it first.'

'Sounds better from your lips,' he said, reaching up and kissing her on the forehead.

The trajectory of their relationship may not have been normal, they may not have gone on dinner-dates or to the movies, but she was certain of how she felt about him. He filled her with happiness in a time of such darkness. He accepted her exactly as she was, something she had never dreamed possible.

Eira inhaled, sighing deep into Cole's mouth as she whispered, 'I love you, Hawk.'

Cole relaxed, brushing a featherlight kiss to her lips. 'I love you too, Eira.'

They grinned at each other, basking in the glow of those words.

'Now, please can I go to the bathroom? I think my bladder is about to explode.'

Cole snorted, extracting himself from her lap and removing the tray. Steadily, Eira pulled back the covers and, on shaky legs, placed her bare feet on the wooden floor. It seemed such a waste of her renewed magic to use it on herself, but she sent a pulse of power through her body to help her stand. Cole braced under her arms as her feet took her full weight. Eira shuffled forward, still feeling weak.

'How have you managed without the immortals' help then, my great Captain?'

'Surprisingly fine, we've coped quite well without superpowers.' Cole's eyes creased in the corners as he stuck his tongue out at her. 'Elowen, Madam Scudamore, and I, took it in turns to watch the three of you. Especially during the day because of Nelka and the baby. As you can imagine, she's been quite protective of Oran, but we bribed her with chocolate. Madam Scudamore and I seem to have reached a truce, and she even smiled at me at one point.'

Eira shook her head in astonishment. 'You seem to have it all in hand.'

Eira was impressed that Cole had taken on all the responsibility, even though she knew he would.

Cole continued, 'The new additions to our team helped greatly. Flint and Tag took it in rotations to cover surveillance. The Major has been checking in with me repeatedly for updates on the Wallflower and preparation for the mission. He is getting quite desperate and is coming to London himself for the mission.'

Eira stopped shuffling to the door and glanced sidewise at Cole. 'You've been informed when the mission is going ahead? When?'

'We move out in five days,' Cole said. 'But that's not important right now.'

Eira reluctantly let the subject drop as Cole gently guided her to the door, unlatching it with his spare hand. They moved into the dimly lit corridor, Oran and Nelka's bedroom opposite the stairs, and the bathroom to the left.

'Now, do you need my help in there or does that go beyond boyfriend duties?'

'I think I'll be fine. But I might need a guard outside if you want to feel useful.' Eira smirked as she walked into the bathroom.

After using the toilet, she glanced at herself in the mirror. Her hair did look like she'd been dragged through a hedge, and her skin was pale, with dark smudges under her eyes. But it was her eyes that caught her attention. Eira bent closer to the mirror over the sink, staring at them. Shimmers of silver moonlight twisted within the deep green of her irises, the same had happened to Oran's white eyes, and she knew it was another effect of the bond.

Eira wrestled her hair into a bun, sighing as she gazed longingly at the shower. It would have to wait. She needed to check on Oran before she did anything else. She splashed cold water on her face, scrubbing the dirt from her ears.

Opening the door to find Cole sitting on the top step, Eira advanced to Oran's room. Cole rose and followed her.

Knocking on the door, Eira whispered, 'Echo, it's Eira. Can I come in?'

When there was no reply, she shrugged and inched the door open, the need to check on Oran overpowering any ideas of politeness. The room was pitch-black, but it didn't take long for her eyes to adjust.

'Two figures on the bed,' Cole supplied.

Eira paused and then smiled to herself realising that Cole had used his black eye. 'See, you do have a superpower.'

He huffed, placing a hand on the small of her back as they stepped inside.

'When was the last time you checked on them?' Eira asked.

'Before you woke up, Madam Scudamore brought Nelka some dinner. Breakfast, I mean. She hasn't moved from the room, but she's been eating and talking fine. I presumed she didn't want to leave Oran. She did seem weaker, but that makes sense with the soul-bond, I guess.' Cole shrugged, worried that he'd done something wrong.

'You've done more than enough, Hawk,' Eira said, placing a hand on his arm. 'Nelka, I'm going to put the light on, okay?'

Still no response. Eira flicked on the muted wall lights instead of the overhead ceiling light, not wanting to blind Nelka with the brightness.

The large, panelled room glowed with the soft yellow light. The ornate bed sat in the centre of the room with Victorian bedside tables either side. Oran was lying face down on the bed. His head was propped on a pillow, and his wings were spread out, one hanging off the edge of the bed, the other draped over Nelka, who was tucked into his side. The top of her indigo head was the only visible part of her. There was an empty tray on one of the bedside tables, which Eira took as a good sign.

She didn't hesitate. Walking around the bed, she lifted Oran's wing and slid underneath it. Nelka was asleep, cradling her bump, nestled into the comfort of Oran's arm. But something was very wrong.

Eira placed a hand on Nelka's arm and instantly withdrew from the chill of her skin. She reached her other hand to Oran; he was chilled to the touch too. Eira knew Oran always seemed colder than she did — gargoyle genetics meant they had a lower blood temperature — but her training told her that this was worrying.

Cole's face appeared under Oran's wing as he crouched by the bed.

'They're both freezing,' she said.

Cole frowned. 'Isn't that how gargoyles are? They are made from stone after all.'

'No, they're colder than usual.'

Eira knew that Nelka would have heard her knock on the door. She should be awake now anyway.

Sending her power into Nelka, she detected no pain. She checked the baby, and her heart rate was steady. Eira trickled a shock of energy into Nelka, whose eyes fluttered open.

'Echo, it's me. Can you wake up for me please? For the baby.'

Nelka shifted at Eira's words. 'I'm so tired. I can't stay awake,' she moaned, rolling back onto her side. Eira looked at Cole, whose face had fallen, his skin ashen. Eira's eyes darted from side to side, sucking her bottom lip. Bending out from under Oran's wing, Eira rushed around to the other side of the bed. Cole followed.

'We need to wake Oran up. I think his weakness, his regenerative sleep, is making Nelka unconscious, which is risky for her and the baby. It must be happening through the soul-bond.'

'How?' Cole asked.

'I will need to use the Bloodstream, but the risk of waking him too early is that his powers won't have fully restored.' Eira paused. 'I'll have to replenish him with mine. I can't risk Nelka and the baby... He would never forgive me.'

Eira glanced at Cole for confirmation. She could see the reluctance on his face, but he took a deep breath and stepped forward, placing a gentle kiss on her forehead. Even though he didn't like it, he trusted her, and her heart swelled with love for him.

Eira knelt and clasped Oran's hand. As with Nelka, she sent a pulse of power into his body, but he was sleeping too deeply to react. Retracing her power, she slowly threaded it along their link, using her mind to push as well. Naturally, his mind was shielded. She could try smashing it open like a battering ram, but then he might react defensively. This needed to be done slowly and carefully.

Their bond felt dormant, and reluctantly, Eira extracted a kernel of his moonlight and bonded it with hers, reigniting the connection. Like knocking on a door, she used Oran's own power to lower his shields and allow her entry.

Oran Light Bringer, you need to wake up now.

Like a slumbering beast, his power stirred, shifting towards hers.

Oran, I need you to wake up. Nelka, the baby, she needs you.

His vast power took form and screamed down the bond in a rush of moonlight and stardust. He was automatically giving her power. Eira exhaled with the force of it; too much and she would drain him again.

Oran, no. Wake up! Eira screamed in his head.

She flared her power, ramming against the tidal wave of his endless reserves, giving him enough to trick his power into thinking that it had regenerated enough.

Eira?

Eira sagged in relief at the sound of his voice in her head.

Please wake up, Oran. Echo needs you. Your baby needs you.

Like a tidal wave withdrawing, his power locked, his mind closed, and she felt him inhale a deep breath, pulling himself from sleep.

Thank you, he uttered before retracting from her mind.

Eira's eyes fluttered open, and she rose to her fee. Oran's strong grip pulsed once in hers before he removed his hand and placed it beneath him, heaving himself up to kneel on the bed. He gently snapped his wings shut and nodded in her direction, his eyes fearful and direct. Eira stepped back into Cole's embrace.

Oran scooped Nelka onto his lap and ran his nose down the side of her face in a gentle, intimate gesture, murmuring in their language. Finally, Nelka stirred, slowly opening her eyes.

CHAPTER 37

‖‖ EIRA

Eira snuggled into Cole's side, repositioning her thigh over his legs, her breasts brushing his chest. He idly drew long strokes up and down her bare back before running his finger along the seam of her underwear. This was as far as they'd got on their lazy afternoon together, their first date of a successful meal and a movie. Neither of them was in any rush given what the morning would bring. Cole read from one of his comics, his steady voice lulling Eira into a sleepy, relaxed state.

Major Stone had given them seven days to prepare, two of which had been ruined by her and Oran's regenerative sleep. Not that they needed the full week. Thanks to Cole's organisational skills and Oran's planning, they probably could have completed the mission with twenty-four hours' notice.

It was the scar left on Oran when Eira woke him up that threatened the mission. His power was fully replenished, and he was at full strength physically, but he was haunted by thoughts of what could have happened if he hadn't woken. Nelka had explained the following evening that if he had been able to turn to stone, he would have regenerated more quickly, and without risk to her health and the baby's. It was Eira's turn to feel guilty then. Deciding that distracting Oran was the best option, Eira came up with an idea.

They both took Oran on in combat, much to his surprise. Luckily, he was quick enough to draw his staff before they both pounced on him, Eira with her Skye sword and Nelka with her moon scythes. It was a battle worth filming. For someone so heavily pregnant, Nelka moved with such fluid grace that Eira had to pause her attacks just to watch her. Oran swiftly adapted, splitting his staff in two and parrying the blows they dealt him. The grin on his face told Eira that it had been a good idea.

'What are you thinking?' Cole's question drew Eira back to the moment, his warm body solid against hers.

'I was just reliving our epic battle against the almighty Light Bringer,' Eira said dramatically, trailing a hand in the air.

Cole sniggered and said, 'You do know I caught part of it on film?'

Eira leant on an elbow to look at him. 'You didn't?' she gasped with surprise.

'You and Nelka were incredible. I couldn't miss an opportunity to film that, could I?' Cole kissed the top of her now tamed and washed hair.

Eira smiled, settling back down under his arm, contentment sweeping through her. Long moments passed before Eira rose on an elbow again, twisting to trace the scar down his stomach.

'What's your favourite colour, Hawk?'

'Huh?' Cole cracked open a hooded eye, the comic abandoned on his chest.

'I was just thinking the other day that I don't know any of the small things about you. Your favourite colour, favourite food, favourite place to visit. You don't know mine either.'

'Right, let me get this in order. Blue would be your favourite colour because of my eye. It's the same as my mum's, by the way. Hot chocolate seems to be your favourite food, you demand it often enough, anyway. Your favourite place is the beach, probably on that island of yours.' Cole ticked them off his fingers as he spoke, a smug grin on his face.

Eira stared at him, shocked that he had got them all right.

She sat up further, and Cole's gaze dipped to her full breasts as the smugness in his face turned to hunger for her. His hand twitched, resisting the urge to grab her. Eira's core burned, yearning for everything that the look on Cole's face was promising. She swallowed, trying to ignore the heat rising inside her. This was important, and she wanted to talk about it.

'I'd say your favourite colour was green because of my eyes. I'm assuming that's only since you met me though, and before me, it would have been black or grey. As for food...' Eira pursed her lips, tapping a finger against her chin. 'Toast and spaghetti from a tin. Your favourite place would be wherever you feel safe. It used to be your grandfather's house or your old training academy, but now it's here, at the gatehouse.'

Cole launched himself at her, taking Eira by surprise, his hand snaking around the back of her head, holding her in place as he devoured her with a kiss. Satisfied that she had got them correct, Eira reluctantly pulled away to gloat.

Cole opened his eyes, his lips swollen, and his breathing ragged. He sighed, rolling his eyes. 'Yes, smartass, all correct. Why do you ask?'

Eira twisted her hands, shrugging.

'I guess because we've gone from slow and steady to declarations of love in such a small space of time, and I want to know more of the little things that make you you.' Eira rolled her eyes and corrected herself. 'What I'm trying to say is, are those things important to this? Or are they minor in the grand scheme of things, when I already know how I feel about you?'

Cole tilted his head to the side, contemplating. Eira reached up and swept his hair from his face, smiling as it tickled her palm. She jolted to her feet, remembering what she had hidden in her backpack. Hurrying to the other bed, she unzipped her case and pulled out the gift she'd bought for Cole. She placed it backwards on her head with a sassy grin, then sauntered slowly up to him.

He was still, his eyes tracking the sway of her hips as she approached with a look of hunger on his face. Her cheeks warmed; she loved seeing his reaction to her, seeing the obvious desire in his eyes. She dropped her glamour so that her skin glowed. She climbed back onto the bed, straddling his waist, and Cole's breath caught as he trailed his hands along her thighs and hips.

'I'm sorry it's not the same as the one in the photo, but I hope it will do.' She reached up and pulled the grey baseball cap off, fitting it on Cole's head, and tucking some of his hair underneath.

He still didn't speak, raw emotion playing across his face. He leant forward and pressed his forehead against hers, letting a tear slip from his eye.

'To me, that hat was a sense of belonging, and that picture was the first time I'd ever felt safe with other people.' He cleared his throat then continued, 'Tagger bought that cap for me as a joke, but I loved it and wore it all the time. This means so much to me. Thank you, my love.'

Eira smiled at Cole, watching as his eyes took on a distant look; she knew he was reliving happy memories with his friends.

'Cole, what happened between your mother dying and you joining the police academy?' It was a question that she had been dying to ask, and this felt like the right time.

She knew that whatever he had to say was full of grief and tragedy, and she suspected it haunted him more than he let on, but Eira needed to know the big stuff too, even if it tore him open and took her with it. There shouldn't be anything unspoken between them.

Shame clouded his eyes as he took a shuddering breath. His voice was quiet, lost to his past as he spoke. 'When my mother died, I had two options: enter the care system or run. At fourteen, I could basically look after myself anyway, so I chose the second option. The Dark was slowly taking control of the government and the police, so it felt like the safer option.' Cole blew out his cheeks, resting his head back against the headboard. 'God, I didn't even know where my father had been taken. I hid and watched his arrest. He was so intoxicated that he didn't even know where he was or what was happening. It wasn't agents who arrested him, it was the police.'

Eira reached forward and wrapped herself around Cole's chest, resting her head on his shoulder. Cole ran his hands through her hair and absentmindedly stroked her back as he rested his head on hers. Eira knew how it felt to watch a parent die and then be utterly alone in the world.

'I stayed at my grandfather's house for two weeks, living off tinned spaghetti,' he said, laughing. 'No one came searching for me, and there were no reports on the radio or TV about my father's arrest. Eventually I became lonely and hungry, so I ventured out to the estate. I had no friends from school and didn't dare go back; I hated that place anyway.' Cole sighed deeply.

'I knew of a gang from the estate — lads older than me — that used younger kids to run errands and paid them in cash. Naively, I thought it was the only option for me. It probably was at the time. They asked me to deliver parcels. Never drugs, I point-blank refused on that front. Weapons, money, anything they needed shifting from one place to another. After that, I started doing some graffiti, y'know, tags and marks for territories drawn between rival gangs. I never drank with them or did any drugs or anything. I started to get a reputation for refusing. Being sober meant I was reliable, and I got more jobs. I enjoyed the parties though. It was so easy to lose yourself in the music there and not worry about anything for a while.' He stared at his lap, struggling to get the next words out. 'I lost my virginity to some girl, whose name I never knew, down an alley behind a warehouse.' Cole ran his fingers up and down Eira's back.

'There were a handful of encounters like the one in the alley. One-night stands, fumbles in the dark, experimentation. Nothing compared to what we share, Eira. Nothing like the love I have for you.'

Eira purred with contentment, tightening her grip around Cole. It surprised her that she needed him to say it.

'As in any organisation, I started to gain favour. I had some leadership qualities which helped me climb the ranks. At that point, I was so far in that I couldn't see a way out.'

Eira understood. He was loyal, and once he committed to something, he saw it through.

'The gang started to change its priorities. Instead of targeting rival gangs, they set their sights on Myths and hybrids.'

Eira stilled, her breathing catching in her chest. He took a shuddering breath and held her tighter. Eira angled her head so she could see him; his eyes were closed, a tear already cascading down his face. She reached up and wiped it away.

'Four of us were sent to set fire to an abandoned house. I wasn't senior enough to know the full intel, but it felt wrong. The others started the fire, but I watched. The flames spread quickly. I can still feel the intense heat and the smoke choking my lungs. I'm haunted by it every day... Because there were people inside, Eira.' Cole choked on the words, tears streaming down his face.

Eira interlaced her hands around his neck and gently kissed the tears away, their salt coating her tongue. Cole clung to her as he heaved another sob and finished the story.

'The house belonged to a dwarf and his human wife. The wife and their infant daughter died in the flames. The worst thing was, that when the others realised there were people inside, they just laughed, swigging from their cans. I tried to get in, to save them, but I couldn't. A window shattered in my face. The others ran. I pushed forward, but the flames were too high, the heat too intense. Then I heard sirens, so I ran as well, and I didn't stop running until I'd left London behind.'

Eira held his face in her hands, comforting him until his tears stopped falling and his breathing steadied. Cole wrapped her in a shuddering embrace, burying his face in her hair. After a long moment, Eira eased back, tracing the scars on his cheek. She knew she couldn't change what had happened, but she could try to reduce some of the guilt.

'Like you've said to me before, Cole, your past is your past. You can only let it shape you. After what happened, you left London and started a new life. One where you save people. You saved me from being consumed by despair after I got the letter from my mother. You let me choose my own path, walking beside me the whole time, even when you don't agree with my decisions.' Eira kissed Cole's lips. 'You do that, Hawk. No one has ever seen and accepted me for what I am without fear. Apart from Oran, but he's just as odd as I am.' Eira shrugged, smiling at him.

Then she took control, kissing away his regrets and his shame. She pressed their bodies together, letting her magic flow through him, connecting them in every way possible. For now, they could enjoy this. Tomorrow, they would change the world.

CHAPTER 38

ORAN

From his vantage point, Oran stared across the misty skies at the grey, decaying urban landscape below. He adjusted his aviator goggles and checked the time on the watch Eira had set for him. The hazy October day was ideal for what they had planned.

He was positioned on top of what Eira called the Walkie-Talkie building, giving him a good view of the Shard and the Thames, as well as the locations of the decoys that they'd planted.

Oran checked the curved daggers on his hips and the staff strapped to his back, flaring his wings as he knelt and activated an Incognito. He could easily become invisible, but both he and Eira needed to conserve their powers for what was to come. He never wanted to experience another burnout again.

Especially when it had placed his Starlight and babe in danger. Another debt he owed Eira.

His night with Nelka had been magnificent. They'd experienced the eve of battle on many occasions, and always made their pairing special. This time though, he'd had a choice in the battle, had decided to take part because it was the right thing to do and not because he was forced to. And it would be his first time without Nelka fighting beside him. She was skilled, but this battle needed to be fought in daylight, something she would never be able to do.

A smile ghosted across Oran's lips with the memory of the lengths the two females had taken to shake him from his stupor. Their battle had been incredible, and it was exactly what he'd needed to get him out of his head.

Tagger is in position, Eira said in his mind.

Phase one started. Oran paused.

Eira, stay safe. Because…

Because I feel the same, Oran. You're my chosen family. We look after one another. See you below.

With that, she faded from his mind. Oran felt warm and cold simultaneously as her words settled in his heart.

Exhaling, he drew the ancient staff and watched Eira's braided green scarf flutter in the wind. Checking that he was under the umbrella of the Incognito, he rammed his staff into the smooth surface of the glass building below his clawed feet.

Channelling his light into the staff, it hummed and glowed to life. He spread his mind out, connecting with each of the decoys; the team had settled on areas that were highly patrolled, hoping they would be spotted quickly.

Oran activated Eira's statue and sent her walking down the street where she used to live. She was wearing Eira's unwanted clothes and even had a band around her head, and he made sure to make her look anxious and on alert, adding to the ruse.

Nelka had estimated that they had two hours before the Heart Stones exploded. Twisting his wrist, he set the countdown on the timer.

Super Healer activated, he told Eira.

They had settled on code names as everyone was freaked out about how lifelike their doppelgangers were.

Make it fun, Light Bringer, came Eira's reply, laced with humour.

Keeping a drop of his consciousness within Stone-Eira, he marvelled at her realistic movements. He instructed the statue to walk down the street past where he knew agents were concealed.

It didn't take them long to notice the golden-haired female, and they started after her, forcing the statue to run. Sending instructions to the decoy, he sought another mind, ready to move onto the next stage.

Oswald was in a shadowy recess opposite the Shard, monitoring the entrance. Within moments, two hover copters rose, propellers spinning, and zoomed east towards the bait, a swarm of drones in their wake. Oran watched through Oswald's glowing eyes as agents streamed out of the building and into two armoured trucks. One agent snagged his attention, and the little beast snarled as Oran himself growled low in his throat in reaction. The agent wore a black suit and black sunglasses, his deformed ear and red scar easy to spot, even at a distance.

Controlling his growing rage, Oran released a deep sigh. Feeling the anger disperse, he sent a message to Eira.

Super Healer is popular.

Laughter greeted him.

Two hover copters and two trucks. At least twenty-two snakes from the nest.

I bet Super Healer gets the most, came Eira's amused reply.

Let's see, my money is on Blue Knight.

Oran waited ten minutes before activating the second and third decoys, enjoying the chase through statue-Eira's eyes. He divided his mind between Tagger and Flint's statues waiting at the docks. With a grin, he made the duo take aim and shoot at a couple of drones above some shipping containers.

Ginger Irish and Big Fella activated.

As soon as the drones were hit, the Dark responded, sending more drones and an armoured truck.

Six drones, one truck, eight agents.

That's slightly disappointing.

Oran chuckled before replying, *Let's make it more interesting, then.*

Oran took control of stone-Flint and stone-Tagger, and sent them sprinting towards a large, rusty shipping freight. He wanted to do as much damage as possible before the backup arrived. He had them place explosives along the ship's hull, then run for cover before pressing a button to detonate them. A deafening boom reverberated around the dock, and the flames spread quickly.

Oh, I love human tech.

I think you're enjoying this, Light Bringer.

Oran sniggered, *I'll raise you another truck and eight more snakes from the nest.*

He rolled his shoulders, planting his clawed feet more evenly, and tightening his grip around the staff. He could feel the drain on his power, but before he could blink, he felt Eira's soothing magic flowing in, filling the void.

Thanks, partner.

No sweat, protector.

Oran grinned to himself.

One final time, Oran flowed his moonlight and mind into the staff and activated Cole's statue. The placement of this one had been the hardest to decide, but they'd settled on Belgravia, near the safehouse where Major Stone and Moyra had placed Tagger and Flint after their infection.

Blue Knight activated.

Cole had been the most precious about his code name. He'd said something about comic books and superheroes. He and Eira had debated and teased each other about it for the best part of an hour before Cole had thrown his hands in the air and told Eira to decide. She settled on Blue Knight because of his eye.

Oran sent Cole's duplicate speeding away from the safehouse and straight into a swarm of drones. Bending the statue's knees, he made the decoy launch itself off the ground in a massive jump. He channelled his magic through the statue, sending out a bright pulse of light that took out all the drones in one swift motion. Landing the statue on the pavement, he sent it weaving down the street and straight into an agent patrol. He used his moonlight again to flatten the trucks and knock over the agents, who'd barely raised their guns.

Blue Knight takes the gold. One hover copter, four trucks, at least thirty-two agents.

You cheat! You used your powers, didn't you?

Oran sent his amusement down the bond.

At least all the hover copters have been activated, she added.

Yeah, good to go, Eira, see you in the nest.

Joy lighting his face, Oran sent final instructions to the statues before withdrawing his consciousness. Sliding his staff back into its sheath, he deactivated the Incognito and pulled his own invisibility around him. Like a diver on the high board, he approached the edge of the building then sprang. Free-falling, he twisted into a stomach-churning spiral, and spread his wings at the last moment, catching himself just before he hit the ground. Oran sped over the murky surface of the Thames, his wing tips skimming the water, his heart set on a cause worth fighting for.

✕ COLE

Cole observed Eira bend, the curve of her hip and bottom making his blood pressure rise, as she sheathed another dagger inside her purple boot. Two elven daggers were already strapped to her shapely thighs. It was hard to concentrate when he was in the same room as her; he couldn't stop thinking about the night before. Cole adjusted the grey baseball cap which was now in pride of place on his head, backwards, and tucked his hair under it.

She had shattered his heart open and then glued it back together again with the simple inquiry into his past, knowing that he needed to get it off his chest. Cole felt much lighter for telling Eira his deepest shame and, as expected, she had been accepting, comforting him through the grief.

Cole shook his head, forcing himself to concentrate. He angled his automatic rifle, sliding the mechanism and checking the scope. He held the larger gun in his hands and had two pistols on his hips. Making sure the large bag across his back was in position and not too tight around his bulletproof vest, he approached Eira. Like him, she was clad in black.

Eira's hair was dyed jet-black again, pulled back into a high ponytail, her curls cascading over her shoulders. She wore a black band around her ears, and she'd applied her makeup as before, muting her intense green and making her eyes appear brown. She wore a dark hoodie under her bulletproof vest, which she was adjusting across her chest.

'What is with you and those purple boots?' Cole mused, dropping his rifle so that it hung at his side.

Eira cocked her head and grinned at him. 'The same applies to your leather jacket. They're more than just boots. These boots,' she said, stretching her leg toward him, 'were the first things I bought for myself when I came to London. Elowen picked them for me, and it cemented our friendship.'

Cole nodded, quirking a smile at her, understanding exactly why they were important to her.

'Do I have to wear this?' Eira huffed, pulling at the bulletproof vest. Cole closed the gap between them, sliding his hands between her vest and her hooded top, satisfied when she gasped.

'You might be a Super Healer, but even you can't dodge a bullet. We can't risk the bullets being infected with the virus, even if your magic can delay its effects. I'm not taking that chance, Doc. Two of your kill zones are protected at least. So don't go getting shot in the head.'

Cole kissed her on the forehead. A cough issued from the far corner of the room. When Eira was with him, he forgot about everyone else. Cole twisted and took in Flint by the door to the basement of the disused office block they were using as a safehouse to meet Major Stone and his generals. Like Cole, he wore a black uniform, a large bag and holdall strapped across his waist. He had two automatic rifles dangling at his sides and a pistol on his hip. Cole rolled his eyes, turning back to Eira.

'Remember how to take the safety off?' Cole asked, lifting Eira's gun and demonstrating for the third time.

'I know, Hawk. Stop fussing. I'd rather fight with a sword, but I can shoot a gun no problem.'

Eira closed her hands around his neck, staring into his eyes.

She recited what he had been repeating to her all morning: 'I know they are blanks. We're shooting to wound if we need to shoot at all. I know to stay close to you or Oran. Stop fretting. If all else fails, I have my magic as a last resort.'

Cole exhaled, wrapping his hands around the back of Eira's neck and resting his forehead against hers. They stayed like that for a long moment until there was a thud on the metal door. They stepped apart to see Flint heave the thick door open.

Major Stone stomped in, his steely gaze sweeping the room. He was flanked by the two generals they had already met and another lanky male who Cole had been told was the hacker. To keep the peace, Cole stood to attention and saluted, Flint following suit.

Major Stone approached Flint, grasping his arm. 'Good to have you back, Lieutenant.'

Flint nodded curtly to him.

Tagger's voice crackled through the earpiece in Cole's ear. 'In position, Captain.'

Cole slid a hand behind his back and gave a thumbs-up to Eira. 'Tagger is in position and is good to go, Major.'

'Good.' Major Stone paced the room, hands behind his back. 'Your plan is solid, Hawk. Immaculately laid-out and if well-executed, we could be moving into a new future we would never have even dreamt of.' The praise was evident in his voice, but Cole tensed for the bite. 'But I do not like being kept in the dark about this diversion of yours, and I don't understand why the doctor is here.'

Cole felt his hackles rise. 'She has a name,' he hissed, his tone sharp.

'Why does she have a gun? You're not expecting her to come with us, are you? She could jeopardise everything,' he continued, ignoring what Cole had said.

A gun sounded in the room, and everyone flinched. Cole turned to find Eira lowering her gun, her face angry. Major Stone turned slowly, staring at the hole in the wall two inches above his head.

'We have a job to do, and I'm coming,' she stated firmly, holding Major Stone's gaze.

Cole grinned at her, winking, before turning back to Major Stone. 'As you can see, our doctor is extremely capable. She is coming with us, no negotiations. If anyone is injured, believe me, you'll want her there,' he said through gritted teeth.

Major Stone looked like he was about to explode with anger.

Eira slung the gun over her shoulder and sauntered past, not even sparing a glance for the League members, who gave her a wide berth. Eira reclined next to the door, the gun hanging loosely at her side, and held up one finger.

'The distraction is underway, Major. That is all you need to know. We have two hours,' Cole said frostily.

Major Stone's jaw flexed as he fought back a retort. Taking his silence as confirmation, Cole folded his arms.

Eira's left foot tapped the wall twice, followed by two quick taps of her right heel on the floor. Her mouth twitched in a smile.

Two hover copters, two trucks. Good start.

'We all know the layout by now, so I won't be going over it again. Major, I presume this is your hacker?' Cole asked, gesturing to the tall brown-haired man who was hesitating by the door, his eyes constantly flicking to Eira.

'Technician Ipcress, Captain Hawkins will take command from here,' Major Stone said grudgingly.

The technician stood to attention and looked at Cole.

'Right, Ipcress, please get set up. I presume you know what to do. Cameras off as we proceed through the nest, and monitoring of all activity on the other floors. I'd like to get a good look at who is left after the bait has been swallowed. Set your watch to leave in two hours and meet us at the collection point.'

Ipcress nodded and moved to the folded-out table and chair, the only furniture in the room. He produced a tablet and headset from his bag and set to work, fingers flying across the keyboard.

Eira pressed two fingers against her own wrist, then raised a finger, totalling three.

'The order of entry will be me, Doc, General Kay, General Bolton, the Major, and then Flint. We all know the drill. Shoot to wound and stun. Our main objective is here.' Cole pointed his gun at the hidden room on the map spread across the floor: the vault of the black stones. It sent a shiver down his spine. 'Gaining entry to this room is the only unknown. Hopefully, Ipcress will be able to help with this detail. Gasmasks on when inside the room. Gather the black stones and leave the canisters.'

Everyone nodded, even Major Stone, though his eyes were teeming with anger. Cole knelt and folded up the plan, stuffing it inside his bulletproof vest.

Eira tapped her right foot once, her hand fisted and then opened.

One truck, drones.

'Any questions before we head out?'

'Extraction?' General Kay asked, shifting her hands to her hips.

Eira tapped her right foot once more, a smirk on her face.

Batman is having fun.

Cole nearly grinned. Keeping his expression neutral, he folded his arms, glancing at Flint, who he knew was following Eira's messages as well.

'We escape across Tower Bridge to the waiting transport. They'll be using Incognitos so will not be seen. The Dark will be drawn to the destruction we leave in our wake, hopefully giving us time to get out.'

'Isn't that too exposed, Captain?' General Bolton enquired gruffly, a sneer on his face.

Eira produced a fourth finger. The last bait had been set.

'It's unwise to stay on this side of the river. The bridge is the closest escape route. Unless you have an inflatable raft in that uniform, General?' Cole asked, condescending.

General Bolton glowered at him without answering.

Cole continued, 'We couldn't risk transport directly outside. The idea is to slip out on foot and then disappear using our invisible transport.'

Eira tapped her left foot once, then her right foot four times. Her eyebrow was angled, mouth twisted in amusement. Their eyes locked, her eyes creasing in the corners.

One hover copter, four trucks.

Blue Knight had been triumphant. Cole owed Oran some money if the gargoyle even took human currency.

'We're good to move out. Ipcress please check the cameras.'

Major Stone and his generals bent over Ipcress's shoulder to view the cameras. Cole glanced back at Flint who looked smug. Eira's eyes met his again and they danced with delight. Cole winked at her as she pushed herself off the wall and stalked back to his side, glancing at the tablet as she passed.

The brief surprise that flickered across Major Stone's stern face almost made Cole smirk. He kept a neutral expression as Major Stone nodded, letting them know all was clear.

'Tagger, we're ready to proceed. Get your team into position,' Cole said over the intercom.

'*Affirmative, Hawk.*'

Cole breathed in, bracing his gun against his shoulder, then marched to the heavy door without waiting for Major Stone's approval.

Cole walked along the service corridor, pushing on the bar of the exit, and swinging the door open. Jumping down onto the gravel rail track in front of him, he angled his gun left to right, scoping for danger. Relying on his black eye to pierce the darkness, he risked switching on the torch on his rifle, keeping it angled towards the ground. Gravel crunched as Eira dropped down next to him. She nodded, letting him know that they were clear to continue.

Cole moved forward along the curved wall of the underground, keeping his steps light. Oran, despite his intense fear of enclosed spaces, had scouted out the tunnels leading from the London Bridge underground to find the best way to enter. They needed the element of surprise. They had scheduled the mission around the trains into London Bridge with Tagger interrupting and stealing the shipment due to arrive at the Shard.

Cole set an even pace through the tunnel, glancing back occasionally, to check everyone was keeping pace. After about half a mile, a yellow glow spilled across the curved wall. Cole turned off his torch, gesturing at the others to do the same.

He slowed his pace, crouching against the wall, and peering around the edge of the large opening to the platform. His normal human eye picked up no agents, but his black eye picked up the almost imperceptible movement of four figures on the other side of the platform.

Cole raised four fingers to Eira, gesturing to their location. Eira's eyes shone in the dark as she nodded. They split from the group, keeping below the edge of the platform. Cole stopped near one of the centre columns where two figures were standing and silently climbed up. Eira already had her back to the cold stone, her gun cocked to her shoulder, when Cole glanced her way. Eira nodded, and they moved as one around the edge of the columns. Cole aimed and shot the moving agent square in the hip, causing him to shout and fall to the ground. Turning, he fired at the one braced against the column, hitting him in the kneecap. Eira had taken out her two targets without even lifting her gun. She sprinted in with inhuman grace, placing her hand against one agent's arm and catching him as he fell to the floor, asleep. Turning to the agent clutching his kneecap, she touched his head and he too slumped backwards.

'You're hot when you're making bad guys fall asleep,' Cole mused as he swept past, touching her hand briefly. He swept his eyes over the rest of the space, checking for any more threats before walking to the unmarked door that he knew led to the labs. He knew that Flint would deal with the bodies, dragging them down the tunnel so they wouldn't be easy to find.

Leaning against the door, Cole spoke quietly into his earpiece, 'Ipcress, door entry.'

He held his breath, waiting for Ipcress to trick the door into thinking an access card had been inserted. The door buzzed green, and Cole pulled it open without delay. Eira proceeded to the landing, monitoring the stairs below. The two generals and Major Stone slipped inside whilst Flint took over guarding the door. Cole proceeded to the lead and angled his gun down the stairs as he made the descent, Major Stone at his back.

There was a rumble from above, and Cole smiled to himself, knowing what had caused it. Major Stone glanced back up the stairs, concerned. Keeping his focus ahead, Cole whispered, 'Part of the plan.'

Major Stone huffed but turned back and continued down the stairs.

Winding around the stairs, gun angled forward, Cole reached the bottom landing with the double-doors ahead. He glanced through the viewing panel and saw no movement.

Over the earpiece, Cole contacted the technician. 'Ipcress, confirm status of bottom corridor.'

'No agents, Captain.'

'Have we been detected?'

'Negative.'

'Access please.'

As before, the door buzzed open, and Cole let out a sigh of relief. So far so good. They had gargoyle backup as well if the rumble was any indication. Cole pushed through the door, placing a foot against the grey panel to allow Major Stone and the generals access to the sterile corridor with its white tiled floor and glaring overhead lights.

Flint was next through, extracting a large metal bar from his bag to wedge the door open against the opposite wall with a grunt, extending the bar to keep it taut. A pause, and then Eira entered the corridor, her eyes locked with Cole's.

Cole nodded to the group, then angled his gun and stalked down the long corridor. One turn and they would reach their objective.

There was a flash of green light in his peripheral vision and a scream. Cole turned in an instant, his heart racing.

'What the fuck?' said Major Stone.

A green laser cage had appeared, blocking the corridor, the huge figure of Oran trapped inside.

CHAPTER 39

||| EIRA

The scream died on Eira's lips. It wasn't Oran's appearance that caused the shock, it was the severing of their bond, which left her grasping for breath. An agonising pain ripped through her body, locking her in place. She had never felt pain like it.

The loss of Oran's power left her breathless, and her own power surged outwards, seeking him. Holding onto her mind before it ripped her in half, with a grunt of effort, she wrestled her power back under control, reinforcing her glamour to hide her glowing skin.

Gritting her teeth, she sent her power flowing through her body, easing the pain, and clearing her mind.

Oran was on his knees in front of her, his wings spread wide. His body trembled with the pain devouring him. His eyes were wide with fear when they met hers, and it made her heart seize.

'Eira, are you okay?' Cole's voice was sharp in the silence.

Taking short breaths, Eira looked beyond the hunched gargoyle. Cole had his back to her, his grey baseball cap and large black bag visible. He had his gun aimed towards the members of the League, who were staring at Oran in horror with their guns raised. He was standing his ground, ready to protect his family.

'Eira, answer me.' Cole's voice held an edge of desperation as he glanced at her.

'I'm fine, Hawk,' she said, her voice strained from the pain.

Cole cracked his neck, turning back to Major Stone. 'This is our backup, Major. He might not be what you were expecting, but we would be dead if it wasn't for him.'

Major Stone didn't answer, just cocked his gun, and kept it trained on Oran.

'If you want to shoot him, you're going to have to shoot me first. So, let's just move on and complete this goddamn mission.' Cole's voice was steady and direct, and Eira could imagine the look on his face.

Major Stone gulped, his eyes flicking between Cole and Oran, deliberating. Finally, he lowered his gun and nodded. Cole sighed and lowered his gun slightly, giving Flint a look that spurred him to move forward. Cole spun around to look at Eira, his calm facade cracking, and a question in his eyes.

Eira ground out, 'I don't know what to do, Cole.' Her body twisted in pain whilst her magic battled to soothe it.

'My power triggered it,' Oran grunted in Elven, his chest heaving with the strain of talking.

'I can't feel your power, Oran, I can't feel you,' Eira blurted out, panicked. Oran shook his head, trying and failing to reply.

Eira tried to quell the rising panic and think clearly. She needed to get Oran out, but the clock was ticking, and every second they spent down here meant a second closer to being discovered and having their plan ruined.

'Hawk, you need to go. Complete the mission. I'll find a way to get Oran out.'

Cole shook his head, a pleading look on his face. Eira knew he wouldn't want to leave her there, but she squared her shoulders, shooting him a determined look. Cole clenched his jaw but then nodded once at her. He placed two fingers to his lips, kissing them, then turned his palm towards her. Locking eyes with Oran, he nodded again before shouldering his way to the front of the group.

'We move on,' Cole thundered, not looking back.

The others glanced at one another and then fell in behind him. Flint hesitated, looking at Eira with concern, but she just flashed him a reassuring smile, and he turned and followed too.

Eira turned back to Oran, examining the web of green surrounding him.

'Don't get too close,' Oran gasped, holding out a hand. 'If it senses your magic, it might ensnare you too.'

'Can you explode it from the inside?'

'I can't sense my magic, Eira,' he said, panic lacing every word.

Eira stared at the cage, trying to work out a way to dispel it. The matrix seemed to come from a green stone embedded halfway up the wall.

Pursing her lips, Eira considered the options. She stepped back and fired her gun at the stone, rocking on her feet from the impact. The bullet ricocheted off the stone, falling to the floor with a ping. The stone was intact and unmarked.

Oran hissed, the tendons in his neck stretching. 'Use your Skye blade, Eira. It's loaded with ancient magic.'

She nodded at him and pulled out the dagger from her boot, holding it in front of her. Concentrating, she took a deep breath and flicked her wrist, sending the weapon soaring through the air. It embedded itself in the stone, small fissure-like cracks spidering outwards. The cage flared once and then disappeared. Oran fell forward bracing his hands on the floor, taking great heaving breaths.

Eira rushed to his side. Hands flaring with her magic, she sent her healing power flowing through him. She inhaled quickly as her pain subsided as well, and she felt Oran's presence inside her head once again.

What was that?

Oran shook his head, bracing a hand on his knee to help him stand, spreading his wings wide.

'Do you need more power?' Eira asked in concern.

'No, it didn't consume my power, only blocked it. I've never experienced anything like that, and I think it was made worse because of our bond. My magic was seeking yours, and it seemed to home in on that.'

Eira nodded, understanding.

A low humming sound filled the corridor. Oran spun around, staring at the blade vibrating in the broken stone. He walked up to it and pulled it free.

'It's hot, like it absorbed the energy from the stone.' Shock filled his face as he studied the blade, turning it over in his hands. 'It can't be, can it?' he whispered, almost to himself.

Eira didn't know what he was talking about. She opened her mouth to demand he tell her when Oran's head jerked back up, staring along the corridor.

You trust me? he asked in her head.

Always, she replied.

The blade needs to expel the power it has absorbed.

Eira's eyebrows drew down in question.

I think there are more green stones down there. And I think Cole needs your help.

She grabbed the blade from Oran and rushed down the corridor. About two metres down the hall, she spotted another stone and effortlessly threw the dagger, sinking it into the middle once again. She didn't pause as she walked past, pulling the weapon free and stalking ahead.

The team had gathered around a door at the far end, and Cole was speaking gruffly into his earpiece, frustration marring his face. Major Stone hovered nearby, his eyes trained on the corridor. He spotted her and flinched at the fierce look on her face.

Cole turned, following the others' glances. When he saw Eira, relief flooded his features, and he started towards her, but she didn't go to him. Instead, she focused her attention on the last two green stones set in the wall ahead of her. Pausing a few paces from the first target she flung the dagger, only stopping long enough to extract the blade before proceeding to the last target. From the corner of her eye, she saw Cole falter, his head cocked to the side.

Completing the process on the final stone, the blade burning her flesh, she sprinted towards Cole, her spare hand gesturing for him to move.

Eira shouted, 'Everyone back. Now!'

Everyone in the corridor moved to the side as Eira came level with Cole. She grabbed his hand, angled her body and flicked her blade at the door. The blade struck true, humming, and vibrating on impact.

'Now, run!' Eira yelled as she turned, dragging Cole with her.

She saw Oran at the bend in the corridor, his hands spread wide with a growing light flaring between them. His eyes shone silver in the bright light and static rose on his flesh and hair.

Get down.

Eira forced Cole to the floor with a grunt, and the others instinctively followed. She glanced at Cole, whose eyes were wide with shock.

Oran's light flared down the corridor as the humming became a rumble.

Eira glanced back at the door. The blade was vibrating so much that it was a blur. With one last violent shudder, the blade broke free of the door, rocketing across the corridor to embed itself in the opposite wall. The door exploded in a blaze of light.

Eira expected Oran's light to shield them, but instead it expanded, catching the door, and smothering the explosion to keep it as contained as possible. Eira felt Oran draw on their combined power as he gritted his teeth, holding the form. The globule shrank in size, drawing the green light into itself until there was nothing left. Then it blinked out, stardust falling through the air in the aftermath.

Eira stood, holding onto Cole's hand, and helping him up. They both stared at Oran, braced against the wall, and panting heavily.

'What in living hell was that?' Major Stone hissed, a hand pressed to his chest. The generals were still spreadeagled on the floor, too shocked to stand up.

Eira released Cole's hand and retrieved her dagger from a deep groove in the wall, as Oran approached, a tired smile on his face.

'That was one way to get the door off,' he said dryly.

'You definitely know how to make an entrance,' Cole joked, grinning despite himself. He turned to the others and stated, 'Explanations later, we need to finish this!'

For once, the humans did the work. Oran, cloaked in his invisibility, kept watch on the platform above. Eira made herself useful by setting the detonators along the corridor. Cole and the others worked efficiently to fill their bags with the black bullets, knives, and anything else they could find.

Big Fella and Ginger Irish are sacrificed. Took out the remaining truck, so agents have no way to return. All drones down. I would start the extraction.

'Hawk,' Eira's clear voice rang through the corridor.

Cole came to the door, peeling off his gasmask and wiping the sweat from his face.

'We need to start the extraction.'

Cole nodded, dropping his gasmask on the floor. He replaced his cap on his head and said to the team, 'Time's up. Roll out.'

Swinging the now full bag onto his back with a grunt, he proceeded forward. Flint followed, carrying two large bags. Eira reached out to take one, but he shook his head and hoisted it higher onto his shoulder.

'We need you mobile, Doc.'

Eira glanced down the corridor to check the others were following then sprinted after them.

Taking the stairs two at the time, Eira emerged onto the platform, eyes alert for danger. Oran stepped out from behind a column, nodding in her direction. Cole approached and laid his head against hers briefly, whispering, 'Are you okay?'

Eira nodded, kissing him on the nose. He quickly withdrew as they heard the footfall of the rest of the team approaching.

'Bloody hell, what is that?' Major Stone jumped back as he saw the heaped rock in front of the door. Oran had moulded the ground in front of the door to stop it from closing.

'Ipcress, we're coming back. Be ready for extraction,' Cole said into his earpiece, pausing to listen to the reply.

'Right, let's make this quick,' he grunted, adjusting the bag on his shoulder then jumping down from the platform. Eira followed quickly, and Flint lowered himself down over the edge with a groan as he braced the weight of the bags. Eira drew on Oran's magic and created a globule of light, sending it further down the tunnel to light their way. She picked her way after Cole, mindful of the sleeping agents slumped along the wall. Major Stone came next, surprisingly nimble despite the bags he was carrying. Both generals followed, looking nervously at the floating light in front of them. Oran brought up the rear, his body tense and alert.

They sneaked along the tunnel at an even pace, long shadows bending up the wall from Eira's light.

'Tagger, extract now,' Cole ordered through the earpiece at his second-in-command. He tilted his head, listening to Tagger's reply.

'Tag's mission went to plan,' Cole whispered to Eira.

As they approached the door to the office, Oran rushed ahead. He reached up and yanked the metal door from its hinges, throwing it down the tunnel.

'Cheers, Batman,' Cole muttered.

'Permission to sacrifice the other decoys, Captain?'

'Of course, Light Bringer.'

Oran closed his eyes, and Eira felt a tug on her magic as he drew some power from her reserves. She closed her eyes, allowing the magic to flow out of her.

A warm body appeared behind her as Cole took her elbow. She fluttered her eyes open, feeling suddenly tired. Oran braced his hands against the wall, looking drained as well.

'It is done,' he grunted.

'Thank you,' Cole said earnestly, clasping the back of Oran's neck for a second.

Oran pulled himself through the door not wanting to spend any more time in the underground tunnel than necessary. Eira followed him into the service corridor as he pulled the door open, causing Ipcress to screech and jump back.

'No time to explain, come on,' Cole spoke from the doorway. 'Great support by the way,' he added.

Ipcress had gone pale, but swallowed and nodded, steeling himself.

Cole pushed past Oran, leading the way to the service stairs winding up to the deserted office above. The next moments were a blur of movement, Eira keeping pace with Cole's long legs as he ascended the stairs, aware of Oran at her shoulder, his claws scraping on the stairs.

They entered the ground floor, the boarded-up windows screening the street from view. Cole paused at the door, peeking through the crack with his gun cocked. 'All clear,' he said. 'Right, it's a quick hop across the park to Tower Bridge. Is everyone ready?' Cole glanced at them all.

Major Stone grunted. Flint nodded.

'Everyone, stay alert. Flint, be ready to detonate when we're clear.'

With that, Cole opened the door and slipped outside, glancing up and down the street. Oran pulled his aviator goggles over his eyes and followed suit. The overcast day had turned to rain, and it tracked down Eira's neck, soaking her hair and blurring her vision. The rain suddenly stopped, a shimmering forcefield encasing her. She could see the raindrops running down the invisible outline and glanced at Oran who shrugged, a glint in his eye. The rest of the party joined them. General Kay flinched as the shield expanded and sealed around them.

Hunched over, they ran down the street, keeping as close to the buildings as possible, their feet splashing in the surface water.

Cole led the party across the street, entering a small park overlooking the Thames. Oran disappeared, and Eira knew he was scouting above the building line. She didn't have time to marvel at the slanted, glazed City Hall, or the trees nearly stripped bare of their autumn leaves as they jogged through the park. The impressive structure of the first bascule bridge in London came into view, with its four towers and curved blue metal suspension wire, it was quite a sight.

Cole leaned against the stone wall leading to street level, his breathing heavy but steady. The rest followed, lining up with their backs flat against the stone.

'Flint, if you could do the honours,' Cole said to his friend.

Flint stretched stiffly, fishing a device from his pocket.

'Tag detonating in five ... four ... three ... two ... one,' Cole instructed into his earpiece.

Flint pressed the button in his hand.

Two booms sounded across London. One to the west along the Jubilee line, the orange inferno and smoke lifting into the misty cityscape. The second from the direction they had come.

The noise made Eira's sensitive ears ring, and she clapped her hands over them, hissing. The smell of sea salt washed over her as Oran landed by her side, folding a protective wing around her shoulder and strengthening the shield around them all.

They stood silently watching the Shard, the city's tallest building, shatter into a thousand mirrored panels which rained down on the streets like glittering stars. A deeper boom sounded. The Dark's laboratory caved in, taking the remaining skeletal structure with it in an explosion that ruptured London's skyline and sent shock waves pulsing through the city, as a black cloud drifted into the air.

'Well, that was impressive,' whistled Flint.

Cole merely nodded, his mouth set in a thin line. Eira knew that he took no joy in destroying such a monument.

He adjusted his bag, then turned and walked up the stairs. Eira followed, Oran close at her side. Cole set a much steadier pace this time, leading them across the open bridge in the riskiest part of their mission.

A few goods vehicles sped across the bridge, and some humans on the opposite side turned to stare at them briefly. They passed under the shadow of the first stout brick tower.

Incoming on the left, came Oran's warning in her head.

'Hawk, to the left,' Eira said.

Like Oran, Eira had detected a disturbance across the churning waters of the Thames. Cole ducked into the shadow of the tower, his eyes squinting to make out the threat.

'Do we have time to make it to the centre?' he asked, eyeing the distance.

'There's a hover copter and a handful of drones. If they've discovered us, they'll just keep coming,' Oran said, staring into the distance at the approaching danger.

'I can maintain the shield while Oran takes them out,' Eira added.

'We proceed,' Cole concluded.

Oran sprinted forward, gesturing for everyone to follow. Eira took control of the shield, keeping it solid around them as they ran.

Suddenly, Oran stopped halfway along the exposed section, where the suspension was lowest, the blue and red paint once regal and historic, now chipped with neglect. He jumped onto the suspension wire, his claws grating on the metal. A black mass appeared on the horizon, the low hum of drones audible even to the humans.

Cole stopped below Oran.

'Everyone to the next tower,' he said, gesturing with his gun. Flint powered past with Ipcress and Bolton on his heels. Kay twisted and tripped, and Cole caught her, helping her to safety, head low.

The thud of the hover copter was deafening, the spray off the Thames divided in its wake.

Major Stone paused, fear gripping him. Eira tugged on his arm to make him move, one eye on Oran as she saw him bend his knees, his staff gripped in his hands. She could make out the agents in the cockpit.

'Move, Major,' she urged.

Eira pushed him forward, but he didn't budge. She met Cole's frightened gaze from the safety of the second tower. He hesitated and then started to come back to them. Fear gripped her.

Eira felt Oran draw on their bond, and she pulled the shield back to cover herself, Cole, and Major Stone since the others were safely at the next tower.

Oran launched himself from the wire, a thundering boom echoing from his wing clap. Despite the danger, Eira couldn't help but stare in awe at him. One strong beat of his wings powered him forward like a missile, staff pointed like a lance towards the aircraft. His power glowed around the point as he aimed straight for the cockpit, his wings tucked in. Eira saw the surprise on the agents' faces as Oran smashed through the windscreen in a shower of glass and continued his trajectory through the craft. The hover copter splintered, the shredding sound echoing off the surrounding buildings. It caught fire in an explosion of light, plummeting to the depths below. Oran spread his wings to slow his acceleration, wings flagging against the wind. With a flash like a whip, his starlight arced out and incinerated the drones.

A screech sounded behind Eira, and she turned to see two black trucks careening diagonally across the road.

'Run, Major!' she shouted desperately.

Eira ran forward and grabbed Major Stone, dragging him along behind her. Cole had halted, firing shots at the approaching trucks to cover their retreat. The sound of doors slamming and boots scraping on tarmac reached her, and Eira turned her head in time to watch Cole take out several agents.

A shot sounded, and Major Stone slipped from her grip with a grunt, his weight pulling her down with him. Peering down, she found Major Stone clutching his shin, blood flowing between his fingers. His eyes met hers, wide with pain and fear. How had the bullet pierced the shield? Then she saw it. The black tendrils creeping along Major Stone's flesh.

'They're using black bullets,' Eira shouted to Cole. Oran sent his light flashing at the agents, blinding them as Cole shot, but he had to turn back to meet the second hover copter. Moonlight shot from his hands like lightning, piercing the aircraft in multiple places. Eira watched as it tail-spun through the air, and Oran leapt up at the last minute to deal it a crushing final blow.

Eira cursed, ripping Major Stone's trouser leg and drawing on her healing power. She went to place her hands over the wound, knowing her power would recoil from the virus, but halted, her breath catching. The black veins had retreated. Major Stone's wrist glowed with a faint light.

'The bracelet,' Eira breathed. 'You were lucky, Major.'

Without further hesitation she placed her hands on his leg and extracted the bullet, closing the wound.

Eira registered his confusion as he dragged himself to his feet and rushed for the safety of the tower. Then she turned angrily and drew on Oran's power, throwing streams of moonlight at the remaining agents.

The force knocked them and the trucks backwards in a flare that momentarily blinded her.

Impressive, came Oran's amused comment.

Breathing hard, Eira stalked to Oran and Cole's side.

'We're not finished yet.' Cole gestured to their left where a third dot on the horizon was approaching at speed. He winked at Eira despite their predicament. 'How're your power levels?'

'Stable.' Eira nodded her reassurance.

'There's another to the right,' Oran remarked.

Without another comment, Cole jogged to the others and gestured to move out.

They ran to the next tower, trying to avoid attack. Bolton braced Kay under an arm, her bag now slung across his shoulder. Flint powered on without complaint, barely breathing heavily. Ipcress and Major Stone brought up the rear. Suddenly, Oran bent and scooped Eira up and into his arms. He landed under the next tower, setting her down in anticipation of the attack to come. The hover copters had changed course, heading straight for them.

Taking a central stance, Oran flared his great wings, his back to hers.

'What's the plan, Light Bringer?'

'You take one, I'll take the other.' Eira stared, horror etched on her face as Oran sniggered. 'Feed me your power, steadily.'

He'd barely finished speaking when he gasped, pivoting, and pulling Eira to his chest. His wings encircled them as he strengthened the shield, his power glowing like moonlight. Something pelted the shield, raining down like hailstones. Oran's body tensed and then sagged. Rain immediately soaked her, dripping into her eyes.

Eira lifted her head as Oran's ragged breathing tickled her ear. Her eyes widened. Oran's wings were peppered with bullet holes, the skin shredded and torn, black blood seeping from the wounds and pooling with the puddles on the ground. She quickly assessed the main spines of his wings and noticed two bullets lodged in them. The black lines spiderwebbing out from the wounds told her exactly how the bullets had bypassed his shield. 'Shit! Shit, Oran, stay awake.'

Panic gripped her as she rose, bracing her feet. She sent her soothing magic down the bond, hoping to keep the gargoyle conscious.

He was wearing the bracelet, and the magic in his veins would keep the virus at bay, so she knew she had time.

Pulling on their combined reserves, Eira faced the two oncoming aircrafts.

Suddenly, Cole stepped forward, putting himself between Oran's prone form and the hover copters. He stood, legs braced, as he stared calmly down the scope of his rifle. He pulled the trigger, his body rocking with the impact. The hover copter spun out of control, the engine smoking. Cole took aim and fired again at the second aircraft, hitting a propeller, and causing it to drop towards the Thames. The pilot regained control though, pulling it to the side and firing on them.

Eira watched in horror as Cole fell backwards, slumping near Oran with a grunt of pain. A scream ripped from her lungs.

She was paralysed with fear, a swell of rage building inside her. Oran's power surged, filling her up. She threw her head back with a shout as glittering moonlight erupted from her in a wave, crashing over the hover copter and incinerating it in a flash.

Eira rushed to Cole and dropped to her knees, seeking out the bullet wound with her hands and her magic. Then she saw the black veins on his flesh.

'You idiot,' she said, worried.

Cole groaned, his hand latching onto hers. His eyes were scrunched in pain, his flesh paling. Eira fed her power into him, easing the waves of agony washing through his body. His eyes opened and he gazed at her, a look so filled with love and adoration that she almost kissed him.

Then her breath caught. He had given his bracelet to Major Stone. With trembling hands, Eira ripped the bulletproof vest from her chest and unzipped her black hoodie, fishing out her necklace.

Gripping it in her palm she went to apply it to the wound, but the black lines had receded.

'Oran,' Cole groaned, lifting his wrist to show her the glowing bracelet.

Eira deflated with relief, laying her head against his chest before shooting upright again. If Oran had given his bracelet to Cole, then that meant he was unprotected.

Turning, she saw Oran hunched on the ground, the virus spreading like roots through his alabaster wings.

Flaring her power, she pressed her hand to Cole's shoulder, drawing out the bullet and sealing the wound. Before the skin had even knitted, she was on her feet and rushing to Oran's side.

She knelt beside him, gently lifting the goggles from his eyes and pulling his eyelid open. She let out a sigh of relief when she saw that they were still white. But his wings were almost entirely black. Either the Dark had worked out how to accelerate the virus, or the number of wounds had caused it to spread far more quickly. Not giving herself time to think about what might happen, she pressed her necklace to his wing, willing it to work.

The opal flared under her palm, and the black veins travelled back through his wing and into the necklace with a loud boom. Eira threaded her power with Oran's, hoping to wake him up like she had when he was in the regenerative sleep.

Oran.

His consciousness shifted, and she saw his eyes flicker under his eyelids.

A foreign power stroked hers, but it wasn't Oran's moonlight. Instead, it felt like a vast cavern full of sparkling, fractured crystal, alive with knowledge and infinite possibilities. Eira latched onto it and drew it down the bond, desperate to heal her protector. She gritted her teeth, squeezing her eyes tight as the combined power became all-consuming.

Firm hands gripped her waist, and she felt weightless as she was lifted off the ground. But she still maintained the flow of power into Oran, the need to save him overwhelming.

Her ears rang. She was conscious of raised voices, screeching brakes, and gunshots.

Eira, let go of the power.

At Oran's voice in her head, her eyes snapped open. Oran had her elevated above the ground, his arms wrapped around her waist.

But you're hurt, infected, she said back fearfully.

I'm healed, now let go. Expand the power.

His voice seemed strained. Eira looked at Oran, his entire form shimmering, his white skin glowing from within. His misted white eyes were streaked through with silver.

With a gasp, Eira looked at her own hand gripping the opal, glowing as well. The opal was burning her palm, and fear gripped her. She turned it over to examine it and saw that it was pitch-black, completely void of light. She screamed, back arching as the power surged from her in a sphere, her lungs burning. Oran gripped her, roaring in pain as the power surged through his body too.

The rippling silver moonlight exploded over the bridge.

Cole stood his ground, head angled into the wave, confident that it wouldn't hurt him. The light swept along the bridge, upending cars, and knocking people to the ground. It seemed to linger on the infected, shimmering around them before moving on. Bolton bent over Kay for protection whilst Stone watched in astonishment, hand braced on the stone edge.

As quickly as the light flared, it blinked out.

Eira felt weightless as her body sagged in Oran's grip. Their combined power flowed into her, strengthening her numb limbs. Oran lifted her, pressing his lips to her forehead and whispering something in his language. The words tickled something in her memory, but she was too exhausted to work it out. He wiped at her nose, his brows furrowed. Oran's ivory hands appeared in her vision, a black liquid staining his fingers.

She felt her numb hand clutching something warm and smooth. Her vision blurred and then refocused again as her head drooped. Eira vaguely recalled Cole's frightened face, a caress over her head, and his firm nod as she was lifted skywards before she blacked out.

CHAPTER 40

⟨ COLE

Cole sat in a familiar room in Bramshill House, his feet on the table, legs crossed at the ankles.

This time, he had part of his team with him. Tagger stood to his right, arms folded in his camouflage gear, attention trained on the door. Flint was on his left in a similar stance. They had been disarmed and shoved in here like common criminals, but at least they hadn't been cuffed. They were still wearing their sodden clothes, and the room was unheated.

It was early evening when they'd finally made it safely to base. Cole couldn't help replaying everything that had happened in his head. From Oran becoming trapped in the green cage and then nearly getting infected again, to the huge wave of magic that had ripped from Eira's body.

He had stood in the centre of the wave, watching it divide and flow around him, keeping him safe. He knew it was the sworn oath that had protected him and left him unharmed. The magic had sought out the Dark's agents, swirling around them and curing them of the virus.

Oran had flown off with Eira, so Cole knew that she was safe. He needed to keep his focus on the here and now, to diffuse the situation with Major Stone.

The door opened, and Major Stone entered, flanked by five heavily-armed officers. He didn't stand, instead giving them a brief nod. Tagger and Flint stood in stony silence beside him, waiting for his lead.

Major Stone stared at Cole, slamming his fists on the table in front of him. 'Hawk, what the fuck was that?' he shouted. 'Yes, the mission was a success, but I didn't approve the involvement of those...' he trailed off, a look of shock and disgust on his face.

'Those what, Major? Those creatures who saved your life and made the mission possible in the first place. Without them, we would all be infected with the virus now and be puppets to the Dark. And this...' – Cole waved a hand around the room – '... would have been compromised and infiltrated by now too.'

'You put us in danger! You sent us on a mission without giving us the full details. We were reliant on creatures we weren't even aware of, and it could have caused the failure of the entire mission,' he spat. His face was bright red, a vein pounding in his temple.

'If I had informed you, what would you have done? Sacrificed the mission because you refused to work with them? We've finally achieved something that we haven't been able to do for a decade. They were fundamental in that. They didn't need to get involved, didn't need to put themselves at risk for the sake of humanity, but they did.' Cole clenched his fists, controlling his rage.

Major Stone huffed, pushing off the table with a groan. He placed his hands on his hips and turned to stare at the wall. 'What are your demands, Hawk?' he asked, getting straight to the point.

Stone wasn't stupid. They both knew that the League had resources that Cole needed. But Major Stone also knew how powerful Cole's team was now, and Cole knew he would want to take advantage of that.

'An alliance between us and the League. Look at what we achieved today, and trust me, that's only the beginning,' Cole said calmly.

The door behind crashed open, and Major Stone spun quickly, a hand on his gun. Cole smirked as Oran strolled in, huge wings flaring around him. Eira was cradled against his chest, but she was awake and taking in the room, much to Cole's relief. Oran set her on the floor, and she sauntered straight to his side, leaning a hip against him and squeezing his shoulder. Cole had to stop himself from grabbing her and pulling her into his lap; he couldn't show Major Stone how much she meant to him.

Instead, he lifted his head, his eyes searching her face for any signs of pain or discomfort. But she looked calm and determined, the only sign of her fragility the dark smudges under her eyes.

Oran took a defensive stance directly behind Cole's chair, arms crossed and wings out. Cole's heart swelled as he sat there, surrounded by his chosen family. The people who would protect him at all costs, and those he would die for in return.

With a sigh, Eira moved and sat to his right, near Tagger who winked at her, a devilish grin on his lips.

'You want us to work with that *thing*?' Major Stone spat, gesturing at Oran.

Cole shot to his feet, anger pulsing through him. 'That *thing* has a name. This is Oran Light Bringer, chief of the Crescent Clan, and you'd better start showing him the respect he deserves,' Cole demanded. 'And whilst we're on the subject of respect, the doctor also has a name, and you owe her your life.' *We all do.*

He tilted his head to Eira.

Eira turned to Major Stone, bracing her elbows on the table.

'My name is Eira Mackay. My mother was Rosalind Mackay, head of the Equal Rise party. She was assassinated over ten years ago by the Dark.' Eira's voice was strained, tired.

Major Stone's eyes flared in recognition at her words.

'Her vision was to create harmony between the races in a selfless act to make the world better for her daughter, a hybrid. She was the first to start the fight against the Dark and was the reason many of the groups like the League exist. But her vision has become blurred over the years, with humans forgetting the plight of the Myths and hybrids. I've never placed myself in her shoes until now, until a solution presented itself where we can combat this evil.' Eira shook her head, sighing heavily. 'We apologise that you were deceived, but we couldn't risk your refusal.'

'Does Moyra know?'

'No, she doesn't, but I think she has always suspected.'

Major Stone nodded, leaning back, and stroking his moustache. 'What's your offer, Hawk?'

Oran replied, 'We offer my clan's protection. Several of our best trained warriors with incredible fighting skills and power to aid in your fight against the Dark. An alliance, a partnership, as the captain has stated. I offer this on one condition.' Oran raised a long finger, his gaze direct. 'That my warriors are treated with respect, equality, and honour by your team.'

The threat in the gargoyle's voice told Major Stone exactly what would happen if this rule wasn't followed.

Major Stone gulped under Oran's stare. Cole sat, tapping his fingers on the hard surface.

'What do you ask in return?'

'Until we can create an antidote to the virus, we request a safe location for our scientists to conclude their work on the production of more bracelets. These will be issued to all Myths and humans in London, and before you ask, yes, they are Myths as well.' Cole leant back, folding his arms.

'We also ask for transparency, aid, and commitment to a cause that we're both fighting for,' Eira added.

Major Stone leant back in his seat, mirroring Cole's posture and folding his own arms.

They waited.

'You've backed me into a corner, Hawk. I need time to consider and speak to the other directors.'

'That's bullshit, Major. We all know that you make the decisions and everyone else nods along,' Cole fired back.

Major Stone choked in surprise at Cole's disrespectful tone.

'Decide now, or we walk. And we take those vans with us.'

Cole hated threatening Major Stone, but he couldn't risk him taking the loot and jeopardising what they'd achieved so far. He had Eira to care for, their goals and future to plan for.

Major Stone was still as he contemplated. Cole was starting to get nervous when Major Stone finally stood and nodded.

Cole rose himself, edging past Flint to meet Major Stone halfway along the table.

'How do we seal the deal?' Stone asked.

Cole held out his hand to Major Stone, who grasped his forearm. 'A binding of sorts, a fealty to the common cause of solidarity and equality. It's an oath made with trust and friendship to meet the objective and give each other support when needed. To give respect and honour to Oran's clan members, we will do the same in return.'

Oran had moved without anyone noticing and clasped their joined hands, his light flaring. Major Stone flinched. Oran had told Cole to put the oath into feelings, a binding created by himself. So, Cole repeated all he had said in his mind, reinforcing it with the love he now felt for Eira, the loyalty and respect from his two best friends, and the admiration and kinship he felt to the gargoyle, binding the promise.

The silver-white light intensified and then winked out. As before, Cole felt the oath created between him and Major Stone like a phantom limb. He turned his wrist to find another mark on his forearm under the moon. Cole gasped with surprise. Instead of a crescent moon, the engraving was a hawk in flight. His nickname. Major Stone looked at his own wrist, the mirror image of Cole's, his stern mouth set.

Cole held his wrist to Oran, amazement on his face.

'You shaped the magic. I was only the battery charger,' he said with a grin.

||| EIRA

Eira lay face down on top of an unfamiliar bed, breathing in the freshness of the duvet. This was where she had collapsed when entering the grand room in Bramshill House. She had sedately taken in the majestic proportions of the room, the panelling on the walls, four poster bed, and the ornate furniture. She knew there was a bathroom to the side of the mahogany armoire, but she didn't have the strength to venture into it.

Her hearing picked up on the door opening, booted feet crossing the soft carpeted floor. Eira knew who it was from his scent alone. She was surprised it had taken Cole this long to find her. She turned to look at him as the bed dipped beside her.

Cole whistled, taking in the room. 'The Major must be trying to make amends since he put you in here.' He unlaced his boots and kicked them off. 'You should see my digs. It's like a box compared to this.'

'Since you're taking your clothes off, does that mean that you're staying with me?' Eira said as he removed his cap, placing it on the nightstand. 'If that cap is staying there, you definitely are.'

Cole winked as he slid out of view, sauntering behind her. 'I'm done pretending,' he said, leaning over her.

Her stomach tightened in anticipation, but he just bent and lifted her leg, undoing one of her boots and pulling it off. His hands wrapped around her ankle and ghosted up her shin to her thigh. Eira sighed, melting into the duvet.

'I'm done pretending I don't know you, don't know every inch of this perfect body,' he said, stroking her thigh tenderly, sliding her dagger free. 'Anyway, I've tied the Major into the oath and I'm pretty sure I'm not part of the League anymore. So, I really don't care if they know you're mine.' He pushed up her top and placed a delicate kiss on her back.

Eira braced herself on one arm to peer at Cole over her shoulder. 'Does that make you sad?'

Cole shrugged as his hands skimmed her bottom, removing the other dagger from her thigh. 'Not as much as it should. I've got a new home, one where I finally feel settled. I think if Tag or Flint had decided to stay here, I would have been sadder.'

Angling his head, Cole tracked his hand down her other leg and Eira bit her lip to stop herself from demanding more. Cole knelt, unlacing her second boot, and placing it next to the other. He then slid up her trouser leg, unsheathing her last dagger.

Eira tracked Cole as he advanced around the bed to the other nightstand and placed her weapons on it. He hesitated with the Skye blade, turning it between his fingers.

'If we hadn't had this, it could have all gone wrong,' he said, staring at the blade.

Eira huffed, flipping onto her back to stare up at the draped, teal canopy above. Her necklace rocked with the movement as it slid to one side. Eira knew the questions that Cole was building up to — they were the same questions that Oran had asked after he took off with her.

Cole flopped down onto the bed with a sigh, his hand instantly finding hers and tracing circles on it. Eira knew he was being patient, letting her gather her thoughts, content to just lay beside her.

She sighed, knowing that it would be better to get it out in the open instead of letting it fester. 'Oran thinks I have a set of welkin swords,' she said, staring at the canopy above her.

'The race from the sky? Like Oran, but more angel than demon with the golden, feathered wings?' Cole asked.

'Yep, those are the ones. He thought that Storm was one, remember?'

Cole turned his head to look at her and nodded, encouraging her to continue.

'He said that the exploding dagger proved it. The blades are ancient, infused with power like his staff and this necklace.' Eira picked up her opal then let it fall back onto her chest. 'They're a set of blades lost from the welkin over two decades ago. They have the ability to absorb energy and turn it into kinetic power, raw and explosive. Oran said, with the correct genetics and training, they can be mastered.'

'We'll figure it out together.'

Cole squeezed her hand again, and Eira tilted her head, so they were nose to nose. He leant up and kissed her forehead.

'What about the power surge?' Cole urged.

'Again, Oran only has a theory, he couldn't give me an actual answer,' she said, grabbing her necklace and twisting it around her finger. 'Did I ever tell you I nearly threw this into the Thames once?' Eira continued after a brief pause.

Cole angled his body sideways against hers, propping an elbow under his ear, and watching the opal spin. 'No, you never said.'

'After I accidentally used it to heal you, I was so overwhelmed and anxious that I was convinced the Dark would find me. So, I knew I had to hide it. On the way to the deposit, I had a split second when I thought maybe it would be easier, safer, to just get rid of it. I came to my senses at the last minute. God, imagine if I had thrown it into the river. None of this would have happened.'

Eira glanced at Cole, who was staring at her with solemn eyes.

'You can always question the ifs, the maybes, the possibilities. If Lofty hadn't shot his mouth off then we wouldn't have been attacked. If you hadn't used the necklace, I would be a sleaze-suit right now. If you hadn't slipped me the scalpel, I would have been reinfected. If you hadn't put that dagger in your boot, we would have been captured,' Cole said firmly. 'I don't believe in a higher being. We're the manufacturers of our own fate. But it doesn't mean that our actions aren't guided, and this is the world's way of changing the course it was set on. Everything that has happened is too much to be a coincidence, so don't go blaming yourself.'

As always, Cole had made her feel better so easily. Tears threatened to fall as she stared at his handsome face, taking in his scar and his mismatched eyes — things she knew were her fault. But maybe he was right, they were changing something bigger than them, and maybe everything that had happened was the universe's way of balancing it out.

Eira twisted so their bodies aligned, placing a hand on Cole's cheek, and kissing his nose. He quirked a half-smile, a dimple appearing beside his mouth.

'Oran's theory is that, in my desperation to heal him, I used the Bloodstream to draw on the opal and whatever ancient power is locked inside it.' She held the necklace up to him. 'It was vast, Cole. I've never felt anything like it. It was completely foreign but so familiar at the same time. I apparently merged our powers into it and amplified my intent.'

'Who would think there was so much might in this little stone?' he mused, stroking the opal.

'What happened? What did I actually do?' she asked.

Cole's eyes flicked to hers, reading the guilt there. 'You didn't hurt anyone, so you don't need to worry about that,' he reassured her, placing a hand on her neck.

Eira nodded, unconvinced but wanting to show him that she was trying.

'The power only seemed to seek those who needed healing, those who were infected. Whilst you were doing your ... glowing thing, we had company. Two more trucks. The power surge flattened them. The silver light became black as it surrounded the agents, so I can only assume that it was drawing the virus from them. I'll admit that we didn't hang around to see if it had worked.'

Eira was still shocked, even though Oran had said the same thing.

'Do you think you could do it again without burning out?' Cole enquired.

'That's the odd thing, Hawk. We'd both expended a vast amount of power leading up to that point, and yes, I was probably close to burnout, but the magic from the opal healed us too, boosted our reserves.' She shrugged and continued, 'I think it would need to be more controlled if we tried again.'

'It would certainly make a difference if we're able to cure a whole group of people at once,' Cole suggested, interlacing their hands.

Eira agreed, but the thought of it terrified her.

'But we'll cross that road if, and when, we come to it. Together, Eira,' Cole emphasised, kissing their joined hands.

The mattress shifted as Cole stood, his fingers still interlaced in hers. He gently nudged her arm, so Eira lifted her head in enquiry.

'Now, let's get you cleaned up. You should see the size of the bath in there,' he said, gesturing at the bathroom. 'And if you're lucky, maybe I'll join you,' he added with a cheeky grin.

Eira allowed Cole to pull her from the bed, following him into the plush bathroom, needing his care and attention.

ORAN

Oran pressed his palm to the mechanical scanner that Eira called a biometric reader. He was exhausted to his core. His strength and power were stable but, like Eira, he was contemplating the gravity of the new developments and what could have come to pass. Oran never usually let such things worry him, but he couldn't stop replaying the things that could have gone wrong.

Oran had reacted calmly when Eira finally asked her questions, but he was just as overwhelmed as she was. The fact that the Dark had been able to create the cage that trapped him and blocked his magic, was almost more worrying than the newfound power in Eira's opal.

Collecting his thoughts, Oran pushed open the secret door, hunching over to fit through the frame. He had chosen to return to the gatehouse to monitor the situation with the Dark. And he needed to see Echo. He knew that the Dark would be looking for him now; he wasn't exactly hard to miss.

The door swung open on silent hinges. He sighed as he entered the dark room, pulling off his goggles and placing his staff on the side table.

He knew the females were in the sitting room, his bond to Nelka telling him exactly where she was. The smoky scent that drifted to him confirmed that Elowen was with her.

He walked to the sitting room, finding them and Madam Scudamore around the fire. All three jumped to attention as he entered, worry etched onto their faces. Nelka had risen from the orange armchair, Oswald draped around her neck like a scarf, her wings hooked over her shoulders. Elowen was in a similar position having vacated the other roll-top armchair, her hands wringing in front of her. Madam Scudamore floated between them, the glow from the orange fire flickering through her grey outline.

'I'm honoured you ladies stayed up to see my safe return,' Oran drawled with a smirk.

Nelka crossed her slender arms, claws drumming on her exposed forearms. He could tell that she was annoyed. She'd either felt his pain when he was shot or was frustrated at the cryptic message he had sent her earlier.

Oswald flared his membrane wings and, with a growled greeting, flew lazily to his shoulder. Oran tickled the little beast under his chin, and he grumbled in delight.

'What happened, Oran Light Bringer?' Nelka's tone was sharp, but the concern on her face confirmed that she'd been worried about him.

'We did it. There were a couple of hitches that we weren't prepared for, but everyone is safe.' He raised a hand as Elowen opened her mouth to ask something. 'Eira and Cole are staying with the League for a couple of days to sort out the particulars of the deal we made. The Major accepted our conditions.'

Elowen collapsed back in the chair, her full fringe obscuring the relief in her dark eyes.

'I have some steak if you're hungry, gargoyle,' Madam Scudamore stated, drifting to the kitchen, her full skirts dragging along the floor.

'That would be much appreciated, poltergeist. Thank you for considering me.' His stomach growled, and he realised how hungry he was.

Madam Scudamore gave a curt nod. 'Elowen, can you come and give me a hand please?'

Elowen looked up, eyes darting around the gathered group. She jumped up and followed her into the kitchen, leaving Oran and Nelka alone.

'Starlight, tell me why I felt your pain, not once, but twice. What happened?' Nelka asked, her eyebrows pulled low.

Oran reached her in one stride. He leant down and pressed a kiss to her brow, his hands tracing her exposed bump. He switched to Gork and filled her in as briefly as he could before Madam Scudamore and Elowen returned. Whilst Elowen was aware of some of what was going on, he knew that Eira was protecting her from the more dangerous aspects.

His soulmate tensed as Oran relayed the story. She turned away when he finished, wrapping her arms around her chest. 'I'm afraid, Starlight,' Nelka said finally.

Oran started. It was the last thing he had expected her to say. She was afraid of nothing.

Wrapping his arms and wings around her, he encased her in his warm embrace. 'I know your fear is rooted in how the virus can infect immortals and this new threat that can block our magic. It poses a huge threat to us and our clan. As does our involvement in this fight. But I will return to our clan and claim my seat. We will unite the clans and face this together,' Oran stated defiantly.

Nelka nodded, wrapping her own arms around his. Finally, she said, 'You need to tell Eira the truth. You owe her that much. She has saved your life more times than I can count.'

CHAPTER 41

‖ EIRA

A rainy October gave way to a blustery November, and the rust-coloured leaves crumbled to the ground.

The days Eira and Cole spent at the League base gave them a hint of a normal life, a future they might have one day if the Dark didn't exist. If the world wasn't prejudiced against Eira's kind; if they could be open and free.

When they weren't in logistics meetings, they spent their time wandering the vast grounds of Bramshill House. They strolled arm in arm through the courtyard gardens as Cole explained how the League, and the police academy before them, used the walled gardens to grow fruit and vegetables to be self-sufficient. How some of the twisted fruit trees espaliered along the walls had been there since Victorian times.

They explored the banks of the ornamental lake, and Cole told her how he used to spend his summers swimming in the pleasant waters. When Eira joked that they should take a swim, she was shocked to see him strip off his clothes and run straight in. She burst out laughing at his loud yelps as the freezing water engulfed him. He ran out minutes later, and Eira wrapped her arms around him, sending her magic into his body to raise his body temperature.

They spent an entire afternoon lost in the ancient forest, climbing the gnarled branches of the yew trees which grew there wild and untamed; Eira climbed to the top of the tallest trees with ease, leaping from branch to branch. Cole told stories of his training adventures through the forest, the pranks they would play on new recruits. The majestic forest was Eira's favourite place, the ancient oak tree with a cave-like hollow being their retreat from the world.

They shared the small things with each other in those moments, creating cherished memories. They never discussed the future, wanting to live in the moment for as long as possible.

When Cole was in meetings, Tagger or Flint would find her, and they would explore the house together, telling her embarrassing stories about Cole.

Her mood seemed to swing from moments of blissful happiness to states of distress and agitation. She didn't know what they would face once they left, and it worried her.

The reaction from the League members was not helping her resolve either. She was used to the stares and the whispers behind her back, but it was the looks of fear and hostility on their faces whenever she walked into the dining hall that hurt. It was only Cole's hand in hers and the kind reassurances of Major Stone that stopped her from running back to her room.

Stone's change of mood had improved the relationship between him and Cole, stripping away the tension which had arisen between them. It turned out that Major Stone could be quite charismatic and humble, even if he was serious and stiff.

Eira knew that the reactions to her were affecting Cole as well. He had made good his promise and had been openly affectionate to her, no longer hiding their relationship. Whenever he caught someone looking at her, he glared at them and led her away. Eira knew it was important that Cole didn't make enemies within the group, even though he wasn't a member now.

'Doc, did you hear me?' Cole enquired, wrapping his arms around her waist. 'You seem distracted.'

Eira was. She knew she had drawn into herself the past day or so. She had started to avoid the crowded communal areas, wearing her band around her ears and, despite the pure bliss of having Cole beside her at night, her sleep had degenerated, and her nightmares had returned.

'Sorry, Hawk, what did you ask?'

'Will this do? Will this be comfortable for the Alchemists?'

'It has windows,' Eira stated dryly.

They stood in the abandoned game lodge on the banks of the ornamental lake, the forest spreading out behind them. It was a large warm space, a fire already blazing in the fireplace. Sheepskin rugs were dotted around, and a small neat kitchen stood in the corner.

'Right, Eira,' Cole said sternly, turning her to face him. His hands clasped her cheeks, forcing her to look into his eyes. 'This isn't you. So what if some ex-military personnel are afraid of you?

You're strong, and defiant, and powerful, and kind. It's their loss that they won't get to know that about you.' His eyebrows knitted as he continued, 'But that's not all, is it? You've been off since the mission.'

As always, he knew exactly what was wrong with her, but she didn't know how to put it into words.

'Let's start with the basics,' Cole whispered, sensing that she needed his help to talk about it.

His hands slid from her cheeks and threaded into her braid, blindly undoing the knot at the nape of her neck. He leant back and unwound the black scarf from her head, running his fingers up her exposed ears, sending sparks and chills racing down her spine.

'You do not hide who you are when it's safe. Even here when those bastards are staring at you. You're better than that. Just imagine you're a gargoyle and give them your best snarl.'

Cole gave an exaggerated impersonation of Oran, making Eira smile weakly. He rested his hands on her hips, the scarf wound around his arm.

'They need time to settle into this, Eira. I'm not making excuses for them, but this is a lot for the average human to take in. And if they can't deal with these,' he said, gesturing at her ears, 'then I don't know how they'll take to a bunch of gargoyles.'

Eira flicked his nipple playfully, making him jolt back with a curse.

He continued, 'You've won over the Major, the rest will follow. I promise you this will work, okay?' Eira nodded. 'I've packed our meagre belongings, and we're heading home this afternoon. I'm missing my leather jacket too much and I need to protect my socks before Oswald uses them all to make a nest.'

'I do miss that leather jacket,' Eira mused.

'So, you do remember how to speak then?' Cole squeezed her waist, bending over her as he laughed onto her neck, a grin lighting his face. 'I was worried I was going to have to run into that freezing lake again just to get a reaction from you.'

Eira raised her eyebrows; she would have loved to see that again. 'I've enjoyed our time here, Cole. I really have been happy spending time with you, exploring the grounds, and learning more about you.' Cole needed to know that it wasn't all bad. 'The moments of simply being normal, of being a couple, will stay with me,' Eira said truthfully, laying a hand on his cheek.

'It has been fun, hasn't it?' he said with a grin. 'But I'm looking forward to the lit fireplace, the stern housekeeper, and our friends. I'll miss the bathtub though.'

She kissed him, slow and sweet, savouring their last moments there. Eira slid her hands between them and made them glow with her healing magic. 'I'm scared. I don't know how I'll cope with another change to this.' She waved her glowing hands. 'And I'm not sure I want to know the truth.'

Her breath hitched as Cole reached up, grasping both her hands. 'Firstly, fear makes you strong. It gives you a conscience, it doesn't make you weak, Eira. I was scared on that bridge, afraid we wouldn't make it, but I would have fought for our freedom until my dying breath. I wouldn't let them recapture me, not again. That's why I protected you both in front of the hover copter. Why you did what you did. It was out of fear for Oran's life,' Cole whispered, his gaze intense. 'Fear made Oran give me his bracelet. Never hide your fear; embrace it.'

Cole kissed her joined hands, steadying her, and she knew that whatever was to come, they would face it together.

'If you really don't want to go back, we won't. We'll just need to make sure that the triplets get here safely,' Cole suggested. 'Oran has secured us safe passage under the city with the bridge trolls' guidance. We can even bring the old gal right to the front door.' Cole shrugged, grinning. 'I won't lie, the Dark are looking for us, and security is tighter. Oran suggested that we return with him and Nelka to his clan.'

Eira gasped. Whilst she had been moping, Cole and Oran had been planning ahead, organising the next steps.

Eira desperately wanted to see Oran's world, to see the place where he grew up. The fact that Cole was willing to go with them made her heart melt. He would be surrounded by powerful, potentially dangerous, gargoyles in an unknown place, but he would do it for her. 'You would do that?' Eira asked, needing to hear him say it.

'Of course, Doc, because it needs to be done. And I'm stoked to see a magical kingdom. Can you imagine the fun we could get up to when they're asleep during the day?' Cole's mischievous grin sparked Eira's own.

'You're so weird. But wonderful.'

'I'll take that as a compliment.' Cole leant his forehead against hers, growing serious. 'We'll deal with any developments in your power together. I'm sure Oran is just as scared as you are.'

Cole exhaled. Eira waited for a solution to the part she dreaded the most.

'Scared to ask them the truth? I presume you mean your family?' Cole asked. 'I have a solution for that as well if you're happy to talk to your family. It's either that or you run into the lake butt-naked,' he said with a cheeky smirk.

Eira grinned, shocked, but the weight seemed to have lifted from her shoulders. She simply kissed Cole and whispered, 'I love you, Hawk, more than you can ever know.'

After pulling back, she grabbed her phone and snapped a photo of Cole pressing a kiss to her cheek as she smiled at the camera. She added it to the folder she'd been collecting while they'd been away.

Cole flicked his hair over his black eye, staring nervously at the screen in front of him. He fiddled with his shirt, wishing he had his leather jacket for comfort.

Eira, who was sat cross-legged next to him, reached over his lap and snagged his discarded cap. Running her fingers through his hair, Eira placed it backwards on his head, and traced her fingers down his face. 'Now who's scared?' Her eyes shone with delight. 'If I'm not hiding then neither are you!'

Cole knew he had brought that spark back to her, and it filled him with joy.

Eira had insisted that he stay with her whilst she made the call. It had taken an hour or so to set up a secure outside call with her aunt and uncle, but they had done it.

Whilst the screen loaded, Eira leant back, her head tilted to the side so her braid draped over her shoulder. 'How have you and Oran been communicating?'

'That would be telling,' Cole said, tapping the edge of his nose. Seeing the fire build in her eyes and wanting to avoid another flick to his nipple, he quickly added, 'Stone Nightingales. Apparently, they're more gargoyle-friendly when the receiver is a technophobe.'

The screen lit suddenly, and Cole only had a second to register that he was about to meet his girlfriend's family before two faces appeared on the screen. Eira's aunt was so like the photograph he had seen of Eira's mother that he jerked. Her chestnut hair was run through with grey, straighter than her sister's, but with the same tone. Her face was rounder, tanned and lined with age, clearly the face of someone who lived their life outdoors. It was the eyes that were different, honey-brown, friendly, and welcoming, not defiant and determined like her sister or niece. She wore an old-fashioned apron over a practical blouse.

Catriona launched into a scolding as soon as she saw Eira. 'Where have you been, Eira? No contact for over a month. Just a weird stone creature talking with your voice,' she reprimanded.

Her eyes widened when she finally spotted Cole, then flicked back to Eira, her hand going to her throat in shock.

'Love, your ears... And who is...' her voice trailed off as she glanced between the two of them.

'What my wife is trying to ask is, who is the handsome chap next to you?' Fergus Ross stated in his thick Scottish accent, clasping his wife's hand.

Cole immediately liked Eira's uncle. He had the tanned and weather-beaten face of a sea captain, a hooked nose, and deep-set sea-blue eyes twinkling with raw humour. He was sitting on their small worn sofa in a kilt and warm jumper. A thick, unkempt beard wrapped around his strong jawline, and a mop of red hair came almost to his shoulders.

Eira plastered on a patient smile and settled her hands in her lap. 'Hi, Auntie Catriona, Uncle Fergus. This is Cole Hawkins, my boyfriend.' She spoke confidently, placing her hand on Cole's knee for emphasis.

Cole swallowed, raising a hand and waving. 'Hey,' he managed to say before Catriona launched into another speech.

'Your boyfriend? Since when? How did this happen? He obviously knows about your heritage. Does he know about your other abilities?' Catriona moved closer to the screen as if she might climb right through.

Fergus placed a hand on her knee, an apologetic expression on his face. 'Let Eira take a breath, my love,' he said placatingly.

'I know how special Eira is, and what she can do. She actually saved my life – that was how we met,' Cole supplied to Catriona's shock.

'And you're comfortable with this?'

'More than you would believe.'

Cole grasped Eira's hand and raised it to his mouth, pressing a gentle kiss there. He needed them to know how much he cared about her.

'But … his eye is black, love,' Catriona's eyes narrowed, horrified.

'I healed the virus from him, Auntie. Well, something I possess healed him. But that's a question for later.' Eira held her hand up as Catriona went to speak again. Cole noticed Fergus's eyes take in the sun mark on her wrist. 'Before you ask, I'm safe. I'm no longer at the Wallflower. I'm at the Nightingale, well not right now, but that's where we're staying. My identity has been compromised. Cole works for the police; he's a captain. He knows all about my past, my mother, and my training. I'm happy and settled with him. I love him. Yes, we're sleeping together but we're taking all the necessary precautions.'

Cole choked at that, a blush lining his cheeks.

Catriona remained quiet, lips pursed as she sat back on the sofa, Fergus giving her knee a squeeze. Apparently, they were used to Eira's defensiveness.

Cole settled in for the next round as Eira said, 'I apologise that I haven't been in touch and I won't lie, I'm involved in something dangerous, something life-changing. I've met others like me who have the same goals.'

Catriona sucked in a sharp breath, covering her mouth with her hand. Cole saw the horror in her eyes and knew she was reliving everything that had happened to her sister.

Fergus leant forward, a worried look on his face. 'We've tried to protect you from this, Eira. From going down the same path as your mother.' His tone was soft, direct.

'I know you've given up your lives for me, Brathair-mathar.' Eira held her hands to her chest. 'I've only started to appreciate the implications of that in the last few years. But you should see what I've achieved with the Nightingale and my work at the Wallflower. I've saved so many people's lives in a way I never thought I would be able to.' Eira's breath caught, and she laced her hand with Cole's. 'But I'm not a child anymore. I'm capable of making my own decisions and will live with the consequences.'

'But do you really understand them, Eira? Your mother was killed because of those choices.' Catriona's voice broke.

'I know that grief, Piuthar-màthar. It ripped me open as a child and it still does. I won't put you through that again, but this is bigger than us. And it's already underway.'

Eira's look was stern, defiant. End of conversation. Cole had been on the receiving end of that stare and knew how intense it could be. But Catriona held her own, her eyes narrowed.

'I opened my mother's safety deposit box and I need answers to some questions I have please.' Her voice was quiet but determined.

'That's good wee'un,' Fergus said, shifting closer to the camera, a hairy knee exposed from beneath his kilt.

Eira inhaled, straightening her spine. Cole traced his thumb over the back of her hand and gave her a reassuring smile. She opened her mouth and then closed it again, trying to organise her thoughts into coherent questions.

Then she held up her right forearm. 'Do either of you recognise this symbol?'

'No, love,' her aunt replied.

Cole observed how Fergus's blue eyes widened then narrowed.

'Or this?' Eira raised her Skye dagger, facing the hilt towards the camera so they could see the symbol. Both family members shook their heads. 'This blade, and another like it, were in my mother's safety deposit box. A man named Storm gave me the symbol on my arm; he seemed to know my mother. A source close to me thinks he was a welkin. Does any of that mean anything to you?'

Her aunt and uncle had both recoiled at her words. Catriona looked to her husband.

'What did he say, Eira?' Fergus asked sternly.

'Why don't you tell me, Brathair-màthar?'

Cole wasn't surprised that her sharp senses had picked up on her uncle's reaction.

Fergus sighed, bowing his head. 'We don't know much, pet. He goes by many names; Storm is only one of them. He was fundamental in your escape from London and relocation to the island. You should recognise the symbol.'

ROXAN BURLEY

Eira twisted her arm to stare at it, brows knitted together. She shook her head.

'It's carved on the entry stone to our island. It's faded now, but it's the same symbol. It protects our island from outsiders and takes the blood tax from those we allow to enter.'

Eira sucked in a ragged breath. She turned to Cole, eyes wide. 'Do you think he was the one who set this in motion? My training? Protecting me?' she asked. But before he could answer, she turned back to the camera. 'What are his other names? Have you seen or spoken to him at all?'

'We haven't seen him since the day he dropped us all at the island, love. I promise you. I'd forgotten about him until this conversation.' Catriona pursed her lips, wringing her hands in her apron. 'All he said was that he knew your mother and father very well. We were to protect you until you were ready to leave the island.' She took a quick breath, reaching for Fergus's arm. 'He was the one who gave us the key. Do you remember, Fergus?'

'I remember, love.' Fergus patted his wife's hand.

'What are his other names? Did you know he was a welkin?' Cole enquired as Eira grew still.

Fergus clicked his fingers trying to remember. 'Sun, or something related to the weather. Shine, maybe. I can't remember. I'm sorry.'

'Solar,' her aunt said quietly. 'Solar Storm, that was his full name. He looked human, but then again, they can. He looked older than his years. His eyes were filled with storm clouds. That's how I remembered his name.'

Cole nodded to Eira, wrapping his arm around her shoulder. She was pale and trembling. Catriona's description matched the man they'd met.

'Did he state his exact relationship with Rosalind?' Cole asked on Eira's behalf.

'You must remember, Captain,' Fergus said, 'that it was a traumatic and upsetting time. We had just lost Rosalind and were thrown into this new world. We had no choice but to trust strangers to protect Eira. So, no we don't know, I'm afraid. I wish we did.' His face dropped when he saw Eira's reaction.

'Believe me, Fergus, I know that feeling well. You do things in the moment that you didn't even know you were capable of,' Cole said with a sympathetic smile.

440

'I appreciate the information you have given me, Brathair-màthar. I really do,' Eira said sincerely, staring at her aunt and uncle.

Cole leant in and whispered to Eira, 'We know his name now, and you have a way to contact him.' He stroked the sun mark on her arm. 'If all else fails, I'm sure Oran will be able to track him down.'

Eira gave a shallow nod before turning back to her family. 'Are Pyke and Etta about?'

'We haven't seen them since your birthday about six months ago. Since you don't need them anymore, they aren't around as much.'

Cole did the mental maths, counting back to April to work out Eira's birthday. Spring suited her. *Date?* He tapped onto her arm in code. 'I'll make sure she comes back for her next birthday,' Cole assured Catriona.

10, Eira tapped back.

Cole committed it to memory. Eira tapped his arm twice, not code, but he understood what she wanted to know. He smirked at her as he tapped: *December 18*. Cole was rewarded with a smile which lit Eira's face. He hated his birthday and, if he had his way, it went uncelebrated. Cole had a feeling that next month would be very different.

'I finally have a photo of my father,' Eira said, turning back to her family. 'But the letter with it doesn't make sense, Piuthar-màthar.'

Catriona nodded numbly, lost for words, but understanding her niece's frustration.

Eira reached behind her neck and pulled her opal from her top. 'Did my father give this to my mother?'

Cole scratched the scar on his cheek absentmindedly. Fergus followed the direction of his hand, and Cole withdrew it, feeling self-conscious.

'Yes, we think so. She only came back once before your father disappeared. Rosalind had a giant bump and that necklace around her neck. Did you know that you came early? You were born here,' Catriona stated.

'I didn't know that,' Eira said, shaking her head. 'I always thought I was born in London, and that my father was there.'

'Sorry, love. Your mother returned after you were born. I wish she had come back when your father disappeared.'

Cole saw the hurt flicker across Eira's face. She inhaled deeply and asked, 'Do you know anything about it?'

Fergus shook his head, his wiry beard shifting.

'I'm sorry, love, but your mother was secretive about that side of her life. All you need to know is she loved your father very much,' Catriona said kindly.

Cole could tell that the conversation had only sparked more questions for Eira, instead of giving her the answers she needed.

CHAPTER 42

ORAN

Oran heard the throaty rumble of the two-wheeled vehicle that Cole called a Harley Davidson approaching. He stalked to the tunnel entrance, wings hooked around his shoulders. As soon as he exited the tunnel, he took a deep breath of fresh air. Whilst he was able to control his fear now, he still didn't enjoy being underground in the tight tunnels. The lashing rain had finally ceased, leaving a deep earthy smell in its wake.

Oran turned his head to the frail light battling through the grey clouds, his eyes closed as he basked in its warmth. He still couldn't believe that he had grown accustomed to the sun. If he had been told a year ago that he would be standing here in daylight, he would have laughed.

Cole drew the motorbike up next to him, kicking the stand, and killing the engine. Eira unwound her arms from his waist and swung effortlessly off the bike. Oran was glad to have her back. Whilst the Bloodstream still connected them, the miles between them made it feel weaker. He'd still been able to catch glimpses of her feelings though: laughter at a frozen lake, contentment surrounded by trees. But there was also fear and anxiety threaded through it all, tugging at the bond, and making Oran want to go to her.

As Eira shook her braid free from the helmet, her green eyes met his and Oran felt her anguish. Before he could say anything though, her walls came up, and she pulled her emotions from his mind.

Oran knew he would be adding to Eira's troubles soon, and the thought hurt him. He could see how overwhelmed she already was.

He turned to Cole as he approached, arm outstretched. They clasped forearms, smiling at each other.

'Go easy on her, Batman,' Cole whispered, knowing full well that Eira could hear him. 'She spoke to her family today, and we didn't really get any answers, just more questions.'

Oran nodded, releasing his arm. 'What were they like?' He knew there were more important questions to ask, but he wanted to know about her family.

Cole's eyes narrowed in confusion, but he answered with an easy grin. 'Her aunt is like a trained interrogator. She was concerned about Eira putting herself in danger. Her uncle seemed solid and humble, the kind of guy you can rely on.' Cole looped his bike helmet over his arm and added, 'Apparently, we're spending Christmas with them.'

Oran chuckled. He had come to respect Cole and he enjoyed his company. He always knew how to lighten the atmosphere, and he was fiercely loyal, something Oran appreciated. His love and devotion to Eira was clear enough.

Eira was hanging back which was unusual. Oran couldn't get a read on her mind, her block on the bond still in place. He brushed his mind against hers, registering the calming power lying dormant behind the link.

Eira retracted slightly, and Oran asked, *What's up?*

He didn't show.

Who?

Solar Storm, she replied sullenly.

Oran was at Eira's side in an instant. She didn't flinch, reading his intention before he moved. 'How can you contact him, Eira?' he snarled.

She held out her arm, and he gripped it, turning it over and pushing up her sleeve. He swore as he saw the outline of a shining sun on her skin.

'Why didn't you confide in me?' Oran couldn't hide the hurt in his voice.

'He marked me with this before we escaped through the tunnels. Then the whole Cole thing happened, and we needed to get into the Dark's compound. I just never found the time.' Eira shrugged. 'He said that if I ever needed to contact him, all I had to do was think of the sun. It's all I've thought about for the last few hours, and I've heard nothing from him,' she said, her voice breaking with a sob.

Oran hauled her into a crushing hug. He turned to Cole with a question in his eyes, but all he got was a shrug in return.

'I thought coming home might help,' Cole said. 'We've worked through some of her fears, but there are still some lingering. Oran, we need to find Storm.'

'Why didn't he answer, Oran?' Eira's voice was muffled against his armour.

Oran pulled back, bracing her slender shoulders. Her face was tight with the effort of holding back tears. 'What have I told you about bindings and oaths?'

Eira's shrug was pathetic, and the look she shot him told him that she didn't want to play guessing games.

He growled in frustration. 'An oath is made with power and emotion, whereas a binding is made using blood and pain.'

'You definitely haven't told me that,' Eira said tartly. Oran looked over his shoulder at Cole for support.

'Doc's correct, Batman, you haven't told us that,' Cole said with a smile.

Oran rolled his eyes. 'How was the mark made?'

Eira shrugged. 'It was done so quickly. It was dark, and there was an orange glow like fire.'

'That confirms who he is. His power, the fire you felt, was elemental. He can harness the sun. Did he cut you or himself?'

Eira jerked back from his grip, eyes wide with accusation. 'You know who he is?' she hissed.

Oran spread his palms, titling his head so that his braids hung over his shoulder. He took a steadying breath, knowing that he had to tread carefully or risk setting off her temper. 'Only when you said his name, Eira.' When she didn't reply, he pushed, 'You believe me, don't you?'

Eira's shoulders slumped, she bowed her head to the gravelled floor beneath her purple boots, her sun-kissed braid sliding over her shoulder.

Of course, I do, Oran, she answered in his head.

Oran let out the breath he had been holding.

'How does the way the marks are made affect the outcome of them?' Cole asked, giving Eira time. He had moved so he was now perched on the edge of his bike, his long legs outstretched, and a hand on Eira's lower back.

'When blood is used, it's like a command. That was how these were made.' Oran pointed to the corners of his eyes, now smooth without his crescent moon markings. 'Callan used his blood to make the binding so he could control the outcome. When he tried to enforce his will on me or give me a command, his blood strengthened the binding, forcing me to obey. Bindings are normally one-way, like the Bloodstream should be. Oaths are a bargain. You put your trust in the other person or people involved. They're still strong, though. They're normally used to keep a secret or make a promise, and it needs to be mutual.'

'So, a binding is like an instruction?' Eira asked. 'That seems the most likely. He didn't ask my permission or anything, so it couldn't be an oath. But it still doesn't explain why it didn't work.' Eira chewed her lip. 'Who, or what, is he, Oran?'

'He goes by many names. Solar Storm, Suncatcher, Inferno, The Golden One. He's a welkin; he used to be their king, or Wing Leader as they call them. About two decades ago, he just disappeared. The welkin cities were destroyed after he left. I've never met him, but his power with fire was legendary. As was his skill with his blades,' Oran finished, his eyes on Eira.

Eira slumped into Cole's side with a groan.

'I presume those blades are the ones that Eira now has?' Cole asked dryly.

Oran nodded in answer. 'If the stories are true, Solar was …' – Oran tightened his jaw, correcting himself – '… is one of the good ones. He was part of a small group from the high races, Callan included, who were instrumental with helping humanity in World War II. They obviously get the blame for the race's decline as well,' he finished bitterly.

Cole wrapped his arms around Eira, kissing her temple.

Oran folded his arms. 'Why do you need to see him?'

'For answers. My aunt and uncle confirmed that he was the one who arranged my escape from London, and my protection on the island. I think he even went as far as organising my training and education. He knew both my parents.' Eira rubbed her face and sighed. 'I need answers, Oran. I can't go on not knowing.'

Oran stepped forward, arm outstretched, but was interrupted by a gruff voice before he could speak.

'There were rumours that you were housing some misfits, Nightingale. But a gargoyle?'

Oran whipped around at the low whistle from the person behind him.

No, Oran, Eira said quickly into his head.

Oran remained motionless, but his body was still tense, his fangs exposed in a snarl, and his wings beating the air around him. He glared at the stout dwarf in front of him, ready to pounce if necessary.

He's an acquaintance, she reassured him.

'Franklin, meet my new guard dog,' Eira said with a chuckle.

Oran contemplated turning his rage on Eira, but the relief he felt on hearing her normal sarcastic tone nearly made his knees buckle.

Shadows peeled away from the edge of the tunnel, and two large trolls approached them. Even from a distance, the warts that covered their body were obvious, and their amber eyes glowed. The smell of damp and sewage wafted over Oran, and he had to stop himself from covering his nose in disgust. He let his guard down slightly. The trolls were expected, the dwarf wasn't.

He stared down at the little immortal, flaring his nostrils and trying to read his scent through the stench of the trolls. He was old for one so small, and he had an earthy scent tinged with iron. No trace of power. His wiry soot beard was plaited and tucked under his belt, drawing Oran's eye to the bronze hammer and clan symbol he had on it. He wore solid, black steel-toe-capped boots and a long coat. Franklin flicked a coin across his knuckles as he stepped from the tunnel entrance, his dark eyes creased with amusement.

'He's a beautiful specimen, isn't he?' Eira slid a hand down Oran's shoulder, twining her fingers around his bicep with a mischievous smile. Oran registered Cole on his other side, cap on backwards and gun loose in his hands, looking calm and relaxed.

'Presume these are the tour guides?' Cole drawled.

'Picking up cocky mortals to add to your collection as well, I see,' Franklin said, grinning at Eira.

'Would you believe that this one is the true threat?' Eira laughed.

A snarl came from the tunnel, and both trolls flinched, stumbling against the curved archway. Franklin tilted his head, eyes squinting into the gloom as a creature padded towards them.

'Actually, *that's* our guard dog,' Eira corrected, pointing at the creature advancing towards them.

You've been busy, Light Bringer, Eira said into his head.

Couldn't let the Heart Stones go to waste, he replied.

447

The skeleton dog stalked forward, its deep chest and pointed nose giving it the look of a greyhound. It had long, slender legs and eyes that glowed. Pulling back its lips, it stepped up to Franklin, growling in his face. Along its scaled back was a pair of membrane wings, tucked against its sides.

Do you have to give everything wings?

Oran snorted but didn't answer.

The creature paced in front of them, never taking its eyes off the dwarf and trolls.

'You seem well-informed, Franklin,' Eira said, feigning disinterest.

'The powers are growing again, and the big players are on the board,' he stated, flicking the coin towards them.

Oran caught the spinning disc midair. Laying it on his palm to inspect it, his breath hitched. The bronze disc was oval-shaped, small, and roughly made. He lowered his hand to show Eira, who paled as she stared at the familiar markings on it. The jagged line scoring the surface.

'Obviously, the human is already familiar with the symbol,' Franklin said, gesturing at the scar on Cole's cheek.

'What is this, dwarf?' Oran snarled.

'So, the White Daemon does speak,' Franklin said slyly. Oran stared at him, eyes narrowed, his body coiled and ready. 'Yes, I do know about the famous disappearing Keystone of the Crescent Clan whom no one can track. And now he apparently walks in the sun.'

Oran stepped closer, his fangs bared. A warm hand rested in his palm, stilling him. Eira snatched the disc and walked forward, his monstrous creature trailing close behind her.

She held the disc between her fingers, a blade in her other hand. 'You've always known too much, Franklin. Always been there when least expected, nosing around my business. I never told you my real name, but you knew it. I'm fed up with people hiding things from me,' she hissed, stalking closer.

The dwarf was slammed into the side of the tunnel and pinned to the arch by his stomach. Oran's arm was wrapped around Franklin's chubby waist. The trolls behind Oran rumbled, but a shield of moonlight appeared in front of them, blocking them from the dwarf.

'My bargain is with your Sunna, your Queen. We mean you no harm and would like to fulfil our bargain when this matter is dealt with,' Oran growled, his head tilted towards the trolls. 'Does that bargain still stand?'

Both trolls nodded their thick heads and stepped away from the shield.

'I prefer White Daemon to Batman,' Eira mused, folding her arms, and tapping her blade on her forearm.

'Much better than Blue Knight,' Cole chuckled from behind them, his gun angled downwards.

Franklin made no effort to escape Oran's grip, instead sweeping his eyes across all three of them.

'Franklin, you've always been kind to me and the Alchemists. You're respected amongst the Myths of London, but I'm frustrated at being lied to in the name of protecting me. These two,' – Eira said, indicating Oran and Cole – 'are the only ones who have given me trust and respect, and don't seek to control my actions.'

Oran smiled a toothy grin at her words, his nose just inches from the dwarf's.

'Now, my gargoyle does love slamming people into walls, but I'd rather we talked this through without any more violence. It seems you've already heard of the Keystone of the Crescent Clan, so I'm sure you know what he is capable of. I want straight answers, and you will give them to me. Now.'

Oran eased the pressure on the dwarf's stomach, and Franklin nodded. He let him slide gently to the ground, dispelling his light shield. His stone creature sat on its hindlegs, tail wagging, and tongue hanging from its mouth.

'Does it have a name?' Eira asked, stroking a hand over its slender head, giving Franklin a moment to compose himself. 'It's like stroking a bone.' The dog creature woofed once and licked Eira's hand.

Oran shook his head in disbelief; of all the topics to start with, Eira wanted to know the name of their new pet. Stalking to the far side of the tunnel, Oran leant on the curve, folding his arms and wings, impatient to get going. He knew this conversation with Franklin was important, but they needed to get to the canal.

You name it, he told her.

'Ernie,' Eira said confidently.

449

Cole snorted, a smile tugging on his lips as he stood in the centre of the tunnel, his hands behind his back, legs spread in an even stance.

Ernie yawned once and lay down, his head resting on his front paws, unbothered by his new name. Oran smiled, tutting to himself. When Cole received his gift, he hoped he wouldn't let Eira name it.

'Right, Franklin, let's get straight to the point,' Eira said, sheathing her dagger and folding her arms. 'You know who I am and were placed in my block of flats to protect me or watch me by Solar Storm. Correct?'

The dwarf's wiry black brows knitted together in confusion as he shook his shaggy head. 'No, chick. But if that welkin has flown into the picture, then the power play's begun.'

Eira tilted her head in confusion.

'You smell ancient, dwarf. Have you been around since before the war? What is your involvement in all this?' Oran enquired, an ivory hand gesturing around him. He was always suspicious when the high races were involved.

Franklin inhaled a deep breath, expanding his broad chest. He rested his hands on his belt, thumbs wedged against his coat. 'I'm a guardian of the Pure Stone, that opal which hangs around your neck.'

Eira flinched, letting her arms fall to her sides. Her hand twitched, and Oran knew she wanted to grip the necklace, but held herself back, not wanting to give anything away.

The dwarf knew too much about Eira, and Oran was worried it would put them in danger. He clenched his jaw, resigning himself. He would do whatever was necessary to protect them, even if it included eliminating the dwarf.

He risked a glance at Cole, who nodded once in his direction, his finger tapping twice at his side, signing *yes*. He understood.

'This disc, this symbol, represents the Pure Stone?' Eira asked steadily, holding up the oval coin. Franklin nodded. 'Its origin is elven, isn't it? The creation of the first three elves.'

The dwarf seemed taken back but again gave a curt nod.

'How many guardians are there? Is Solar one of them?'

'At the beginning, there were six guardians, but now only three remain. Solar is not one of them.'

'Let me guess, the other two are called Etta and Pyke?'

The stout dwarf bowed his head and slumped against the wall.
'You always were a sharp one, chick,' Franklin said wearily.

'So, my training and education were organised and overseen by guardians of the stone. What were they doing, preparing me to be its bearer?' Eira demanded, face contorted in anger. Cole had edged closer to her, already anticipating Eira's mood.

Where does Solar fit into all this? Eira asked desperately in Oran's head.

Before Oran could answer, Eira murmured, 'Was my mother a bearer?'

'What, a human?' Franklin scoffed.

'Watch your tongue, dwarf,' Cole barked, his body angled in front of Eira.

Franklin shook his head, arms raised. 'I didn't mean any offence, master human. A mortal would be unable to carry the power and the might of the stone.'

'Well, my mother did for ten years. It was gifted to her by my father,' Eira replied haughtily, stepping forward.

Franklin wrung his podgy hands in front of his ample stomach, confusion marking his broad face.

Oran stalked the width of the tunnel, his shadow casting Franklin in shade. 'Who was the bearer?' His voice was icy.

'There has only ever been one bearer of the stone. That bearer was your father, Eira. The stone was created for him and him alone. It seems his kin are able to unlock its power in the same way he could.'

CHAPTER 43

||| EIRA

'You knew my father?'

Eira noticed Franklin had used the past tense. Maybe her fears were realised, and her father was dead. Hope had evaporated like a wisp of smoke when Solar didn't appear. He had been her only link to her parents, her past. But perhaps the dwarf held the answers she so desperately needed? She nearly asked for her father's name, but she knew it would make her seem desperate, vulnerable. Eira had trusted Franklin, but he knew too much about her for comfort.

Warm arms encased her, the presence of the solid body against hers helping to ground her. Cole stroked her waist and pressed his lips close to her ear, whispering, 'It's okay, my love. Whatever happens, we'll face it together.'

The endearing term he used sent fire shooting up her spine, and her power flowed to the surface, pulling the Bloodstream wide open.

Franklin flinched back a step on seeing her eyes flare with silver tendrils. Oran's power surged, responding to hers, sparks of moonlight illuminating the tunnel. She glanced at Oran who stood with his head bent, his silver hair obscuring his eyes. His body rippled with tension.

She knew that he was feeling her pain and distress and poured her healing magic through them to calm them both down. She didn't want Franklin to know about their connection, and Oran's reaction to her emotions would be a dead giveaway.

'Like all the guardians, I've known your father since the creation of the Pure Stone,' Franklin stated.

It didn't exactly answer the question, but Eira swallowed, taking a breath before asking, 'What does the stone do?'

'It's a store for knowledge which gives the bearer the answers they seek. It holds a vast power of raw magic which, if unlocked correctly, can create a balance between what can be achieved and the impossible. It allows them to perform miracles.'

'So much for no immortal cryptic messages,' Cole chuckled, holding Eira's hand.

Does that mean anything to you? Eira asked Oran.

Oran didn't reply. Eira turned his way to find him immobile still, his fists clenched.

'What does it actually do though, Franklin?' she asked.

'You tell me, chick. You used it on that bridge.'

Eira tensed. 'I'm not sure what you mean,' she said, guarded.

She knew that Franklin had asked the triplets to record their journey from the flat to the abbey. It didn't surprise her to know that the dwarf was aware of Tower Bridge, which made her even more suspicious of him. But the need to gain information on her father replaced her apprehension.

'From the footage I've seen, a light surged out of you, knocking over cars and agents of the Dark. You disappeared with the White Daemon here, and then those that were infected with the virus rose, healed but confused.'

'What happened after?' Cole asked, eyeing the dwarf.

'The Dark swept back in and reclaimed them.'

Cole cursed, closing his eyes. 'Such a waste. We should have extracted them all,' he muttered in an undertone.

Eira squeezed his hand, trying to ease his guilt, even though her eyes never left Franklin. 'We didn't have the capacity. More than one of us had been hit, and we needed to get out. So, don't ever carry that guilt, Hawk,' she whispered. 'You're the one who said that we can't worry about the what ifs.'

'I know, Doc,' he replied, angling his head to kiss her cheek.

'The stone traces power,' Oran said, his voice hollow. 'It basically assumes the power of the wearer and mimics it, retaining the knowledge it learns from them and using it to give the bearer what they need.'

Eira and Cole turned to Oran, eyebrows raised. Of course, their gargoyle had solved Franklin's cryptic answer.

The stone is so attuned to your power. It stirred when you needed it the most. You needed to know how to cure the virus, and the stone provided the answer, he told her, deflated.

Then the bond was severed. Oran lifted his head. His mouth was set in a thin line, jaw tight, his swirling white eyes distant. He raised a shaking hand to his pointed ear, tracing it once. Eira jerked towards him, catching a glimpse of his distress before he blocked the bond.

'I need to fly for a moment, catch Lunar as she rises,' he spoke above their heads to the tunnel wall. 'I'll return in fifteen minutes, I promise,' he said, glancing at Eira briefly before turning away.

Eira nodded, knowing he needed some time away, but not understanding why.

As he stepped to the entrance of the tunnel, he turned and glared at Franklin. 'If you dare hurt either of them, I will make sure that the dog takes your head.'

Ernie instantly sat up, snarling at the dwarf. Oran vanished, launching himself into the air with one stroke of his powerful wings.

'You have leashed a mighty fine warrior there, chick. What does his clan chief have to say about it?' Franklin wondered.

'That is none of your business, Master Dwarf,' Eira snapped, letting her irritation show in her voice.

Oran's words settled in her mind. Could her magic really have activated the opal? Had it been learning from her all these years? This thought unnerved her the most, and she nearly reached for the necklace to throw it at Franklin's feet. He could have it back. But she knew Oran spoke the truth. Her power combined with the opal could heal the virus. It had given her the solution when she had needed it the most.

'What happened to the true bearer? Where is he?' Cole asked. Eira knew on her behalf. It didn't go unnoticed that Cole avoided using the word "father". There was still a chance that Franklin was lying.

She felt the warm pressure of Cole's hand on her lower back. He had repositioned himself, so they stood shoulder to shoulder, a united front.

'History is repeating itself with you. Your father fell in love with a mortal,' Franklin said sadly, his gaze piercing.

'My mother,' Eira breathed, a hand going to her mouth.

'He was one of the first elves, wasn't he? One of the most powerful to walk the Earth?' Cole enquired, level-headed.

Ernie sat on his hind legs, his bony body pressed against her knee, head tilted as he gazed up at her. Eira knew that Oran was listening to everything through his ears.

'He was one of the three, along with his brother and sister. The symbol is always shown with the central, vertical line slightly higher, representing his power,' Franklin recited, tugging on his plaited beard.

If her father was that powerful, it made sense that Eira's magic was as strong as it was.

'What is his power?' Cole asked.

'Mind. He could look inside people's heads, control entire villages using illusions or suggestions. The Pure Stone was made for him to store that knowledge, use it to harness the power to make decisions.' Franklin tutted. 'It sounds bad, but your father was one of the most selfless individuals I've ever met. He never once used his power for ill-gain or control, even though he was capable of it.'

Eira tensed. Her mind powers had amplified since her bond with Oran, but maybe they had always been that powerful and she simply didn't know how to access it. Eira shuddered at the thought of being able to control people's minds. It must have taken an incredible amount of self-control for her father to have not used it for his own gain. If Franklin was telling the truth.

'You keep using past tense, Franklin. Is he dead?' Eira asked.

'I don't know,' he said, puffing out his cheeks. 'It all changed after the war. Your father and most of the other high-race leaders were the reason the Myths got involved with the human war, and it led to our exposure. Your father, and his brother and sister, disappeared at the end of the war, just like that.' Franklin clicked his fingers. 'The brothers resurfaced, but their sister never did. They were broken in their own way. Divided in opinion about how to deal with humans once they knew of our existence. The races fractured, each looking after their own. After the war, I remained at your father's side, but then one day he never returned. That was about sixty years ago.'

Franklin sighed, placing a heavy hand on his hammer, pacing back and forth.

'I searched for him for three decades, through every magical kingdom I could find. Your father could easily hide using his mind powers, manipulating people's minds to make them forget him. Just over twenty years ago, I registered the magical signature of the stone. The bearer can mask the stone's magic so that it can't be tracked, but it had flared in the centre of London. Your father wanted to be found.' Franklin licked his lips.

Eira opened her mouth to speak, but Franklin continued before she could say anything.

'I found him with a family. He had a wife and a toddler – you. For the first time in his life, he was happy. In love...' Franklin sighed.

Eira caught her breath. That part of her childhood had at least been true. The photograph of them in Hyde Park came to mind.

'But the threat of the Dark was rising, and it wasn't safe for you to remain in London. We planned to get you all to safety, but then he disappeared again. Just vanished. To this day, Eira, I swear on that stone you have around your neck that I don't know where he went or who took him. I don't believe for one second that he would have left you or your mother. The Pure Stone's trace disappeared as well. I presumed that he had it on him. But you said your mother had it?'

Eira nodded numbly, trying to take in everything she was being told. Her mother's letter was starting to make sense now, so she knew Franklin's account was true. Her mother spoke of her father's disappearance and fleeing London when Eira was two years old. One sentence sprang to mind: *Your father gave me his heart and soul, his care. But forces were at work to separate us. Our love was forbidden.*

Cole leant his head against hers, his arm now around her waist. She was trembling, unable to accept the answers she had so desperately wanted.

'Eira, your mother was a powerhouse.' Franklin whistled. 'When your father disappeared, instead of breaking down, she immediately went on the defensive.'

Cole chuffed, 'I know that feeling well.'

Eira smiled at him.

'Instead of chasing a vanishing ghost again, I decided to remain with your mother as she was refusing to move. She always believed your father would return. I created my own life here, working undercover with the Myths and your mother. Her campaign grew until she became a threat.' Stepping forward, he grasped Eira's hand in his weathered calloused ones, looking up at her, his eyes sparkling with tears. 'I'd been called away when it happened, chick. I promise you, if I'd been in London, you would have seen me first. I would have protected you,' he said, his voice choked with emotions.

Eira searched the clouded memories of her childhood in London. Did she know Franklin's voice, his face? It sounded like he had been a fixture in her early years. She shook her head; trauma had stolen those memories from her.

Eira felt her own tears responding to the ones cascading down Franklin's cheeks and glistening in his shaggy beard. Eira bent and hugged the dwarf as he shuddered at the painful memories. Cole ran a soothing hand along her exposed neck.

Ernie whimpered at her side.

Franklin drew back, using his wrinkled hands to wipe his tears. 'But it was too late, wasn't it? I was taken before you could get to me. I think Solar Storm had a part to play in that. I'm not sure how he fits in with the story. Have you ever met him?' Eira asked gently, a hand on the dwarf's shoulder.

'I never met him whilst I was in London. I definitely would've recognised him.' Franklin pulled a handkerchief from his pocket and loudly blew his large nose. 'At one point during the war negotiations with the humans, he was your father's closest ally.'

Eira turned to Cole. He shrugged, a sympathetic smile on his face. 'At least we know more than we did,' he said sadly.

'So,' Eira said to the dwarf, 'I presume that Pyke and Etta were able to track me down somehow and were looking after me? Franklin, you need to know that I was with family, and I was well cared for,' she reassured him.

The dwarf took a shuddering breath and shrugged. 'I'm not sure why Pyke and Etta came after you. We parted ways after your father vanished a second time. They might have been drawn to your necklace, or Solar might have had something to do with it. I never knew that you knew them.' The candour in Franklin's voice was enough for Eira. 'I remained in London despite your mother's death and your abduction, just in case you turned up.'

Eira nodded her understanding.

'I also had a life. A very secretive one, but I was doing something good. Then two years ago, I felt it again — the tug from the Pure Stone. I followed it, and there you were, lost in the tunnels. You were so much like your parents that it took my breath away.'

'So, it wasn't coincidence that you found me that day?'

'Sure wasn't, chick.'

'Why didn't you say something? I've known you for years now.'

'How could I? You would have thought I was crazy. You had to find your own way, discover it for yourself. Anyway, you were so fresh and full of life. I knew you had come to find answers, but you weren't ready for them until you'd experienced some of the struggles of mortality. But I never expected you to bomb the glass tower,' he said with a laugh.

Eira rose, dusting the dirt from her knees. She felt lighter; she finally knew as much about her father's disappearance as she could right now. What Franklin said had confirmed what was written in her mother's letter: her father loved her, and he wouldn't have left if he'd had a choice. But it still didn't answer the nagging question of where he was now.

'I've finally started to experience life, Franklin.' Eira laced her fingers with Cole's as she spoke. 'I know what needs to be done, and I will see it through.'

'I understand, and that's why I'm here.' He knelt, head tilted towards her, sincerity on his ancient face. Three fingers raised, he pressed them against his chest. 'As a guardian of the Pure Stone, I offer you my protection and guidance. I offer you my hammer.' He held his weapon towards her. 'As the new bearer of the Pure Stone, I am yours to command.'

Eira, stunned, looked to Cole, who shrugged, teasing, 'You're the immortal. This is more your wheelhouse than mine.'

She cleared her throat, stalling.

The scent of sea salt filled her nose, and she felt a pressure on her shoulders, a kiss to the crown of her head. Oran didn't announce his presence. He was allowing her to deal with this one herself, but he was there.

Eira sighed. 'Thank you, Franklin. I appreciate the struggles you've been through in your long years. I don't need more protectors, but I do need Myths on our side. The local Myths trust you. Will you help me with their recruitment?'

Franklin rose, bronze hammer in hand. He twisted it, inserting it back into his thick belt. 'I'll see what I can do, Eira. For you. For the future.'

⋈ COLE

Cole found himself walking next to Franklin, slowing his gait to match the dwarf's. The tunnel trolls lumbered ahead in the gloom, wheeling his motorbike between them, much to his apprehension. It had taken much reassurance from Eira to allow them to even touch it, but he trusted her.

Franklin had fallen into leisurely conversation with Cole after the initial tense standoff. He spoke openly about his involvement with the Myth network, smuggling goods in and out of the city, regaling Cole with tales of slip-ups and close calls.

A globule of light floated above their heads, casting them in a silvery hue, their shadows elongated and curving around the roughly hewn tunnel. Despite their smell, Cole was glad to have the trolls guiding them; alone, he would have quickly been lost in the labyrinthine tunnels.

Cole glanced over his shoulder at Eira, Ernie at her side. Her face was tight with concentration, but she looked lighter, less troubled since the conversation with Franklin.

The light was the only indication that Oran was with them. Cole guessed that he was probably speaking to Eira through the bond, giving her an update on what had happened since they'd been gone. He sighed, wishing he was able to join in their telepathic conversations.

Turning back to the dwarf, Cole asked, 'How old are you?'

The dwarf rumbled with amusement. 'Older than your underwear, sonny.'

Cole laughed. 'Come on, you must be thousands of years old. I thought the lifespan of a dwarf was close to that of a human?'

'That's true, but I linked my life to the stone. While the stone exists, so will I. I can be wounded or killed like any other, but I heal faster and can withstand more,' he said with a wink.

'How are you linked? Is it an oath or a binding?' Cole asked, remembering Oran's lesson on such things.

'Sounds like you've got experience in such matters, boy,' Franklin said, raising a bristly eyebrow.

Cole slid up the sleeve of his top, exposing his forearm. 'Experienced in receiving them and making them.'

Franklin chuckled. Without breaking stride, he too slid an arm from his bronze, buckled jacket and rolled up his shirtsleeve. His shoulder held a raised mark of three vertical lines.

'Oath and binding combined. Painful but effective. There's no breaking this one, only my death will release me.'

'Well, I can raise you two to your one,' Cole said, amused.

'Not that one,' Franklin indicated the mark under his black eye.

Cole found his eyes flickering back to Eira. He knew that she and Oran would be listening to the conversation. His eyes held Eira's as he answered, 'No, that one was a mistake. A life-altering mistake which just happened to save my life.'

'I see,' Franklin stated, following Cole's gaze. 'It was made by the stone though, so it may still hold some power.'

Cole stored that information away, his eyes returning once more to Eira, whose eyes flickered to where Oran was camouflaged. 'Why did you choose to serve the stone?' he asked.

Franklin was quiet for a moment as they continued along the tunnel. The sound of running water filled his ears, and he hoped they were nearing the canal.

'It was a decision I didn't hesitate in making. At the time, my choices were limited, and it was a good offer. I've become accustomed to it after all these years. Though it's hard to live so long and watch everyone you care about wither away and die in front of you.'

Cole didn't need to turn around to know that Eira's eyes were on him. They hadn't discussed that part of their relationship yet, not wanting to taint their time together with talk of death and loneliness.

'That didn't exactly answer the question, Master Dwarf,' Cole joked as he eyed Franklin from the side. Franklin tutted, eyes sparkling. The tunnel's gradient slowly increased, and light spilled from ahead. A rush of air nearly blew Cole's cap from his head. He cursed, slapping his hand on top of it to keep it in place. Ernie cantered by, nearly taking Franklin out.

'Let me guess, that was the White Daemon? Does he need to be invisible right now?' Franklin huffed, looking disgruntled. The two trolls grumbled their own annoyance.

A warm hand laced into his as Eira placed a kiss on Cole's scar.

'He has his reasons, Franklin. It's a skill I wish I had,' Eira replied, easily joining the conversation.

Cole wondered if it was something she would be able to master over time, as she and Oran learned more of the Bloodstream.

'How are you so at ease with these creatures, mortal?' Franklin asked, confused.

'We've had our arguments about that,' Eira reflected, squeezing Cole's hand.

Cole wasn't going to forget that argument or where it had led anytime soon. 'I've been told I'm special.' He grinned, shoving Eira lightly with his shoulder.

The trolls disappeared over a rise, the chopper with them. Cole instinctively pulled Eira along as his beloved bike vanished from view. She obeyed, following with a giggle, leaving Franklin to bring up the rear.

The tunnel ended abruptly, and they stepped outside, back in London. Cole wasn't sure exactly where in London they were, but he could see that they were under a large bridge, three huge barges moored and bobbing on the black water.

Oran stood at the jetty, his pale back to the tunnel's exit, his wings snapped in tight to his muscled body. He bent down to three hooded figures in robes. Ernie flapped his bony form and sat on the cabin of one of the rusty barges.

Eira gasped, rushing to the three small figures. They had kept this part a surprise for her.

Cole exited the tunnel, grabbing his bike from the trolls and wheeling it far enough away from them that he didn't have to worry about them accidentally crushing it.

Breathing a sigh of relief, he approached Eira as she spluttered, 'I thought we'd missed you!' She grabbed all three of them and drew them into a tight hug, Isaac, hooded, squashed in the centre. 'We've scouted out where you're going to stay, and I think you'll like it,' Eira signed. 'It even has windows.'

Darwin grinned, flashing his yellow teeth, ears wagging with his eager nod.

'I know we are asking a lot of you, to move and everything,' Eira signed, her hands pausing for a second as she thought of what she wanted to say.

Cole placed a hand on her shoulder, knowing that she needed a bit of help. 'But we owe you our lives and are indebted to you all. Without your skillset, we wouldn't be able to accomplish what

461

we have planned,' he finished for her. She smiled gratefully at him and signed what he had said.

Eira squeezed his hand quickly before signing to the gnomes again. Whatever she said, it had them hugging her again. Isambard stepped away and pulled a fabric bag out of his pack, presenting it to Eira.

Eira's hand shook as she took it, the contents clinking together. Opening the pull-string, she reached inside and pulled out a bracelet like the one Cole wore.

'You made these already?' she said in astonishment.

The triplets nodded enthusiastically.

'Clever boys,' Eira said, a wide grin on her face. She turned to Oran and held one out. 'Here, put this on, and don't go taking it off again.' She threw a bracelet at Oran who caught the glittering bangle, securing it around his wrist with an eyeroll.

She pulled another from the bag and strode to Franklin, tying it around his wrist. 'You'd better have one too, Franklin.' She also pulled out the bronze disc from earlier and handed it back to him. He accepted it gratefully, tucking it carefully into his pocket.

'What is this?' he asked, studying the bracelet. His mouth popped open in shock when he saw the engraving on it. 'Have you been able to do what I think you've been able to do?' Franklin was in awe.

Eira stepped forward and smiled. 'It just needs to be charged.'

Cole watched as she wrapped her hand around the bracelet on his wrist and her palm glowed. She poured her power into it until it was warm and thrumming with magic.

Franklin's face sagged, wonder in his eyes.

'This is for you, Franklin, as a thank you for everything you did or tried to do for me.'

He nodded his thanks, unable to speak.

Eira walked back to Oran and the triplets. She placed her hand over Oran's wrist, hand glowing. Cole watched as Oran bared his teeth in surprise and took a sharp intake of breath. He tried retracting his hand, but Eira held firm. Cole tentatively stepped forward to find three Nightingales in flight raised on his opaque flesh.

'That's too much, Eira. You give too much,' Oran said, his voice husky and raw, his face twisted with emotion.

Cole, a hand on her back, whispered in Eira's ear, 'Did you just create an oath with the White Daemon?'

From the corner of his eye, he saw Oran herding the Alchemists along the jetty to their designated barges, but he didn't take his attention from Eira. Ernie watched from the cabin, glowing eyes tracking Oran's path.

Eira's lips twisted into a playful grin as she eyed him. 'Are you jealous, Hawk? I can mark you someplace special if you like.' Her blonde eyebrows lifted as her hands moved towards his crotch.

Cole jerked, heat spreading from his neck to his face. He nuzzled her neck with a small moan. 'I'll hold you to that promise later, but you already have my heart so it would be for decoration only.' Eira sniggered as she stroked his neck. 'Seriously though, what did you do? When did you learn to do that?'

'I promised my protection to him, Nelka, and the baby,' she said in an undertone. 'I don't know how I did it. It kind of just happened. I've seen and experienced enough of these oaths now that I took a risk and winged it.'

'Well, that was a very personal gift, Eira. You already protect each other without fear, so to extend it to his family is something special, and something I'm sure he appreciates, even if he isn't good at expressing it.'

Eira nodded, watching the last preparations for the triplets' departure. Oran flew back to the jetty, arms full of last-minute supplies.

Franklin stepped from the walkway, hauling his small frame up onto the last barge where Ernie still sat, tail wagging. 'I'll see the triplets safe out of London; I know these waters better than most,' he called from the stern. 'When I return, we'll discuss the recruitment of the Myths.'

'Are you sure, Franklin?' Eira stepped closer to the edge of the jetty. 'It might be dangerous travelling at night. You have the Incognitos and a water escort, but there might be heat drones…'

'Even more reason for it to be me then, chick.' Franklin winked, ending the conversation.

'Water escort?' Cole asked, joining Eira and waving to the dwarf.

'Have I never mentioned the Mosasaurus that lives in the Thames? She saved my life when I went to rescue that damn tablet of yours,' Eira mused, staring out at the water. 'There she is now,' she added, pointing into the depths.

Cole followed her gaze and jolted in fright. A huge scaled body breached the surface of the water, its mouth filled with razor-sharp teeth. The creature stared at Eira and blinked its intelligent eyes, acknowledging her. Then, with one powerful sweep of its tail, it turned and followed the boats, dropping beneath the water's surface until only a blue fin was visible.

Cole gulped. 'How exactly did she help you?'

'I rode on her back to safety.' Eira shrugged as if riding an extinct reptile was an everyday occurrence.

'You do amaze me, Doc,' Cole muttered, interlacing their hands, twisting them so he could kiss their joined fingers.

Eira's eyes sparkled in the dim light. Cole sighed, glad to see her happy, even if it was only for a short while.

'When you're ready, Light Bringer,' Eira called, lifting her free hand to the curved brick ceiling.

Oran nodded, gracefully spreading his wings, and launching himself into the narrow space above the lead barge. Hovering for a split second, his great membrane wings clapped together, then he propelled himself forward, flying high above the barges. He sent his moonlight shooting towards each vessel, activating their Incognitos and hiding them from view.

Grumbling, the trolls grabbed the chopper off the wall and turned back towards the tunnel, ready to leave.

Eira looked out over the water as Oran landed next to them. 'What about our new pet?' she asked him.

Oran chuckled. 'Don't worry, we'll get him back when he's finished serving the triplets. I have another surprise at home which I'm sure the captain will not want you naming.'

Cole quirked a smile at that, intrigued.

Eira unthreaded her hand from Cole and, throwing one arm over his shoulders, she wound the other around Oran's waist, sandwiching herself between the two of them.

'Homeward bound then, boys. I'm looking forward to the heated fire, Madam Scudamore's cooking, and that very narrow bed,' she mused. Cole threw his head back on a laugh, earning a chuckle from the other two.

CHAPTER 44

ORAN

Oran leant against the wooden divider between the kitchen and living room, hoping his weight wouldn't cause it to fall.

They had woken up as Lunar rose, illuminating the chilled sky. It had been easy to slip back into their familiar routine of waking during nocturnal hours whilst Cole and Eira had been away.

Oran glanced down at his soulmate, his arm slung along her back, drawing half-moons on the skin of her indigo wings which she had locked under her collarbone. Nelka nursed a hot chocolate balanced on top of her exposed bump, watching the others. Cole's hot chocolates were delicious, and he'd missed them while he'd been away. They would probably have to take a crate home for Nelka, who'd developed a taste for it.

Nelka's restlessness was due to her confinement in the gatehouse. She was craving the feel of the wind in her wings, the sight of the blanket of stars surrounding Lunar. He knew because he felt it too. But they were set to leave by the end of the week, so it wouldn't be long before they were able to experience it again.

He was excited to show Eira his home but nervous about seeing Callan and accepting his place as clan chief.

Hearing Cole's hiss, Oran lifted his head to hear Eira snap, 'You let me slice your arm open several times in front of your best friends without flinching, but a needle you baulk at!'

'You were dulling my senses then! This is different.'

He looked over and saw Eira leaning against the kitchen worktop, a needle in hand, Cole's worn, leather jacket over a baggy top. Her hair was scrunched up in a tight ponytail, her curls rippling down her back like honey-coloured silk.

A challenge sparked in her eyes as she mused, 'You face down an enemy hover copter to protect us, but you won't let me stick a needle in you. I can make you sleep and then do it,' she said, raising a glowing hand threateningly. Oran had noticed she had stopped glamouring her power around them, showing how comfortable she was now.

Cole pulled back, staring at her accusingly.

'Come on, Captain, we've all had a turn. You're the last,' Elowen teased from the other side of the kitchen table.

Cole turned to Oran, hoping for his support. But Oran only shrugged and said, 'You're on your own with this one. I've already given my blood for her experiments.'

Cole sat up straighter on his chair, rolling his sleeve up higher. Eira slid the needle into his skin, pulling back the plunger and drawing his blood.

'That wasn't bad at all,' he exclaimed. Then comprehension filled his face. 'You're reducing my pain, aren't you?'

Eira chuckled, amused. Removing the needle, she touched his arm, and the wound healed itself. Sauntering past him, she cooed, 'Who's my brave boy?' Cole slapped her ass in return.

Oran chuckled. Eira seemed more herself after the emotional revelations from Franklin. He had listened to the dwarf's account via his latest creation that Eira had named Ernie. The distance between them allowed him to get a handle on his own emotions without hers clouding them.

He looked down at the metal on his wrist, with the three nightingales below it. Three lives for her to protect, a promise that she wouldn't leave them. She had promised too much.

Nelka said something in Gork that Oran didn't register, but he turned and crouched next to her anyway, stroking a hand over her swollen tummy.

'Sorry, Starlight, my head was in Lunar,' Oran replied in Gork. Nelka tutted and shoved his shoulder, but Oran didn't move.

'Is it safe for us to give a sample of our blood to Eira for her experiments?' Nelka gestured to Eira, who was putting Cole's sample into one of her machines.

'Yes, it is, Echo,' Eira replied in perfect Gork, without looking up from her work. 'I'm good with languages,' she added with a smile at the confused looks on their faces.

'Since when?' Oran asked in Gork, shaking his head in disbelief.

'Since our bond has gotten stronger.' Eira shrugged, studying the equipment.

Oran understood magnified stuff. Cole narrowed his eyes, head moving between them.

'I have a natural talent for languages. I'm fluent in most human languages, ancient Elven, Scottish Gaelic, sign language, and now Gork, it seems. I had a very isolated childhood.'

You do amaze me, Oran said in her head.

Hawk said something similar, she replied, her amusement clear.

Eira turned away from her microscope, and Cole caught her eye, lifting his eyebrows in question.

'It appears our doctor can speak our language, so all my flirting conversations with my Starlight will have to be done behind closed doors,' Nelka chimed in English, her dark eyes narrowed.

Cole sucked in a surprised breath, opening his mouth to ask a question when Oran supplied in Gork, 'But our doctor still has access to my head in those moments.'

Nelka's melodious laugh filled the room, and at Eira's blush, Oran's rumbled through too.

'I don't even want to know, do I?' Elowen asked, rolling her eyes.

'You know I would never do that,' Eira exclaimed, ignoring the humans for a second.

'I know, Eira.' Oran chuckled, glancing down at Nelka, who rolled her eyes, huffing. 'I know you wouldn't dare.'

Eira still looked put out but returned to her work.

A noise caught Oran's attention, and he turned, ducking with a snarl as a huge stone bird soared over his head, skimming his scalp with its claws.

'Can't let the immortals have all the fun, can I?' Cole grinned. A stone bird perched on his shoulder, feathers clanking as it rustled its wings, clicking its beak and staring at Oran.

The stone hawk had been Oran's gift to Cole, a way to offer him some protection if he wasn't there.

Oran straightened and grumbled, 'Well played, Captain.'

Cole sniggered, stroking the hawk he had named Hawkeye under its beak. Apparently, it was named after a superhero from one of his comics, but Oran still wasn't sure what those were. The stone hawk was programmed to protect Cole and follow some simple commands, via taps against Cole's hawk marking. He couldn't speak to them the way Oran could, or give a direct command, but it was close enough.

Static broke through the companionable silence. Elowen picked up her walkie-talkie, pressed the button and said, 'Elowen here, over.'

'Urgent medical assistance required, over,' came the reply.

Elowen rose and went into the living room, holding the walkie-talkie to her ear.

Eira followed her friend with her eyes, head angled to listen. Oran stepped to the screen to observe. Elowen paced in front of the fire, replying in short phases over the static on the other side. She ended the conversation and sighed.

'I'm needed at Macclesfield Bridge,' Elowen said, pulling on her shoes.

'Do you need me to go instead?' Eira asked, walking towards her.

'Hell no. You're a wanted criminal. It sounds like it's only a foot infestation which should be easy enough to sort.'

'Macclesfield Bridge, isn't that where the nightclub is?' Cole asked, still sitting at the table.

'Yes, it is,' Eira said over her shoulder.

'Elowen's depriving you of a night out then, Doc,' Cole sniggered.

Eira rolled her eyes to her friend, before suggesting, 'Why don't you take the van? It's not far, and the new heat camouflage has been tried and tested against the thermal drones. I don't like the thought of you being out at night. Take a couple of trolls with you too.'

Elowen contemplated her friend's advice before nodding her agreement. She gave Eira a quick hug before adding, 'Remember, we need to discuss my plans for the virus protection rollout when I get back to the Nightingale. I've been in touch with Moyra, and she's on board with the rollout at the Wallflower.' Elowen stepped back, her eyes intense. 'You need to tell her the truth, Eira.'

'I know and I will,' Eira said, giving Elowen's shoulder a squeeze.

'Take Hawkeye as well,' Cole piped up from the back.

Oran cursed, bending again as the hawk flew over his head and alighted on Elowen's elbow. He growled at Cole's gleeful smile.

'Be safe,' Eira said, giving Elowen's shoulder one last squeeze before she disappeared through the hidden door, Hawkeye perched on her arm.

Oran stalked back and sat next to Nelka, dropping a kiss onto the top of her head.

Silence filled the space for the next few moments whilst Eira worked, and Cole observed. Oran, content to be by Nelka's side, watched and waited as well. He wasn't sure what they were waiting for, but he could tell that Eira was close to whatever discovery she needed.

After a few minutes, Eira gasped, grabbing Cole's arm, and gripping it tightly. He looked up from the comic in his lap, brow furrowed.

Oran stood and moved to Eira's side. Her face was clouded with uncertainty, but she laid out several slides, stained with liquid, onto the table.

Cole leant forward on his stool, elbows on his knees, eyes trained on Eira. Nelka approached as well, taking a seat at the other side of the table.

'What I'm trying to experiment with is how the virus infects different blood types so that an antidote can be produced,' Eira said, staring down at the slides on the table. 'If it was for just one group then it would be easier, but with all the different types it's almost impossible.' She paced back and forth before Cole grabbed her hand and ran a soothing thumb over her knuckles. 'Let's start with the basics. These slides hold samples of different blood, and the microscope magnifies the samples so I can see them clearly.'

Oran nodded, starting to understand the technology.

'Oran, can you find the ones which have any traces of power in this first set?' Eira asked, indicating the first row of nine slides.

Oran moved closer to the table and leant forward, focusing on the slides that Eira had pointed out. He held out a hand and ran it over the samples, his moonlight glowing slightly in his palm. Using a long, pale finger, he pointed out the five which held traces of magic.

Eira nodded. She brought the five Oran had identified to the front of the table, moving the other four away. She touched the first of the slides Oran had rejected; all were coated with a red liquid. 'These are human blood,' she said, pointing to the first three. 'Elowen, Tagger, Flint.' Tapping the last one, she said, 'This is dwarf blood from Franklin.'

'How the hell did you sneak that one in, Doc?' Cole asked, impressed.

'I already had it from when I used to make him growth potions,' Eira answered, turning to look at him. 'I thought there was no harm in recycling.'

Cole snorted.

'The five that Oran pointed out get more interesting.' She looked at them, indicating the first in the row, a sample of black blood. 'This is gargoyle blood, Nelka's to be exact. The next one is gnomish blood from one of the triplets.' Then she picked up a black sample and held it out to Oran. 'This is hybrid blood. Have you ever seen your blood up close, Oran?'

Oran shook his head, dread creeping into his gut. Eira slid the sample into the microscope and gestured him forward.

Come on, it's nothing to be frightened of, she said telepathically.

Oran swallowed and approached the scope, bending and pressing his eye to the eyepiece. He staggered back with a sharp intake of breath.

'I can imagine it is even clearer with your acute vision,' Eira whispered from his side. 'What can you see?'

Oran licked his lips and approached again. 'I see black and silver metallic circles. They appear to be moving. It's fascinating,' he said, his voice awed.

'Those are your blood cells. The black is your gargoyle heritage, and the silver ones are your elven. Look, I'll show you mine.'

Eira slid the sample out and pushed another one under the scope. 'What do you see now?'

'Red and silver metallic circles, but there's a pulse of blue. Human and elven?' Oran looked at her in wonder.

'Until I met you, I wasn't certain what the silver in my blood was. I'd only guessed that it was the part of me which was elven.' Eira shrugged, leaning against the bench. She pulled another from the table and slid it into the microscope. 'Tell me what you see on this one,' she whispered.

Oran cocked a white eyebrow, wondering what had made her look so afraid. Obliging, he looked through the eyepiece again. 'I see mostly red, and silver. A blue hue again.' Oran inhaled sharply and looked up at Eira. 'And black,' Oran whispered.

'That's my blood now. After the bridge incident. I don't know what it means though,' she said, her eyes wide and pleading.

Oran grasped her hand.

It must be the Bloodstream, he said soothingly.

But why is it that I've taken on your blood, but you haven't taken on mine? And I don't know what the blue hue is, either.

Eira bit her bottom lip, and Oran saw the panic on her face.

'I don't know, Eira, but we'll figure it out, I promise,' Oran said aloud, squeezing her hand.

Cole had risen, looking concerned. He pushed past Oran and glanced down the scope. Pulling back in shock he said, 'That's why the bleeding from your nose was black?'

Eira nodded. Oran stepped back further, allowing Cole to enfold Eira in his arms. He stroked a hand down her back. Nelka caught Oran's eye, looking concerned herself.

'I'll tell you later, Starlight.'

Cole placed his forehead against Eira's, a hand to her cheek. 'We have this, don't we, Doc?'

'Yes,' Eira breathed, closing her eyes.

'How about the fifth sample?' Nelka asked, filling the silence. She flicked it across the table with a sharp, blue nail.

Oran retrieved it, holding it between his finger and thumb. The blood within was red. That only left…

'Me?' Cole breathed, his head still against Eira's. 'My turn for a shock, hey?'

Eira traced her fingertip across Cole's scar. 'You have magic in your blood. Oran only confirmed what the science told me.'

'But that can't be right? I don't have any superpowers,' Cole exclaimed, his own eyes closing.

'Cole,' Oran said, 'mortals can carry power, if you remember our conversation from a few weeks ago. They might not be able to access it like we can, but it's still there. When we first met, I thought I sensed power in you, but I put it down to the virus still inside you.'

'It would explain why he's so comfortable around us,' Nelka supplied.

'Okay, Light Bringer. How about now, what do you detect?' Cole said sharply, moving in front of Oran.

Oran backed up slightly.

'Cole, the science proves it, and your blood might hold the key. Look.' Eira grasped his arm and steered him towards the table. 'These samples are the ones which have been infected with a live strain of the virus.' Eira indicated the top five which were totally black. 'Three human blood samples were immediately consumed by the virus. It's not surprising really as it was created to attack human genes. It took a little longer for the dwarf sample, but it still succumbed eventually. The gnomish sample resisted a bit longer with the magic in their veins. But this is where it becomes interesting,' she said, picking up the next two samples, which were totally black as well.

'These are Oran's and Nelka's. It's hard to tell as their blood is already dark. Nelka did you want to look?' Eira glanced at Nelka.

Nelka nodded, rising, and walking to the table. Cole reached out a hand to her. If it had been any other male, Oran would have protested, but Cole had his complete trust. As Cole allowed him to show affection toward Eira, Oran gave Cole the courtesy to do the same to his mate. He looked on as his soulmate rested a hand in Cole's, and he gently guided her around the table, a supportive hand on her back.

Eira inserted the slide and gestured for Nelka to look. She raised on her tiptoes, twisting her body to keep her bump out of the way.

'That is beyond weird,' she stated to Oran.

Eira inserted the other slide and Nelka bent to view it. 'What Echo is seeing is how magic fights off the virus. Neither of your blood samples have surrendered to its effects yet. But we know that it can affect gargoyles. I've seen it spread quickly in Oran the more times he was hit. We just don't know whether it would take full control in the end. Hawk, if you could do the honours on the next one?'

Cole pushed off the table and approached the scope.

'What do you see, Hawk?' Eira whispered, a hand to his back.

'The same colours as before in your blood, but they're mixed with the virus. There's something shimmering that seems to be fighting it off,' Cole said, stepping back. He took his cap from his head, running his fingers through his black hair with a sigh before fitting it back on and waiting for the next slide.

Eira inserted it. Cole slowly angled his face to the eyepiece and went still, barely breathing. Eira leant her head on his shoulder and whispered, 'When I first sent my power into you to heal you, it detected a shimmering substance fighting the virus around your wound. At the time, I didn't know what it was. That shimmering substance is what you can see under the microscope. It's your power defending your body,' Eira said tenderly, kissing his temple. 'Whatever power I have in my blood, you share it too, Hawk.'

Cole blinked, withdrawing from the scope. Oran was lost for words. It now made sense why they were so well paired.

Power calls to power, he mused in Eira's mind.

She flicked her head up in confusion.

'Never mind, Doctor,' Oran smiled.

'That's why the gas didn't work on me,' Cole said, a hand raised to his chest. 'I wasn't immediately infected like the others. It took the actual virus piercing my body for it to take effect.'

'I've only seen this on one other occasion.' Eira swallowed, taking Cole's face in her hands, grief clouding her eyes. 'A young boy, stabbed like you were. His body was fighting off the virus, but he died of his injuries before we could save him. He must have had a drop of this type of power in his veins. He had a comic on him when he was brought in, and do you know what we nicknamed him?' Eira said, looking between Oran and Cole.

'Batman,' Cole whispered.

'Ironic, wouldn't you say?'

'Am I the end of some joke again,' Oran sighed exasperatedly, bracing his arms around Nelka. 'As I secretly like that term.'

'Don't worry, Oran. Batman is a badass. You can borrow my comic from upstairs, and it will answer all your questions.' Cole laughed, throwing a wink in his direction.

'So, what does this mean?' Nelka asked after a while, both hands gripping his forearms.

'It means that my talented Doc needs more of my blood.' Cole winced, grazing his mouth against Eira's lips.

Oran hummed, kissing his own mate on the temple, pleased with the progress that had been made.

Suddenly, his vision blurred, and the room spun. Oran staggered slightly, hissing, a hand going to his temple. Eira snapped her head in his direction, breaking contact with Cole and staggering towards him.

As quickly as the pain came, it receded. Oran shook his head to clear it, snarling angrily; he knew the feeling and exactly what would follow. He had been a coward for not telling her sooner, and now it was going to come out. Icicles fused his spine together, the breath he was trying to take wedged in his lungs as he panted.

His wide eyes met Eira's confused gaze as she froze partway across the room. Nelka tensed, rigid in his arms.

Oran willed his magic around him, gathering it in like a comforting blanket. He coated himself and Nelka in invisibility, making them vanish before Eira and Cole. He heard Eira catch a sharp breath before he built a fortress around his and Nelka's mind, severing the Bloodstream.

CHAPTER 45

||| EIRA

The packet crinkled in Eira's lap as she grabbed the marshmallows from inside. She popped one into her mouth, twisted her hand, and slid one into Cole's mouth; he latched onto her fingers and sucked, humming contentedly. In any other circumstances, she would have indulged his flirting, but she was too on edge.

It had been just over an hour since Oran and Nelka had disappeared. They should be used to it by now, but this had been so unlike any other time that it had happened. The fear in Oran's eyes, and the pain he had blocked her from, had been so sudden and unexpected that it had taken her breath away.

Eira pushed at the wall between her and Oran, sending her power battering against it, but it didn't budge. Sighing, she looked at the coffee table, stacked neatly with piles of paper and binders. Elowen's neat, precise handwriting, crosses and ticks beside names. Her friend had continued the research into the Dark network whilst they had been away.

Extracting another fluffy treat from the bag, she ate, laying her head against the arm of the rolled armchair.

'We need ice cream,' Eira declared.

Cole snorted, tilting his head so their noses brushed. He was sprawled in the armchair, his head resting on the curved back, his long legs crossed at the ankles towards the fire. Eira was cradled in his lap, her legs bent over the other arm. Music played softly in the background, and Cole tapped her thigh to the beat.

'I didn't know you had rhythm,' she said to him with a smile. 'I'd love to see you dance.'

Cole sniggered, his breath tickling her nose. 'Believe me, you never want to see that. My fingers might have rhythm, but my body certainly doesn't.'

Eira wound a hand around his neck. 'I'm sure you'd surprise me.'

She nearly dared him to show her, knowing that he would never turn down a dare, but it didn't feel like the right time.

Neither of them had discussed the gargoyle's disappearance, unsure what to say. Oran's staff and blades were still on the table near the door, and she would bet that his armour was still in his bedroom. The fact that he had left without his defences scared her.

'They need to return before daylight, for Nelka's sake,' Cole voiced his own concerns. He tried to rise, shifting his bottom back into the seat so his feet were flat on the floor, his knees moving Eira up. 'Come on, we should get to bed.'

'I need to finish this bag of marshmallows. A few more minutes, please, Hawk.' Eira fluttered her eyes in his direction, pulling a marshmallow from the bag and sliding it into her mouth with a devilish grin. Cole rolled his eyes, relenting.

Do you trust me? Oran's voice in her head had her frozen in shock.

Always, she replied instantly.

Access my memories, Eira. Take them away. Take my memories away, that's the only way it will stop.

Oran withdrew. A pinprick of light remained at the end of the Bloodstream like a lifeline.

Eira didn't hesitate. She channelled her power and threaded it towards that lifeline. The pain Oran was bearing was excruciating. Eira nearly pulled back from the feeling of a thousand knives stabbing inside her. She gritted her teeth, her body jerking within Cole's arms. She barely registered Cole's gasp, holding her tightly as her body locked.

Her power instantly fed into Oran, giving him the strength to mute the pain. It was enough that he opened his eyes, his vision hazy.

She saw tall, blurry figures in front of him, felt solid stone beneath his knees. He tilted his head, growling. Nelka was pulled in tight to his side, paralysed by his pain.

Protect her. Take them, Eira. Take my memories. NOW!

The last word was guttural, a desperate plea to protect them. Eira weaved her magic with his starlight, knitting it together and smothering his memories. She felt herself sucked in, watching his memories flash past her like a film on fast-forward, flowing down the bond. Like fireflies at night, Eira caught them in a light-infused net and pulled them to her, hiding them away in the bond. Then she built a solid granite wall in front of Oran's mind, infusing it with their strength.

476

Eira spasmed as another wave of pain washed over her. Oran opened his eyes, giving her a brief glimpse of his location before the pain overwhelmed them again. The opal at her neck heated, and she grasped desperately at its power, drawing it into herself along with the ancient knowledge of how to defeat the threat Oran was facing.

⋈ COLE

Cole couldn't hold Eira any longer, her body a dead weight in his arms. Cursing, he carefully lowered her to the wooden floor, the marshmallows spilling from the packet, forgotten. Panic gripped him. He knew that Eira must be experiencing Oran's pain, and that his friend was in danger. But he couldn't think about Oran right now; he needed to concentrate on Eira.

Cole bent, smoothing the escaped curls from her face with a trembling hand, his knees smeared with the discarded marshmallows. She had gone pale, her body rigid. Her eyes were closed, and her face contorted with so much pain that Cole could hardly bear it.

'Shit. *Shit*!' he swore, feeling helpless. He pulled her head into his lap, looking around the room desperately, trying to work out how to help her. This wasn't something that he could shoot, and it made him feel weak. What was the point of the drop of magic in his blood if he couldn't use it to save the people he loved?

A REQUEST FROM THE AUTHOR

Thank you so much for taking the time to read Bloodstream of Moonlight. I hope you enjoyed it.

I've always thought that if just one person read my work and couldn't put it down, that would make it all worthwhile. I still hold to that, but it takes a lot of energy and time to write a book, and I'm secretly hoping that more than one person enjoys it. The truth is that without reviews, most books become forever lost and are not enjoyed to their full credit.

Leaving a review on the major online stores, lights the way for others to discover their work. Readers are more likely to buy a book from an unknown author that lots of others are rating, even if it is only a few words. So, if you do have a moment, I would really appreciate it. The link below should take you to the Bloodstream of Moonlight review page.

You can also become a Liberator of the Dark and join my mailing list at roxanburleyauthor.co.uk, and be first to hear what happens next in the Equal Rise journey.

Review Here:

ACKNOWLEDGMENTS

I would like to thank my parents, Zena, and Gary, for first introducing me to the world of fantasy — those first books you read to me inspired my imagination. For continuing to instill in me the belief that I can do anything I set my mind to.

To my mother-in-law, Chris, for reading my very first draft manuscript, for being surprised I had even written it, and for encouraging me to publish it.

To my wonderful sister, Ashton, for always being my number one supporter and champion. You seem to always shine the light within me.

To my husband, Jon, for letting me write. All the evenings I have spent on the laptop letting the story come to life, and you have not complained once. You have supported me without question.

To my wonderful daughters, who have fully embraced the characters and constantly ask what is happening in the book.

To my friends Sam, Allie, and Kathryn. Your friendship is treasured in the highs and lows of life.

To Becky Jones from Opal Grove Editing. Your professionalism and knowledge have been invaluable.

And to you, dear reader. I hope you enjoy reading my debut novel as much as I have enjoyed the writing process.

ROXAN BURLEY

AUTHOR

Roxan Burley is an author who delves into the intense world of dystopian fantasy, one where the segregation of magic has a powerful resonance on her characters' abilities to change society. She also runs her own business as an interior designer. She lives in rural Devon, where she is converting a barn with her husband, two children, and their many pets. She spent her childhood lost in the world of magic and the possibilities it could create. She finally put pen to paper, despite the challenge of being dyslexic, with her debut adult novel *Bloodstream of Moonlight*, the first in her Equal Rise series.

BV - #0040 - 070125 - C0 - 229/152/28 - PB - 9781068787409 - Matt Lamination